Nihal de Silva

The Far Spent Day

Vijitha Yapa Publications
Sri Lanka

For
Shirlene,
Shanik & Shernal -
my world.

PART ONE

Onslaught

The Assyrian came down like a wolf on the fold,
and his cohorts were gleaming in purple and gold.

Lord George Byron
Destruction of Sennacherib

1

All he did was try to break up a brawl.

The graduation day celebrations at Serendib International had gone well. The principal, Peter Jeffries, made his customary speech boosting the stock of the school in the hope that the listening parents would have younger children waiting in the wings. The certificates had been distributed and the head girl was reciting her litany of praise when Ravi was ushered into the hall.

The lawful medium of education in the country, at least for those institutions assisted by the Ministry of Education, was Sinhala or Tamil. Parents who wished to send their children abroad for further studies had no choice but to place them in one of the 'International' schools that followed the curriculum of the British public school system. Dozens of these institutions had sprouted up all over the country. Serendib International in Colombo was one of the better ones.

Ravi watched the assembly breaking up and the students escorting their parents out of the hall and into the waiting cars. He stood quietly at the back wondering what he was doing there. Tilak was pushing his way through the throng, shouting and waving.

'Hi Rav,' he yelled exuberantly, making people turn and stare. 'So you finally decided to come.'

Tilak was his childhood friend, practically his foster brother. They had been together in junior school and then in parallel classes at Serendib. When their parents agreed to send them abroad for higher studies, they had both picked the University of Warwick in England. Now they were back, Ravi having read for a degree in economics, Tilak in computer science.

'I'm here,' Ravi smiled wryly, 'and wondering if this is a mistake.'

'Naah,' Tilak said dismissively, pulling him by the arm. 'Just wait till the party starts. You'll love it.'

Tilak was still the irrepressible spirit who could not resist any lunacy that struck his fancy. And he always dragged Ravi along. They had been in some mad escapades during their three years in Coventry, hair-raising at the time but great fun to recount afterwards.

It was Tilak's idea to attend the student's social that followed the graduation day celebrations at Serendib. Past pupils were allowed to attend and often did, strutting around the dance floor and showing off. Tilak was anxious to check out the current crop of girls, but Ravi having seen the head girl, was not optimistic.

Tilak led him down to the gymnasium where preparations had been made for the party. It was gaily decorated and a DJ with a phony accent was checking his equipment in one corner. The kids started to drift in, having tactfully got rid of their parents. There was an excited buzz, then the lights were dimmed and the coloured spots from the crystal ball began floating lazily around the room.

Tilak located the bar.

He went on the basis that there had to be booze available at these functions and asked around till he made the right contact. Tilak knew these things. It was set up in the van belonging to the DJ, which was parked under a tree behind the gym. Two kids who didn't look more than eighteen were running the operation. All they had was vodka and arrack served in plastic cups. A shot of vodka was going at Rupees 100/- for 25ml with a teaspoon of tonic thrown in free. The enterprising little bastards were making a fortune.

They knocked back a few and were ready. Loud music came blasting out of the gym and they knew the action had begun. They fixed two girls to dance with, using just hand signals. Ravi found himself with a smallish girl with a pageboy haircut and a toothy smile.

More visitors and Ravi recognized several batch mates he had not met since they left school, four years ago. He began to relax and enjoy himself. His partner went off to chat with friends, and Ravi went back to the bar for another watered down vodka. Tilak was there already and had brought a girl with him. Ravi could just make out a tall, slim girl with short hair parted in the center and falling over her ears, Madonna like.

Tilak introduced her as a past pupil, but junior to them. Tilak and the girl were sipping from the same cup.

They chatted for a while and Ravi went back inside, walking around slowly looking for familiar faces. Their batch had scattered all over the globe, a few to the States and others to England. Some had stayed behind to work in their family businesses. It was great fun to catch up and he was glad now that Tilak had pushed him to come. Little pageboy was bouncing around the dance floor with a boy in spectacles. She saw Ravi and waved.

There was a commotion at the far end of the floor, raised voices and a scream. Someone turned off the music and put the lights on. Ravi heard Tilak's voice, unmistakable over the chatter.

Ravi pushed his way through the crowd. The dancers had moved away and there were three people standing in the centre. The girl, Tilak's lady friend, was arguing with a stocky man who had his back to him. Tilak was standing by them with a smile on his face. He looked pretty relaxed … and half pissed.

Ravi knew that look.

The man swung his arm in a short arc and slapped the girl. The ugly "splat" sound rang through the deathly silence of the room. The girl spun around with an anguished cry and fell to her knees. The man stepped close to her menacingly when Tilak, standing by his side, took a clumsy swing at him. Ravi was already running towards them when the man raised his left shoulder, dug his chin into it to evade the blow and then hit Tilak in the chest, sending him staggering.

Ravi came up behind the man, wrapping his arms around him, trapping his arms against his body. The man grunted with surprise and struggled powerfully to break loose. Tilak came back with a rush, his eyes glittering in the spotlights.

'Cool it machang,' Ravi panted. 'Piss off somewhere!'

Tilak wasn't listening. He took one more step and punched the man solidly in the face.

The man let off a roar of anger and redoubled his efforts to free his arms, almost lifting Ravi off his feet as he swung from side to side. Then the girl joined the fray, pushing Tilak aside and trying to whack the man with her handbag. Ravi had to hang on now, because the man was almost berserk with fury and would have done some real damage if he were released.

The security guards arrived, four of them.

Ravi released his grip and jumped back as the man turned quickly and took a swing at him. He had his first clear look at the man. A round, cherubic face spoilt by an ugly scowl and a split lip. Heavily built and going to fat. Late twenties. The guards surrounded the man, trying to usher him out of the room.

Ravi thought the big fellow was going to take them all on. He struggled violently for a minute, throwing the guards around in a bizarre dance. When he realized the odds were too great he stopped struggling and allowed the security men to hustle him out of the building. He stopped when he came to Ravi, stared at him balefully and then stalked out without a word.

All the kids began chattering nervously. The girl had caught a good one. Her cheek was puffed and red, and her left eye was nearly closed due to the swelling. Ravi found some ice, wrapped it in his handkerchief and tried to hold it against her cheek but she would have none of it. She grabbed her bag and turned away saying she'd drive herself home.

When Ravi found him, Tilak was standing in the centre of an admiring circle of kids, regaling them with the details.

'Let's get out here,' Ravi told him. 'I've had enough of this.'

'Relax pal,' Tilak drawled lazily. 'This is a great party. Let's just have another drink and forget about that bastard.'

It had always been like this.

Tilak never consciously looked for trouble but he seemed to gravitate to it. Once he'd sucked down a couple of pints, he was ready to take on the world. It wasn't that he was a troublemaker; he just wouldn't back off and he did fancy himself as a tough guy. He wasn't and Ravi had collected a few bruises over the years to remind him of Tilak's recklessness.

Ravi went out towards the van at the back and bought himself another Vodka. He found some younger kids huddled together passing a joint around. He felt dated, far removed from these giggling idiots, bored and now sorry he had allowed Tilak to persuade him to come.

He sat on a chair overlooking the playground and found another to rest his feet on. He looked up at the sky, so clear and cloudless and saw bat shapes labouring across. Giant fruit bats that sheltered in the Vihara Maha Devi Park during the day were already out foraging the outskirts of the city for food. These must surely be stragglers.

Ravi had loved, and hated, his three years at University in England.

He thought of his parents, struggling so hard and sacrificing so much, to give him his opportunity. Earning Rupees to finance a university education in England was not an easy task, but to do it in a crumbling economy where Sterling gained against the local currency month after month, had been heartbreaking.

They had been very comfortably placed when his father worked for John Keells. He'd enjoyed a princely salary, a new car of his choice every three years and ample perks that extended to the family. Ravi had taken the privileges very much for granted. He had moved easily with friends who came from genuinely wealthy families and had become accustomed to a lifestyle that revolved around The Hilton.

Ravi had never imagined that the good times would end.

Then David Perera retired and their standard of living plummeted. To compound the problem, David had sunk all his money into a business that had never really prospered.

There were times when Ravi thought he'd have to chuck it in and get back. His dad had not always been able to come up with the fees in time to register for the term, and Ravi had to speak to his tutor for an extension. Sometimes the remittance would come in only at the end of term, long after the cut-off date when everyone else had paid up. At the end of his second year he had come home for the summer vacation without having paid his fees for the previous term. His dad had managed to scrape the funds together only when he returned at the end of September.

The final year had been a nightmare. David had strained the small family business to the maximum, siphoning its working capital to make up Ravi's tuition fees as the conversion rate from Rupees to Sterling rocketed with heart-stopping regularity. Ravi had worked in a bar in Coventry every weekend during term and then every day during the Christmas and Easter vacations in order to bridge the gap. He hadn't been home for ten months. In the end and after periods of excruciating suspense, he had made it. He now had a degree in Industrial Economics, with a second upper to cap it.

And the world was at his feet.

Tilak came out of the gym dragging two giggling girls behind him.

'What the hell are you moping here for?' He demanded loudly. 'The party is starting to really take off now.'

Tilak introduced the two gigglers who happened to be twins, mixing up their names. It turned out they were current students, just finishing school. They'd never taken alcohol before and took turns to sip off Tilak's cup.

They sat chatting for a while and then took the girls inside the now pitch-black gym to dance some more. Ravi found that his partner giggled a lot less once she was separated from her sister and turned out to be quite good company. He was beginning to enjoy himself. She was allowing him to hold her just those few vital inches closer when the DJ closed the party down by stopping the music and turning the lights on.

All the revelers yelled at the DJ, pleading for him to carry on for just a little longer but then accepted the inevitable philosophically. They broke up into little clusters and chatted for a few minutes. The twins took off with their brother, a former student Ravi had not met before.

'What about checking out The Blue?' Tilak put his arm across his shoulder. 'You are not tired are you?'

The Blue Elephant was a nightclub located at the Hilton. It was a popular hangout for young people with more money than good sense. The kind of people Ravi had always hung out with.

'No, machang, I'm not tired,' Ravi marveled at Tilak's resilience. The brawl was history to him. 'But I've had enough excitement for the day. I'm going home.'

'Ahh, don't tell me you were put off by that cheeseburger?' Tilak laughed at him. 'You are getting to be a cautious old coot.'

They walked out of the gate and onto the road. They had arrived late for the prize giving and had to park some distance away. The old rain trees on either side of the road gave welcome shade in the day, but at night the thick canopy screened the streetlights and forced them to watch their step.

A man stepped on to the road from behind a white van, blocking their path. Ravi looked up casually and went rigid when he realized it was the cheeseburger himself. Before he braced himself, he heard heavy footsteps behind him and then they were fighting for their lives.

Ravi thought there were at least three others besides cheeseburger. They were heavy men smelling of stale sweat. And they were armed with brass knuckles and iron rods. Ravi used his arms to protect his head, but still took some crunching blows on his face and on his forearms. The assailants had them backed up against the van so they were unable to run … or fall. They escaped serious injury for a while because their assailants were crowding each other in their anxiety to inflict the maximum damage.

Then the whole scene was lit up by a vehicle that turned into the road from a bylane. There was a sound of brakes and confused shouting. Ravi took a crushing blow on the side of his head and felt himself falling.

2

Ravi knew he was not dead only because the pain was so awful. He laboured with half breaths to minimize the knife thrusts in his chest. He wanted to open his eyes, but the daylight streaming in from somewhere only intensified the throbbing in his skull. He was conscious of voices close by, but couldn't make out what was being said.

He drifted off.

When Ravi woke up again the light was fading and his headache had subsided marginally. Breathing still required a ghastly effort. He opened his eyes and was not surprised to find himself in a hospital ward. Two rows of metal beds with a half wall on either side, then another row of beds in the corridor defined the ward. Ravi knew it was the General Hospital. Despite the outward squalor, this hospital had the best emergency services in the country. Some Samaritan must have brought him to the accident service.

Ravi turned his head slowly to his right and saw that the sun was slanting into the ward. He had no way of knowing if it was morning or evening. An old man who gave him a cheerful, gap toothed smile occupied the bed on his right.

'Mahaththaya nägittadha?' He croaked. jauntily. 'Mama hithuwey märennna yanawa kiyala.'

Have you got up then, sir? I thought you were about to die.

Ravi managed a weak grin but even that hurt. He turned with infinite slowness and looked at the bed on his left. He felt a flood of relief, and a return to normalcy, when he saw Tilak lying there. He seemed to be still asleep. Or unconscious! Tilak's face was a mess. A broad strip of sticking plaster ran over his left eyebrow. The rest of his face was bruised and swollen.

Ravi turned back to the other bed, grimacing at the stabbing pain in his chest. He spoke to the old man in Sinhala.

'Were you here when we were brought in?' He spoke slowly, using a minimum of his facial muscles.

'Yes. They woke me up when they brought you in late last night. Your people were all here at lunch time but you were unconscious.'

'Mm.'

'You don't remember me, do you?' He cackled. 'Didn't you come to the Golf Club those days?'

'I am still a student member,' Ravi said without interest. 'How did you know?'

'I'm a caddie. I have seen you on the course.'

A nurse came bustling up and took Ravi's pulse, then checked the strapping on his chest. She then turned to Tilak in the next bed, bending over him solicitously. He was lying on his back with his eyes closed and his right arm hanging over the side of the bed. As Ravi watched, he saw Tilak curl his hand round the back of the girl's knee and gently fondle the back of her thigh.

The young nurse skipped back with a startled squeak. She looked furiously at Tilak, ready to give him a dressing down, but the bastard had his eyes closed and appeared unconscious. The nurse stared at him uncertainly for a moment and then flounced off. She muttered under her breath as she went away.

'Kupardiya.'

Cad.

Ravi felt a surge of relief. If Tilak had the balls to pull off that little trick he couldn't be dying.

'Open your eyes, you bastard,' Ravi whispered. 'The nurse has gone.'

He did then, and his eyes sparkled with the kind of manic glee that had always been irresistible.

'Was she pretty, that one?' Tilak's voice was hoarse, as if he had a bad cold.

'Never mind the nurse. How badly are you hurt?'

'I don't know,' Tilak ran his hand over his chest. 'My whole body hurts like hell …. my head as well.'

A senior nurse came bustling out of the cubicle at the end of the ward, her spectacles flashing as it caught the evening sunlight streaming into the ward. She was a short, stumpy woman with a face like a bullmastiff. The little squeaker must have complained because the head nurse made straight for Tilak's bed and he, wisely, shut his eyes and contorted his mouth. With years of practice Ravi could see inside his head. This was Tilak's depiction of some war victim he had seen in a movie.

But it worked.

The nurse came striding up briskly breathing fire but stopped uncertainly when she saw that Tilak appeared to be on the verge of passing on. She stared at him for a moment, then checked his pulse, pretended to look at his bed head ticket and marched off.

Ravi looked at him fondly. Tilak was his brother. Almost. He yearned to talk to him but couldn't risk it now.

His thoughts drifted.

Tilak had lost his mother when he was quite young. His father Suren Wettasinghe was a young lawyer, struggling to build a practice with little time for his only child. They lived at Clifford Place, two houses further down from Ravi's home and the two were classmates at St. Peter's College. It was natural that Tilak spent most of the day, even study time in the evening, at Ravi's house.

Tilak was seven months younger than Ravi and a year older than Ravi's brother Jith. They had been inseparable, the Clifford Place gang of three. Ravi was the oldest but Tilak was the idea man, always ready with some zany project for the weekend or school vacation.

Taping coins and other metal items on the railway track had been one of their stock amusements. They'd look for new items to be flattened by the train and started a trophy collection to show off to their schoolmates.

Stealing milk bottles from Mrs. Chinniah's doorstep was a weekly activity. Mrs. Chinniah had been a bad tempered old lady who lived near the end of the lane. She would complain about Tilak to his father whenever she had the chance, claiming that he was "growing wild". Tilak would get his own back from time to time by stealing her milk when the Elephant House van had rattled off after depositing a fresh pint in the early hours.

The three of them would sit by the railway line and take turns to sip off the bottle, commenting on its creamy taste and great nourishment. They'd quietly replace the empty bottle on Mrs. Chinniah's doorstep knowing full well that she'd call the company no sooner their office opened, to give someone a rocket for failing to deliver her milk.

Then there was the *bothal karaya*. This was a Tamil man with a bad squint who came down the lane during the weekend, to buy empty bottles and newspapers. Tilak disliked the man for the reason that some adventure story he'd been reading at the time had a squint-eyed villain.

One lazy Sunday morning Tilak heard the familiar cry of *'bothal … paperrrr'* at the top of the lane, and gathered the gang. They had hurriedly climbed a Kottang tree by the side of the road near the gate of the Dias house.

Old Quintus Dias had a fierce crossbreed dog in his garden that barked furiously at the boys whenever they ran down the road. That morning they had hidden themselves in the dense foliage of the tree till the bottle man was just passing the gate. Then Tilak used a stick to lift the latch of the gate and push it open. The dog came charging out. The man uttered a startled cry of alarm and dropped his bag of empty bottles with a huge crash. The noise distracted the dog long enough for the man to race off and disappear along the railway line.

He never came down their lane again.

Jith had cut his foot while playing cricket on the road near the bottom of their lane. They had not taken any special notice except to rub spit on the wound. A few weeks later Jith was dead of tetanus.

Ravi was twelve at the time.

Ravi's mother Jacintha had been inconsolable, living for months like a ghost, lost in her world of regret. Jith had been her life.

The same year, Tilak's father, Suren married again and Tilak became a fixture in Ravi's house, often staying over for days on end, especially during holidays. Ravi had seen without realizing the implication, how his mother had slowly climbed out of her well of despair by emotionally adopting Tilak in place of her lost son.

It had been Jacintha who'd rushed Tilak to hospital when he'd broken his arm, after falling off the Araliya tree in the back garden. She had been the one who'd slept over at the hospital when Tilak had his appendix removed.

They'd been inseparable, Tilak & Ravi, first as schoolmates at St. Peter's and at Serendib International in Colombo. Then they'd chosen the University of Warwick as their first preference when applying to UCAS.

Now they lay in adjoining beds, trying to repair their bruised and broken bodies.

3

A rising babble of voices woke Ravi. People began filing into the ward. They came in, mostly women carrying food and clothing in shopping bags and rushing anxiously to the patient they'd come to see. He turned painfully to look at Tilak and found him awake, grinning gamely through his swollen and discoloured face.

Then Ravi's mother hurried up to them, striding between the two beds. The long walk had brought on her wheeze and Ravi could hear her gasping for breath, unable to speak. She gripped his hand for a moment and then turned immediately to succour Tilak.

Tilak took charge. He always did.

'Sit down, aunty,' he patted the edge of his bed. 'Get your breath back and don't look so anxious. We're both ok.'

Ravi's father, David, came up then. It was obvious that Jacintha had hurried ahead of him in her anxiety to see the boys. Despite his measured approach, Ravi saw that the old man was shocked by their appearance.

'How are you? Are you still in pain?' David's voice was shaky.

'It's ok, dad,' Ravi cleared his throat to speak steadily. 'Just a few bruises. We'll be all right in a few days.'

Once she was sure the boys were not seriously injured, Jacintha started looking around her, and not liking what she saw. The accident service catered to all comers, but of course most of the patients were victims of motor accidents or brawls, poor folk who couldn't afford a private hospital anyway. Ravi watched fondly as his mother drew a cologne-scented handkerchief from her bag and held it delicately to her nose. He knew it wouldn't be long before she suggested moving them to one of the more elegant private hospitals.

They had more visitors then. Peter Jeffries, the head of the school, and another teacher. Chaos reigned for fifteen minutes. Ravi and Tilak

14

struggled to answer all their questions, and conceal at the same time, their own pain and discomfort.

How did the brawl start?
Some outsider assaulted a girl who was with Tilak.
Did they know who that man was?
No.
Was it the same man who assaulted them on the road?
Yes.

The Wettasinghes' came when the visiting hour was nearly over. Aunty Ruki, Tilak's stepmother, had accompanied Suren. She did not speak much, looking as if she just wanted to spend the obligatory ten minutes before running away. Like Jacintha, she also gave the impression she wanted to cover her nose with a perfumed tissue. Uncle Suren was a successful lawyer now, portly and rather full of himself. He doted on the two daughters he had with Aunty Ruki, and treated Tilak kindly but without too much interest. He looked disapproving now, as though he knew that Tilak had been responsible in some way for his own predicament.

The police came soon afterwards, a sergeant from the Cinnamon Gardens police station, accompanied by a constable from the police post at the hospital. The sergeant, a grey haired man with an air of quiet competence, introduced himself as Liyanage and started questioning each of them in turn. He then wrote it all down in Sinhala on an A4 sheet, read it out to them and had them both sign the document. He promised to have the statement pasted in the Information Book down at the station.

When all the visitors left at long last, Ravi found Tilak looking at him, his smile lop sided in his swollen face. But his eyes were alive, dancing with the familiar mad gleam.

They were finally able to discuss the extent of their aches and pains, satisfying themselves that despite their current discomfort, neither was seriously damaged. Ravi was anxious to put the whole incident behind him and get on with his life, Tilak much keener to identify and punish their assailants.

After awhile they discussed their plans for the future.

'I prefer to work for someone, join a Bank maybe,' Ravi said slowly, 'but dad will be happy if I came into the family business.'

'How is it doing?' Tilak had always been interested in the small fruit drink business into which David Perera had sunk his life savings.

'Not too well. The market is there but we're very short of working capital. It's a daily struggle to keep going.'

'Perhaps you should bring in a partner,' Tilak jested. 'Better still, why don't you marry a rich girl and pump the dowry into the business?'

'I might do just that,' Ravi thought of Dilu. She was wealthy enough and Tilak knew it.

'And you?' Ravi asked gently. He had always known that his father's business would not support them both and so had not discussed the matter before. 'What will you do?'

'I have a project I'd been meaning to tell you about,' Tilak said slowly. 'There's an institution called Oxford Learning that specialized in correspondence courses for a variety of diplomas and degrees. I have a deal with them to design interactive courses on the web for Sri Lankan and Indian students.'

'Come on,' Ravi chided. 'Computers are not used widely enough by students here to make that viable. You know that, surely?'

'I've thought of that. Each lesson in the form of a tutorial will be E-mailed to the student, so he can download it onto a floppy. The student will work on it at his own convenience and mail it back to us. Our software will record the mail and route it to one of our tutors. The corrected tutorial, with the next lesson attached, will then be mailed back to the student.'

'I suppose you might be able to make it work,' Ravi said doubtfully, 'but all the infrastructure and marketing will cost a lot. Is Uncle Suren coming up with the capital?'

'No. My college fees were his final contribution towards my welfare. I'm on my own now.'

'So where's the money coming from?'

'Do you remember Mukesh Chawla? He's putting up the money and handling the Indian part of the project.'

Ravi remembered Chawla, plump and spectacled, from a parallel batch studying Computer Science at Warwick. He was from Mumbai, and rich.

'How far have you gone with this?'

'I've made an application for approval by the Board of Investment,' Tilak said. 'I meant to tell you about it but didn't have the chance.'

Ravi didn't reply, slightly hurt that Tilak had gone this far with the project without a word to him.

'I wanted to surprise you with it,' Tilak said. 'We've kept a place for you on the Board. Mukesh agrees.'

Ravi smiled fondly at him, mollified. 'No. My dad needs me to help him out, so I'll stick with the fruit juice business while you make your millions in IT.'

'Come on, machang. Uncle David will be able to manage. This project has real potential.'

'No,' Ravi said firmly. 'Thanks but no.'

Ravi drifted off to sleep soon afterwards.

4

Ravi woke early the next morning, pleased to find he was able to raise himself up and sit on the edge of his bed. Tilak was still in a Valium induced sleep, but the old man on the other side was awake.

And chatty.

His name was Eetin and he lived by the railway track near the Golf Club. He had started life as a 'Ball Boy', picking balls at the driving range but was now a full-fledged caddie. He cheerfully admitted he'd been beaten up in a drunken brawl.

'*Mama dope eka gahapuhama harima chandiya,*' he grinned widely. '*Ethakota thamai gutikanney.*'

I am quite a tough guy when I'm drunk. That's when I get beaten up.

Ravi looked at the old man with reluctant curiosity. Eetin was a short man with stick-like arms and legs fixed awkwardly on a rounded potbelly, quite like the clay figures Ravi had made in nursery school. His face was covered with purplish bruises and his left arm was heavily bandaged from wrist to elbow. But his eyes were bright with amused intelligence.

They spoke in Sinhala.

Eetin had married young but his wife had run away with another man. He then took another woman and had one son who was in prison for manslaughter. He lived with his common law wife in a shanty by the railway line, between Model Farm Road and Castle Street.

He earned good money as a caddie. Members had to pay Rupees 150/- to the starter before each round, and came through with a tip of another Rupees 100/- most of the time. A caddie could secure at least one turn a day on weekdays and two during weekends and holidays. It was a fair income for a man with just his wife to feed, but he cheerfully admitted that he pissed away most of his money betting on the horses.

And illicit booze.

David Perera was the first visitor that afternoon and he was clearly upset.

'I've just been to the police,' he told Ravi. 'Liyanage wasn't in but the OIC seemed to have lost interest in the case. Just brushed me off saying they'd let us know.'

'Cops are cops, dad,' Ravi soothed. 'They take their time.'

'We are taxpayers and have the right to be protected from thugs and gangsters. We are only asking the police to do their duty. The job they are paid to do.'

Ravi glanced at Tilak and saw him wink. Once David got started on the subject of lethargic officialdom, he could go on for hours.

Mr. Arumugam came limping into the ward. He was an institution at Serendib International, having been the senior Math teacher there since inception. He had coached Ravi and Tilak for the A Levels and had been fond of them despite the devilry Tilak often got up to. Ravi was surprised to see him just the same.

'Ahh, Mr. Perrah,' he said cheerfully, seeing David. 'I see these rascals have got themselves in trouble again. Always like this, no? Trouble, trouble, trouble.'

'Mr. Arumugam, isn't it?' David asked. 'It is so kind of you to come. I know these fellows gave you a hard time in the old days.'

'Vaat hard time? I could manage them and I knew their hearts were good. No?' Old Aru waved his hand dismissively. 'Here, I brought them some Kolikuttu from my own garden. Good for gas.'

'Thank you, sir,' Ravi took the comb of fat bananas. He was deeply touched, knowing the old man had come all the way by bus.

They chatted awhile and then Mr. Arumugam prepared to leave.

'Mr. Perrah, I must tell you in confidence that the school authorities have decided to drop the case. They have withdrawn the complaint they lodged with the police.'

'What? What?' David spluttered in bewilderment. 'Why on earth did they do that?'

'They say it was a drunken brawl. They don't want to take sides.'

'But that man was a gate crasher,' Tilak said angrily. 'He assaulted a girl on the dance floor. Afterwards they beat us up on the road.'

Arumugam didn't answer for a moment, looking down at his shoes. Then he looked into David's eyes.

'They have found out who the assailant is. It's Shalindra Premasiri. The son of Mudalige Premasiri.'

Mudalige Premasiri was the Minister of Education.

'Mr. Perrah, I came here to advice you to be careful. It's best for you to drop the matter and let these boys get on with their lives. We Tamils have learnt to live peacefully without offending people with power. In this case you should do the same and hope that the matter ends here.'

David stood seething quietly as the tutor nodded and walked away.

'So that explains why the cops had lost interest. Well I'm not going to stand for that rubbish. I shall write to the IGP and, if necessary, to the President.'

'Dad, it's not worth the hassle,' Ravi hated seeing his father so upset. 'Why not just drop this?'

'No,' Tilak intervened. 'No. That means thuggery pays off. Uncle is right. Minister or not, these bastards must be exposed.'

'I agree with Tilak,' David said firmly. 'It's because every victim suffers meekly that these beggars are able to terrorize the population. Someone has to take a stand.'

Ravi knew in his heart that his father was right, morally anyway. But he was uneasy. Because of the threat of assassination by the separatists, each government Minister was given a contingent of trained policemen to act as personal bodyguards. These cops, all dressed in civvies, were very much beholden to the Minister, and often acted as a private goon squad. Even a motorist who failed to move aside quickly for a Minister's motorcade was sometimes threatened and roughed up. Anyone getting into a physical confrontation with a Minister would certainly get flattened. The security was also extended to the Minister's family. If a family member got involved in a dispute with an outsider, the Ministerial Security Division (MSD) would be ready and willing to play a leading role.

Mudalige Premasiri had a grown son.

'Dad, those thugs who beat us up could have been MSD. I think Old Aru was right. We should walk away from this.'

David stared at his son for a long time then slowly shook his head.

'No, son. There are times when we have to take a stand and this is one of them. We can't back out of this.'

'You are right, Uncle David,' Tilak said staunchly. 'These politicians carry on like this only because people are scared to stand up to them. I'm sure my dad will back you up if you want to take this to the top.'

Soon afterwards Dilu walked in with an enormous basket of fruit, and her mother. The whole ward paid attention. A bubbly girl, small and fair, filled to her eyebrows with energy. And eyes, mischievous with a hint of sexuality. She was not his fiancée, not yet anyway. His mother had selected her from a host of possibles, and with the full backing of Dilu's parents, contrived several meetings for Ravi.

Ravi had found his initial amused tolerance of the matchmaking swept aside by his growing interest in Dilu.

Mallika Dunuwila was a cheerfully plump woman with a motherly way about her. Ravi had heard that her husband Denzil had worked overseas for many years. He had taken early retirement and come back with the cushion of a Dollar pension. Denzil was now acting as a consultant, Jacintha had told Ravi proudly.

'Ravi, who was responsible for this?' Mallika asked anxiously. 'What are the police doing? Have they arrested anyone yet?'

'I don't know, aunty. They are still investigating. We'll find out soon enough.'

'Are you badly hurt?' She fussed. 'Are you in pain? What do the doctors say?'

'He looks alright, Mum,' Dilu seemed faintly amused by the whole incident, taking it as just another prank. 'Don't fuss.'

She calmly hopped up and sat on the edge of Ravi's bed, chatting easily. After a while she opened the basket of fruit and took out a bunch of green grapes from it. She began pulling grapes off the bunch, swishing each one delicately in the tumbler of water at Ravi's bedside and popping them in his mouth. She managed somehow to have a private conversation with Ravi while her mother stood a few feet away chatting awkwardly with David.

Then the spectacled nurse walked around shooing the visitors out.

Dilu touched his nose with her finger, waved, and was gone with the rest of them.

'So that's Dilu,' Tilak said wonderingly. 'She's going to be a handful, pal. If you lose interest in her, just let me know.'

'Shut up.'

But Ravi knew Tilak was impressed, and that pleased him most of all. Normally it was Tilak who collared the prettiest girls.

Tilak stood up, grimacing painfully, and limped off to the loo.

'*Sir. Jāthi missy ne?*' Eetin was seated on his bed, grinning. '*Sirgeda?*'

That's a fine girl. Is she yours?

Ravi was torn between annoyance and amusement. It was a highly inappropriate remark from a stranger. Normally he would have taken offence at it. But the cheeky bastard had such a mischievous look in his eye that Ravi was disarmed.

'*Ow. Magey missy thamai.*'

Yes. She's my girl.

'*Hondha joduwa. Magulata matath kiyanna. Honda drink ekkak dānda puluwan.*'

You are a nice couple. Invite me also to the wedding. I can have a good drink.

'*Oyata bonna hondhadha?*' Ravi laughed. '*Mata āhuna cirrhosis rogaya thiyanawa kiyala.*'

Is it all right for you to drink? I heard you had cirrhosis.

'*Eh okkoma boru. Le titak giya kiyala mung okkoma baya wela. Honda adiyak gāhuwoth okkoma hari.*'

All lies. Just because I bled a little, they have all got frightened. A good drink will put me right.

Ravi had turned towards Eetin's bed. The old man raised his eyes to look over his shoulder and Ravi saw his expression change in the strangest way. He turned to find a man standing by his bed looking down at him.

'You are Ravi Perera?'

'Yes.'

The man stood and stared at him silently for a while. A dark man in his mid thirties, well built. He wore black trousers and a cream tunic type shirt with a Nehru collar. A political collar.

'I am Sergeant Sudesh Pathirana from the MSD of the Minister of Education,' he had a pleasant, gravelly voice. 'I have heard about the incident at the Serendib school. Where is the other boy?'

'He has gone to the toilet.'

'You can convey my message to him as well. We are sorry about what took place. It was unfortunate. But now it's over. Don't try to take it any further. It will only lead to trouble for you and your families. Drop it now. Do you understand what I am telling you?'

'I understand what you want. But that is unjust. You are a policeman. Surely you see that?'

He obviously wasn't a patient man. Ravi saw his veneer of civility vanish in an instant to be replaced by an angry snarl. The man switched to Sinhala to express himself better.

'Don't talk to me of justice. Our job is to protect the Honourable Minister and his family. If you people inconvenience them, you will regret it for the rest of your life. Tell that to your father. I will not warn you again.'

He turned abruptly and stalked away.

Tilak, on his way back to the ward, saw him leave.

'Who was that arsehole?'

'Sergeant from the MSD. He warned us not to press charges. Says they will retaliate against our families.'

'Ah, they are bluffing,' Tilak said dismissively. 'They want to frighten people into doing what they want. What can the bastards do if we go ahead?'

Ravi was silent for a minute, deeply disturbed. 'I don't know, machang. He threatened my family. I don't want to expose them to harassment. They have suffered enough.'

Tilak sat on his bed and smiled confidently. 'You worry too much pal. Let's get out of here first. Then your attitude will change.'

5

'I am not going to be scared off by these goons,' David Perera said stubbornly.

'But dad, you are risking so much for so little,' Ravi was desperate. 'Nothing positive will come of it anyway.'

'You are wrong, Ravi. When it is a matter of principle, you cannot step aside. Anyway it is too late. I have already written to the President about this and copied the letter to the Inspector General.'

'Oh no, dad. When did you do that?'

'Yesterday. I had the letters delivered by hand so let's just wait and see what happens. Leave that alone now, Ravi. Tell me what your plans are.'

'I offered him a good opportunity, uncle,' Tilak piped in. 'But he turned it down saying he wanted to join you.'

'Is that true, son?' David was clearly delighted and trying hard not to show it.

'Uh. Yes, dad,' Ravi looked fondly at the older man. 'I'd like to join you, if you'll have me.'

'Of course I will,' David seemed uncertain. 'It's a very small business, you know. Are you sure you want to do this?'

'Yes. Yes I am sure.'

They were seated in the open rear verandah of their home at Clifford Place. Ravi and Tilak had both been discharged from hospital the previous day, more Ravi suspected, to free the beds in the ward, than because they had fully recovered. They were glad enough to leave anyway. Jacintha had insisted on Tilak coming to her home for a few days till he was fit enough to get about.

She called them in for dinner.

'So Tilak,' David asked as they sat down. 'What's this big operation you are involved in?'

'It's a distance learning project Uncle. We plan to offer courses in a variety of subjects through the net. Our project will cover pupils in India and Sri Lanka. Lessons in the form of tutorials will be sent to each student by E-mail. The student will download it on to a floppy and E-mail the finished tutorial back to us. We will recruit retired teachers who will work from their homes to correct each lesson,' Tilak glowed with enthusiasm as he rattled on. 'I have the overseas investors lined up. We just need the BOI approval to get started.'

'That's marvelous, putha,' Jacintha looked at Tilak fondly. 'I'm sure you'll be very successful.'

Their conversation drifted to the General Election that had been announced the previous day. Although the election itself was to be three months later, David was worried about the inevitable violence that would take place all over the country, and disrupt business and other activities.

'Maybe the government will change,' Tilak said lightly, 'then old Mudalige will be out of power and unable to attack us.'

Tilak excused himself soon afterwards to go to his home and sort some papers. He still stood up gingerly and walked with a slight limp.

David turned to Ravi after Tilak had left. 'I suggested to Tilak's dad that we should both sign that petition to the President. He declined. Said Mudalige Premasiri's brother was a client of his and that put him in an awkward position.'

'My goodness dad, do you mean you wrote that on your own? I thought at least uncle Suren had supported you in this. You will be a marked man now.'

'Well, I couldn't force him, could I? Stop worrying about this son. It will work out alright, you'll see.'

They had been careful to avoid talking about the problem and David's letter in front of Jacintha. As far as she was concerned it was over and done with. When she came into the dining room again she had another matter in her mind.

'Dad told me that Dilu had come to see you,' Jacintha smiled at Ravi. 'Well?'

'Well what, mum?'

'Well how did it go?'

'Fine, mum! She fed me grapes,' Ravi was faintly embarrassed.

'Yes, I heard about that. What I want to know is, do you like her?'

Ravi hesitated and said. 'Yes. Yes I like her. In fact the old rogue in the next bed described her as a *jāthi missy*. That about sums her up.'

Jacintha was pleased. 'I'll call Mallika. I'm sure she'll be delighted.'

'Ahh mum! Don't rush it now,' Ravi was alarmed. 'Let things develop quietly.'

'I'm not rushing anything. I'll just tell Mallika that you like the girl. There's no harm in that, is there?'

'No, mum! I suppose not,' Ravi accepted the inevitable.

'Did you know that Denzil Dunuwila worked for the UN for many years? He retired on a Dollar pension only last year. He is very well off and Dilu is their only child.'

'You know I am not interested in all that stuff,' Ravi hoped his mother would drop the subject.

'You youngsters always say that but some wealth is just as important as a good family background. You will realise that only later. Remember then that I have warned you.'

'Right mum.'

Ravi looked fondly at his mother. He knew, from early photographs, she had been tall and beautiful when she was young. The years had not been kind to her. She had developed a stoop, and asthma had brought a hollow cheeked gauntness to her face.

Ravi would have liked to pursue Dilu on his own terms. She made his blood race and the thrill of winning her might have been even greater if her own mother disapproved. But Jacintha was an incorrigible matchmaker and Ravi had not seen her so animated in a long time.

He let it rest.

6

Two days later David Perera received a call from the Cinnamon Gardens police station. They had been instructed to conduct an identification parade. Would he come with his witnesses? Could he come that afternoon?

David had been at the office showing Ravi around. The office was really a small house David had rented at Sulaiman Terrace in Colombo 05. He used the garage and another room at the back to store his cartons of fruit juice. Dealers would call there to settle accounts, return the empty glass bottles and collect new stock. David proudly introduced Ravi to his staff, six faithful old hands.

Ravi wondered if their small business really needed, and could afford, an office in Colombo. Surely they could operate from their factory at Meepe on the High Level Road? That would save on rent, overhead and some staff cost. He had been wondering if that was a good time to discuss his idea when the call from the police came through.

David was delighted, feeling vindicated and confident that some satisfactory action would follow. But they couldn't locate Tilak. He had gone out that morning with a loaded briefcase and had not returned. David was getting worried, thinking they'd miss the opportunity, for it was nearly 11.00 now and the parade was fixed for 2.00 in the afternoon.

'Dad. I think I can find Tilak,' Ravi assured him. 'I'll meet you at the police station at 2.00. Have some lunch and come there quietly. Don't worry.'

'Are you sure? Maybe I should call the police and ask them to postpone.'

'No. Let's try to get this over with. I'll find Tilak.'

A three-wheeler took Ravi to the World Trade Centre in the Fort. Taxis were not allowed close to the building due to terrorist threats, so Ravi had to get off near the security barrier and walk up to the entrance.

A fat woman at the information counter told him that the Investment Promotion section of the BOI was on the 24th Floor, West Tower.

The receptionist at the BOI didn't have a clue, so Ravi walked round the entire floor peeping into cubicles. No sign of Tilak. Ravi was beginning to get worried when he spoke to the receptionist again – did the Investment Promotion department extend to another floor?

'Why, yes sir,' she said brightly. 'You might try the 27th floor.'

And there he was, speaking animatedly to an officer in the very first cubicle.

'Ravi. What the hell are you doing here?' he asked when Ravi tapped him on his shoulder. 'Are you spying on me for a competitor or are you are also working on a new project?'

'I can't tell a lie. Bill Gates is very worried about your project and wanted me to check you out,' Ravi then explained why he had come.

Tilak didn't seem overjoyed at the prospect of leaving his business meeting to attend an identification parade at a police station. Just the same he stuffed the files into his briefcase and told the officer he'd come back the next day. They stopped for a sandwich and a coke at the deli on the ground floor. Ravi noticed again that Tilak seemed unusually preoccupied.

Another three-wheeler took them to Cinnamon Gardens. They got off and walked towards the OIC's office. David was waiting for them.

The police station was situated at the apex of the fork between Reid Avenue and Guildford Crescent. Although it was a sprawling complex, buildings appeared to have been constructed without any plan or central concept, giving the impression of an urban slum. When they entered the office, a broad shouldered man seated behind the scarred wooden table introduced himself as Inspector Gamage, the officer in charge of the station. Sergeant Liyanage stood by the side of the table.

The Inspector did not offer them a seat. He told them to wait, nodded to the Sergeant and walked out of the room. Liyanage smiled briefly at them and followed the Inspector. They had been waiting about five minutes when Liyanage came back and asked Ravi and Tilak, the two witnesses, to follow him. David was told to stay where he was.

They were taken to large room at the back of the building. Although sunlight streamed in through a row of windows on one side, all the fluorescent lights in the room had also been put on. Against the far wall were a number of young men standing in a row. Ravi glanced at the men casually and realized with a start that HE was there. Shalindra Premasiri in person, glowering malevolently at them. He was a heavily built man with a thick neck running into an equally broad jaw. Not as tall as Ravi or Tilak, but broader at the shoulder and hip.

'I have been instructed to carry out an identification parade in connection with your complaint,' Gamage said loudly, as if for the record. 'I want one of you to remain behind, while the other goes to the next room. You have to study the men standing there and identify any person guilty of assaulting you on the night of September 1st.'

Sergeant Liyanage escorted Tilak out of the room. Inspector Gamage looked at Ravi.

'Well? Can you identify your assailants?'

Ravi looked carefully at all of them in turn. It was of no use. He hadn't seen the other men who had beaten them on the road well enough to identify them.

'That man,' Ravi finally pointed to Premasiri. 'He was the one who started the fight in the dance hall and then led the gang who assaulted us on the road.'

Ravi saw Premasiri's jaws clench when he pointed at him and knew he had crossed an invisible line.

'Can you identify any of the others?'

'No.'

'All right! You can wait in my office.'

The Sergeant accompanied him up to the door and then called Tilak. Ravi went to the Inspector's office and found David pacing the floor impatiently.

'What happened?' David asked anxiously. 'Were you able to identify anyone?'

'Shalindra Premasiri was in the lineup. I pointed him out. I couldn't make out any of the others.'

'Where is Tilak?'

'He was taken separately.'

'That's good,' David said. 'When they have two positive identifications, they will have to prosecute.'

The Inspector came into the room followed by the Sergeant. Tilak came after them but didn't enter the room. He stood just outside the room, looking out of the window.

'The other witness couldn't identify anyone in the lineup,' Gamage looked at Ravi. 'Now it's just your word against the accused. We can't prosecute on that.'

His words hung in the air, like the cloud of dust following an explosion.

'Tilak. Is this true?' Ravi asked urgently. 'Surely you saw Premasiri there?'

Tilak didn't look at Ravi or answer him. He shook his head and turned away.

'Tilak. You'd better have a good reason for this. Why don't you answer me?'

Gamage interrupted them. 'You'd better discuss this outside. I have work to do.'

Tilak walked away from the office. David and Ravi followed him outside. Ravi caught Tilak by his shoulder and turned him around.

'What the hell is going on? You owe us an explanation.'

There was a stricken look in his eyes when Tilak finally turned to face them. 'I'm sorry. I am so sorry. My project needed clearance from the Education Ministry. They ... blocked it!'

'So you betrayed us in order to get your project passed?' Ravi's voice was cracking in pain. 'That was the price, was it?'

Tilak didn't answer but his eyes were anguished. 'You must understand, Ravi. You have your family business to fall back on. I have nothing. This project is my only hope for the future and they wouldn't ... wouldn't approve it.'

Ravi stared at him for a minute without speaking.

'I'll pack your things and leave them near the gate. Take them away and don't come to our house again.'

Ravi turned and led his father away. He heard Tilak call his name but didn't turn around.

David didn't speak at all till they got into his car.

'What are we going to tell your mother?' David's voice broke at the end. 'It will kill her if she finds out what Tilak has done. I still can't believe it myself.'

'Let's not tell her. At least for now.'

'We treated him as if he was our own son.'

'Yes, dad, I know. But that's over now. We have to get through this by ourselves.'

During the last summer vacation Ravi had persuaded David to get rid of the old sliding door and fit an automatic roller door to their garage at home. Jacintha managed the house without servants except for Marimuttu, the gardener who came in twice a week. Opening the heavy old slider was much too difficult for her, and the roller door although quite expensive, had made their lives much easier. Ravi drove straight in, shut the door and went into the house.

Jacintha was sitting in the rear verandah, calling instructions to old Marimuttu who was clipping a hedge of Madras Thorn. They normally spent the whole day arguing about everything from how much water was needed for the bougainvilleas to whether or not to fertilize the mango tree.

'Oka kapala thiyenney äddheta neda? Noolak thibba nam kelling ganna thibuna.'

Haven't you cut that hedge crooked? If you had drawn a string, you could have got it straight.

Marimuttu was a man of indeterminate age with thinning white hair over a coal black face now shiny with perspiration. And he was a man of spirit. He kept his head down and spoke to the hedge he was trimming.

'Hevaney indang väradhi hoyana ayata väda lesi,' he muttered, yet loud enough to be clearly heard by Jacintha. 'Äs penimath adu äthi, dhäng wayasa nisä.'

Work is easy for those who criticize while sitting in the shade. Anyway her eyesight must also be failing, now that she is growing old.

Jacintha was drawing a deep breath to make a scathing reply when David and Ravi came out.

'Ah David. What happened at the police station? Had they caught the culprits?'

'No, mum,' Ravi answered quickly. 'We couldn't recognize a single one of the suspects. It was a waste of time.'

'I thought as much. The police are totally useless. Anyway it's a good thing you came back because I want to do some marketing. Do you need the car now?'

Seeing both men shake their heads, Jacintha picked up her handbag and left the verandah. She looked over her shoulder and caught Marimuttu looking up slyly.

'*Mama gihama boru karannney nähä, ähunada? Ávilla wäda balanawa.*'

No shirking when I'm gone, do you hear? I'll check your work when I return.

Marimuttu glared at her and muttered something, but this time he made sure she couldn't hear him.

'Ravi, ask Tilak whether he'll stay to dinner,' Jacintha called over her shoulder as she left.

Ravi heard the garage door rumble down. He left his father slumped in an armchair, staring sightlessly at the garden and went up to the room that had been Tilak's ever since his brother Jith died. He found a traveling bag and started packing Tilak's clothes.

Then his hands started shaking and he sat on the edge of the bed. It finally hit him that without Tilak his life would never be the same again. They had been there for each other from as far back as he could remember. And now Tilak was gone.

Forever.

Ravi felt tears rolling down his cheeks and couldn't stop himself. The aching sense of loss was almost more than he could bear.

Ravi took the case downstairs and instructed Marimuttu to deliver it to the Wettasinghe residence down the road. The old man complained that when the madam returned she would find fault with him for not having finished his work. He picked up the case just the same and left through the side gate.

But when Jacintha returned her mind was not on her garden or

Marimuttu.

'David. I met Mallika Dunuwila at Keells and tried to talk to her. I wanted to tell her that Ravi was interested in Dilu,' Jacintha was clearly upset. 'Would you believe that she just looked through me and walked away?'

'Are you sure she saw you properly?' David asked. 'She struck me as a very nice person. What could have made her act so rudely?'

'Dad, didn't you tell me that Denzil Dunuwila was a consultant to the Minister of Labour? Maybe the talk in the grapevine is not to have anything to do with us.'

David looked at him in surprise. 'Surely not? Denzil didn't appear to be a man who would be intimidated easily. And they were so keen on an arrangement between Dilu and you.'

'Maybe we are jumping to conclusions. I'll call Dilu. From the reaction we'll know what's going on.'

Mallika Dunuwila picked up the phone when Ravi called.

'It's Ravi, aunty. May I speak with Dilu please?'

'I ... I'm sorry, Ravi,' Mallika was flustered. 'My husband feels that it is best for you not to speak to her right now. Please .... please don't call again.'

Ravi put the phone down without speaking further. The thought that Dilu was lost to him as well was another body blow. Subconsciously he had seen this coming.

The word was going round that they were to be ostracized.

7

They trashed the office at Sulaiman Terrace on Sunday night.

Champa handled the accounts for their family business, Jaci Beverages. She was sobbing hysterically when she called David on Monday morning.

'Sir, okkoma office eka kudu ... kudu karala.'

Sir, the office has been reduced to bits.

David tried to calm her down but failed. The girl kept repeating, 'Mokuth ithru karala nā. Aney okkoma ivarai!'

Nothing has been left. All gone!

Ravi drove his father to the office. They didn't speak, each one stifling his anxieties. The school traffic on Dickman's Road was unbearably tangled, more frustrating than usual. They finally turned into Sulaiman Terrace, a normally quiet backwater with few pedestrians, and were shocked by what they saw.

Dozens of people, neighbours and bystanders, were loitering at the gate, craning their necks to see what was going on. Ravi used his weight to clear a path for himself and his father.

The chaos was indescribable.

The garage adjoining the main building had been used as a store for their finished products - fruit drinks in glass bottles packed in corrugated cartons. The door opening to the house had been ripped open, the hasp holding the padlock hanging at an angle from the doorjamb. Cartons of drinks had been thrown down and smashed. Broken glass and sticky orange, green and yellow fluid covered the floor of the garage and the open area outside.

David stood there with his mouth slightly open, unable to take it in.

Walking carefully around the mess, Ravi entered the main hall. This had been their sales room where dealers from all parts of the country would come to buy their products. Not any more! The salesman's tables and the small reception counter had each been dealt a powerful blow with some heavy club. The veneered chipboard had split neatly in the center and collapsed inward. The computer used for raising sales invoices looked as if it had been blown up by a bomb. Files and loose papers covered the floor.

Ravi heard David come into the room.

'My God,' he whispered despairingly. 'What have they done to us?'

Champa came out running with two of the other girls. All were in tears and talking incoherently

'Aney sir, balanna mey karala thiyana dhey,' Champa wailed.

Oh, sir, see what they have done!

Ravi glanced at his father and was dismayed to see the change in David. His face had a whitish tinge. His lips were moving but no words came out.

Ravi grasped him by the arm and took him to the garden.

'Kädichcha näthi putuwak thiyanawada?' Ravi called to Champa. *'Bonna wathura tikakuth geynna. Ikkmanata.'*

Is there an unbroken chair? And bring some water. Quick.

The girls seemed to pull themselves together now that there was someone to tell them what to do.

One girl came running with a plastic cup filled with tap water, another with a wooden stool. Ravi eased David into it and gave him the water. He saw his father's hand trembling as he raised the cup to his lips. Ravi looked away quickly. He knew how shameful David would find it.

Once Ravi thought his father was looking a little better, he left him sitting there under the shade of a stunted mango tree. He walked through the rest of the premises, three rooms that included his father's office. They had spared nothing. Computers and all other equipment had been destroyed beyond any hope of repair. Filing cabinets had been wrenched open and tipped over. The files were taken out, papers ripped and strewn all over the floor. The destruction was total and even in his shattered state Ravi realized that the vandals had taken their time over it, to make sure they did a thorough job. They must have made a lot of noise, yet had been confident that no one would interfere. Or call the cops.

Ravi found a few unused cardboard boxes that had somehow escaped destruction. The three girls had finally pulled themselves together and stopped crying. He instructed two of them to collect all the papers from the rooms and put them into the boxes in as much order as they could manage.

He called Champa, the senior girl, aside.

'Has anyone called the police?'

'No, Mr. Ravi.'

'Find me a directory. This comes under the Thimbirigasyaya station, does it?'

'Yes, Mr. Ravi. I think so.'

As she turned to go, Ravi asked, 'who is your insurance agent? Can you locate his number?'

'Mr. Arangala. Yes, I have his number.'

Ravi called the police on his mobile phone. He found the response unimpressive. The duty sergeant listened to his description of the damage without comment and finally agreed to send a constable to investigate. However, they had no transport at the moment as the OIC had gone out in the Isusu.

Would the complainant provide transport?

Ravi drove over to the station on Elvitigala Mawatha and spent another fifteen minutes waiting patiently till the constable was ready. He spent the time trying to locate the insurance man, Arangala. The man was not at home and his mobile phone was not responding. His wife promised to have him call back.

The constable was a tall man, thin and gloomy. On the way over, he complained about the long hours of work and how rarely he was able to get a few days leave. Now that the elections were approaching, the situation could only get worse.

When they entered the office Ravi found his father had regained his composure and was supervising the cleaning operation and the recovery of documents.

The constable, who introduced himself as Somasiri, was clearly taken aback by the extent of the damage and the ferocity of the vandals. He chased the loiterers away and examined the broken padlock on the front gate. It was clear that the vandals had entered the premises by forcing it open. They had not only used a powerful lever to wrench open the heavy front door but also smashed the folding glass doors that ran along one side of it. They had not worried about the noise.

'Do you suspect anyone? Have you dismissed any employees recently?'

'No.' David answered. 'Definitely not!'

'Any enemies?'

'No one who would do anything like this!'

'What about your competitors?' The policeman persisted.

'No.' David was impatient. 'We are too small for anyone to worry about.'

Ravi, standing near them wondered if he should tell the cop what they were up against when he noticed an old gentleman coming through the gate and walking hesitantly towards them. Ravi took in the thin, sharp-featured face, with neat grey hair parted in the centre, immaculately brushed down.

They all turned and looked at him expectantly. The man addressed David in a cultured voice.

'I am Winslow. I live upstairs, across the road.'

'David Perera. I've seen you around the street, although we never had the opportunity to speak.'

'This is a terrible thing,' Winslow looked around at the carnage. 'I saw the men who came last night!'

'What?' Ravi felt a shiver of dread, as if the information brought those faceless thugs closer. 'When did they come? Can you identify them?'

'It was well after midnight. The noise of breaking glass woke me up and I looked out of my window,' Winslow said. 'There was a Pajero type vehicle and a double cab parked near the gate. One man was standing there but I couldn't see his face.'

'*Varhaney nombara gattadha?*' The constable asked.

Did you get the vehicle numbers?

'No, it was too dark.'

'Go on,' Ravi was impatient. 'What else did you see?'

'They had put the lights on and … they were making a lot of noise. You know, smashing things up. I heard thuds and breaking glass. They were shouting instructions to each other. They didn't seem worried about the neighbours.'

'What did you do?'

'I called Police Emergency on 2433333. I told them what was happening. They said they'd send a squad car.'

Ravi waited.

'But no one came,' Winslow went on. 'After awhile the men came out, five or six of them with some iron rods and clubs in their hands. They got in their vehicles and drove away. They were … laughing.'

After Winslow left, the policeman shut his notebook, indicating that his work was over. Ravi noticed a subtle change in his attitude after he heard Winslow's story. He knew that the police were highly politicized so the constable might have realized that there was more to this than simple vandalism. The off-road vehicles, the bold, uncaring thugs and the failure of Police Emergency to respond, all pointed to a powerful hand somewhere, and he wanted no part of it.

He seemed to be in a hurry to leave, and Ravi couldn't be bothered dropping him. He just gave him some money to take a taxi and saw him off. Ravi knew very well the bastard would get a trishaw driver to drop him for free and pocket the money anyway.

Ravi had the feeling that he would never see that cop again.

David went inside to see how the girls were getting on. Ravi stood near the gate trying to get his thoughts in order, form some plan. How could a small family resist such an overwhelming force?

They were clearly the victims. There had been an unwarranted and brutal assault and all they had asked was for justice. Justice that should have been their right.

But even a victim seeking justice seemed to be an intolerable affront to these people.

All the friends Ravi thought he could count on had deserted them. They were totally alone.

His mother was not in the best of health and Ravi felt that his father could not take many more of these blows. His reaction that morning, when he saw the devastation of his beloved office, had frightened Ravi. His father had been a rock, a person he had looked upon as a colossus. But Ravi knew that he was getting old and he was not equipped to cope with vicious opponents who were not restrained by any civilized norms.

Ravi knew it was up to him. He had to take the initiative.

Standing near the gate looking sightlessly at the destruction inside their storeroom, Ravi was startled by a mocking voice in his ear.

'Impressive damage, isn't it?'

He turned angrily to find himself looking into the eyes of Sergeant Pathirana, the MSD man from the Ministry of Education.

'Why are you here?' Ravi wanted to smash the man's impassive face. 'Haven't you done enough?'

'I'm here to warn you for the last time,' the man said calmly. 'You are being very foolish in thinking that you can go on with this. We have dealt with people like you before. Normally, I don't bother to warn them more than once.'

'What are you trying to say?'

'I will be open with you. Elections are coming up and we don't want our Minister bothered by these matters,' snake eyes bored into Ravi. 'Stop now and go on with your lives. I will make sure you are left alone.'

'If not?'

'You and your family will be destroyed.'

'How can you people do things like this?' Ravi was stung into asking. 'There are laws to protect citizens. You will have to answer for your crimes.'

'You have been away for some time, so I'll be patient with you,' Pathirana said disdainfully, as though speaking to a child. 'Laws are there to settle disputes between citizens, but the Minister is the law! When you have a dispute with a Minister there are no laws to protect you.'

Ravi just stared at the man.

'If you persist in this campaign to damage the Minister's interests we will have no choice but to … remove you,' Pathirana's tone was menacing now. 'We can do that easily. Do you understand?'

'Yes.' Ravi kept his anger concealed with a supreme effort, knowing further argument was futile. 'Yes. I understand.'

The man stared at him for a moment, then he said softly, 'I come from a tiny village called Uru Udiyandaluwa near Chilaw. I was a beggar till I got into the Police. Now the Minister has given me a place in life. If you threaten that, I will kill you myself.'

He turned and walked away. Ravi watched as he climbed into a Land Cruiser parked further down the road and was driven away.

David came downstairs followed by two peons carrying cardboard boxes filled with papers. He supervised loading the cartons into the boot and rear seat of their Nissan.

Ravi saw that his father had recovered his poise and was trying to take charge of the situation. He decided not to tell him about Pathirana's visit just yet.

'We'll have to move the office to our house for a while,' David told Ravi. 'We've collected whatever papers we could.'

Ravi nodded. 'Why don't you tell the staff to take the rest of the day off? They can report to the house tomorrow.'

'We can't keep this from mum. What shall we tell her?'

'Let's tell her the truth, dad. How can we keep this a secret?'

'Yes,' David fought to keep his spirits up. 'I don't know how we can carry on though. We have lost all our stocks and even the records of our debtors. We will need money quickly. Did you get through to that insurance fellow?'

Ravi called again and got the same reply. Arangala was out of reach.

They got a new padlock for the gate and closed the office. The staff looked on anxiously as they drove away.

The manager of the Bank of Lanka branch at Milagiriya, Mr. Nonis, was sympathetic. David introduced Ravi to him. He greeted them politely and ushered them into his office. He was clearly shocked to hear about the destruction of their office and the loss of their stock and records. He was generous with advice, which they didn't need, and tight with his money, which they needed desperately.

Ravi knew that his parents had already mortgaged their home to raise both a term loan and working capital for the business. The house was really his. Ravi's mother had gifted the house to him when he turned twenty-one. He had readily signed the papers to mortgage it when his dad needed funds for the business. But his father had taken an appalling risk in using borrowed capital to build a factory on leased land. Nonis was quick to explain that they had reached the absolute limit of what they could borrow against their house, for they had already fallen behind, and had been forced to restructure the loan. The bank was not willing to go further.

Ravi was mortified by the way his father had to plead for some accommodation by the bank, for David was a proud man. He knew also that David valued his, Ravi's, opinion of him and would have been traumatized by the humiliation of it. More so when his pleading proved to be of no avail, for Nonis was adamant. No money without more collateral.

They drove home without speaking, utterly depressed. Marimuttu opened the gate before they could operate the automatic switch.

'*Nonata saneepa nähä,*' he snapped accusingly as Ravi got off the vehicle. '*Ath pone ekata gatta gatta. Off karala thibuney.*'

The lady is not well. I called and called on your hand phone but it was switched off.

They rushed upstairs and found Jacintha lying on the bed with her eyes closed. Her head stretched back and the tendons of her neck stood out like violin strings every time she gasped for breath. A nebulizer was clutched in her hand and she raised it to her mouth as they came through the door. Then for a while her breathing eased but Ravi knew it would get bad again.

Dr. Jayaweera was a family friend, one who was moreover particularly fond of Jacintha. And he'd seen this emergency before. When he finally left, Jacintha's breathing had eased and she was resting with her eyes closed.

Father and son sat by her bedside in the darkened room.

'An ... awful ... fellow ... called.'

Ravi was startled to hear his mother speak.

'Don't try to speak, Jaci,' David said gently. 'We can discuss this tomorrow. Just rest.'

Ravi had never heard David address his mother like that before. It had always been "mum" when the boys were around.

'No. I am better now. Is it true our office has been destroyed?'

David hesitated. 'Yes,' he said finally.

'The man said so .... on the phone. He said this is only the beginning.'

'I am so sorry, Jaci. I ...'

'No David, you did the right thing,' Jacintha's voice was firmer now. 'Is it true what the man said? Have we lost everything? Our stocks and our equipment, is it all gone?'

'Yes.'

'How will we manage?'

'We'll find a way. Don't worry about it for now.'

'No. I want to know. How are we going to pay the suppliers and the staff?'

'We have to make some collections from the dealers.'

'Have you got the debtors list?'

David was silent.

'No.'

'So it won't be easy to collect the dues, will it?'

'No,' David sighed. 'No, it won't.'

'Did you go to the bank? Did you meet Nonis?"

'Yes.'

'Did he help at all?'

David didn't answer, his humiliation still rankling.

'No. We won't get any help there. They want more collateral.'

Jacintha didn't say anything for some time and the silence hung over the room like a blanket. Ravi felt he was a bystander, watching and listening but unable to help.

'That man who called me said he had warned you not to pursue this,' Jacintha spoke so softly that Ravi had to lean forward to pick up the words. 'He says if you don't stop now, it'll become much worse.'

'Sergeant Pathirana wasn't it? The man who came to see Ravi in the hospital. I thought he was bluffing. I should have dropped the whole thing.'

'No, dear. You did the right thing. We have always taught Ravi that he must stand up for his principles. What will he think if we run away just because some thug threatens us?'

'Where is Tilak?' Jacintha asked suddenly. 'Why isn't he here?'

'He has gone to Matara, mum,' Ravi said quickly before David could say anything. 'He'll be away for a few days.'

'It's strange he didn't tell me,' Jacintha murmured.

The evening died slowly around them. Father and son sat in the darkened room till Jacintha's breathing became steady again and she drifted off to sleep.

8

Ravi woke up late. Going downstairs in search of coffee, he found his mother curled up on a chair in the rear verandah talking to Marimuttu. She looked better but not really well, the skin on her face seemed to have been stretched across her cheekbones till it looked transparent. She was huddled in the chair, feet tucked under her with the nebulizer on the table by her right hand. The old man was seated on the steps in front of her, speaking in an undertone.

No quarrels today.

Ravi went to the kitchen and made himself a cup of coffee and a cheese sandwich. When he went to join his mother in the verandah he found his father there as well. Normally a talkative cheerful man, David was preoccupied. Ravi thought worriedly that his father appeared to have aged overnight.

'Ravi,' his mother called out before he could sit down. 'There is a box on my bed. Bring it here.'

It turned out to be a small leather case with a good lock and a handle at the top. The weight of it surprised Ravi. Marimuttu had wandered off to the garden when he placed it on the coffee table. When Jacintha opened it Ravi realized it was her jewellery case.

'David,' Jacintha looked directly at her husband seated across from her. 'I want you to take this to the bank. The pawning section will value it. It will give you enough to keep going.'

David was scandalized. 'No, darling, there is no need to pawn your jewels. We will go to the dealers and collect our dues.'

'You know very well they will not pay immediately, besides when they realize your records are gone, they will cheat you,' Jacintha's breathing had quickened. 'You will need money now.'

David was moved and close to tears. 'We'll find a way, Ravi and I.

Let's keep this till we have tried everything else.'

'No, David. You have already tried everything,' Jacintha was getting agitated. 'I don't have the strength to argue with you but I want you to do this.'

The staff, all six of them, were at the gate by half past eight. Ravi put the peons, Wije and Sena to rearrange David's small office room. Once the seating was arranged, he put the staff to work, sorting the papers in the cartons they had carried home the previous day.

The news of the attack had been reported in the press. The carton supplier called asking about outstanding bills. David put him off, but the supplier of fruit for the factory, Mahinda Sirisoma of Weligama Farm, was not so easily convinced. They had started supplies on the basis of thirty days credit but over time the credit period had slipped to nearly sixty days. Now Sirisoma was worried, wanting to hold deliveries till the oldest bills were cleared.

A very dark skinned man with unusually white teeth stood smiling at the gate when Ravi answered the bell. He introduced himself as Arangala.

The insurance man.

'I was out of town, Mr. Perera,' he sat down and fanned himself. 'I came as soon as I got the message.'

'Yes,' David said sourly, walking behind Ravi. 'Yes. You have always been prompt when the premiums were due.'

Arangala's smile slipped a bit but he let it pass.

'Champa told me that the office had been attacked,' he said. 'Had they taken anything away?'

'No, I don't think so. Why do you ask?'

Arangala hesitated: 'Mr. Perera, your policy … only covered fire and robbery. You have no cover for malicious damage.'

David stared at him, his jaw falling in surprise. 'What … what do you mean? Are you saying the insurance company will not pay anything?'

'I'm sorry, sir. There will be no payment unless you can prove loss through robbery.'

Ravi was shattered. Although they had never discussed it, he knew his father was depending on a good settlement to clear his dues to the bank and have something left over to revive the business.

David argued for a time, talking about taking Arangala and the insurance company to court, but his heart was not in it. Ravi ushered the man out soon afterwards and shut the door on him. He came back to the drawing room to find his father staring gloomily at the carpet.

Bowing to the inevitable, David drove to the bank. Ravi sat at his side with the jewel case on his lap. Most banks now had a separate department to handle pawn broking, a section for the damned. Here people without other collateral and desperate for quick money would pawn their last scraps of gold and valuables.

And now they had to squirm with shame as the man at the counter sorted through the box, examining each item in turn. Most of the heavier pieces, Ravi knew, Jacintha had inherited from her own mother and rarely used.

The valuer complained about the old fashioned cut of the stones, which he said diminished the value. That was his job, of course. They finally settled at two hundred thousand. David decided not to deposit the funds in the company account, knowing the bank would select that moment to squeeze down on the overdraft. He put the money in his personal account and they spent another hour converting it to a joint account with Ravi.

*

The office staff was ready to leave that evening when the doorbell rang again. Ravi had answered the door himself throughout the day because of a vague fear that the MSD men might come calling. He knew his father was not fit enough to cope with them just yet.

Standing outside was a young woman he had never seen before. Tall and slim in a loose shirt-like blouse of some pale material hanging outside tight fitting blue denims. A long sling bag and wedge heeled shoes; sunglasses pushed back over brown streaked hair completed the picture.

Pretty in a hardboiled way! A regular ten-minute egg.

'You must be Ravi,' she had a slightly nasal voice. Confident though.

Ravi just nodded.

'I'm Tanya Koch. I am a feature writer working for the Sunday Statesman.'

'Do you have any identification?' Ravi asked cautiously.

'Yes.' She had the grace to look amused as she fished out a visiting card from her sling bag.

'It says you are a freelance writer.'

'That makes no difference. The Statesman prints my stuff. You see, I know about your problems. I can help you.'

Ravi hesitated, asking himself if this was more trouble. He finally shrugged and stood aside, leaving room for the woman to walk inside. He gestured for her to sit in the drawing room and went to find his dad.

David was seated in the rear verandah, cup in hand but lost in thought. Jacintha was curled up again in her favourite chair, looking a little better now and taking an interest in Marimuttu's work.

'Dad, there's a woman in the hall, says she's a reporter for the Statesman. She wants to interview us but I'm not sure it's a ...'

'Mr. Perera. I'm Tanya Koch.'

Ravi realized angrily that the pushy woman had followed him and had been standing behind him all along.

'I know you have had a problem with the Premasiri family and they are now using the MSD to harass you,' she went on before Ravi could butt in. 'The only way to control these thugs is to expose them publicly. You know my newspaper is not afraid of politicians! Give me an interview and I'll splash the story next Sunday.'

'Dad, it'll only cause more trouble. Mum and you can't take much more of this. Just let it go.'

David looked uncertain. Ravi saw that his hand was shaking again when he reached out to place the cup on the stool by his side.

Jacintha put her feet on the floor and sat up straight. 'No putha, we must not be frightened of these bullies. We are in the right. We must expose them.'

'Mum, that man came to see me again. Sergeant Pathirana from the MSD,' Ravi was desperate. 'He said he would have us killed if we threaten the Minister's interests.'

'You didn't tell me that,' David was surprised. 'When was this?'

'When we were clearing the office. He must have been with the gang that did the damage.'

'Mr. Perera, that is their style and fear is their weapon,' Tania Koch interrupted earnestly. 'As an individual you have no chance against them. By telling the country about their activities we can stop them going further.'

'They will attack us again,' Ravi told her rudely. 'My parents have suffered enough. I feel we must stop this right here.'

'Ravi, I know enough to write the story anyway. But I'd rather do it with your consent.'

She calmly pulled up a chair and sat down facing David.

Ravi didn't answer, resenting the pushiness and her familiar use of his first name.

'Remember Mudalige Premasiri is facing an election,' she tapped the arm of her chair for emphasis. 'My paper is doing everything possible to help defeat this corrupt government, and Mudalige Premasiri is the worst of them. You can help me prepare a damning story. Just remember if the man loses his position, he will not have security thugs to help him harass you.'

David looked at the woman, clearly undecided. Ravi was about to ask her to leave when Jacintha spoke. 'Ravi, I want you to tell this young lady the whole story. We must stand up for what is right. At least we can prevent the same thing happening to someone else.'

Tanya Koch looked pleased, and she clearly wasn't going to hang around for a second invitation. She reached into her sling bag and fished out a small dictaphone and a notebook. She placed the recording device on the stool between them and turned to Ravi.

'I hope you don't mind my recording the interview. I'll take notes as well but I want to have a reliable back up. That ok?'

Ravi didn't answer.

'Tell it from the beginning. Start with the function at Serendib school.'

Ravi hesitated, caught his mother's eye, and finally gave in. He started with the brawl in the school gymnasium and went on to the beating they got on the road outside. Jacintha uttered a moan when he related Tilak's perfidy at the police station.

'Ravi,' she wailed. 'I can't believe that my Tilak would do that. Is that why he hasn't come here?'

The look on his mother's face was a white-hot needle in his brain. Ravi knew that she had lavished all her love on the boy, more perhaps than on her own son.

'I'm sorry, mum,' he wished that he could find a way to soften the blow. 'It seems Tilak needed the Minister's approval for a business project, so he did what he had to. I've told him … not to come here again.'

Jacintha gave him a stricken look, seemed about to protest, then changed her mind and remained silent.

Ravi related the rest of the story and found the Koch woman a good listener. She sat attentively with her arms crossed, and the end of the little finger of her left hand in her mouth. She took some notes and didn't interrupt with questions.

When he was done she sat for a while looking towards the garden, seemingly lost in thought. She nodded finally and stood up, putting her dictaphone away carefully. She promised to return the next morning with a cameraman for pictures of the wrecked office.

9

Ravi had to walk to the top of the road to pick up a copy of The Statesman. The story was spread over most of page nine and the one-inch headline read, "Mudalige crushes family – Victims face financial ruin." The story that followed gave a clear, if biased, account of the trivial incident that took place at the school and the massive retaliation it had triggered. The photographs of the vandalized office were particularly damning.

Tanya Koch had kept her promise.

Ravi found his mother seated once again in her favourite chair in the rear verandah. It was Marimuttu's day off and she was alone. The exposé brought a rare smile to her face. She had been ill again after the Koch woman's interview, her asthma apparently brought on by the shock of Tilak's betrayal. She was better now but the frequent attacks had taken their toll. It tore Ravi's heart to see that her stoop was more pronounced, and her movements slower and more measured now, than they had been before all this trouble started.

They were inundated with calls from family and friends who tended to be, Ravi felt, more curious than sympathetic. David had walked to Frankfurt Place where some of his cronies had arranged a game of bridge, so Ravi handled the phone.

Then Reshane called.

'Machang, it seems like you are in a war,' he said happily. 'Anyway you are a media star now, so I'll buy you a beer. I'll pick you up in half an hour, ok?'

Reshane was another batch mate from Warwick, one of the rich ones. Rich enough but not one to flaunt it too much, so they had been friends.

'Hi Resh,' Ravi was inordinately pleased to hear a friendly voice at last. 'I'd love that, sure. I'll be ready.'

'Will Tilak come too?'

They had always been two for the price of one. All their friends knew that.

'No. He's out.'

'No worries.'

Knowing his mother was not up to handling the phone, Ravi tried leaving it off the hook but after a while the instrument gave a loud whistle. He found he could simply switch off the ringing tone; then only the little red light blinked and that was easy to ignore.

Reshane tooted outside and Ravi couldn't help but admire his new Toyota sports utility. The smell of new leather inside was intoxicating, and they used the drive time to happily discuss the more outlandish features of the vehicle.

The fairways of the Royal Colombo Golf Club came into view when they passed through the slums that nestled round the railway gate on Model Farm Road. Ravi thought it was rather like walking through a public lavatory and stumbling into a field of wildflowers.

'Have you been here before?'

'My dad was a member in the old days. I think I'm still a student member,' Ravi smiled without embarrassment. 'I can't afford to up it to full membership.'

'Yeah. Membership costs Rupees 100,000/- now.'

'I'm a student member at the Nuwara Eliya Golf Club as well. I haven't been there in years, though.'

They sat in the open verandah overlooking the eighth green with frosted glasses of Lion Lager in their hands. Ravi felt at ease for the first time in several days, and Reshane with his jolly spectacled moon face, was a good company. He must have guessed that Ravi didn't want to talk about his troubles so he prattled on about mutual friends and who each was currently paired off with.

Reshane turned to speak with someone and Ravi watched a perspiring foursome work its way up the eighth fairway. Another group were coming up the eighteenth fairway on his left. The game looked easy enough to an

untrained eye, but Ravi saw that the players were making an awful hash
of it, digging up huge divots with each stroke and sending the little ball
shooting off in all directions, except towards the green.

A wrinkled face, covered from ear to ear with a gap-toothed grin,
appeared over the flower trough in the foreground. It took Ravi a moment
to recognize the man. Eetin the caddie!

'*Ahh, sir,*' he called out cheerfully. '*Däng saneepadha?*'

Sir, are you all right now?

Ravi was pleased to see the old rogue. He also seemed to have recovered
from his beating.

'*Ow, Eetin. Däng Hondai. Oya kohomada? Adha vädä keruwadha?*'

I'm fine. How are you? Did you work today?

He knew that caddies were not employees but were registered by the
club and offered their services directly to the members.

'*Nä, sir,*' the man said woefully now. '*Magey väda navaththala
thiyenney.*'

No sir. They have stopped my work.

'*Mokada ehema karey?*'

Why did they do that?

'*Tikak dope eka gahala vädata āvai kiyala,*' Eetin had his infectious
grin switched on again. '*Podi deyak neyda, sir?*'

Just because I came to work a little drunk. It's a small matter, isn't
it?

'*Väda vitharak nevai, umbawa ellanna thiyenney,*' Ravi said with a
laugh.

Stopping your work isn't enough. You should be hung.

'*Dawalta kanna issarawela adiyak gähuwey näththang kämath rasa nähä,*'
Eetin ignored Ravi's comment. '*Mata podi support ekak denawadha?*'

If I don't have a tipple before lunch, even the food doesn't taste right.
How about a small 'support'?

Ravi gave him Rupees 50/- just as a course marshal came to shoo the
old man away from the clubhouse.

'*Mama inney rail pāra langa,*' the man called as he allowed himself to
be led away. '*Ona welawaka ethanata ävith ahanna, mama innawa.*'

I live near the railway line. Ask for me there. I am available at any time.

Ravi waved him away.

Reshane looked at Ravi, 'That bastard is a good caddie, but he's always pissed. Where the hell did you meet him?'

'In the accident ward. He was in the next bed. He'd been beaten up as well.'

'The bugger probably deserved …,' Reshane stopped suddenly, looking over Ravi's shoulder.

Ravi turned casually to see what had attracted Reshane's attention, and felt a jolt of apprehension. A group of golfers were walking tiredly towards the clubhouse from the eighteenth green. Leading them into the entrance at the end of the verandah was the unmistakable figure of Shalindra Premasiri.

Ravi turned away quickly. The last thing he wanted was another confrontation. He heard them sit down close by, discussing the game and calling on the losers to pay up.

'This bugger missed a two foot putt on the seventeenth,' the disgusted voice must have belonged to Premasiri. 'Any idiot could have just tapped it in, then we would have been all square.'

'My caddie said right edge,' the other man said defensively. 'I played a line and …'

'Bullshit. You had the yips,' the first man interrupted. 'Anyway I want a beer. Boy!'

Another member came towards them, a thin middle-aged man with unnaturally glossy black hair and an ugly wart on his cheek. Ravi cringed when he realized it was Leo Dias, a man his father was acquainted with.

But Dias had his eyes on Premasiri.

'Hey Shalindra,' he called out. 'You are featured in the paper today. Are you having trouble with these people?'

'Hi Leo.' The loud voice was Premasiri's all right. 'No. How can they make trouble for me? I've stepped on a thousand worms like that.'

Leo laughed.

Ravi felt chilled by the confident arrogance of the man, and annoyed that Leo found it funny. Looking up he saw a lady in a lavender dress coming towards him holding a sprightly little girl by the hand.

'Ah, Maduri. Your husband is in a bad mood because he's lost the game,' Leo called out.

'Aiyo, thaathi. Is it true? Did you lose?' chirped the little girl.

'No, darling,' Premasiri growled. 'Thaathi never loses. You know that, don't you?'

The child wriggled free from her mother, ran towards Premasiri and jumped on his lap.

'Ravi, do you really want to take these people on? You've been away a lot so you don't know the score. These are bloody dangerous bastards,' Reshane said quietly.

'I am beginning to realize it. If it were up to me, I'd have dropped it. But my parents ... they think we shouldn't back off when we are in the right.'

'That's true, of course. But, in this country today, there is one law for us and another for ... them. That fellow is right. He can step on you whenever he chooses to.'

Reshane called for his bill. Ravi kept his face carefully averted as they walked out of the clubhouse towards the car park. They had to go past the security hut to the outer area where Reshane had parked his vehicle. Some men were standing there. Ravi glanced casually at them as they walked past and felt a shiver of anxiety.

Two of them were in dark trousers and white short-sleeved shirts. And Nehru collars. The hangers-on who sucked up to politicians always wore Nehru collars. The MSD favoured them as well.

One of the men glanced at Ravi without interest, looked away and then snapped his eyes back. Ravi let his own gaze slip away and walked quickly past, before the man could speak. He looked back when Reshane was manoeuvring his vehicle out of the car park and found that the man had turned around and was still staring suspiciously at him.

Ravi stayed home that evening. David came in just after dark, having spent a carefree day at the bridge table. He seemed more relaxed than he had been for some time, and Ravi was glad. Jacintha came downstairs, still breathing heavily, but insisted on preparing their customary Sunday dinner of soup and sandwiches.

They sat together at the kitchen table and discussed their day. Jacintha had stayed in bed for most of it and Ravi was unwilling to report his near meeting with Shalindra Premasiri, so they listened contentedly to David descriptions of finesses and end plays.

Ravi looked fondly at his parents and felt his earlier unease ebbing away. He was cocooned in the cozy domestic scene. He became convinced that if they had each other, no permanent harm would befall them.

And they didn't talk of Tilak.

10

They had driven almost up to Kalutara without speaking, each busy with his own gloomy thoughts. Although traffic going out of Colombo at that time was relatively light, private buses coming in to the city often swung over to their side of the road to overtake, and Ravi had to use considerable skill and mumbled swear words, in order to avoid a head on collision.

Sirisoma of Weligama Farm was David's old friend, but he hadn't been friendly when he called the previous day. He was no longer able to supply their fresh fruit and he wanted full settlement of outstanding invoices. He'd rung off immediately, rudely cutting off David's outraged protests. When David called the farm office moments later, a girl told him that "Sir" had gone out. They called till late that night but couldn't reach him.

Had someone forced Sirisoma to make that call? A regular supply of fresh fruit, just ripe enough for juicing, was the lifeblood of their industry. They had no chance of survival if their supply was cut off suddenly.

The southern coastline had a grandeur that overwhelmed Ravi every time he saw it and he knew he would never tire of it. He allowed the passing scene to seduce him till the road curved past the old shallow water port at Galle, and then turned gently southeast towards Weligama.

They caught Sirisoma as he was leaving the office for lunch. Ravi saw a thin man with a full head of silver grey hair and a pronounced stoop. A kind face behind gold-framed spectacles perched on the end of his nose.

'Ah, Mr. David. Yes, I was expecting you. Please come into my office.'

David introduced Ravi as Sirisoma ushered them into his office, a small room near the entrance with barely enough space for two visitor's chairs.

'I am sorry about this, more than I can tell,' the old man spoke so softly, Ravi had to lean forward to hear him. 'You have been my good customer for many years and I consider you my friend.'

He kept staring at the table as if he was unable to raise his eyes.

'What happened? What did they do?' Ravi queried.

'Two men. I think they work for Chandrasena, the local MP. They told me that I was to make no more supplies to you. If I disobeyed them ...,' Sirisoma choked.

'Yes?' Ravi persisted. 'What did they threaten?'

'My daughter is a first year medical student at Peradeniya,' his voice had sunk to a whisper again. 'They laughed and said ... they said she was such a pretty girl ... there would be many volunteers when they arranged to ... to have her molested.'

The old man looked up and Ravi saw his face crumple in pain. There were two glistening lines of tears on either side of his nose.

'I .. I cannot bear it. She is my only child!'

David had not spoken at all. He stood up now and walked around to Sirisoma's side of the table. He reached down and squeezed the man's shoulder, turned and walked out of the room. Ravi followed him quietly.

Sirisoma sat without moving as the tears rolled down his face.

David walked out resolutely, but when he reached the car Ravi saw his shoulders slump.

'What are we going to do? How can I run our plant without fruit?'

'Don't worry about it now, dad,' Ravi tried to comfort him. 'We'll work something out. At least we know the position now.'

'Yes. We know where we stand!'

When they reached the main road, Ravi asked for directions and found the resthouse soon afterwards. The charming hostelry was set up in a large tree-filled garden overlooking Weligama bay. The decaying mansion on Count de Mauny's island dominated the center of the picturesque cove, but its charm was lost on Ravi that day. They ordered a snack and two beers, but when the insipid looking chicken sandwiches appeared, David pushed them aside. The dining room was empty except for one other family.

The resthouse keeper was an immensely fat man with a round hairless head, perched on several chins resting directly on his shoulders. If he had a neck, it had dissolved long ago.

'Oh yes,' he nodded his head for emphasis. 'I know of at least two farms that grow fruit. One of them is at Henegama, the other near Akuressa. There may be others.'

'Are those places far from here?'

'No. Not far. Maybe 20 miles to Henegama and another 15 to the second place.'

David had agreed without much enthusiasm, so they had left the coast and driven inland from Weligama. The road soon deteriorated and Ravi found the journey tiresome and unrewarding. Both farms focused on their dairies, the supply of fruit being limited and seasonal, unsuitable for their type of business. Tired and depressed, Ravi took the road through Imaduwa to Galle and was just in time to witness the sun setting over the little harbour as they drove through. David stared steadfastly at the road ahead and didn't seem inclined to chat. Ravi concentrated on getting them safely through the evening traffic.

It was after 10 o'clock when they finally reached home. Ravi parked the car, shut the gate and walked into the sitting room thinking the day couldn't possibly have been worse. David paused to collect his files. The lights in the sitting room were on.

Jacintha was sprawled face down on the carpet.

'MUM!' Ravi yelled as he ran towards her. He heard his father drop his files and utter a strangled cry behind him. Ravi reached her first and gently touched her hand. Finding no response, he turned her over as his dad knelt on the other side. Her eyes were closed and her head fell back.

'Call Dr. Jaye,' David said. 'I'll lift her onto the sofa.'

David was gasping for breath, his eyes wide in panic. Ravi gestured for him to get the phone and knelt down by his mother. He was surprised by the frailty of her body, how featherlike her weight was.

But she was cold!

Ravi heard his father speak on the phone, his voice high with tension. He surreptitiously held his mother's wrist and ran his thumb along the upper side of it, trying to find her pulse.

He felt the horror rising within him from his belly to his throat, like a vast bubble of noxious gas. He had an uncontrollable urge to scream.

'Dr. Jaye is on the way. How is she?'

Ravi stood up. He felt the tears dripping from his chin as he turned to face his father.

'She's gone, Dad,' Ravi's voice came from far away. 'She's gone!'

'No,' David's face went rigid with shock. He pushed Ravi aside and knelt by the sofa, cradling Jacintha's head in his arms. 'Oh no. No. No'

Ravi knelt beside his father and placed one arm across his shoulders. He felt the older man's body shaking as he hugged him.

The doorbell rang soon afterwards and Ravi rose to let Dr. Jaye in.

11

Marimuttu sat on the ground at the foot of the coffin and refused to move.

Dr. Jaye had signed the death certificate confirming that Jacintha had succumbed to heart failure, following a severe attack of asthma. Reshane had driven Ravi to Raymonds. It was night, and raining heavily, when they finally released the body and Reshane followed the hearse as it proceeded in its stately way down Bullers Road, and then to Galle Road. When the hearse backed into their garage, Ravi saw Tilak standing by the gate. He had no umbrella or hat and had made no attempt to take shelter from the downpour.

Ravi had wanted to avoid meeting Tilak, but when Reshane stopped his vehicle, he had no choice but to get off and that put him face to face with his erstwhile friend.

Tilak looked at him as he stepped out of the vehicle. His hair was plastered to his face and his clothes were soaked. Ravi guessed that he'd been standing there for a while.

'You broke her heart, you bastard,' Ravi heard his own voice coming from far away. A stranger's voice. 'If you come near her coffin I will kill you.'

Tilak looked stricken. He stood staring wordlessly at Ravi for a moment, then turned and walked away.

Tanya Koch came to the cemetery.

Ravi saw her standing on the far side of the open grave, her eyes concealed behind brown tinted dark glasses, as Father Thomas from Jesuit House conducted the service. Ravi had his arm under his father's elbow and he felt a shudder pass through the older man. He turned and saw another teardrop run down his cheek and suspend itself at the end of his jaw.

To Ravi, his father had always been a rock, a man who could handle any situation, overcome any problem. Out at sea in a hired fishing boat, when the engine packed up in a squall, lost while trekking in Horton Plains, crashing down a steep hillside when a passing truck hit their car, Ravi, a small boy then, had never felt panic or even serious concern. He had always known that his father's calm strength and clear mind would see them to safety.

But they had broken him now.

David's shoulders were slumped in defeat as he stood there. When the priest signaled them to throw the first handful of soil on the coffin, David bent over with seeming difficulty and might have fallen if Ravi had not held him firmly by the shoulder.

They stood side by side as their friends and relatives came by to mumble their unintelligible condolences. The endless line finally dwindled and came to an end. Tanya came up shepherding an old man.

Mr. Rasiah, a widower who lived across the road.

'Ravi,' Tanya said slowly. 'I am truly sorry about your mum. I really am.'

'Thanks.'

'I think you should listen to what Mr. Rasiah has to say.'

Ravi looked at the man with some curiosity. He had been a teacher now long retired, a short, slim man with feathery white hair. He lived alone, Ravi knew, since his two sons were settled abroad.

'How are you Mr. Rasiah?' Ravi asked politely. 'I am sorry I haven't come to see you since I returned.'

'I'm well, Ravi. Thank you. Please accept my deepest sympathies.'

'Thank you sir.'

'Tell him what you saw,' Tanya intervened.

'That night, the night she died,' Mr. Rasiah began hesitantly. 'Some men came … they parked their vehicle down the lane near the railway line and two of them walked back to your house. They banged on the garage door till your mother opened it. They were there for only a short time, ten minutes maybe. Then they left, but Jacintha didn't come to the door to let them out. They left through the side exit.'

'What time was this?'

'It might have been about 8.00 o'clock.'

'Will you be able to identify the men?'

'I don't think so. No. I couldn't see their faces clearly. I noticed that they wore white shirts and dark trousers.'

Ravi felt a shiver pass up his spine. He let his eyes slip away from the old man and saw Tanya looking impassively at him.

'Her Nebulizer was missing.'

'What?'

'Her asthma puff … you know, the device she inhales to ease her breathing when she has an attack. She always had it by her side,' Ravi said slowly. 'I looked for it all over. It's not in the house.'

'They took it away,' Tanya stated evenly. 'They frightened her and that brought on an attack. Then they took her Nebulizer away.'

Mr. Rasiah looked shattered. He mumbled his excuses and hurried away.

'She was murdered, wasn't she?'

'Yes, I'm sure she was,' Tanya answered. 'The question is, do you want to take this to the police?'

'No. No, I don't think so. It won't do any good and poor Rasiah will probably get killed as well.'

'I can write the story.'

Ravi looked at her. The afternoon sun was falling on her face and she had pushed her sunglasses to the crown of her head. He noticed that her eyes were not black but had a greeny tint.

Steady expressionless eyes, unblinking.

'Write it and let's see what happens. We have nothing more to lose.'

'All right.'

Tanya turned and walked away.

12

Jaliya, the man who managed the factory at Meepe, finally located Ravi at Reshane's house. He was covered in perspiration and gasping for breath. From his distended eyes Ravi knew that some serious crisis had occurred.

'*Sirta gahala salli aragena,*' his voice was shrill with emotion. '*Sirta thuwalai.*'

Sir has been attacked and the money stolen. Sir is injured.

Ravi felt his heart stop.

Although the plant at Meepe was idle, the staff had to be paid and David had driven off with the money that morning. Ravi had offered to go with him but David, knowing that Ravi had a job interview to attend had scoffed at the idea. David seemed to be recovering slowly from the loss of his wife and had been quietly making plans to re-establish the business. But he had encouraged Ravi to secure a job for himself and Reshane had arranged an interview with a stock broking firm.

'What happened? Where is he?'

'A man from the village came and told me that sir's car had gone off the road and was in a drain. He told me there was no one in the car,' Jaliya's voice was still hoarse with emotion and his eyes seemed to bulge from under his brow. 'There was a crowd of villagers around the car when I got there. They had found sir in a thicket nearby ... he was unconscious ... bleeding from a cut on his head. His briefcase had been forced open and the money was gone.'

'Was he badly hurt? Where is he?'

'I hired a van. We took him to the accident service.'

'Is he all right?'

'I don't know.'

Reshane knew an intern at the General Hospital. She was off duty but he had managed to locate her at her quarters. Dr. Anula turned out to be a plump girl with a dimpled smile and the face of an angel. She hustled them past the security officers at the gate and into the accident ward.

The ward was like a war zone on that day. Men with broken arms and legs, some with hastily bandaged heads, lay on the beds. The nurses attended unemotionally to the victims of brawls and beatings, others perhaps injured in road accidents.

David Perera was at the far end of the ward. His head was almost covered with a bloodstained bandage. His eyes were closed.

'Dad, are you awake?'

Ravi felt a rush of relief when his father opened his eyes.

'Ah Ravi,' he spoke softly. 'They took the money. We can't pay the staff now.'

'Don't worry about that dad, I'll take care of it. How badly are you hurt? What happened?'

'Pajero forced me off the road … some men pulled me out of the vehicle and … they had iron rods in their hands… went on hitting me.'

David closed his eyes.

Ravi looked at Anula who had the bed head ticket in her hand.

'He has bruises on his hands and body, but they are not serious. One cut on his head has needed four stitches, and he is suffering from concussion,' she said. 'He will be all right. He needs to rest.'

Ravi touched his father's hand, now lying lifelessly on the sheet.

'They said *meykath pattarey dapang. Apita kamak nähä.*'

Put this also in the newspapers. We don't care.

Ravi wanted to throw up.

He stood in the corridor outside the ward staring sightlessly at the yard. He knew this was his own fault, his bad judgment. He had told Tanya that they had nothing more to lose but he had been so dreadfully wrong.

Tanya's expose had appeared on the 24th, the Sunday following the funeral. The banner headline, "Victim of MSD violence dies mysteriously" had stirred up a hornet's nest. The telephone didn't stop ringing as friends and relatives called to express their outrage. Ravi had expected some retaliation but when a week went by, and nothing happened, he thought they had dealt the enemy a lethal blow.

And now Ravi realized his father had paid the price for his folly.

'We must go now. He needs to rest,' the doctor said.

Ravi squeezed his father's hand but there was no response. They left the ward and went outside. Dr. Anula promised to check on him regularly.

Ravi was still at Reshane's house when the phone rang. Reshane picked up the phone, listened for a moment and said, 'We'll come over right away.'

When he put the receiver back and turned around, his face was grave.

'I'm sorry, Ravi. Uncle had a heart attack. He's been rushed to Intensive Care.'

Ravi felt utterly crushed by the new blow. Just when he thought nothing worse could happen, it did, and the succession of devastating blows, one after another, was more than he could bear.

'He'll be all right,' Reshane said. 'Anula is there with him.'

Ravi was unable to answer, choking with worry. They didn't speak again till they reached the cardiology unit on Kynsey Road. Reshane called Anula using his mobile phone and she came to the gate to escort them past a scowling gatekeeper.

She turned and looked at Ravi only when they had reached the lobby of the main building.

'I'm sorry, Ravi. Your father suffered another massive attack. They did everything possible. He ... he passed away a few minutes ago.'

Ravi felt the light fading away and his world go black. His leaned against the wall and let his knees fold up beneath him as he slid to the floor. He sat with his back to the wall, his head resting on his knees, curled like a foetus.

His mind was numb, unable to grapple with the final crippling blow.

PART TWO

Riposte

*You only have power over people as long
as you don't take everything away from them.
But when you've robbed a man of everything
he's no longer in your power –
he's free again.*

Alexander Solzhenitsyn
First Circle

13

Tanya Koch was not in her seat when Ravi walked in to her office, but a fair girl with a bad attack of acne assured him she was somewhere in the building. Would Ravi wait?

Ravi pulled a wobbly chair from behind another vacant desk and sat down. It was an untidy room crammed with too much furniture. The pimply girl now had a phone jammed between shoulder and chin. She started scrabbling through the piles of paper scattered untidily all over her table. Tanya's desk was a stark contrast with just one thin stack of papers under a glass paperweight on one edge, and a glass of water on the other side.

Tanya walked up and stood behind her desk, studying him impassively.

'Hi.'

No smile – just Hi.

'Hello.'

'Have you settled your affairs then?'

'Yes.'

'Specifically?'

'I closed the business and found a buyer for the house. When he pays up in a couple of days I'll be able to settle the bank.'

'Will you have anything left?'

'Not much. Enough to get by till I find a job.'

Tanya looked at him steadily for a while.

'What's happening to the Police investigation? Have you had any news?'

'They insist that mum's death was due to natural causes,' Ravi was mildly surprised that he was able to speak without choking up. 'About dad ... they have no witnesses and no leads. The file is not closed but the investigation is going nowhere.'

'The Police are a bunch of prostitutes. So long as Mudalige Premasiri is in power they won't move against him, or his family ... or his thugs. He can do anything and get away with it. These minor scandals are useless – people read the stories, whisper about it to their neighbours and ... nothing happens. In a week it's history. All our efforts to get at the truth, all the risks we take to publish, all forgotten. Useless.'

'Yes.'

Tanya was silent for a while, looking down at her hands held open on the table.

'The Statesman is committed to toppling this government and Mudalige is the key.'

'So?'

'We must make sure he loses his seat. That will be a big blow to them,' Tanya went on thoughtfully. 'We have a common interest there. If he loses, he won't have the power to harass you.'

Ravi just looked at her.

'Yes, I see what you mean. But what can we do? If people don't believe what they read in the newspapers, what else can we do?'

'Oh, they believe it all right. It's just that the Minister attacking some family in Colombo is not an issue for the voters in his electorate, in Pananpola. They have to see something affecting their own lives.'

'So?'

'I'm going down there on Monday to look around. The opposition candidate is Upali Tennakoon. I know his organizer, a fellow called Sandika. You can come along, if you like'

Ravi hesitated, trying to gauge the woman's thoughts but she stared back impassively. He noticed again that her eyes had an unusual greenish tinge when the light caught them.

'Yes. Yes I'll come.'

'Good,' Tanya nodded. 'We have to leave very early. Can you get here at 5.00 on Monday morning? The office van will drop us at the Pettah bus stand.'

'No worries.'

68

'All right then. Come prepared to stay over, in case there's a story to follow up.'

She stood up abruptly and escorted Ravi out of the room.

*

The bus stand in Pettah was nearly deserted when a sleepy office driver dropped them off. The coach, built to seat forty passengers in what passes for comfort, carried just a handful of people outward bound from the city. The driver took off at 5.30 and they were soon racing along the deserted sections of Galle Road, till they reached Mt. Lavinia. The driver, an unwashed ruffian in a blue T-shirt, fiddled with the tuning switch of a radio with his left hand, trying one station after another till he found one that was playing music to his taste. Sinhala love songs at eighty decibels. Ravi found the look of tortured distaste on Tanya's face almost enough to compensate for putting up with the awful racket.

She had been silent at the beginning of the journey, taking the window seat and staring at the ghostly scene falling behind them.

Ravi hated periods of silence because it made him more conscious of the knot of fury in his stomach. It had grown and grown after each crushing blow, till he felt as if it filled his entire midriff. And he was afraid of it. Afraid to look too closely, afraid to take it out to the light of day and examine it. Afraid that if he let it out, he would be driven mad by grief and hatred.

One day retribution will come to you, you bastards. I don't know how or when, but you'll pay for your crimes before that day ends.

Tanya turned and looked at him.

'You are taking this very well,' she said with a ghost of a smile. 'Is it possible you are not quite the wimp I took you to be?'

Ravi was surprised to find that her praise, backhanded though it was, still pleased him.

'No. I am still numb,' he said honestly. 'I want to do something massively destructive but don't know how to get about it.'

'That's what all dumb asses want to do to their enemies. Run up and kick their faces in. But that doesn't work. The idiots end up losing their own teeth.'

"So? You have another solution?'

'You can't succeed with a frontal assault. It's like charging the front gate of a fortress. The defenses are in place and they are expecting you. You will be playing to their strength.'

'So you attack from the rear?'

'Or the flank. Anywhere you're not expected.'

There was enough daylight to see her face now. Ravi was surprised to see that her normally impassive face was animated. The subject excited her and her expression showed it.

'That sounds logical enough but we don't have the weapons even for a surprise attack. What can we do that will really hurt them?'

'Secrets! A man like that has secrets for sure,' Tanya asserted confidently. 'These bastards imagine they're going to be in power forever so they do the craziest things. You'll be surprised at what you can find once you start digging.'

The traffic built up thereafter slowing their pace, and it was nearly 7.00 when they crossed the twin bridges over the Kalu Ganga. They got off the bus at Kalutara.

The bus to Kalawana hadn't come in yet so they sat on the half wall of the bus stand and watched the buses from the interior disgorge passengers. Tanya was again dressed in faded denims and a man's shirt with button down pockets. She wore sensible walking shoes and had her hair tucked under a cap. Tanya Koch was a Burgher, a misnomer given to descendants of the Portuguese and Dutch, who had settled in the island in colonial times. With her brown streaked hair and fair complexion, Ravi thought she might easily pass for a European tourist.

Ravi bought a small comb of bananas and a packet of cream crackers for their breakfast. They were brushing the biscuit crumbs off their clothes when they heard a man shouting *Kalawana, Karawita* and knew their bus had come in. Ten minutes later they were rattling along the road towards

Matugama and Kalawana.

They had nearly sixty kilometers to travel, and Ravi knew it would take at least two hours to reach Kalawana. The bus was half empty and the journey through miles of shady rubber plantations was a pleasant one. It was mid morning and the sun was unpleasantly warm on their backs when they got off at Kalawana. Ravi made inquiries at the bus stand about getting to Pananpola. A bearded loafer told him they'd have to take a bus to Potupitiya, the nearest town, and try their luck from there.

It was nearly noon when the crowded van they had boarded at Potupitiya turned round a blind corner and entered the main street of Pananpola.

There were burning tyres on the road.

Columns of black smoke rose up and the acrid smell of trouble drifted through the van as it came to a halt. The passengers were murmuring worriedly to each other as they collected their belongings and stepped out of the vehicle. Locals had gathered in small groups looking at a shop that had been gutted, the roof collapsed inward and smoke still rising from the rubble.

Ravi and Tanya shouldered their backpacks and walked with the other passengers towards the market area.

Sandika, it seemed, had gone out but would be back soon.

A worried looking middle-aged man was sorting posters with four young men in the small National Alliance office that opened into an alley near the town centre. They looked suspiciously at the visitors but Tanya's awful Sinhala soon convinced them that the visitors were harmless.

Ravi sat down on a bench by the side of the front door while Tanya went over to examine the posters. The office comprised one large room leading to the alley with two smaller rooms at the back. He was not surprised to see a collection of steel rods and wooden axe handles leaning against the wall behind the front door.

A stocky young man with close-cropped hair walked in accompanied by two other men. His face split into a grin when he saw Tanya.

'Ahh, Miss Tanya. Hondai adha āpu eka. Däkka nedha ung karana deval?'

Ah Miss Tanya. It's good you came today. Can you see what the other side is doing?

'Tell me what's happening? I'll report it in the papers.'

'The campaign was normal till last week and we were doing well. There were small incidents when our boys putting up flags and posters were assaulted in some places and we did the same to them. Nothing serious till they brought some thugs from outside, men with guns. They started attacking our meetings. Last Friday they killed Chamath, one of our key organizers. He had been shot and his body had been thrown in a paddy field.'

'Who are these men? Haven't you gone to the police?'

'*Huh!*' Sandika snorted in disgust. '*Ung ämathithumagey puka imbinawa misak, wena mokuth karanney nähä. Arpu aya ämathithumage security kārayolu.*'

Huh! The police do nothing except kiss the Minister's arse. We hear the outsiders are from the Minister's security.

'*Pathirana kiyala minihek thamai ungey näyakaya.*'

A man called Pathirana is their leader.

'What happened last night?' Tanya had her little dictaphone balanced on the table and was also taking notes.

'Matara Mudalali was one of our strong supporters. He had an electronic goods store on the other side of the road. They broke into his shop last night and set it on fire.'

'What about the burning tyres on the road?'

'Oh. That was us.'

Sandika went on with a litany of wrongdoing by the Minister's supporters.

Tanya listened intently and finally said, 'I can write about this but it isn't enough. All the government MPs are resorting to thuggery. It isn't real news. I need to print something that will shame him. Some secret people don't know about.'

Sandika looked at his boys. A long haired fellow raised his eyes, '*Eyāgey hora lee business eka nang harima sarui.*'

His illicit logging business is very prosperous.

'What logging business?' Tanya asked eagerly. 'What does he do?'

The man looked faintly embarrassed that he was the centre of attention but continued doggedly in Sinhala, 'They are cutting down timber in the forest. There's a big camp and a sawmill in the jungle. They run the machines with generators. They bring the sawn timber out in big trucks and the Minister arranges permits for the vehicles.'

'Where is this being done?' Ravi knew very well what the answer would be.

'South of here,' the man said simply. 'In the Sinharaja.'

Tanya's quick intake of breath indicated that she also realized that this was news indeed. The Sinharaja forest was the largest lowland rain forest in the country and covered some eight thousand eight hundred hectares. It had been declared an international Man and Biosphere Reserve by UNESCO and was considered a national treasure. It had many unique features, the Sinharaja, but to a timber thief it would be heaven, for the trees of the canopy towered one hundred and fifty feet above the ground.

If they could prove that illicit logging was taking place, and that the Minister was heavily involved, the news would raise a storm of protest around the country.

'I want to film the camp and the saw-mill,' Tanya said calmly. 'Can you take us there?'

Long hair turned and looked at a bearded fellow standing next to him.

'The only way to the camp is along a cart track that goes through a village called Koskulana. But all the villagers there work at the logging camp and the track is guarded by armed men,' the bearded man said. 'They will not let outsiders go near the saw-mill.'

'Can't we cut through the forest?'

'Miss, you haven't seen this forest,' beard shook his head. 'It's far too thick. The road is the only way in.'

'Can't you write about it?' Sandika asked anxiously. 'We can find witnesses.'

Tanya shook her head impatiently. 'No. I need proof that there is a saw-mill and proof that the Minister is involved.'

The men shuffled their feet. No one had any new ideas.

Tanya wanted to video the burning building and the tyres on the road. Sandika walked with them. Some of his men sauntered into the market area behind them.

'Wait till the bus is here,' Sandika told Tanya quietly. 'Take your pictures at the last moment and then leave.'

Tanya looked at him for a moment and nodded.

'We think there is a traitor in our office. Whenever we plan something, even a cottage meeting, the Minister's thugs know about it in advance.'

'You are not going to defeat the Minister like this.'

'No,' Sandika sounded depressed. 'No, we need help.'

A small bus came creaking down the road, swinging gingerly to the grass verge to avoid the smoldering tyres. It picked up speed again only to stop before them, raising a cloud of dust. Tanya whipped her camcorder out of its case and quickly shot pictures of the gutted building and the columns of black smoke spiraling up from the tyres. Minutes later they were jammed uncomfortably into a seat at the back as the driver took off with a jerk.

Ravi had spoken very little while they were with Sandika.

'We can get to the logging camp from the other side.'

'What?' Tanya pulled her sunglasses on to her nose and peered at Ravi over the rim. 'What are you talking about?'

'I know the Sinharaja. I know the birding trails.'

'What the hell is a birding trail?'

'The Sinharaja is the largest lowland rain forest in the country. It is famous for very rare bird species. There are footpaths through the forest that birdwatchers use.'

'And you know these … birding trails? You think you can find this camp?'

'Yeah,' Ravi said confidently. 'I can find it.'

'You're not just bullshitting me, are you?'

'No. No bullshit.'

Tanya was silent, mulling over what she had heard.

'Burgher blood is running thin these days,' Ravi said softly.

'What?'

'In my dad's time, he told me that the Burghers were an adventurous lot. They knew every inch of the wild places in this country. They wouldn't have needed a Sinhalese to lead the way. Now …'

'Now what?' Tanya's voice was dangerously quiet.

'Now they've gone soft. They just want safe city jobs. They don't want to know anything about the country.'

'Listen, you arsehole ...' Tanya stopped when Ravi started laughing. She glared at him angrily for a moment and then turned her face away.

'Fine! Maybe you have a point but remember, I hate smug bastards. So what's your plan? Can we really do this?'

'We've brought clothes and toiletries for staying overnight, haven't we? If we hop off at a village called Weddagala on this road, we can walk up to the forest department office at Kudawa. From there it is an uphill slog to Martin's place. We can get help there.'

Tanya kept silent, waiting for him to go on.

'Martin?'

'Martin is a real character. He is a former forest guard who is now a self-taught expert on the flora and fauna of the Sinharaja. Professors from foreign universities travel to Sri Lanka just to consult him.'

'How come I've never heard of this man?'

'Burgher blood is thinning ...'

'Shut the fuck up about my blood.'

Ravi saw a road sign and yelled at the driver to stop. They paid their fares and stepped on to the dusty road at Weddagala. A narrow road branched off to the left and Ravi knew this led to the Kudawa camp and the entrance to Sinharaja.

He walked into the least rundown grocery shop and listed the provisions he would need. Bread, a tin of mackerel, biscuits and some chocolates. He also picked up a two-cell flashlight, matches, a knife and a roll of nylon cord. He added two little vials of Siddhalepa, a herbal balm and a box of mosquito coils. Tanya seemed faintly amused by it all but did not comment as Ravi packed his purchases away carefully in his backpack.

They were lucky to hitch a ride in a van that dropped them near the Kudawa office. The steep and badly broken road leading to the forest reserve started there. Ravi knew another route, a footpath that was even steeper but considerably shorter than the main track, and went ahead of Tanya to show the way. It was nearly noon and the sun was blazing down on them as they struggled up the incline. They were streaming with perspiration and panting heavily when they reached Martin's lodge.

Martin, a short barrel-chested character in a sarong and sleeveless banian, was standing near his gate watching them labouring up the slope. He owned the only place that visitors could stay over and remain within walking distance of the main gate, but he, Martin, decided who would be taken in as a guest.

And who not.

And how much each person should be charged. All decisions were made on the spot by looking at the visitor's face. Hot shots driving up in powerful vehicles often got the "No Vacancy" handoff. If he thought you were a researcher or a young person keen on birds you got in almost free.

Ravi wasn't sure if old Martin would remember him but he need not have worried. As soon as they were close enough, Martin called out.

'Ahh, mey apey Ravi podi mahaththaya neyda? Kālekata passé.'

Isn't this the young gentleman Ravi? After a long time.

'Ow Martin. Mama rata giya iganaganna.'

Yes. I was abroad for studies.

'Padan witharack karala nähä. Suddiyekuth allagena thiyenney.'

You haven't only studied. You've caught a white woman as well.

Ravi started laughing when Tanya said coldly:

'Mama suddiyeck nevei. Mama muge gäänith nevei.'

I am not a foreigner. I am not this bugger's woman either.

That shut Martin up. He looked at her with his mouth open for a moment but recovered quickly. He ushered them into his lodge.

Martin's dining cum sitting room was brilliant. It was situated on a ridge with a breathtaking view of the forest falling away into a valley and then climbing up the far slope. He had wisely built an open hall with a half wall going round it. The furnishings comprised three crude dining tables with benches on either side. And a few armchairs!

The other buildings were slums.

Martin had built a two storey monstrosity with stuffy little rooms and toilets at the end of a corridor. He was architect, builder, plumber and electrician.

And it showed.

Ravi told Martin they'd come to look at some of the amphibians of the Sinharaja. And would stay for a day or two. Could they have a room?

'*Prasneyak nähä. Dennatama panseeyai – käma ekka.*'

No problem. Five hundred for both, with food.

Generous rates indeed! Ravi realised that the old man was still fond of him.

Martin led them to a room on the lower floor and left to organize lunch. The room was a poorly ventilated box with one double bed. Ravi knew that many of the rooms had two beds and realized that the old rogue was either trying to establish a romance or get his own back at Tanya for the snub he'd received.

Probably the latter.

Tanya looked at the room with distaste.

'Not the Hilton, is it?'

'The old Burghers would have loved this place.'

'Shut up! I want to shower and change. Can you bugger off?'

Tanya stared at him icily till he left the room.

Ravi found Martin in the living room playing with one of his grandchildren, a little fellow of four or five with a running nose.

Did Martin have a lightweight tent and a couple of sleeping bags? Extra binoculars? They were thinking of camping out for a night to look at frogs and stuff.

'*Ona ekkak dennang. Häma deyma thiyanava.*'

I can give you whatever you want. I have everything.

Ravi knew that lots of the foreign researchers who came to the Sinharaja presented Martin with gear they no longer needed, and the man had a good collection of stuff, lovingly maintained.

He had selected what he wanted, pleased to find a small compass as well, when Tanya came up seemingly in a better frame of mind. He left her with Martin and went for his turn under the shower.

When Ravi got back he was mildly surprised to find Tanya and the old man chatting comfortably. Martin spoke good English, when he wanted to. And he was immensely knowledgeable about the flora and fauna of the Sinharaja.

'Missy say you are still on test,' Martin called loudly when he saw Ravi. 'She will give a break if you are nice to her.'

'Missy only saying that. I'm always nice but still no break.'

'Ah, you young gentlemen don't know how to get round young lady,' Martin replied with a yellow-toothed leer. 'If I was young I would have given a try myself.'

'Even now you are more handsome than this fellow,' Tanya joined in the banter.

'No. No.' Martin said. 'Too old. But tonight in the tent, maybe missy give him a chance, eh?'

'What tent?'

'I borrowed a small tent. Just in case we have to sleep rough tonight,' Ravi pacified her hurriedly, ignoring the quick frown. 'I'll explain later.'

Martin's meals were unique in their own way. When the food was ready it was brought out in cauldrons and placed on a long bench. Pauper or king, you ate what was on the table. No special dishes for anyone. Pick up a plate, serve yourself and eat with your fingers, then wash the plate carefully and place it back on the rack for others to use.

Tanya was right, of course. It wasn't The Hilton, but the food was wholesome and they were hungry. Tanya looked around surreptitiously for cutlery and finding none, wrinkled her nose and settled down to eating with her fingers. When they were done, Ravi asked for two parcels of food to take with them.

It was just after 2.00 p.m. when they left Martin's and began to climb the gentle slope to the gate. Ravi knew that Martin did not for a moment believe his story about looking for frogs. The old man probably thought it was an elaborate scheme of his to get into Tanya's pants.

The walk up to the main gate was uphill and there was little cover from the sun. Their backpacks were bulging with provisions, the tent and sleeping bags adding to the load. They were covered with perspiration once again when then reached the entrance to the forest reserve and presented their papers to the guard on duty. Fortunately the road was mostly flat and shaded thereafter and they were able to make better time.

And enjoy the surroundings.

Batu Nā, Keena and Beraliya trees rose above the road, forming an almost seamless upper canopy. Another distinct layer of shorter trees formed a sub-canopy, while dense patches of shrubs and ferns covered the ground. The forest throbbed with the shrill chirping of cicadas.

Thirty minutes of trekking brought them to the Field Research Station. A large area, an acre at least, had been cleared and a single solid building stood in the centre of it. On one edge of the clearing stood a couple of open, shed-like buildings. Someone had told Ravi that the sheds belonged to some group called the March for Conservation.

They sat on the steps of the main building to rest and drink some water.

'So, what's the plan then?'

'We have to locate the saw-mill first. It'll be a long walk so we won't have time to get back to Martin's before dark. It's best to camp out tonight.'

She didn't dance for joy. Ravi had a feeling that she was even less anxious to go back to the dingy room at Martin's and figured the tent was a better proposition.

'All right, but how in hell will we find a saw-mill in this huge forest?'

'There's a peak called Sinhagala up ahead. It's probably not too far from the area where they're doing the logging. If we can climb a fair way up, and look in the right direction, we might be able to spot it.'

She was silent for a while, thinking about it.

'How do we get to this Sinha ... whatever?'

'There's a footpath and then up, along a stream bed.'

'How far?'

'I don't know. It's a long way.'

She smiled grudgingly, but still a smile that washed away the severity of her normal expression. Ravi was mildly surprised to find that she was very much a foxy lady when she smiled.

'You are not quite the twerp I'd taken you to be,' she said lightly.

'Oh, thanks,' Ravi tried to inject some sarcasm into his voice. 'First I graduated from being a wimp, and now I'm up from twerp. How much further can I go?'

It was wasted on her.

'I'll keep you posted.'

They followed the gravel road as it swung across a small bridge and then continued in an easterly direction beyond the Research Station. The thick canopy of the forest stretched across the road in its quest for sunlight and gave them some respite from the early afternoon sun. This was an area that had been selectively logged when a brain dead government had given a Canadian company permission to extract timber for supply to a local plywood factory. A storm of public protests had halted the project but the affected areas had produced a regenerated forest, slightly different in character to the virgin rain forest.

On account of the thinner vegetation, it was easier to spot birds there. That's where they ran into a feeding flock.

The forest that seemed to be dozing quietly in the mid-afternoon heat suddenly burst into life. A feeding flock of birds is a unique feature of the Sinharaja. Flocks of birds, many different species, were moving through the forest in an orderly way, feeding noisily as they went.

Ravi tried to identify them.

Orange-billed Babblers were in mid canopy, chirping lustily. He saw Black Bulbuls, Yellow-naped Woodpeckers, an Azure Flycatcher and a couple of Crested Drongos flitting about. A Laughing Thrush was rooting in the leaf mould on the forest floor. Then he caught a glimpse of the rare and wonderful Red-faced Malkoha in the upper canopy.

Ravi explained how the flocks fed at different levels of the forest, and helped each other. The birds feeding on the forest floor picked up any succulent tit-bit that was dislodged by the birds feeding above them. Insects the ground feeders disturbed when they foraged on the forest floor were picked up by the birds feeding in the trees above!

The Drongos were warrior-bandits. Two or three of these jet-black birds kept watch, faithfully guarding the feeding flock against predators. But the feeders had to pay a price. If one of them unearthed a particularly succulent grub or moth, one of the Drongos would execute a power dive to snatch it away from the finder.

Species by species, the birds crossed the road over their heads and moved away into the forest, their incessant twittering gradually fading away. Then the forest was quiet again, except for the droning of the Cicadas.

'It's very ... impressive,' Tanya said grudgingly, as if the compliment was forced out of her. 'Is it always like that?'

'Mm.'

'How did you learn this stuff? About the birds, I mean?'

'My dad ... taught me,' Ravi words caught in his throat when it hit him again that they would never visit the forest together again. 'He was very keen on wild life. Especially birds. He planned trips for the holidays ... Mum hated them, but Tilak and I, we lived through the whole school term just counting the days till the next trip'

'Hmm.'

The gravel track came to an end and narrowed into a footpath.

Leech country. The curse of the Sinharaja!

Leeches had not been a problem so far as they had stayed on the broad gravel track, but the footpath would be different. The rotting leaves on the forest floor harboured endless hordes of leeches that seemed to smell the approach of a nice red blooded human. They'd be sucked dry if they weren't careful.

'Fold the ends of your pants and push them into your stockings.'

'I'll look like a jockey,' she grumbled sourly.

'Female jockeys are quite sexy.'

'Bugger off.'

But she bent over and did as she was told. Ravi did the same and then fished out a vial of Siddalepa balm he had purchased earlier. He used his fingers to daub the aromatic paste over their shoes.

'Does it work?' Tanya was suspicious, clearly put out by the greasy stains on her white walking shoes.

'It does, really,' Ravi grinned up at her. 'But you still have to check all the time. You don't really want these creatures crawling up your legs.'

Tanya just looked at him.

The footpath wound its way through the forest that now seemed oppressively close. The sky was almost covered by the canopy and they were moving in a tunnel. But the leaf mould on the path was soggy with moisture, and crawling with leeches. The Siddalepa must have been effective, because only very few actually clung to their shoes and tried to crawl up. Ravi insisted on regular checks but despite their precautions he had one oozing red patch where a leech had managed to find his skin through a lesion in his stocking.

They finally came to a rocky stream cascading down from their right. The water splashed and channeled its way through a moonscape of boulders that disappeared up the hill.

That was their road to Sinhagala.

Sinhagala was one of the mountains within the forest that soared to some two thousand five hundred feet. Clothed with impenetrable forest on all sides, the only way to assault the peak was along the stream.

And it wasn't a walk in the park!

Ravi led the way and picked a route. The boulders were huge, most of them with moss laden, slimy sides. He knew that one slip would result in a serious injury so they had to pick their way with extreme caution. Unencumbered, it would still have been a stiff climb but with their heavy packs it was a nightmare.

They were exhausted when they came to the small plateau that Ravi had been making for. He remembered the place from a previous visit and had planned to make camp there.

Tanya sank to her knees, dropping her backpack on the ground.

'Is this it?' She asked wearily. 'We camp here?'

'Yeah.'

She didn't seem impressed. The rock strewn clearing by the side of the stream was small and surrounded by trees and heavy undergrowth. The trees on the hillside were different to those in the valleys, not quite as tall but making up for that by their sheer density.

'There aren't many clearings in this forest. Come on. Let's get the tent up.'

'You can't spot the logging camp from here,' Tanya pointed out. 'Are you planning to climb a tree?'

Ravi shook his head.

'There's a spot further up where you are able to see over the forest,'

'More climbing? My knees are wobbly already.'

'The old Burghers ...'

'Cut that out.'

Half an hour later they were perched on a rock some distance above the camp. The streambed traversed the northern face of the mountain, and by looking down the path of the stream they were able to get a fine view of the forest to the north of the mountain. Their own tent was tiny in the foreground and the mountain fell away beyond it. And further on, like a billiard table, the green canopy stretched out towards the horizon.

Ravi began scanning the forest with Martin's binoculars.

He had thought it would be easy to spot a clearing from their vantage. He knew that, if Sandika's story was accurate, the logging camp had to be north of Sinhagala and near the two villages that bordered the reserve on that side. He was high up, and looking in the right direction, but there was no obvious break in the sea of green treetops. He began to scan the forest slowly from side to side, starting near the base of Sinhagala and slowly working his way outwards. He began to get worried when he completed a full survey and found nothing.

Start again. Nothing.

He was on his third scan when he saw a tree crown sway in the wind. He passed over it and moved on. Then it hit him. There was no wind to speak of, and only that tree had moved.

Back!

Ravi managed to locate the movement again as the crown of a tall tree continued its list to one side and then sank out of sight. He noted the spot, not very far from the foot of Sinhagala, in relation to a distant mountain and then again with a tree in the foreground. Putting his binoculars aside, he took a careful compass reading. He made it five degrees west of north.

That was it.

Thirty minutes later they were scrambling down the bed of another small rivulet that took them down the mountain in a more northerly direction. Ravi found that the compass reading was going to be less useful than he had expected once he was submerged in the forest and had no view of his reference points. But it was better than nothing.

When they finally reached the foot of the hill the stream meandered off in a northeasterly direction, so they had no choice but to scramble through the forest. Going over rocky overgrown terrain was very hard and Ravi began to wonder if they would miss the camp altogether and get lost.

They found the camp only because the logged area was so extensive that they stumbled into a clearing. It was easy from then on to follow the high-pitched drone of the chain saws and the thud of a generator.

'We can't walk in the open,' Ravi said. 'We'll have to stay in the trees.'

Tanya had mud stains in her pants, oozing leech bites around her ankles and scratches on her arms, but her eyes were dancing.

'Yeah, ok. I want to get as close as possible to the mill.'

In each clearing they passed through, Tanya videoed the surrounding forest first to demonstrate that they were indeed in the Sinharaja. Then she scanned the telltale stumps in ruined clearings to show the devastation.

The saw-mill was located in a shallow valley. Ravi made a wide circuit and approached it by crawling over a wooded ridge on one side. Although the tall trees had been cut down, the under canopy and shrub gave them enough cover to reach a small rock outcropping that emerged from the ground near the edge of the cleared area.

'The greedy bastard,' Ravi breathed. The conservationist in him outraged by what he saw before him. 'They are destroying this ... this jewel.'

There were two tractors hauling trimmed logs into the yard. Ravi saw two work elephants in the distance. Sawn timber was being loaded onto a truck at the far end. Men were moving about with urgency, as though they had a quota to fill.

Tanya worked her camera carefully, zooming to get details of the operations going on. Finally she turned to Ravi and whispered, 'we can show that there is a large scale logging operation going on in the Sinharaja. We can show it is by Sinhagala and therefore near the Minister's electorate. But we can't show a direct link to him.'

'Yes, I know. But we can't stay here much longer. We have to get to the camp before dark.'

'How much time do we have?'

'Fifteen minutes maybe. We can come back in the morning.'

Tanya took some footage of the men washing up after work and put her camera away. They crawled up the gentle slope till they got over the ridge. Once they were able to stand up, Ravi used his compass to set a course due south.

14

Martin's tent was a parachute silk affair with barely enough crawl space to shelter two persons. The feature that pleased Ravi was the ground sheet that could be connected to the upper section by a zipper. That kept leeches and even snakes out of the picture.

They were very tired, but Ravi pushed himself to find enough driftwood along the edge of the stream to build a fire. His years of scouting had at least taught him how to get one going. Find one piece of relatively soft dry wood and use your penknife to shave off strips of kindling. Make a small wigwam with the kindling and set that pile alight with a match. Feed dry leaves and twigs till you have a healthy flame. Then lay larger twigs around the flame. Place the longest logs upwind so they will last the night.

Tanya had found a pool with about a foot of water to sit in. She had washed her clothes and spread them on a rock. There wasn't enough light for Ravi to see what she was wearing and she called out to him before he got too close.

'Push off. This area is for ladies only.'

'What ladies? I only see one Burgher bimbo.'

She said something unprintable.

Ravi found a spot further downstream and stripped down to wash his clothes. His ankles and calves were covered with dried blood but the leeches were long gone. He lowered himself into the surprisingly cold water and let the weariness wash away with the grime and blood.

They ate immediately afterwards, famished by the day's exertions. Martin had parceled their afternoon meal but supplemented it with a splendid dry fish *thel dala*. They drank water directly from the stream.

It was early, not quite 8.00 in the evening. Ravi tended the fire and then lit a few mosquito coils and placed them in a circle. He stretched himself out on the rock and looked up at the sky directly above. The Sinharaja had a very high rainfall but, fortunately for them, it was a clear night and the sky was jeweled.

Tanya had worn a flimsy pair of shorts with a loose T-shirt.

Long, long legs.

Ravi felt sensitized by those legs. How had he never noticed or even thought about them before?

She came over and sat down nearby. After awhile she also stretched herself out on the rock, her hands under her head.

'Will anyone see our fire?'

'It can't be seen from down the hill, the trees are too thick. Someone would have to come really close to see it.'

'Would they?'

'Only a crazy man would climb these hills at night. It's a good way to break a leg.'

They saw a shooting star just then.

It might have been just a bit of space debris re-entering the atmosphere or it might have been the real thing. What they did see was an immensely bright object streak across the sky.

'You can make a wish, you know,' Tanya said seriously.

'Really?'

'Sure. Make one.'

'All right.'

They were silent for a while.

'So? What did you wish?'

'You first.'

'I wished this shitty government gets thrown out. No. My wish is that I get the scoop that ruins the bastards.'

'Mm.'

'Your turn.'

'You'll laugh.'

'Try me.'

'Well, you know ... I wished for something very simple,' Ravi said slowly. 'I just wanted to rest my head on something soft.'

'You idiot!' Tanya laughed derisively. 'When you could have wished for anything, you wish for a pillow? You really are a mutt!'

'Actually I wished you'd let me rest my head ... on your lap.'

Silence.

'Do you see the three bright stars in a row?' Ravi asked in the void, worried he had gone too far. 'That's Orion's Belt.'

'Really?' The voice came straight out of a freezer compartment.

'The sword that comes at an angle from the centre of the belt always points south,' Ravi stumbled on bravely.

'All right.'

'What?'

'All right,' Tanya said quietly. 'You can put your head on my lap.'

Ravi couldn't hear the frogs anymore. Either they'd stopped suddenly or the blood rush had burst his eardrums.

Tanya was now seated with her legs stretched out and leaning against a rock. Ravi crawled over to her, lay down and gently lowered his head.

She wore a pair of shorts made of some silky material. He felt the material slipping over her skin under the weight of his head. It made the faintest rustling sound. The indescribable girl scent assaulted his senses making his head swim. He felt as if his body had been transfixed, every nerve end raw and tingling.

He turned his head slowly and looked into her eyes. He thought they had the strangest expression. But it might have been just the dancing flames. Or his excitement.

He raised himself and kissed her cheek, then her forehead and eyes, the tip of her nose and then finally her mouth. An Irish barmaid in Coventry had taught him how, and he had been a willing learner.

Tanya seemed to like it. He could tell.

After a while he put his hand under the front of her T-shirt and touched the edge of her breast. He didn't have a chance to enjoy the moment. Tanya took a fistful of hair at the back of his head and yanked his face off her.

'Ow.'

'Kissing is ok, baby. But no more ... unless you're really serious ... about us.'

Ravi calmed himself with an effort. It took blood and time.

'Tani, I like you,' his voice was steady when he finally spoke. 'I like you a lot but there's too much anger in me to be serious … about anyone. You understand that, don't you?'

'Yes, I understand.'

'What do we do now?'

'You can kiss me some more,' she smiled calmly, as if asking him to pass the salt. 'If you like.'

He liked.

And did.

He had to knock it off when she complained that her lips were hurting. He put his head down on her lap and again felt the eroticism of her girl smell engulf him. He wanted to scream that he loved her, that he'd marry her.

Anything!

Tanya must have known what he was going through, yet all she did was taunt him. 'That's about as close to the jackpot as you're likely to get, sweetie.'

But it made him laugh and the laughter released the tension in him. Tanya laughed too, leaning over his face and smothering him. She didn't laugh often but when she did, it was a throaty gurgle.

He liked that.

They talked for a while and then decided to get some sleep. They heard a Sambhur bell in the valley below, a haunting 'Donk' as Ravi got up to tend to the fire and prepare for the night.

Tanya made fun of Ravi's sarong, a gaily-printed batik.

'Bloody Sinhalese,' she jeered. 'Can't you find anything better to wear than a tube of cloth, like a woman's dress.'

'The sarong is an unmatchable garment in case of diarrhoea,' Ravi said stoutly, 'and for fornication.'

'Well, you'd better hope for diarrhoea, because fornication is out.'

'Don't be so sure. I might get scared in the night and cuddle up to you. Who knows what might happen then?'

'I know for sure what will happen. You'll spend the night in the open.'

The tent was semicircular in cross section, but less than three feet high. They crawled inside and zippered up the entrance. Netting on either side provided some ventilation and kept the mosquitos out, but the space inside was just enough to roll out two sleeping bags, with about six inches of free space in between.

They both decided to sleep on top of the bags rather than creep inside. The air pillows, courtesy of Martin's visitors, made them reasonably comfortable.

But she was very close. Ravi felt the tension building again.

'If you promise not to touch me,' Tanya said, 'I'll kiss you goodnight.'

'Are you trying to drive me mad?'

'Sure. Why not? All men are pigs anyway.'

'You're a sadist. Did you know that?'

'Do you want to be kissed or not?'

'Yes. I like suffering.'

She was chuckling when she leaned over and kissed him.

Gentle, almost sisterly.

'Good night, honey.'

15

They broke camp very early. The sun had just cleared the highest trees to the east of them when they negotiated the ridge above the logging camp. Minutes later they were concealed, once again, behind the rocks at the edge of the clearing.

They had traveled light.

Ravi had hidden most of their gear in a pile of rocks near the base of the hill. The streambed they had climbed down turned sharply to the east there and Ravi thought that would help him find the spot again. If, on their return, he came to the base of the hill and there was no stream, he'd have to turn east to find it. If he came upon the stream flowing east, he'd have to follow it upstream to find the spot.

An open truck came up the road with about a dozen men standing at the back. Minutes later a tractor came rattling up the track hauling a trailer full of more men. Workmen from the village. The generator started with a thudding roar and the sawmill came to life. Some of the workers climbed into the trailer once again and were taken deeper into the forest.

Tanya, who'd been morose and grumpy all morning, was now all business and focused on the job. Ravi scanned the clearing with his binoculars, cupping his hands over the end of the lens so the sun wouldn't catch the glass and give away his position.

Nothing new.

After a while they got tired of crouching behind the rocks, staring down at the clearing. They took a break to eat biscuits and drink some water.

Back to the watch.

It was getting towards noon and Ravi began to feel they were wasting their time. It was hot and humid and the flies were tormenting them. How much longer?

The growl of a vehicle coming up the track broke the monotony. They scrambled back to their position behind the rocks just in time to see a gleaming silver Montero come into the clearing and pull up in front of the mill. Tanya aimed her camcorder at the vehicle as the driver got off and ran round the front of the vehicle to the passenger side. He was just in time to hold the door open for a heavy set man who stepped down from the front seat and stretched himself, as if to get rid of the kinks of a long journey. Thick frame, broad shoulders, fat jowls and unmistakable close-cropped hair.

Shalindra Premasiri himself.

Wow!

A man in trousers and a singlet came running out of the mill. He clasped his hands together and bowed to Premasiri in the best traditional manner. Premasiri put his arm over the man's shoulders and led him into the mill.

'I've got the bastard,' Tanya breathed. 'Got his face and vehicle number, with the saw-mill in the background. We have the connection.'

A querulous voice came from behind and above them.

'Eyii, monawada methana karanne?'

Hey, what are you doing here?

Ravi turned. A bare bodied man in a sarong was standing at the top of the hillock behind them, probably on his way to the mill. He was staring at them with deep suspicion.

'Sir, Sir. Menna kauda photo gannawa.'

Sir. Sir. Someone's taking photographs.

The man made no attempt to get closer to them. He remained where he was, some thirty feet above them, calling hysterically to the men in the mill. Ravi heard confused shouting behind him and turned to look. Men were streaming out of the mill and leading them was Premasiri's bulky figure.

They heard the man roar:

'Unwa allaganing. Mama langata geneng.'

Catch them. Bring them to me.

Tanya had stuffed her precious camcorder into its case at the first sign of trouble. Ravi grabbed her by the shoulder and picked a rock in his other hand. He then charged the man on the hill.

The man looked to be middle-aged, slightly built and timid. He had carefully kept his distance while alerting the others but now he was blocking their best escape route. The man's mouth opened in alarm when he saw the intruders running towards him.

Ravi heaved the rock at him, missed and hit a tree.

The man yelped once, turned and ran along the ridge, out of their way. Ravi got ahead and led the way through the forest. He knew they couldn't outrun their pursuers. These men knew the forest better than he did, they would be fitter and with Premasiri there in person, they couldn't afford to fail.

Ravi knew they had to get away from the cleared area, reach the heavy forest and hide, but to do that they had to get out of sight. Their pursuers were too close so he set a hard pace, scrambling over rocks, pushing his way through thickets and sliding down mud banks. Tanya kept up with him doggedly, but when he stopped to help her up a steep incline he saw that she was gasping for breath, near exhaustion. She couldn't go on.

He saw a jumble of rocks a little further up the incline, boulders the size of trucks piled together and festooned with giant ferns and greeny yellow lichen. He half dragged, half carried Tanya up the incline.

There were plenty of hiding places among those rocks. But by the same token, anyone seeing it would realize that it was the most likely place they'd choose to hide in. A plan was forming in his head but he had to know something first. Were they coming in a bunch or had they spread themselves in a line? If a line, how far apart were they?

Tanya was crouched against a rock, her head resting on her arms. He climbed on to one of the larger boulders and carefully surveyed the surroundings with his binoculars. Sinhagala rose steeply behind him, roughly to the southeast. Their pursuers would be coming up from the north, from the valley below them. He tried to think like them. What would he have done in a similar situation?

First he'd send a couple of men racing to cover the path to the Research Station and cut off their retreat. There was no other easy way out of the forest. Then he'd spread his men out, like beating for game, and flush them out of their hiding place.

The forest was dense and he couldn't see anything. Had they given up? He kept sweeping the forest down the slope.

No movement.

Then a small flock of Babblers took off from a thicket and flew away with squeaks of alarm. Ravi focused on the area and finally made out the figure of a tall, unshaven man in a pair of dark cutaway pants and a dirty singlet. He used the kathi in his hand to ease his way slowly through the undergrowth. He had his eyes on the ground, looking for signs of their passing. Ravi saw in him the look and carriage of a man who knew his way around the forest.

But he was alone.

Ravi knew that his guess had been right. Their pursuers had spread out in a line and were making a thorough search. He would have preferred a headlong chase because it would have been easier to escape by hiding, but there were some positives even in the current situation. The man was alone and he was coming up slowly.

Tanya had recovered her breath and some of her poise.

'They have spread out,' Ravi whispered. 'One man is coming up the hill.'

'Will he find us here?'

'He is tracking our footmarks. Yes, he'll find us.'

Ravi looked around but couldn't find anything he'd be able to use as a weapon. He hurriedly yanked off one of his track shoes, removed his thick cotton stocking, and pushed his bare foot back into the shoe. He stuffed the sock with sand and small stones hastily scraped up from the ground. He then explained to Tanya what he wanted her to do and climbed back on the boulder he had used earlier to scan the forest. Tanya retreated further into the crevice, but kept him in sight.

Not a moment too soon. A careful peep through a bed of ferns showed that the man had come quite close and was studying the pile of rocks. He then looked carefully at the ground and must have seen some sign of their passing because he walked forward confidently.

He went a few steps past them, then stopped and turned back.

He stopped again and stood for a moment looking thoughtfully at the crevice.

Ravi signaled Tanya. Obediently she tossed a pebble against a sloping rock face. It was a faint noise but the man heard it. He shortened the grip on his kathi and stepped into the gap. He went forward very slowly and very carefully.

But he didn't look up.

Ravi had the free end of his rock filled sock firmly wrapped round his hand. As the man went past below him, Ravi leaned forward and swung his cosh at the man's head. The man took it squarely on the back of his skull and collapsed without a sound.

Tanya crept out of her hiding place and looked up at Ravi.

'Is the bugger dead?'

'I don't know. Hop on to this side first.'

But she couldn't. The body of the man was wedged in the narrow crevice and blocked the way.

'Step on him and jump,' Ravi ordered. 'Do it now.'

Tanya hesitated, then placed her foot on the man's back and scurried across. Ravi jumped down and went to the crumpled figure. He reached for one of his wrists and tried to find a pulse. He couldn't find any sign of life at first but forced himself to concentrate and try again. He felt it then, a reassuring thud in the vein. He turned the man's head to a side so he wouldn't suffocate and backed out of the fissure.

'Are you all right?' He put his arm on Tanya's shoulder and felt her tremble.

'I'm ok. What do we do now? Won't the others look for him?'

'No. They have spread out in a line. I don't think they will miss him for a while.'

'Is it safe to go to Martin's?'

'No way. They know we came from there. There's no other way in.'

'So?'

'They'd have rushed a couple of men to the Research Station to cut us off. They might have even sent men by road to wait at Martin's.'

'You mean we have to hide in the forest?' Tanya seemed aghast at the prospect.

'If we did, they'd catch us in the end,' Ravi said slowly. 'They went westwards, towards the Research Station. If we go the other way, we should cut across a footpath that leads to some villages on the southern border of the reserve. Premasiri won't expect us to get out that way.'

'Have you been on this footpath?'

'No. Someone told me about it long ago.'

Tanya just looked at him.

'What about our kit?'

'Sinhagala is on the way, almost. We can pick our bags up.'

'What about Martin's stuff?'

'We'll have to take it with us. I'll send it back to him through someone.'

They were exhausted and near panic when they finally found the narrow overgrown footpath. They sat on a rock to examine their feet and were horrified to find their socks covered with wet patches of blood. They both found bloated leeches inside their shoes. Tanya rolled her trousers up to check and yelped when she saw a slimy creature attached to her calf.

Ravi lit a match from the box in his pack and let the flame touch the leech. It fell to the ground immediately leaving a bloody patch. It struck him again how lovely her legs were, smooth and fair and rounded.

He leaned forward and kissed her on the knee. She looked at him with amused tolerance:

'Are you still trying to get my pants off?'

'Yeah,' he laughed. 'There's always hope.'

'If you had lied to me last night, you might have had a chance,' she grinned. 'Why didn't you?'

'What the hell do you think I kept asking myself all night?' Ravi snarled morosely. 'I must have been crazy.'

They reached the little hamlet of Mediripitiya. An old man told them it was a long walk to the main road but they might be lucky enough to get a ride on a tractor. They sat in the shade of a Tamarind tree to wait.

The old man came back after some time and shyly offered them something wrapped in a newspaper. Ears of corn freshly boiled in salt water. Ravi had never eaten anything sweeter.

They got a ride in a cart drawn by two bullocks. The cart was piled high with vegetables but the carter, another white haired man with betel stained teeth, made room for them to sit at the rear of the cart facing backwards. The cart swayed and rattled through tiny rustic villages as the track wound its way through fields of paddy and other crops, all green and shimmering in the noonday heat. An hour later they reached a main road the carter referred to as *"bavely para"*.

A signboard put them right. The road led to Beverly estate. Going in the opposite direction would get them to Deniyaya.

The bus rides were endless. South from Deniyaya to Matara, then an "express" from Matara to get them to the outskirts of Colombo soon after dark.

'You'd better come home with me. Stay the night.'

Ravi looked at her in surprise but she was looking out of the window.

'Won't your parents object?'

'Whatever for?' Now she looked surprised. 'People are always coming and going in our house. Mum doesn't mind.'

'Where is your home?'

'Dehiwela. We can get off this bus at the junction and take a three wheeler.'

Tanya's family lived in a single storey house midway down Campbell Place. The house was well kept but quite dated, with an old fashioned porch leading to an open verandah. It had a comfortable look to it.

'Hi pop,' Tanya bent to kiss a middle-aged man with a lined face who'd been stretched out in an armchair, reading a newspaper.

'Hullo chubby,' the man greeted her with a pleased smile. 'Did you get your story then? And who's this fellow?'

'This is Ravi. He helped me get the scoop. Ravi, this is my dad, Richard. Ravi is staying the night.'

'Oh Good. Can put a drink then. You better wash up and come.'

Tanya led the way through a cluttered sitting room to the combined pantry-kitchen. Ravi noticed with amusement that there were no formalities in a Burgher household. He was not asked to wait in the drawing room while the family dressed up to meet him.

'Can I call you chubby?'

'Only if you want your balls cut off,' she threw back over her shoulder.

A plump woman in a printed housecoat was chopping onions and tomatoes in the kitchen. A spindly young girl with the face of a cherub had been arguing with her mother and stopped short when they walked in.

'I'm back mum. This is Ravi. He's helping me with my story,' Tanya turned to Ravi. 'This is my mum, Pam and the little horror is my sister, Tammy.'

'Hullo Ravi,' the tubby woman smiled, waving her knife perfunctorily. 'Stay and share our meal. We're having string hoppers.'

Tammy made a face at her sister.

'I've asked him to stay the night,' Tanya stated. No explanation.

'Camp cot in the hall then,' Pam Koch responded placidly, as if this happened all the time. 'Where were you last night, baby?'

'In the jungle. In a tent, with Ravi.'

'Darling, you mustn't. I mean, it's not ...,' Pam's flustered voice trailed off.

Richard Koch walked into the pantry with another man.

Tanya said: 'Ahh, don't worry mum. Ravi can't do it.'

'What's that?' Richard asked. 'Ravi can't do what?'

'They spent the night in a tent together,' Pam said uncertainly. 'But Tani says it's alright because Ravi can't ... you know.'

Tammy asked, 'Ravi can't do what?'

'Shut up, Tam.'

Richard and the other man, a bald headed coot with two missing front teeth, found it extremely amusing. Ravi felt his cheeks flush when the two men commiserated with him.

'Never mind, son,' Richard said kindly. 'Happens to everyone now and then. Don't take notice of these women.'

'Let's have a shot, Dicky,' the other man said. 'Pour this bugger a stiff one.'

That broke them up.

They laughed and laughed like hyenas, with even Pam and Tanya joining in. Ravi gritted his teeth and kept a smile on his face.

'What can't Ravi do?' Tammy's childish voice cut through the laughter like a knife.

'Shut up, Tam.'

Dinner was a noisy affair with Uncle Conrad, the bald man, relating stories about his escapades as an engine driver in the railway. Some of the stories were quite funny. Ravi was glad enough that their attention was elsewhere for he'd had his fill of frivolous advice about his imaginary malady. And the food, string hoppers, kiri hodhi and curried squid, kept him busy.

After dinner they sat in the darkened verandah and chatted. Ravi and Tanya sat on the front steps, away from the rest.

Richard Koch called, 'What are you two whispering out there?'

'Let them be, Dicky,' Conrad the bald coot said. 'Our Tani girl is safe with that bugger.'

More laughter.

'You are going to pay for all this,' Ravi whispered angrily, 'the next time I catch you alone.'

Tanya laughed, then put her hand on his knee and gave it an affectionate squeeze.

'Ahh. We're just fooling. Don't get mad.'

'I am mad, and I plan to get even for this.'

Tanya laughed again.

'You'll get even only when I let you!'

Ravi realized that Tanya's character had changed in a subtle way once she entered her home and was surrounded by her family. It seemed as if her prickly public persona had been peeled away like a layer of an onion to reveal a somewhat different character underneath. As if she had left her protective carapace at the gate.

They sat quietly for a while, listening to the night sounds.

'What's happening about your house? When are you selling it?'

'The buyer will take possession on Thursday.'

'Where will you stay then?'

'Reshane has asked me to stay at his house, for a time anyway.'

'Premasiri will come after you.'

'Yes. They'll come after you too.'

'No. The newspaper is my protection,' Tanya said confidently. 'You are the one they will want to attack.'

'Yes, but they have already destroyed everything of mine. What more can they do?'

'They can beat you up. Inflict permanent damage. Or ... kill you.'

'Mm.'

'They'll go berserk when I break the story on Sunday. It's best if you stay out of sight, you know, till things cool down. Reshane's place will be too obvious.'

'I'll have to find a room somewhere.'

'I can fix you up at Aunty Nora's.'

'Who?'

'Mum's aunt, mum's friend really. She lives alone at Elfindale Avenue in Bambalapitiya. Keeps cats.'

Ravi knew Elfindale was a narrow lane opposite Holy Family Convent. It was a dead end but very centrally located. It would do very well.

'Will she take a boarder?'

'She's hard up. She'll take you if you pay her something. I'll ask mum to call her.'

16

Ravi walked the short distance to the Bank at Milagiriya.

He had taken to Aunty Nora from the start. She was a tiny birdlike creature, amazingly sprightly for her eighty something years. Since her husband died she had lived alone with only her beloved cats for company. She had plenty of them and they had the run of the house.

Ravi had been given a small front room. Tanya and her mum had helped to clean and dust the room and settle him in. Aunty Nora was delighted with his offer of Rupees 2000/- per month for the room.

It was a good place, Ravi decided, once you got accustomed to the cat fur on the furniture.

The Sunday Statesman had devoted a double spread for Tanya's scoop. Ravi had read the story in the seclusion of his room, but his elation was mixed with a measure of dread. The exposé was devastating. It boldly accused Minister Mudalige Premasiri of large scale logging inside the Sinharaja. Photographs of the Minister's son, Shalindra, set against the saw-mill were clearly shown. The article also offered the police and the authorities copies of the video if they wanted further proof.

The revelation would create a storm of protest around the country. Sinharaja was a national treasure and one of UNESCO's world heritage sites. For a Minister of the Government to be directly involved in raping this gem would be considered sacrilegious.

And the man was facing an election in six weeks.

Shabbir, who bought his house, had deposited a draft at the bank on Thursday. The manager Mr. Nonis, in his cautious way, had asked Ravi to come by on Monday in order to give the bank enough time to recover all its dues and credit the balance proceeds to Ravi's account. Ravi wanted to withdraw his balance, a better part of a million rupees, and deposit it elsewhere.

Mr. Nonis saw him outside the room and signaled him to wait. Ravi thought he looked particularly nervous and harried that morning, but perhaps he always looked like that. Ravi sat in the waiting area outside the manager's room and leafed through a magazine.

Nonis kept him for nearly forty-five minutes and then summoned him.

'I am sorry, Mr. Perera,' he said, 'I have received instructions from head office to freeze your account till you get clearance from Inland Revenue.'

'What are you talking about?' Ravi asked angrily. 'This is a joint account. I can withdraw funds at anytime. My father had no outstanding tax liabilities.'

'I'm sorry. I cannot release your funds till I get clearance.'

'Show me the account seizure notice from the department.'

'I … don't have it,' the man looked uneasy for the first time. 'It must be at head office.'

Ravi had the urge to push the man's face in but restrained himself with an effort. He knew very well there was a hidden hand behind this.

'Whom should I see in head office?'

'The AGM Corporate Affairs.'

The morning traffic was still heavy on Galle Road as Ravi stepped out of the bank. He noticed that a vehicle was parked by the side of the road directly in front of the door and thought it strange. The traffic police did not permit parking on the seaside of Galle Road till after 12.00 noon.

The rear door of the vehicle facing him was open but the seats were not occupied. He glanced idly at the man seated next to the driver and felt a tremor pass through his body, as if he'd touched a live wire.

Sergeant Pathirana, staring at him balefully.

The man made no attempt to get off the vehicle but his eyes shifted from Ravi to someone behind him. In that fleeting instant Ravi knew he was in mortal danger. Nonis had betrayed him. He had been instructed to tip them off when Ravi came to the bank, then to keep him in the bank till they were ready for him outside.

The door of the Pajero was open for his body!

He swung around to find two men converging on him. One man had receding hair and a heavy black moustache, the other clean-shaven. Nehru collars and black trousers. The uniform!

Ravi knew it would only take them an instant to pick him up, throw him into the back of the vehicle, climb in and drive off. If that happened, he was as good as dead. Whatever he had to do, he had to do right now.

As one of the men reached out to grab him by his shirt, Ravi clutched his chest with both hands, contorted his face and sank to his knees.

Both men hesitated for a moment.

'Uta papuwe amaruwakkda?'

Is he having a heart attack?

Moustache came closer and leaned forward.

Ravi brought his clenched fist off the ground and drove it into the man's crotch, rising to his feet at the same instant, using all the power of his leg muscles. The man was almost lifted off his feet by the force of the blow. He shrieked and bent over, clutching at his groin. Ravi shoved him onto the other man, turned and ran along the pavement towards Wellawatte, knowing they wouldn't be able to turn the vehicle to follow him.

He saw a gap in the traffic and glanced back. Pathirana and the other man were coming after him but they were not built for racing. He dashed across the road and vaulted over the centre railing, crossed the road and then raced down Hildon Place. He finally slowed to a walk, made a wide circuit through Duplication Road and finally went back to Aunty Nora's.

He felt anger swirling in his chest. The hard ball in his belly seemed to swell and swell with each new attack. He struck his bedroom wall with his clenched fist to vent his frustration.

But part of his mind was cold. Gradually the cold side took control and he was able to take stock of his situation.

He had the money from the sale of household goods and furniture safely tucked away in cash. Enough to keep him going for a few months. The money from the house would have been very useful but there was time enough to sort that out.

Pathirana was a major threat. The man was clever and ruthless, utterly without conscience. Ravi knew he had been very lucky. His assailants had been overconfident and that had given him a tiny chance to escape. But

Pathirana seemed to have turned this into a personal vendetta. He'd keep searching till Ravi was caught. The man had access to limitless resources to do just that.

He had to find a way to neutralize the man.

*

It took Ravi most of the morning to get to Pananpola. There was still an air of tension about the little town. No burning tyres on the road though. Posters supporting the candidates had been plastered on every available space.

Among them Ravi was mightily elated to see one with a picture of Shalindra Premasiri with the saw-mill in the background. The caption read:

"Lee hora".

Timber thief.

Sandika was delighted to see him and all his crew gathered round Ravi to congratulate him. Ravi discussed the status of the campaign. The publicity had helped them, but of course, people in the area had always known that the logging was going on. With six weeks to go till the election they'd need more help to down the Minister.

Ravi took Sandika out to a kiosk for tea. They spoke in Sinhala.

'Have you found the traitor in your office?' Ravi asked.

'No. No yet. But we'll get the bastard.'

'I think we can use him, whoever he is.'

'What do you mean?'

'What about Pathirana and his MSD thugs?'

'They come here whenever we plan a big meeting. They terrorize the outer villages preventing people from coming. Very hard for us to organize a crowd.'

Ravi took the document he had prepared so carefully the previous day and placed it on the table, two sheets of paper with a carbon in between. He turned the letter, hand written in Sinhala, so Sandika could read it.

K.U. Tennakoon,
J.P.,
Wewa Gedera,
Pananpola

Sergeant Sudesh Pathirana
Uru Udiyandaluwa
Chilaw

Dear Mr. Pathirana,

Thank you for your help in the timber matter. Your advice was very helpful and, as you would have seen from the newspapers, we caught the small fellow.

The money has been deposited as agreed and I am looking forward to having more assistance from you in the future. Your support will not be forgotten when we come to power.
With good wishes

Upali Tennakoon

Sandika looked at Ravi in surprise.

'Get the candidate to sign the letter with the carbon in place,' Ravi told him. 'Then destroy the original.'

'And?'

'Leave the copy in the drawer of your desk.'

Sandika looked puzzled for a moment and then a slow grin spread across his face.

'I like it. Oh, I like it a lot.'

17

Ravi had spent two frustrating and largely fruitless weeks trying to get the bank to release his money. He had met a number of officials and written countless letters but was no further forward than he had been on the first day. With every passing day, it became more evident that a hidden hand was blocking him at every turn.

He had refrained from visiting Tanya for fear that there'd be people watching her, and waiting for him to show up. They used their mobile phones to keep in touch.

Ravi was disappointed that the Sunday Statesman did not carry any follow up on the illicit logging story in subsequent weeks. He realized that the election campaign was getting more and more violent and there were plenty of hot stories vying for space. They'd need new material if they wished to resurrect the story.

Ravi had started frequenting Saraswathi Lodge for his meals. Saraswathi served cheap Tamil vegetarian food and had long been the haunt of dead broke schoolboys. It was one place you could be assured of filling your belly for a few rupees.

In the old days Tilak had done it for even less.

The practice there was for the waiter to give you a handwritten bill to cover what you had consumed. On your way out, you just paid that amount at the cashier's counter near the front door. Tilak's technique, when they were short of cash, was to go right to the back of the room and there eat their fill and collect a bill. Then they'd get up and wash their fingers at the sink near the front of the café. Afterwards, they'd sit at another table right next to the cashier's counter and order two cups of tea. The new waiter would duly give them a second bill for forty cents.

After that one only had to wait till there was a bit of a rush, go with the crowd, plunk your bill with forty cents on the counter, and walk out whistling.

Ravi was conserving his funds once again now, so he walked the short distance from Elfindale Avenue to Saraswathi for an early lunch. He surveyed the road carefully for the deadly parked Pajero and ventured out only when the coast was clear. He went to a table at the back and ordered dosai. A man pulled out a chair and sat opposite him. Ravi looked up and his breath caught in his throat, choking him.

Pathirana!

Shit. Shit. Shit. He's caught me this time.

Ravi fought to keep calm. He stared into the eyes of the man, hoping his fear would not show. Pathirana stared back at him impassively for a minute. Ravi had a vague impression that something had changed in the man but couldn't put his finger on it. The anger still blazed in his eyes but the arrogant assurance seemed to have, in some subtle way, diminished.

Ravi waited.

'Wachanayakkwath näthuwa ung māva us keruwa,' Pathirana said slowly.

They sacked me without a word of explanation.

Ravi experienced an explosion of delight. Fireworks and skyrockets burst into living colour – but all inside his head.

He wanted to scream and shout; he wanted to dance on the road and kiss all the old ladies. With a supreme effort of will he managed to keep his face expressionless. He couldn't for a moment believe that the wild arrow he'd shot in the air had found its mark. And the icing on the cake was that this vicious bastard didn't know who had fixed him.

'Who has sacked you? The Ministry?'

'Yes,' the big man said glumly. 'I have been transferred to the Police reserve.'

Ravi waited quietly for him to go on.

'Why have you come to see me?'

Pathirana looked at him for a long time without answering.

'You are trying to bring down the Minister. I can help you.'

'Why?' Ravi felt compelled to ask. 'Why do you want to help me? You were trying to kill me.'

'I did all their dirty work. I've risked the gallows for them. Now they've just thrown me out without a single word. I want them to pay for that.'

'How can you help?'

'I have information. I know the things they've done.'

The words hung in the air as Ravi thought it over.

Could he trust this bastard? Was it all an elaborate trap? Or was it a golden opportunity to strike a decisive blow?

'Will you talk to a reporter?'

'Yes, I'll talk to the Burgher woman,' Pathirana made it sound like an insult. 'I will give her the story but she cannot reveal my name. I am still in service.'

'All right. I'll talk to Tanya and let you know. Do you carry a mobile phone?'

'Yes,' the man gave Ravi the number as he rose to leave.

Ravi remembered something. 'What about my blocked account? Can you help me with that?'

Pathirana smiled wolfishly. 'That order came from the Minister himself. You have to remove him from office to get that money released.'

They left together. Pathirana had parked his motorbike directly in front of the café. He climbed on and spent some time fiddling with his mirrors. Ravi saw a bus going to Dehiwela slowing down as it approached the halt and leapt aboard, hoping to catch Pathirana off guard. He stood in the isle of the nearly empty bus and saw the distinctive cop bike following at a leisurely pace. Maybe he was just going in the same direction. Or maybe not.

Ravi waited till he had passed the flats and came to a stretch of road with an unbroken centre island. He got off the bus, ran across the road and stepped into a three-wheeler going in the other direction. He searched the road behind him carefully but this time there was no sign of Pathirana. He got off near Bambalapitiya junction and took another bus to Fort.

Tanya was excited. 'Are you sure he will talk to me?'

'So he says. Let's think this through. It might be a trap to get us together'

'Yes, that's a thought. Let's just be careful. Can we find out if he really

108 .

has been transferred from the MSD?'

'I called the Ministry and asked for him. They said he wasn't there anymore.'

'That settles it. It seems as if he is genuine.'

'Not quite. What if he's been fired, but is now trying to get back in their favour by bringing us in?'

'Mm. We'll have to be very careful then.'

'Yes.'

They sat there thinking about it for a while.

'I can't believe your letter idea worked. I mean it's really weird,' Tanya looked at him strangely. 'You're getting to be a tricky bastard, aren't you?'

'Are you impressed enough to give me a break?'

'Let's do it then,' Tanya said.

'The sex thing?'

'No you dope. Let's set up a meeting with that bugger.'

*

He had told Pathirana to come to Saraswathi Lodge at 11.00 am.

Ravi stood under the awning of a newsstand across the road and watched him ride up and park his bike. Ravi waited till he had taken off his helmet and punched the send button on his phone. The man stopped in the middle of the pavement and reached for his phone.

'Sergeant?'

'Yes.'

'Turn to your right and walk towards Dickman's Road ...'

'What is this bullshit?' The man snarled. 'Do you think you're directing a movie?'

'We are only protecting ourselves, Sergeant,' Ravi said firmly. 'We will do it my way, or there'll be no interview.'

Pathirana turned and had a good look around but Ravi had made sure he was in deep enough shadow not to be easily seen.

'All right,' Pathirana controlled himself with an obvious effort. 'What do you want me to do?'

'After you pass Vishaka Road you will come to another lane to the left. Gravel. There is a sign with the words Ambal Café. Turn down the lane and go into the café.'

'All right.'

'Miss Koch will be there. And Sergeant …'

'Yes?'

'If you use your phone for any reason, she'll be gone.'

'Listen, you fucking …'

'Just follow the instructions.'

Ravi stayed under cover and watched the man as he turned into the lane. Tanya was already in the café, waiting for him. Ravi's instructions to her had been very detailed. He ran over them again in his mind to convince himself that he had covered every eventuality.

Pathirana had prohibited any recording equipment or photographs, so she was to carry only one small handbag and that was to be left on the table for him to inspect. Ravi told her to wear jeans and sneakers so she could run and climb easily, if the need arose.

It was too early for the midday crowd so the café would be nearly empty. She was to go to the back of the café and sit facing the entrance. Order a coke and keep the unopened bottle on the table. Keep her mobile phone also on the table. Ravi would watch the entrance to the road from under cover. If he saw anything suspicious, like MSD men turning into the lane, he'd call her.

His other instructions had made her laugh.

If he called and gave the alarm, she was to first distract Pathirana by pointing to the entrance, then hit him as hard as she could with the bottle. When the man was temporarily disabled, she was to run through the back of the café and scale the low wall at the rear. A dash through the next garden would bring her to Elfindale Avenue. She was to turn to her left, towards the dead end.

At the very end of Elfindale Avenue was the rear boundary wall of a house facing Bethesda Place. That wall already had footholds made by generations of thieves looking for an escape route. Like Ravi.

Tanya was to get to Bethesda Place, pick up a three-wheeler and get out of there.

Ravi's precautions turned out to be unnecessary.
He called after ten minutes just to make sure.
'Yes?' Tanya sounded calm.
'Is everything ok?'
'No problems,' she said. 'I'll call you when we're done.'
It was nearly noon when Pathirana appeared at the top of the lane, looked around trying to spot Ravi, then went to his bike and rode away. Tanya came out, crossed the road, stopped a three-wheeler and was driven off.

They met, as planned, in the food court at Majestic City. Tanya waved when she saw him.
'How was it?' Ravi asked anxiously. 'Did you get anything useful?'
'Plenty of dirt. Mudalige is a real bastard, worse than I had imagined. The problem is, my editor will never run the story.'
'Why on earth?'
'I can't prove any of it. Pathirana hasn't got any documents and he is not willing to give evidence. Others in the know are all cops and political catchers.'
'So it was useless?'
'Oh no. It's just that I have to investigate further and collect some real evidence before I can write the story.'
'What about?'
'There's not much news value in the beatings and thuggery. Everyone knows about that. There are some cases of bribery. He's taken money to approve setting up International Schools but who'd give evidence?' Tanya asked thoughtfully. 'The teachers are the best chance.'
'What teachers?'
'There are thousands of teachers in government schools. It seems that lots of them want transfers to other schools. Those who pay a fee to the Minister's catcher get their job done right away.'
'Mm. Not much, is it?'
'But if they are young women, and pretty. It seems they don't have

to pay.'

'Really?'

'When the Minister goes on tour his henchmen make the arrangements. The Minister takes over a circuit bungalow, even a resthouse sometimes, and the lady is brought over to spend the night. The MSD makes sure he is not disturbed.'

'Not easy to prove, is it? The women will never admit it.'

'It seems the old lecher is a camera buff,' Tanya's voice hardened. 'He takes photographs of the women in the nude, sometimes of both together ... during ... you know? He often shows the pictures to his henchmen later and they enjoy a good laugh.'

'Mm.'

Tanya sat staring at the table for a while, lost in thought. Ravi noticed that her jaw was clenched.

'Those women may be foolish enough to get sucked into this, but they're not whores, they are not animals to be laughed at. I wish I could bring the bastard down just for that.'

'You know very well we can't prove any of this,' Ravi said then a thought struck him. 'I wonder if he's still at it.'

'Parliament has been dissolved.'

'But he's in the caretaker cabinet, he still has power,' Ravi persisted.

They had been silent for some time, thinking of possibilities.

'Let's ask him,' Tanya said.

Ravi called Pathirana.

Pathirana had said the Minister would not go on circuit when he's busy with the election campaign. He'd check anyway and call back.

They waited, then walked around the shops when they got bored.

Pathirana called half an hour later. 'I spoke to one of the boys who worked for me,' he said. 'I was right. The Minister is not interested in circuits these days. Sorry.'

'Too bad,' Ravi hid his disappointment. 'Let me know if your hear anything.'

'He's spending all his time in the electorate till the election is over. He's only making a visit to Kataragama to make a vow.'

112

Kataragama was an ancient shrine located in the southeastern corner of the country. It was sacred to both the Hindu and Buddhist communities of the country. Devotees made frequent pilgrimages to the shrine to seek divine intervention in their affairs. Mudalige Premasiri wanted to make sure the Gods were on his side when the voting started.

Rich and powerful men often did that, and Ravi imagined that Premasiri's prayer would be something like, "Oh God, I have made an offering of so many gold sovereigns to your temple. Please, please make my wish come true. Ignore the awful things I've done ... and will continue to do. Just count the coins."

'When is he going to Kataragama?'

'The weekend after next,' Pathirana replied. 'He's staying over at Hambantota resthouse on the 26th.'

Ravi thanked him and rang off.

Tanya said, 'Hambantota is a long way. This could be a total waste of time.'

Ravi stood staring at the floor, lost in thought. 'I have a feeling about this, Tani. Men can get hooked on that kind of sex. Let's try to catch bastard at it.'

18

The driver of the office van, Wimal, was a cocky fellow convinced that every other motorist on the road was either incompetent or mentally unbalanced. Siri, a taciturn young photographer sat quietly in the passenger seat, hugging his camera bag.

They had left Colombo soon after 6.00 a.m. hoping to get to their destination by mid morning. It was nearly 11.30 when they turned off the main road and climbed the gentle slope towards the small town of Hambantota.

'Are we going to the resthouse?' Tanya asked.

'No. The staff will remember me from last week. There are other places in town we can use.'

Ravi had come to Hambantota the previous Saturday and spent a night at the resthouse. He now had a clear idea of the layout of the resthouse and its surroundings. A second visit was an unnecessary risk.

As they reached the promontory, the bay spread out before them, picturesque as a postcard, too lovely to be real.

The sea was a deep magnetic blue circled by the white rim of the bay, stretching into the distance on either side. Traditional fishing boats were drawn up on the beach while the ungainly mechanized eighteen footers rocked in the swell.

They parked the van and got off to stretch their limbs. None of the others had been to Hambantota before, so Ravi explained the general layout.

'The road to the right goes past the pier where the boats are anchored. The resthouse is almost opposite the pier. The road goes to the Kachcheri up there and then swings round in a loop behind the resthouse. We'll drive round it in the afternoon.'

The road along the beach was fairly busy. Fishermen and traders going

114

about their daily business, tourists walking about in groups, and a busload of *"puwakmal"* pilgrims. Puwakmal, areconut flowers were traditionally tied at the front of a vehicle carrying villagers going on pilgrimage.

They sent Wimal and Siri off to have something to eat. Ravi bought some fish buns from a bakery and led Tanya to the town cemetery.

'Let me guess. You want to select a burial site in case they catch you?'

'That too, but you know, this is a good spot to have a peaceful lunch,' Ravi sat on the headstone of some long departed soul.

Tanya looked a little scandalized at first.

'You are desecrating someone's grave,' she observed.

Ravi glanced casually at the name engraved on the monument and said:

'No sweat, babe. It's just some dead Burgher. He was probably pissed when he died, so why should he mind?'

'You are really going to lose some teeth if you carry on like this.'

But she calmed down and sat on the coping of one of the graves. The cemetery was planted with some fine shade trees, it was not dusty and there were no loiterers. And the fish buns were surprisingly fresh and wholesome.

Ravi took her hand. 'Come on. I want to show you something.'

He led the way to an ugly grey headstone set in the middle of the cemetery. They read the inscription standing side by side.

In memory
of
H. Engelbrecht.
Died 20th March 1928.
For 21 years guardian of the
Yala Game Sanctuary.
This stone is erected
by the members of the
Game Protection Society
in appreciation of his work.

'Hey, I've heard about him,' Tanya said wonderingly. 'Wasn't he the Boer prisoner-of-war who refused to go back?'

'Mm. When the war ended, all the other Boer prisoners were sent back home on condition they swore an oath of allegiance to the King of England. He refused, so for many years the British had to maintain the prison camp just for one man. They released him finally, that's how he came to be the first warden of the Yala Sanctuary.'

Tanya tilted her head and looked at him quizzically.

'You're a storehouse of useless information, aren't you?'

Her sunglasses were perched on the top of her head and the green tinted eyes were smiling at him for a change. Ravi noticed she'd unbuttoned her shirt for relief from the heat and he had a tantalizing glimpse of the top edge of her bra.

'We have a long afternoon to waste ...' Ravi started.

'So?'

'We can, you know, take a room in one of these guest houses and ...'

Her smile became nasty. 'A double bed is what you have in mind, is it?'

'Well, yes. You'll be scrumptious I'm sure, after a shower.'

'Listen dickhead, you are going to need all your blood in your head tonight, not ... there. So get your mind off that and on the job!'

They found Siri and Wimal standing near the van and set out on a tour of inspection. The road ran past a pier on their left. The resthouse was a long, single storey building that stood on high ground to their right and commanded a magnificent view of the bay. A feature of the building was the wide-open verandah that ran along the front of it. The six rooms all opened to the verandah.

Two cars and a silver van were parked in the spacious front garden, casual visitors for lunch, no doubt. No off-roaders, so the Minister's party had not turned up yet.

The road climbed to the end of the promontory. A gaily-painted lighthouse stood at the end of it like an ice cream cone, and behind it a strange and incongruous tower.

'What the hell is that?'

'Martello Tower,' Ravi said briefly, looking at the cylindrical structure with thick walls and embrasures for placing guns along the upper perimeter.

'Go on. What is it, this Martello?'

'I thought you were not interested in trivia.'

'Shut up and tell me,' she said crossly, seemingly unaware of the contradiction. 'Is it Dutch?'

'No, British. They built normal fortresses in Galle and Matara. Here they built this circular one, one of the very few like it anywhere. I think the design is Corsican.'

The road curved inland and ran behind the resthouse. The building, Ravi thought, resembled an airplane with each wing having three large rooms; the toilets protruded outwards behind each room like engines. The centre of the building extended backwards to house the dining area, kitchen and staff quarters.

The road looped around the high ground and meandered back to the beach further on.

Ravi knew, whatever the outcome of their project, they'd get no sleep that night. In order to cope, they needed to get some rest that afternoon. He had thought they would find rooms in one of the seedy motels that had sprung up all over the town. Surprisingly it wasn't easy, and the first three places they tried were all booked up by backpacking tourists. The fourth was a dilapidated place on the far side of town, creatively named Beach View Inn.

But only two rooms were available, air conditioned though.

Ravi hesitated and looked at Tanya. She just shrugged and picked up the key leaving Siri and Wimal to take the other room. Five minutes later they were ensconced in a surprisingly large room with a double bed and an ancient air conditioner groaning in the window.

'You'd better shower first. I want to take my time.'

'We can shower together, if you like,' Ravi offered.

'Bugger off.'

When Ravi came out a few minutes later Tanya was ready to take her turn. He held the door open for her with exaggerated courtesy but she went in without a word and slammed the door in his face. Ravi threw himself on one side of the neatly made bed and tried to run through his plan again. There were so many unknowns. Would the Minister turn up?

Would he bring a woman? Would the untested plan work?

He dozed off.

As if in a dream, Ravi felt something soft and filmy fall on his face. He took a drowsy look at it and came awake in a flash.

Tanya's silk sleeping shorts!

He turned his head and found her face on the pillow next to him. She'd slipped under the covers with only her head and shoulders showing. She was wearing a pink T-shirt and her eyes were closed.

Had she brought two pairs of shorts? Surely not. In which case …

He held the shorts to his face inhaled the now familiar girl smell of her. It made him as giddy and breathless as it had done that night on Sinhagala. When he looked up he saw that her eyes were open and she was studying him gravely.

Her hair had made a damp patch on the pillow. Ravi thought she looked very young and infinitely desirable. He wanted to savour the moment.

'You're wearing the same native sarong,' she observed finally.

'Yes. I've told you what it was good for,' Ravi grinned. 'And diarrhoea is not a problem at the moment.'

'Don't be disgusting.'

'Did you bring two pairs of shorts?'

'You'll have to find out for yourself.'

'I'll have to come under the covers for that.'

Why had his voice gone hoarse?

'Take that silly sarong off first. You look like a bloody gamarala.'

Ravi slipped under the sheet, pulled off his sarong and lobbed it on to her face. She flung it away with a gurgle of laughter.

Ravi stared at her for a moment but her eyes were unreadable, pools of unfathomable greeny black water. He lifted the covers and ducked his head underneath. As he turned to look at her he realized that she had slipped her head under the covers at the same time. There was light enough under the flimsy white sheet for her to see him. He saw her eyes move and she uttered a shriek when she glimpsed his condition.

Ravi looked at her with horrified mortification, unable to believe his eyes or conceive the extent of her perfidy.

She was a picture of modesty in a pair of faded blue denims.

Ravi launched himself at her with a roar of anger, wanting at the very least to strangle her. She pushed herself away from him with a squeak of alarm and, in trying to wriggle free, fell to the floor with a thud. She cried out as she fell and Ravi tried again to get hold of her but she rolled away. Moments later she was at the other side of the room holding up his sarong like a trophy.

She was laughing.

'Come back here,' Ravi roared peremptorily.

'Not a chance.'

'Come back or you'll be sorry.'

'No!'

'That was a dirty trick you pulled on me. You know I'll get back at you sometime.'

'No, you won't. Anyway you've been saying mean things about the Burghers, now you've been punished. Get over it.'

'At least give my sarong back.'

'You don't need it. Why can't you walk around as you are? I've already seen everything.'

'Oh shut up. Are you giving it or not?'

'Not. Unless you promise not to get physical.'

'No. No promises.'

'Then no sarong for you, gamarala.'

Ravi yanked the covers off the bed and wrapped it clumsily round himself. He charged towards her but tripped on a loose end and went sprawling on the floor. Tanya skipped towards the door and got it opened before Ravi could get back on his feet. She tossed the sarong at his head with a laugh and slammed the door behind her.

*

They were seated together in what passed for a dining room at the Inn. It was getting dark outside and the roomboy cum steward placed a mosquito coil under their table.

'Siri, you know what you have to do?' Tanya asked.

'Yes,' Siri said in his quiet way.

'So tell me.'

'Wimal and I go into the resthouse. We order something to drink and ask about dinner.'

'No alcohol,' Tanya said sharply.

'No. We sit in a quiet corner of the verandah and see if they've brought a woman.'

'And?'

'Which room the Minister is using.'

'Good,' Ravi took it up. 'We'll drop you and come back here. Use your mobile only if there is an emergency; otherwise wait till you've finished your food.'

Ravi drove the van with Tanya in the passenger seat. As they dropped Siri and Wimal near the entrance to the resthouse, Tanya pointed. Parked neatly side by side were two Pajero type vehicles and one gleaming silver Mercedes. Their quarry had arrived.

As Ravi drove away he felt Tanya's hand on his knee.

'Are you sure you want to do this?' She asked. 'If they catch you they will really beat you up. Even if they kill you, they'll get away with it.'

'Why should you care?' Ravi growled, memories of the afternoon still rankling. 'I'll make sure you get your pictures.'

'I care,' she said simply.

Two words were enough to banish Ravi's foul temper.

When she was good, she was very very good but when she was bad she was awful.

'They won't be expecting anything like this and I'll be careful.'

'You'd better be.'

'It's you I'm worried about. You'll be out in front and they'll see you.'

'Ahh, I'm a journalist. They dare not touch me. Anyway it's my job.'

120

It was nearly 9.00 when Siri called.

All he said was, *'Hari.'*

OK.

Ravi picked them up on the road near the pier. Tanya turned anxiously towards the rear seat and asked the one important question.

'Was there a woman?'

'Yes,' Siri said in his quiet way. 'The Minister was already there when we went in. He's using the middle room in the left wing. They sent a security vehicle out a little later. It came back with a girl.'

Yes!

They went back to the Inn to wait. And make their final preparations.

*

Ravi had decided to start the operation soon after midnight.

They had parked the van near the pier after dropping Ravi at the rear of the resthouse. Tanya and Siri would conceal themselves in the front garden.

Ravi had ordered two potions of *"bistake"* at the Inn. He'd cut up the stringy beef into small strips and had the steward pack them in two plastic bags. Siri carried one bag and Ravi the other. If the resident mongrels started barking all they had to do was toss them bits of beef and they'd turn from guard dogs to tail wagging pets.

So they hoped.

They had all worn dark clothes. Ravi slipped through the barbed wire fence at the back with some difficulty and crossed the back yard. There was no moon but the sky was clear and the stars at their brightest. Just sufficient light to see his way.

The western wing of the resthouse had three rooms, now spread out before him. The room in the centre housed the Minister, if Siri had got it right. Each room had an attached toilet that protruded outwards. The toilet had a door leading to the outside to facilitate cleaning, for the man who cleaned the toilets wasn't allowed in through the front entrance. Ravi tried the door and found it bolted securely from inside.

At the centre of the rear wall was a fanlight, a glass pane that swiveled around a central axis. Ravi peered carefully through it but it was too dark to see anything useful. He had the impression that the door leading to the bedroom was ajar.

Ravi took off his backpack and squatted on the ground. He removed the three bundles he had prepared with such care the previous day.

Ali Dongs.

BIG BANGS.

These were the biggest, and most annoying of the fireworks produced in the country. It did nothing except explode with a huge noise. Ravi knew about them because at Christmas time, a cretinous child down his lane persisted in setting off one of those awful devices every half hour through the night, just to make sure no one in the neighborhood got any sleep. Tilak finally got the little moron to desist by threatening to tie his pet dog, a sad-eyed Spaniel, across the railway track when the office trains were running.

They came with long fuse cords, to give the sub-humans enough time to fling them away before their hands were blown off. Ravi had bought thirty of them off a dealer in Pettah. He had tied them in three bundles of ten and carefully spliced the cords of each bundle together, so they could be lit simultaneously.

The *Ali Dongs* were packed with crude gunpowder, a mixture of Potassium Nitrate, Sulphur and Charcoal. When a bundle of ten went off at the same moment, there'd be an impressive blast.

He hoped!

Ravi lit the first bundle and dropped it into the toilet through the open fanlight. The long fuse gave him enough time to light the second bundle and lob it close to the bedroom door.

He got his head down very quickly.

The first bundle went off like a bomb, just as he had hoped. The enclosed space must have accentuated the blast because it blew the outside door clean off, leaving it hanging drunkenly on a single hinge. The second explosion was more subdued but still impressive enough, especially if you'd been fast asleep.

Ravi lit the last bundle with shaking fingers. He dashed into the toilet through the ruined doorway and tossed it into the bedroom.

BRRRAAP.

The room was filled with smoke. Ravi stood at the bedroom door knowing the next step was not in the plan and he was running a huge risk. The toilet door falling open had presented an opportunity and he wanted to capitalize on it. But he had to time it just right.

The Minister would panic and run out of the room. His security officers would rush in to find out what had happened and they'd be armed. But between these events there had to be a gap, a small window of opportunity.

Ravi saw flashes of light reflected from the smog that filled the room. That had to be Siri and Tanya who were to rush up to the edge of the open verandah at the sound of the first explosion. Flashes meant photographs - the Minister had run out of the room.

Ravi went into the room. Smoke still swirled in the cone of his tiny flashlight but it gave enough illumination for him to see the camera mounted on a tripod by the side of the bed. There was confused shouting outside the room and someone switched on the lights in the verandah. He only had seconds to spare.

He struggled to free the camera from the tripod, his hands now slippery with perspiration. It came off at last, heavy with flash. He turned and scurried out of the back, through the broken door of the toilet. The lights in the room came on just then.

His shirt got caught in the barbed wire. He spent more precious seconds, and scraped his back painfully, trying to struggle free. Confused, angry voices came from behind him now, getting closer. Then he was through to the road.

No van. He'd told Tanya not to get too greedy. Get one or two shots and then escape before they realized what was happening. If they hung on long enough to get caught, then the whole project would come to nothing.

123

He began to walk down the road.
Stick with the plan. Depend on the others to play their part. Stay calm.

The van, running on sidelights, was almost on him before he realized it. He scrambled in, lightheaded with relief, and Wimal lost no time in speeding away.

Tanya was squeezing his arm, laughing.

'We got him. The fat bastard charged out of the room stark naked, the woman was naked too. We got them together as they came out of the door. Perfect!'

'Did the security interfere with you?'

'Not a chance.' Tanya was high with excitement. 'They must have been in the other two rooms. We ran off just as they came rushing out. We heard them shouting for us to stop.'

'I've got something too.' Ravi showed her the camera. She knew instantly what it was, even in the dark interior of the van.

'Don't tell me,' she cried in delight. 'Oh, don't tell me. Is it really his camera?'

'Yeah. Parked on a tripod, pointing at the bed. He really is a sick bastard.'

'How the hell did you get in?'

Ravi laughed.

'Bit of luck. The toilet door got blown open by the blast.'

'The government should ban those damn crackers.'

They started laughing.

Peering out, Ravi saw that they had reached the main road.

'Dakunata harawanna,' he called out to Wimal.

Turn right.

'Colamba annith pätthe ney?' Wimal brought the vehicle to a halt.

Isn't Colombo the other way?

'What's the plan?' Tanya asked quietly.

'They'll come after us in the Pajeros. They'll want your camera and the Minister's one. They'll also instruct the Police Stations along the way to detain us.'

'Yes.'

'They won't expect us to go the other way.'

She squeezed his knee and called out to Wimal, *'Ähuna neda? Dakunata yanna.'*

You heard him, didn't you? Turn right.

The van swung on to the deserted main road and turned east, headed for Wirawila. They covered the twenty kilometers very quickly and turned north towards Tanamalwila passing through sleeping hamlets and long stretches of forest. The initial euphoria died down and they sat quietly, busy in their own thoughts.

They'd succeeded beyond their wildest dreams. They had been almost too successful. Ravi wondered again what the reaction would be. He looked back from time to time but the road behind remained clear.

It was nearly 3.00 a.m. when they reached Wellawaya. Ravi spotted a *Rä kadè,* an all-night restaurant, near the bus stand and told Piyal to pull over. They parked and locked the van and went towards the brightly lit entrance.

Having ordered tea, they sat down.

'What now?' Tanya asked wearily.

Ravi studied the road map he had spread on the table.

'We are here now,' he pointed. 'The easiest route is through Beragala, Balangoda and Ratnapura.'

Ravi traced his finger along the red line that skirted the southern edge of the central hills.

'The trouble is, there are other roads from Hambantota that fall on to the same road, here at Pelmadulla. I think they'll figure that as another likely route for us and close it as well. I want to go through Ella and Nuwara Eliya to Kandy.'

'That's a hell of a long way round,' Tanya observed. 'Aren't you over reacting?'

'You haven't thought it through,' Ravi explained carefully. 'Your shots of him running out of a room with a young woman, both naked, will destroy this man. The photos in his camera will be much more damaging. The timber story might be quickly forgotten because people know these Ministers are up to all the rackets. But this is different. I think our people, especially women voters, are more conservative than we think. This exposure will sink him. Not just him, it might be enough to swing the election to the opposition. He was, after all, the Minister of Education and a very senior man in the governing party.'

'So?'

'He just can't allow this to be published. No way! His own party will disown him. He will use all his power to catch us. He might even want us killed.'

'Ravi, come on ...,' Tanya started to protest but her voice trailed off.

'No. This really is serious. It's essential for us to take some precautions.'

'Oh, all right,' Tanya sighed. 'What happens when we get to Kandy?'

'I'll tell you then.'

Wimal looked jaded, so Ravi took the wheel from there. The road to Ella was a steep climb to the southeastern corner of the hills. The road was new though, and well cambered, so they made good time. About three quarters of an hour later Ravi glimpsed a waterfall on his right and eased the van to the side of the deserted road.

He took the Minister's camera and examined it under the headlights. Eleven frames had been exposed. He looked in the back of the van and found Wimal asleep, his head resting on a towel wadded up against the window.

Siri looked at Ravi in his quiet, unassuming way. Ravi gave him the camera and spoke in Sinhala.

'Finish the film and take it out.'

Siri took the camera and fiddled with it for a while. Ravi heard the click of the shutter release button. He opened the film compartment, took the film out and handed it to Ravi. Ravi took the camera, and holding it by the strap, wiped it carefully with a tissue.

'What will you do with it?' Tanya asked.

'Drop it over the side.'

'It's an expensive camera. Can't we return it?'

'If we're caught with it, we'll be arrested for theft. No. It's safer to get rid of it.'

He leaned over the concrete barrier and thought he saw the glint of white foam in the gorge below. He tossed the camera into the void and spoke to Siri.

'Finish the roll in your camera and give it to me. Load a new film in it and take about five shots.'

Siri was not very pleased but then shrugged and did as he was told. Ravi picked up a stone and scraped a cross on the casing of the cassette Siri gave him. He put the two rolls of film away in his pocket.

'What do you want photographed?' Siri asked when he put in a fresh film.

'Anything. I just want the frame counter to show a reading.'

They reached Ella soon afterwards and turned towards Bandarawela. From there Ravi left the main road and turned to the right, towards Welimada. Mist began to drift across the road in faint wisps at first, and as they climbed higher, in great swathes that covered the road and turned his world white.

Ravi tried to keep going by reducing his speed to a crawl and peering carefully at the edge of the road just by his front wheel. He soon realized that was an easy way to get them all killed. He carefully eased the van to the grass verge away from the precipice and killed the engine.

He woke the others.

'Where are we?' Tanya asked rubbing her eyes.

'Between Welimada and Hakgala,' Ravi got down, stretching his arms wearily.

'Why have you stopped?'

'Mist. Can't see.'

'Ahh, it doesn't look so bad,' she said grumpily. 'Do you want me to drive?'

Actually visibility wasn't too bad when the lights were off but once they came on, it was a wall of white snow.

'If you even touch that steering wheel, I'm walking home.'

Tanya walked over and thumped him solidly on the shoulder with her clenched fist.

'Don't try that macho shit with me if you want to stay healthy.'

It was cold.

They walked up and down the deserted road for as long as they could stand it. One by one they retreated to the van.

'What time is it?' Tanya asked after awhile.

'5.30. Sunrise will be in about forty five minutes. The mist will clear away then.'

They were lucky because it began to rain soon afterwards, and the mist was gradually scrubbed away under the drizzle. They got underway again, and a washed out sun was peeping over the trees when they passed a white sign that told them they had reached Nuwara Eliya.

The Hill Station was popularized by Sir Samuel Baker who had, in 1846, made it his home. It was by far the most popular holiday resort in the country.

Tanya couldn't care less.

'I want to use the bathroom,' she announced.

Ravi considered the options. The big hotels would have the facilities but they'd take ages to give them anything to eat. The toilets in the smaller hotels … well you wouldn't want to face those so early in the morning.

19

The Golf Club at Nuwara Eliya!

The Golf links was set in the centre of the little town, almost as if the town had grown in the nooks and crannies left by the fairways and greens. It was said to be one of the most spectacular and challenging golf courses in the world. The club would be open even at that time to cater to "early bird" golfers.

And Ravi was still a student member. He hoped!

'Will they let us in?' Tanya asked, as Ravi turned into the drive leading to the clubhouse.

'Sure,' Ravi said with more confidence than he felt. 'They'll let me in. I'm not sure if they let Burgher girls in these days.'

She gave him a tired grin. 'Burgher girls are welcome anywhere, chum, but seriously?'

'I was a student member but I don't know if I still am. Some of the waiters might remember me. The Secretary won't be there at this time so we should be able to bluff our way in to the toilets.'

There were just three vehicles in the car park. Thankfully the rain had ceased when Ravi put the van in a slot and led them into the clubhouse through the rear entrance. The deserted corridor led past the closed office, the billiard room on one side, and the indoor badminton court on the right. Ravi nudged Tanya towards the ladies changing room and led the others to the men's dressing room at the end of the corridor.

Chelliah was there arranging towels. He didn't recognize Ravi but he didn't question him either. The toilets and showers were at the far end of the room.

Ravi felt much better when he sent Siri and Wimal back to the van and sat in the broad verandah to wait for Tanya. The old clubhouse had been built on a rise in the ground, and looked down on the tree-lined fairways that rolled out greenly in the morning sun.

A man in golfing clothes came out of the caddie master's room and walked down to the first tee, swinging his club from side to side and stretching his shoulders. He kept looking back, as though waiting for someone.

A steward dressed in a crimson tunic came shambling out of the hall. He looked at Ravi, a smile spread across his kindly wrinkled face.

Michael.

Ravi remembered him and, glory of glories, Michael made him out as well.

'Master Ravi,' the man held his hand. 'How nice to see you after so many years.'

'Michael. Yes, I must come more often.'

Tanya came out just then and sat down.

'Is this your missy?' Michael looked down at her.

'She wants to be my missy, but I'm not sure,' Ravi grinned. 'What do you think, Michael?'

'Missy very pretty, but how is golf swing?'

'Like digging potatoes,' Ravi laughed.

'Master better get Sigamani to give lesson,' Michael said with mock severity. 'No marry till golf swing all right.'

Tanya was glaring balefully at both of them but Ravi had a suspicion she was not really pissed off.

'What can I get for master?'

'I've forgotten my number.'

'I will check with office later. Tell what master and missy want.'

They ordered cheese toast, a club speciality. Two potions for now and two to take away.

Another man emerged from the dressing room and walked past them. Ravi had the impression of unnaturally glossy hair perched on an aging face. The man also glanced casually at them, the only other visitors in the club. He turned away to go down the steps to the tee when he checked himself and turned back.

He looked hard at Ravi. 'Aren't you David's son? I'm Leo. Leo Dias.'

Shit! That day at Colombo Golf Club with Reshane, this was the man who'd been chatting with Shalindra Premasiri and his wife.

The man didn't offer to shake his hand, so Ravi remained seated and just nodded.

'Yes, I'm Ravi. This is Sandra, a friend of mine.'

He glanced at Tanya without interest and brought his eyes back to Ravi. 'I'm sorry about your father. But he brought it on himself, getting into battles he couldn't possibly win.'

Ravi felt the familiar fury erupting inside him but throttled it down with an effort.

We'll see who'll win the next battle, you arsehole.

The man turned away and took a few steps towards the front of the verandah and the other man waiting on the tee. Then he stopped and came back!

'I heard about an attack on the Minister at Hambantota last night. That was you, wasn't it?'

'What attack? I don't know anything about that. I'm on holiday with my girlfriend.'

'Bullshit. This must be that reporter woman.'

'You must be a daft,' Ravi replied rudely. 'Why don't you piss off and leave us alone?'

The man's face flushed with anger. Ravi saw his lips tighten and he stood there glowering for a moment, then swung round and walked away towards his friend on the tee. But he stopped on the front steps once again.

'I'm going to the toilet,' he called to his exasperated partner. 'I'll be back in a minute.'

He went past Ravi without a glance and disappeared into the hall.

'Who is that bugger?' Tanya asked.

Ravi looked at her and liked what he saw. She must have showered because her hair was wet and plastered to her skull in uncombed strands, she wore no makeup and her clothes were creased. And she still looked great.

'A good friend of the Premasiri family. He knew my father as well.'

'How did he know about last night?'

'I warned you. This is more serious than we thought.'

'I don't trust the bastard. Let's get out of here.'

'I'll check on the cheese toast. I can eat a camel — or a Burgher, right now!' Ravi stood up and looked speculatively at Tanya. 'Actually I'd prefer a Burgher.'

'Go get the food,' Tanya ordered coldly.

He walked through the hall and across the corridor that bisected the clubhouse. The kitchen stood behind a pair of batwing doors at the end of another corridor. He met Michael coming out with the food.

Michael was carrying a tray table, that is, a full size tray with little legs fitted underneath that could be placed anywhere for the member's convenience. Ravi turned to follow the man and noticed someone leaving the phone booth by the corridor.

Leo Dias.

Ravi thought it strange that the man had kept his partner waiting so long on the tee. He also wondered why he hadn't used a mobile but then realized that hand phones are not encouraged on the course. He wanted to say something about it to Tanya but Michael took the silver cover off the plates. The aromatic slices of toast with the thick covering of golden-brown cheese put all other thoughts out of his mind.

They didn't speak for a few minutes. Ravi glanced idly towards the fairway and at Dias and his companion, now stick figures on the distant first green. Some movement made him look to the left. A dark blue vehicle was coming up the drive. It flashed past a gap in the live fence bordering the eighteenth fairway, and he saw the unmistakable white lettering, POLICE.

In an instant Ravi realized they were in big trouble. The Police force had become increasingly politicized in recent years. They would, to a man, blindly serve their political masters whoever it was in power at that moment. Ravi knew that if they were caught now they would certainly be locked up, and most likely brutalized. Given the humiliation they had inflicted on the Minister, even Tanya's status as a journalist wouldn't protect her.

He picked up the parcel of food, grabbed Tanya by the hand and hurried towards the other end of the verandah that led to the putting green.

'Dias informed the cops. They just drove into the car park.'

They scrambled down the steep gradient to the second green. The four fairways facing the clubhouse lay within a V, formed between New Bazaar Street and Grand Hotel Road. A footpath ran across the fairways to save townsfolk a long walk around. Ravi stayed under cover of the trees and led her towards the exit of the footpath to Grand Hotel Road.

He knew he should be afraid but felt strangely exhilarated instead, as if the danger stimulated him. He felt high.

Tanya turned to him, 'What about the others?'

Ravi thought she looked intoxicating at that moment and there were breadcrumbs still clinging to the edge of her mouth and chin.

He leaned over and licked them off.

'Stop it, you idiot,' Tanya wiped her chin vigourously with her hand. 'What do we do next?'

Ravi dialed Wimal's number. It was picked up on the first ring.

'Wimal?'

'Ow.'

Yes.

'Kosso ko?'

Where are the cops?

'Äthuley.'

Inside.

'Hondata ahaganna. Carpark eka pitipassey boralu pārak thiyanawa. Eken ävith thāra pārata vätenakota vamata harawanna. Api ethana innawa.'

Listen carefully. There is a gravel road behind the car park. When that falls onto the tarred road, turn left. We'll be there.

As they squeezed through the stile at the end of the path Ravi saw the van come out of a gate further down and turn into the road. He stepped back under cover to make sure the Police vehicle wasn't following them.

It wasn't.

They were on the road to Kandy. Tanya sat close to him in the rear seat and placed her hand comfortingly on his knee. Ravi realized she had the rare gift of knowing when not to speak.

He tried to work out their options.

The Police would probably find out that they were in a white van but there were shit loads of white vans on the road. The Police knew they were heading for Colombo and had only two practical routes. They were now traveling on one of them!

So they'd set up roadblocks. The question was, where?

'Where will they put the check points?' Tanya asked.

Clever girl.

Ravi looked at the old map he'd taken out of the glove compartment.

'It could be anywhere. But if it was up to me, I'd set it up at Pussellawa. They have a big force there.'

'All right, genius,' she took away the sting with a faint smile. 'Assume that. What follows?'

'They don't have our photographs, so they will look for cameras.'

'So?'

'Let's drop Siri off at Ramboda so he can take his gear and get home by bus.'

'And?'

'I can't tell from this map but I'm pretty sure we can bypass Pussellawa by using estate byroads.'

They drove past the Ramboda Falls and then the spectacular pass where the narrow single lane threaded its way under a threatening slab of black granite, anchored in the hillside and hanging over the vast precipice on the left. The road worked its way through a series of hairpin bends along the edge of one mountain, over a bridge spanning a narrow gorge and then onto the next mountainside. Magnificent tea gardens spread out on either side of the road following the contours of the hill, like a vast green billiard cloth thrown over a rock pile.

Ravi told Wimal to stop near the bus stand at Ramboda. Siri was glad enough to take his precious camera bag and find his own way back to Colombo. Ravi liked the quietly competent young fellow and was sorry to see him go. Walking over to the shops, Ravi purchased a small roll of scotch tape and two rolls of film.

When they started off again, Tanya looked on with amused tolerance when Ravi took the cap off her head. He took out the two used film rolls from his pocket and carefully taped the cassettes to the inside of Tanya's cap, one on either side. He then took the two new film rolls out of their packing and put them in his pocket.

Ravi was pleased with himself, more so when Tanya stretched and patted him lightly on the head.

'Clever little fellow, aren't you?'

'If you see the cops, don't take your cap off and bow.'

'Teach your grandmother to suck eggs,' she grinned.

They took a long turn to the right and a vast body of water came into view far down in the valley. Tanya was enchanted by the sight and raised an eyebrow in enquiry.

'Kotmale reservoir,' Ravi explained.

Wimal yelled: 'Sir. Sir, Police!'

It was a dark blue 4x4, probably the same one that had come to the Golf Club to find them. The vehicle was dangerously near the rear of the van and closing fast.

These bastards are going to ram us!

He grabbed Tanya by her shoulder and pulled her head down on his lap. He folded his upper body over her and braced his feet against the front seat.

There was a resounding bang at the rear. The van jerked violently and veered sharply to the left on screeching tyres. Ravi raised his head in time to see the stricken vehicle smash through a flimsy guardrail and launch itself into space.

Wimal screamed.

They hit the ground with a bone shuddering jar and bounced up again.

And again.

The van continued to slide downhill under the momentum of the impact, swaying alarmingly from side to side. Ravi realized that they were careening over the tea bushes on the slope. The bushes must have cushioned the impact and was slowing them down.

Wimal was still screaming.

The van fell onto a gravel road, bounced straight across and hit the stone terrace on the far side. Ravi was thrown forward against the front seat and fell, still holding Tanya in a tangled heap between the seats.

We have to get away before those cops get here.

The rear door slid open easily and he crawled out first. Tanya followed him looking dazed but apparently unhurt. Wimal was struggling with the front door that appeared to be jammed.

Ravi tugged at the passenger door till it came open with a protesting squeak. Wimal crawled out and stood staring glassily at him. He didn't or couldn't speak.

Ravi tried to work out the next step.

The van had come blasting down the slope for about fifty yards. The line of ruined bushes told the story. The estate road they were on joined the main road some distance behind the broken guardrail. That meant the Police vehicle would have to back up a good distance before it could turn down their road in pursuit.

And their van was jammed solidly across the road.

Ravi picked up his overnight bag, then Tanya's, and walked away leaving the others to follow.

'Where are we going?' Tanya asked quietly.

She had been shaken by the crash but had recovered quickly.

'Away from the van. The cops will be here any minute.'

'And then?'

'We have to find a vehicle or get a ride.'

'Where will we go?'

'These estate roads are a maze but they all connect up. If we can find our way through the plantations we can bypass Pusselawa and reach the main road further down.'

They were hidden from the main road by a rise in the ground. They came to a fork and took the lower road, taking them further away from the main road. Ravi saw women plucking tea on the hillside below him but no one crossed them on the road.

They heard the growl of a diesel engine. Ravi was through the fight-flight dilemma before he realized that it was coming from ahead.

A postbox red Rav 4 came around the corner. Ravi saw the driver studying them for a moment, and then slow to a halt. A heavy man with a shoe brush like head of black hair and a pepper and salt moustache leaned out of the front window.

'Were you in that crash? I saw it from the factory.'

'Yes.'

'Is anyone hurt?'

'No.'

'Hop in. I'll take you back to the road. You can get a ride to town from there.'

'No, we'd rather go the other way,' Ravi said earnestly. 'Some men were trying to hijack our vehicle. They forced us off the road.'

The man looked surprised but not disbelieving. The lawlessness in the country had reached such proportions that anything was possible.

He hesitated for a moment and then asked, 'Where do you want to go?'

'If we can get to Ulapane, we can get a bus to Gampola from there.'

Ulapane was a small town on the road from Gampola to Nawalapitiya.

The man stared at them broodingly for a while.

'All right! Let me turn this vehicle around.'

Ravi turned to muster his team and found Wimal missing.

Bloody hell! Where had the stupid lout gone?

The last time he'd checked, Wimal had fallen back a bit but had been following them doggedly. He had looked a little dazed but otherwise uninjured. Had he fallen behind and then taken the wrong road or had he stopped to rest?

'Are we going to look for him?' Tanya asked.

'I'd like to, but no, it's too risky. We'll run into the cops for sure. Someone will find him. Don't mention him to this guy.'

The vehicle drove up and they climbed in, Ravi in front and Tanya immediately behind him.

'My name is Devendra,' the big man said abruptly.

'Uh. I'm Ranjan and this is my fiancée Penelope.'

Ravi felt a sharp pain in his side that nearly made him yelp. He realized the Tanya had leaned forward and pinched him.

It wasn't gentle.

Was that for calling her his fiancée or for christening her Penelope?

Probably both.

Devendra didn't say anything till he came to a board that read "Superintendent's Bungalow".

'Let's have something to drink before we go,' he turned the vehicle into the driveway lined with flowering plants. 'You both look like you could use it.'

Ravi was impatient to move on, yet felt it would be churlish to refuse.

'Thank you.'

The large, flower-smothered bungalow came into view as they rounded the final bend. The façade of the building had been built with rectangular blocks of granite into which white casements had been let in a row. A stone chimney stood proudly over the green painted roof.

Devendra suggested tea and the appu, an old Tamil man in spotless white, took the order. Devendra excused himself and went outside. Ravi heard him shout something in Tamil, probably haranguing the men he'd seen working on the slope above the bungalow.

The heady aroma of fine upcountry tea filled the room as appu returned with a tray. The old man poured two cups for them and stayed to chat with Tanya. Ravi was bemused by the strange quirk in her character that kept her cold, almost haughty at most times. But now and then she met a person she, for some unfathomable reason, happened to like and then she turned on her charm. She seemed to have taken to the old appu. She talked to the man about his family and the "*Periya Dorais*" he had worked under.

The rheumy-eyed coot glowed under her attention.

Devendra came back at long last and the old man beat a hasty retreat.

'Thank you for the tea,' Tanya said brightly. 'I don't wish to be rude but we'd really like to be going.'

The big man looked broodingly at her for a moment

'Not just yet,' he said.

Ravi looked at him in surprise for there was a hint of menace in his voice.

The front door opened and two men came in. One was an oldish man with a shock of white hair and a face covered with grey stubble. The other was a squat younger man with a narrow brow and thick ropy arms. Both men carried wicked looking pruning knives in their hands.

138

'Where are the two cameras?' Devendra asked quietly.

'What the hell is this?' Tanya raised her voice angrily. 'What cameras?'

Devendra gave an exaggerated sigh.

'Don't play stupid with me. It's been on the radio. You people are wanted by the Police for staging a bomb attack on Minister Premasiri. There's also a reward for finding the two cameras you stole from him.'

Two cameras? The clever bastards wanted to get hold of Siri's camera as well.

'You are making a mistake ….,' Ravi began.

'No mistake,' Devendra cut him off nastily.

He grated something in Tamil. The younger man came forward and picked their kitbags in his left hand.

Ravi felt the long suppressed anger bubbling up inside him again. Almost subconsciously he found himself measuring the distance he'd have to fling himself to thump the black bastard.

Devendra said sharply, 'Don't. I've told him to cut you if you resist.'

Ravi forced himself to calm down and lean back.

Devendra emptied their two bags on the low table. Clothes and toiletries. No cameras.

He scowled at it for a moment. 'Empty your pockets.'

Tanya was ready to explode but Ravi knew that this was not their moment. He did as he was told and Tanya followed suit. Devendra's eyes widened almost imperceptibly when he saw the two rolls of film Ravi placed on the table. He picked them up and placed them reverently in his own shirt pocket.

Devendra went to the telephone standing on a little table near the door. He lifted the instrument and punched some numbers. He listened for a moment, juggled the cradle violently and dashed the receiver.

'Bloody phone,' he muttered darkly and then stood for a minute, deep in thought.

'Keep your things where they are. Your handbag as well, young lady,' the man ordered and then, turning around and pointing, 'now go into that room.'

He walked forward menacingly with his men following closely behind. Ravi knew that resistance would only result in their getting roughed up. He put his arm round the shoulders of the incandescent Tanya and coaxed her into the room.

The door slammed and Ravi heard the key turn.

Tanya was too angry to speak. Ravi left her to sizzle and quietly took stock of their situation. They were in a large room with windows facing the front of the house. Each of them had steel grills solidly screwed onto the wooden frame.

No exit that way.

A heavy double bed stood on one side of the room with a mahogany wardrobe and dressing table on the other. Two overstuffed chairs with a little coffee table formed a sitting area near the window.

The only other door from the room led to a spacious old-fashioned bathroom. A stained bathtub stood across one wall and a washbasin in the other. There was a narrow fanlight for ventilation that could have accommodated a polecat.

No door to the outside.

Ravi heard a vehicle engine and rushed into the bedroom. Tanya was at the window first but he was in time to see the red off-roader disappear down the curve of the drive.

'He's going for the Police, isn't he?' Tanya asked.

'Yes.'

'Why didn't he take us with him? It would have saved time.'

'I think he's more interested in the reward for the film rolls. If he gives it to the cops, he's never going to see the money. He's going to phone to make a deal about that first, then he'll bring the cops.'

Tanya looked at him steadily. 'So how do we get out of here? You are the idea man.'

'The door and the windows are out and there's no way through the bathroom.'

'So?'

'We can't go down. We can't dig our way out.'

'You mean we have to go up? Through the ceiling?'

They studied it.

The wooden ceiling was nut-brown with age but the beveled planks looked solid and fitted snugly together. High too, at least twelve feet above the floor.

'I can reach it if I stand on the wardrobe. Help me push the dressing table near it.'

The mirror table was heavy but they managed to push it close to the wardrobe and Ravi climbed up. He was not encouraged by what he found.

'I need a tool to prise these planks off,' he told Tanya when he jumped down. 'Let's search the room for something.'

They searched the room carefully, stripping the mattress off the bed and turning the heavy chairs over, but it was hopeless. There wasn't even a coat hanger in the empty wardrobe.

Tanya was looking at him calmly, depending on him to suggest the next step. Ravi fought down the panic he felt in his belly.

Think. You're not going to let them beat you.

He went to the bathroom and studied the fittings there. The bathtub and washbasin had nothing he could use. The old ceramic toilet had a wooden seat and a cast iron cistern mounted high on the wall. Tugging at a long chain hanging from it would work the flush.

The chain was connected to a long metal lever.

Ravi stood on the toilet seat and removed the heavy cast iron cistern cover. Working by touch he tugged and twisted at the device but it took more than five precious minutes, and a painful broken fingernail before he was able to wrench it off.

It wasn't ideal for the job by any means, not having a sharp edge to insert between the planks. But it was a solid piece of metal and it was all they had.

Back on the wardrobe.

Ravi tried inserting the lever between the planks. The strips of wood had warped with age and there were gaps between them, but the edge of the lever was simply too thick to go in.

Time was running out. How long would it take Devendra to come back with the cops? How much time had they used up already?

Tanya had been studying the ceiling in the rest of the room. She now stood in the centre of the room, under the fan.

'Take a look at this.'

Ravi jumped down and joined her. The pattern of the ceiling had been changed in the centre of the room. Thinner strips of a lighter shade of wood had been used to make a design in the form of a square.

And one strip was slightly out of line.

Moving the heavy wardrobe almost beat them. They were collapsing in exhaustion without making much progress when Ravi thought of inserting the coir rug from the bathroom under one end of it. When they put their shoulders to it the next time the ancient dresser began to move.

And stop. And move again.

They finally had it in place, directly under the fan and the dressing table next to it. Time! Devendra could turn up at any minute now. They couldn't stop to rest.

Ravi's head was nearly touching the ceiling when he stood on the wardrobe and the cistern lever slipped easily into the gap left by the damaged strip. He wrenched off the narrow strips one by one and eventually had an opening big enough to climb through.

'I'm coming with you.'

'It could be dangerous on the ceiling. I can open the door for you when I get down.'

'No. I'll come with you,' she said firmly. 'Help me up.'

The ceiling covered the entire building. Light filtering in at the edges was just enough for them to see their way. The high roof enabled them to walk upright in the centre of the building.

How the hell do we get down?

Ravi led the way towards the rear of the building, making sure he stepped on the sturdier beams and signaling Tanya to follow. He saw it then, a line of light filtering through what looked like a crack in the ceiling. He walked carefully towards it.

He should have looked for it in the first place. Of course they'd leave a kind of trapdoor to get into the ceiling if only to check the wiring. Ravi lifted the cover carefully and peeped. The Appu was arranging some crockery on a table directly below the trapdoor in what appeared to be a large pantry. He was alone.

Ravi knew the sensible thing to do was to wait till the man moved away but waiting also had its dangers. He tried to slide the cover away quietly but some faint sound made the man peer myopically at the ceiling.

Ravi flung the cover away and launched himself through the opening. He landed on the table, which collapsed under his weight with a tremendous crash, ruined crockery flying everywhere.

Ravi gathered himself painfully and rose to his feet. He found the appu cowering against the wall, his hands joined together in entreaty.

'Where are those men? Are they in the house?'

'Gone back to field, master,' the man quavered.

'Who is in the house?'

'No one master.'

'If you lie to me, I'll break both your legs.'

'No lies, master. I was worried about lady. I wanted to open door for her but my sir would kill me.'

Ravi kicked the debris of the demolished furniture aside and forced the man to help him bring another table from the kitchen. He placed it under the trapdoor, and standing on it, caught Tanya as she jumped down.

Her cap fell to the ground. Appu bent to pick it up and saw the two rolls of film taped on either side of it. He handed the cap to Tanya without a word.

Ravi forced the appu to come with them to the sitting room. He was relieved to find their belongings still scattered on the table. They hurriedly repacked their bags.

'Is there another car here?' Ravi asked the man.

'No car.'

'Shit,' Ravi turned to Tanya. 'They'll catch us easily if we walk along the road.'

Appu mumbled something.

'What can we do then?' Tanya ignored him, looking at Ravi.

The man muttered inaudibly again.

'What? What do you want?' Ravi snarled.

'Have master's motorcycle in garage.'

Ravi stared at him with his mouth half open.

Hallelujah!

They grabbed their bags and followed appu back to the pantry. He picked the keys off a board and handed it to Ravi, pointing the way. Parked against the far wall of the garage was a mud stained trail bike.

Kawasaki KDX 125.

'Wow!' Tanya burst out enthusiastically, looking at the hefty machine. 'I've always wanted to ride one of these.'

'Are you saying you can ride a motorbike?'

'Sure. Ridden them since I was a kid. What's the matter? Can't you ride?'

'Not very well,' Ravi lied manfully, ashamed to admit that he'd never ridden at all.

Tanya knew at once. She laughed as she swung her leg over the seat.

'Well mister-can't-even-ride, who did you say has thin blood? Burghers or the gamayas who wear sarongs and are scared of motorbikes?'

'Nice girls don't ride motorbikes,' Ravi shot back. 'You have been badly brought up.'

'Right, I'm getting off then. You can push the damn bike and see where it gets you.'

'Stop fooling around, you idiot. The cops will be here any minute now.'

'Then you'd better admit that Burghers are best. Otherwise you can stay here and rot.'

'Never. But I'll agree that Burgher girls are kind of cute.'

Tanya stared at him speculatively for a minute. She grinned. 'I'll take that. You can hop on now.'

Appu touched Tanya on the arm. 'God bless.'

Tanya squeezed his hand and murmured something.

She waited for Ravi to climb up behind her, gunned the engine and rode expertly out of the garage.

Ravi heard furious shouts from the hill above the house, and turning his head, saw several men running through the bushes brandishing their pruning knives. Some of them were running towards the house, others towards the road in the hope of cutting them off.

Tanya could ride all right and there was no vehicle that suited the estate terrain more than a powerful trail bike. She threw the bike down the sloping drive at furious speed, made a sliding turn on to the gravel estate road at the bottom and flashed past the men trying to jump on to the road from the embankment. Their angry shouts faded behind them as they swung round the next corner.

Ravi knew he had to head west to reach Ulapane but he couldn't tell direction from the mid-morning sun and estate road meandered in circles anyway. They saw a man in a dark sweater walking towards them with a heavy bundle of fuel wood on his head. They stopped to ask directions. How would they get to Gampola?

The man told them at great length, instructions as clear as mud, but enough to keep them going for the moment.

'Are we really going to Gampola?'

'Nah, but every little bit of disinformation helps.'

Thirty minutes of bumpy riding with many stops for information/ disinformation brought them to the small board, announcing the town of Ulapane. The estate road ended in a T. The signboard pointed right for Gampola and left for Nawalapitiya.

Ravi said, 'Turn right.'

'What? I thought we were going the other way.'

'Hey, if you're hard of hearing I can do it by touch.'

'Don't you dare!'

Tanya swung the bike to the right and they roared through the busy town centre. The dingy shops dwindled behind them and they were soon in open tea country again. When they'd traveled about a mile Ravi spotted an estate road to leading up the hill to the right and told her to pull up.

'What now?'

'Let's get the bike out of sight. I want to catch a bus going the other way.'

'You mean back the way we came? To Nawalapitiya?' Tanya looked exasperated. 'We could have caught a bus from Ulapane.'

'All the men in that town will remember seeing a girl riding a big bike turn towards Gampola.'

'So?'

'They'd have noted she was a sexy looking bimbo.'

'Oh shut up.'

'The cops will question them for sure. They'll all say we went towards Gampola.'

'And when they find the bike?'

'They'll still think we've hopped on a bus to Gampola.'

What came along was an ancient truck with a ragged canvas cover over its rear. It had been adapted for passenger traffic by having two transverse benches at the back for a lucky few. The others stood in the centre of the truck and hung on to the metal ribs of the hood.

And there were lots of those others in the truck.

Ravi pushed his way to the centre of the motley crowd, dragging a reluctant Tanya behind him. He was almost overpowered by the smell of stale sweat and musty clothing. Tanya knew very well why they had to conceal themselves in the crowd but there was no sign of understanding on her face. She glared venomously at Ravi as if he was to blame for her discomfort and noxious surroundings.

Just before reaching Ulapane, the ancient truck had to swing to the grass verge to allow a vehicle going towards Gampola to cross. Peering through the sea of arms and heads, Ravi could only tell the other vehicle was bright red in colour.

Devendra for sure, hot on their trail. How soon would he turn back?

They didn't cross any other vehicles in the short run to Ulapane and Ravi breathed a sigh of relief when the truck started off again, after a brief but noisy stop at the town centre. It took them the better part of the thirty minutes to reach Nawalapitiya.

The town was much bigger than Ravi had imagined. And dirtier! A sprawling hotchpotch of crumbling buildings and filthy streets clinging to the side of a hill. Tanya was affronted by the transition from immaculate green plantation to scruffy township.

'This place is an ulcer! Why can't these buggers keep it clean?' She grumbled. 'Look at that pile of vegetables. I suppose that's what we have to eat when it gets to Colombo.'

Ravi hurried her past the vast mounds of leeks, carrots and radish piled on the side of the road and surrounded by puddles of muddy water. The bus stand was a teeming mass of humanity but an old man told him there was a bus to Colombo every thirty minutes.

They looked around carefully and, to their relief, saw no policemen. Ravi suggested eating something and earned himself a fastidious glare. Tanya Koch wasn't ready to dine in such a verminous town. Ravi bought a comb of bananas. They ate a couple, nice *Kolikuttus*, and put away the rest for later.

It was nearly noon when an unshaven character, with greasy shoulder length hair and a sheaf of folded currency notes between his index and ring fingers, began chanting, 'Comba, Comba, Comba!'

The bus to Colombo was taking on passengers. They climbed aboard and moved to the rear of the bus that took off soon afterwards.

20

The forty something passenger bus, started off with no more than a dozen. The driver stopped every few hundred yards to pick up others and soon all the seats were taken. They joined the main highway at Ginigathena and turned towards Colombo. Tanya saw the view for the first time and was enchanted.

The nicely cambered road snaked its way along the edge of the mountain to their right. On their left the land fell away in a steep, scrub-lined slope till it ended in a magnificent rock strewn river at the bottom of the gorge. A forest clad mountain rose on the far side covered by a canopy of mighty treetops in every imaginable hue of green with an occasional crimson flamboyant thrown in, as if by an artist, for dramatic effect.

The road wound imperceptibly down into the valley till the river, now a white-flecked torrent, was just fifty feet below the road. Some tourists were trying to negotiate the rapids in an orange dingy and having a hard time staying dry.

Tanya said, 'I need to use a bathroom.'

Ravi pulled the crumpled road map out of his rucksack and had a look. Buses in Sri Lanka don't often make toilet stops. A name swam into his consciousness.

'We must be close to Kitulgala. We can hop off there.'

'That name's familiar. I can't think why.'

'They made a film at Kitulgala years ago. The Bridge on the River Kwai.'

'Really? Who acted in it?'

'Alec Guinness and William Holden. Ever heard of them?'

'Man, the nonsense you carry in your head,' she laughed. 'Of course I've never heard of them. Maybe Auntie Nora will remember. Or her mother!'

They got off and walked the short distance to the resthouse. There were several passenger vans and a tourist coach parked haphazardly outside. The front of the building was inauspicious, but as they walked into the main dining room, a splendid vista opened up before them. The building had been constructed on a bluff headland overlooking the river and afforded a fine view of the torrent rushing whitely through the rock-strewn riverbed.

Tanya came out of the washroom looking wet and fresh once more, and they spent some time looking at the framed photographs of the movie set hung around the dining room. Tanya marveled at the wooden bridge built, according to the movie story, by prisoners-of-war in Burma. It had really been built upriver of Kitulgala and was blown up in spectacular fashion at the end of the movie.

Tanya approved of the place, so Ravi ordered sandwiches for her, and rice and curry for himself.

'Can't you Sinhalese manage without your buth-curry? I suppose now you'll stuff yourself and then want to have a nap. That's the style, isn't it?'

'Of course! Being only a Burgher, you've no feel for the finer pleasures of this life,' Ravi stretched his arms wearily. 'I could really do with a nap.'

The sleepless night, and the unending tension, was beginning to catch up with him. He knew it would be even more difficult to stay alert after a heavy meal and regretted ordering the curry.

'I think it's time to call your Editor. I'm surprised he hasn't called you already.'

'Ah, that's because he doesn't know my number.'

'How come he doesn't know how to reach his star reporter?"

'The stingy bugger refused to pay me a phone allowance, so I don't use it for official work. Gimme your phone.'

'I see,' Ravi took his hand phone out. 'You get the glory, I get the bill.'

'Oh, shut up and give it to me. What do you want me to say?'

'Tell him we are in Nawalapitiya and have this sensational material with us. We're scared the police will catch us and take it away. Ask if he will send a vehicle to pick us up at Kitulgala resthouse in two hours?'

'What are you playing at this time?'

'Just do it, sweetie. I'll explain later.'

She called the Editor-in-Chief, Pali Ranatunga. Squawking noises came out of the phone.

'Yes sir. — We're all right. — Yes, we've got the film. — It's incredible. He came charging out of the room with a young woman. Both were naked. — Yes, we have the shots. —Yes sir, the film is safe.'

Tanya listened for a moment and spoke again. 'The police vehicle rammed us from behind — pushed us over the precipice and tried to kill us. — Arrested? Really? Siri as well? — Yes, all right. Sir, we are very tired. We can get to Kitulgala resthouse in about two hours. Can you send a vehicle to pick us up?'

Tanya listened intently for a while then said, 'I understand. Thank you.'

She rang off and looked at Ravi.

'He says Wimal has been arrested. Siri was also picked up and his camera has been confiscated. We have been accused of attempting to kill the Minister using an explosive device. We are to be arrested under the Prevention of Terrorism Act.'

'Hell. They'd know by now it was only fireworks.'

'I suppose that's for us to prove and they won't give us the chance. They've also accused us of stealing two expensive cameras.'

'What's special about the PTA? How is it different to the normal law?'

'They can keep us locked up indefinitely without producing us before a magistrate or allowing us bail.'

They thought about it for a minute, absorbing the implications. Terrorist was the key word these days. Now that they had been classified as such, every policeman in the country would be after them.

Ravi said softly: 'I'm sorry I got you into this, honey.'

Tanya swung her foot under the table and caught him painfully in the shin.

'Don't start that rubbish. We are in this together. We just have to make sure the story gets published. When the truth is known they won't be able to call it terrorism.'

They tried to wave down another bus and succeeded only when a long distance coach from Badulla stopped at the entrance to the resthouse to drop off some back packing tourists.

They found space at the back and sank gratefully into the seats. Tanya made herself comfortable by the window and rested her head against Ravi's shoulder.

'As captain of the team I now assign the first watch to you,' she murmured. 'See you keep a sharp lookout.'

'Who appointed you captain?'

'You know that I can make you do whatever I want, that makes me the captain. Now shut up and let me sleep.'

He had been sleeping at his post!

Ravi clawed his way to consciousness as if he was climbing out of a deep well. He saw they had pulled up at a checkpoint and a couple of policemen had climbed aboard.

They were caught like rats.

Ravi found Tanya's eyes on him, waiting calmly for instructions. He should have been frightened for there was no escape for them, yet he felt again the strange exhilaration he'd experienced at the Hambantota resthouse, and at the Golf Club. He felt invincible.

'So who's the captain now?'

'Be serious, you idiot.'

'Am I captain or not?'

The cops were halfway down the aisle, questioning the passengers one by one.

'Oh, all right, if it's so damn important to you,' she muttered angrily.

'Right. Act like a foreigner. Pretend you don't understand Sinhala. I'll translate for you. I'll say I'm your guide.'

'They'll ask for my passport.'

'Say you've left it in Colombo. Undo the top button of your shirt to show a little something. And smile!'

She stared at him icily but did as she was told.

The cops were questioning the passengers directly in front of them.

Ravi yanked his backpack from under the seat and took out the battered remnants of the comb of bananas. Tanya understood his intent immediately. She was nonchalantly peeling a banana when the cop turned to them.

'*Kohenda enney?*'
Where are you from?
'*Badulley indang, ralahamy. Mama mey suddiwa tour ekak genichcha.*'
We're coming from Badulla. I took this white woman on a tour.
'*Denna eyāgey passport eka.*'
Give me her passport.
'What's he saying?' Tanya asked indistinctly through a mouthful of banana, raising the visor of her cap slightly to look at the cop. 'What does he want?'
'He want passport, madam,' Ravi said loudly.
'I keep …. passport … Colombo,' Tanya addressed the cop as if speaking to a child. 'Agent say … don't take. Get lost … big trouble.'
'*Suddi kiyanawa …*'
The white woman says …
'*Mata terenawa, modaya! Äyi umba kiwwey näththey passport genna kiyala?*'
I understand, you moron! Why didn't you tell her to carry her passport?
'*Gäni lassanainey, ralahamy. Däkka welawey indan mage hitha hari upset eken inney!*'
The woman is very pretty, officer. From the moment I saw her, my mind is very upset!
'*Umbala okkoma hari kupādiyo. Suddiyanta kelinnamai haddanney.*'
You fellows are all cads. Always trying to screw foreign women.
'*Chance ekak läbunoth kohomada atha arinney, ralahamy?*'
If I get a chance, how can I let it pass officer?
Tanya took another bite of her banana. The cop had a good view of the lacy edge of her bra as he stood above her.
He looked envious.
'*Gunning umbalai bäg.*'

Get your bags out.

He pawed through the two bags perfunctorily, handed them back and moved on.

A young fellow at the back of the bus was carrying a camera. The cop pounced on it and wanted to confiscate it. The owner objected vehemently, screaming abuse in Tamil. He must have been traveling in a family group because his relatives took up the cause, all crying out at the same time and creating a deafening row. The cop held his ground stubbornly but obviously didn't understand a word they were saying.

Another policemen climbed into the vehicle and the situation looked as if it might get out of hand.

A grey haired sergeant followed him a minute later and yelled something in Tamil. Everyone piped down immediately. He picked up the camera and opening the film chamber, yanked out the half used reel. He handed the camera back to the youth, who was staring speechlessly at him, and stepped off the bus before anyone realized what had happened.

They got underway soon afterwards.

'Did you see the arrogance of those cops,' Tanya said angrily. 'They have no right to impound all the cameras in the country. These bastards are crazy.'

'Ahh, the cops will do whatever their political masters tell them to. They're just a bunch of cock suckers.'

'Don't be vulgar.'

'Speaking of which, I wonder if …'

'In your dreams, buster. You've been watching too many crappy movies.'

'Ah, come on, Tani,' Ravi was beginning to enjoy irritating her.

'Do you want a punch on the nose?'

'No.'

'Good. That settles it then,' she said icily. 'That cop called you a *kuppādiya*. He wasn't wrong.'

Tanya turned away, rested her head against the window and closed her eyes.

Was she really pissed or just pretending? Ravi couldn't tell.

They crossed the river at Yatiyantota and turned towards Avissawella. Ravi felt the wretchedness of extreme fatigue spread like a stain inside his body. He felt mildly depressed too and chased through his mind to pin down the cause. Surely it wasn't because he might have offended her with his off colour joke? He watched the shadows under the rubber trees flitting past the window and tossed the idea about in his mind.

How did this girl's mood have such an impact on his world?

'You've been an absolute pig,' Tanya said suddenly, 'so I'm sacking you as captain. I'm in charge now.'

'Hey, you don't have the power to do that.'

'Yes, I have. As long as you're hot for me, I have the power to do whatever I choose.'

She turned towards him, put her head on his shoulder and closed her eyes again.

The bus pulled into the main bus station at Avissawella and the driver told them they'd have a fifteen minute break. Tanya wondered off into the market, stepping carefully over piles of vegetables and fruit spread on plastic sheets, talking to the vendors. Ravi realized that she had the knack of relating to people, of being genuinely interested in their lives and travails.

They heard the conductor yelling, 'Comba, Comba, Comba' and hurried back. The bus was nearly full when they pulled into the main road leading to Colombo some fifty-five kilometers further on.

Traffic built up soon afterwards and movement against the oncoming office traffic slowed to a crawl. The sun was sinking in the west when they passed through Maharagama. They had agreed to get off at Nugegoda, the next main junction, and take a taxi to Tanya's home in Dehiwela.

Ravi's phone rang.

'Hullo, I'm Ranatunga from the Statesman,' a gravelly voice said. 'Are you Ravi?'

Pali Ranatunga, the editor.

'Yes.'

'Is Tanya with you? Are you all right?'

'Yes, she's ok. I'm sorry we couldn't keep the appointment. I'll explain

154

later.'

'Good thing you didn't. The men I sent, they ran into a serious problem.'

'What?'

'They'd been at Kitulgala resthouse, waiting for you. A man had come in saying he had a message from you. He'd said you were afraid to come into the resthouse and wanted to be picked up further down the road.'

Tanya had leaned close to him and placed her ear next to the phone in an effort to hear what was going on. Ravi felt her breast pressing on his elbow and had an urge to annoy her by doing something outrageous, like licking her nose. She must have read his thoughts because when he turned she glared at him angrily.

'Go on,' Ravi said into the phone.

'It seemed reasonable so they went with the man. About half a mile down the road they were told to turn into a cart track. They did. Some men pulled them out of the vehicle and assaulted them.'

'Bloody hell! Were they badly injured?'

'They've been taken to Avissawella Hospital. I don't know how serious their injuries are. They … burnt the car. It's a total write off.'

Ravi was quiet for a while then asked, 'How did they know your people were at Kitulgala?'

'Could they have followed you?'

'No. Positively no.'

'Then they must have an informant at my office. We discussed the project openly at the news desk. The Minister is going to far greater lengths than I expected. Those shots must be explosive.'

'Mm.'

'Is the film safe? Is it with you?'

'Yes.'

"Tell Tanya not to go home. They'll have men waiting for her.'

'Police?'

'Or MSD! Who can tell?'

'I'm not sure I can convince her. Will you speak to her?'

Tanya took the phone, listened for a while and finally said, 'Yes, all right. I'll work something out. We'll call you tomorrow. Yes, on your mobile. Bye.'

She cut the line and looked at Ravi. 'I want to go home,' she said wearily. 'I hope no one's tried to harass my mum and dad.'

'You know it isn't safe, honey. The Police will arrest us for sure. Let's stay out of sight till we find out what's happening.'

'I suppose so. Where can we stay?'

'There's a hotel I've seen at Bambalapitiya, facing the Marine Drive. I think they cater to folks coming from Jaffna. Doesn't look expensive. Shall we try it?'

Instead of answering, Tanya turned away and looked out of the window. After a time she turned back, 'If you register my name as Penelope you'll be sorry.'

'Fine. How about Hermoine? We can be Henry and Hermoine Herft.'

'Oh shut up.'

*

They got off near Dickman's Road and took a three-wheeler to their destination, an ugly square building rather grandly called The Great Eastern Hotel. It stood facing the sea with Frankfurt Place on one boundary and the Bambalapitiya Flats on the other.

The clerk at the reception was a morose young Tamil who looked suspiciously at them but made no comment. Ravi registered as Clement and Horty Ferdinands with an address in Matale. They had to pay Rupees 600/- in advance for the room. The clerk told them they could have vegetarian meals at a restaurant on the ground floor, accessible through another staircase at the rear of the building. Occupancy must have been low because they had no difficulty in getting a room at the front of the building facing the sea.

The room was small with a tiny attached bath. It smelt faintly of incense.

'Horty? Horty? What kind of name is that? Sounds like a bloody car horn. You always try to make me look silly.'

156

'Your given name is Hortense, of course,' Ravi explained seriously. 'The children and I just call you Horty at home. A pet name. I can go down and change it to Hortense if you like.'

'Oh bugger off with your pet names.'

Ravi showered first and Tanya took her turn. Ravi tried to reach Reshane but he wasn't at home and his mobile was switched off. He walked to the window and stared at the western sky, now streaked with reds, orange and yellow. The sea was still as grey-black glass with gentle breakers running onto the rocks below the railway line. The unfinished Marine Drive carried little traffic but masses of fitness freaks were tramping up and down, getting their daily exercise.

Tanya came out of the bathroom already dressed in T-shirt and jeans. She had a towel wrapped around her head. She stood beside him at the window, looking at the scene below them. Ravi put his arm around her and pulled her in front of him taking the towel off her head. He felt a sudden and unexpected rush of tenderness for her as he gently wrapped his arms around her waist. When she put her arms over his and leaned back he began to nuzzle her ear and neck. She smelt delicately, deliciously of Lux.

The queen of beauty soaps or was it the soap of beauty queens? Ravi didn't care.

The tenderness didn't last. He felt the rising heat and knew that she knew. She pushed him away immediately. 'I need to stretch my legs. Let's go for a walk.'

'Ahh, can't it wait till later? I was just getting started.'

'No, you must learn to be patient. It's good for you.'

'There's a wicked streak in you, did you know that?'

'Sure.'

'You'll be sorry for making me suffer.'

'Balls.'

Tanya picked up her cap.

'Shall we leave this here or take it with us?'

'I don't want to leave it in the open and carrying it is an unnecessary risk. Give me a moment.'

Ravi looked around the room carefully. The obvious hiding places were in the wardrobe, under the bed or inside a pillow. He finally fished out the small roll of sticky tape he'd bought in Nuwara Eliya and tore off some strips. He then stood on the bed and carefully taped one cassette on the upper side of one of the blades of the fan. He got off the bed and walked around the room, looking at it from every angle. Satisfied that it wasn't easy to spot, he quickly taped the second cassette on another blade.

'There is such a thing as being too clever. Why don't you just carry it in your pocket?'

'Ahh Burghers don't understand subtlety.'

Tanya just glowered at him silently.

'There have been robberies on the Marine Drive, especially after dark. After all the trouble we've been through, I don't want to lose these to some damn thief.'

They didn't encounter any thieves, only strollers ambling along chatting loudly in Tamil, a couple of serious joggers and a man selling sliced pineapple. A train filled with office workers rumbled past, dual headlights lighting up the track.

A low wall stood between the road and the vast apartment complex everyone called Bambalapitiya Flats. Ugly and horribly old-fashioned three storey buildings had been constructed in some bygone era and stood on prime property between the Marine Drive and Galle Road.

They came to the bottom of Clifford Place, once his home. Ravi felt as if a spear had passed through his belly when the magnitude of his loss hit him. His parents, his home and everything he'd treasured.

Wipe out the memories or you'll go mad.

Tanya instinctively guessed his mood. She slipped her hand through his arm and gripped his fingers, then pressed his arm against her chest. She didn't say anything but he was comforted and weathered the moment.

Walking back to the hotel, Ravi noticed that an eight-foot wall stood between the Eastern Hotel and the rear compound of the flats. A side gate of the hotel opened to the Marine Drive and allowed public access to their restaurant.

A heavy man wearing a black beret and a grey security uniform greeted then near the main gate.

'Ahh sir la ävidinna giyada?' He asked cordially. *'Koi palatenda enney?'*

Have you been for a stroll? Where are you from?

'Matale indala.'

From Matale.

'Sir lata policiath ekka prasnayak nä ne?

Surely sir couldn't be having problems with the police?

Ravi felt the back of his neck grow cold.

'Nähä. Äyi ähuwey?'

No. Why did you ask?

'Jodu ärwoth policiyata dannanna kiyala thiyanawa. Reception eken dänatama kiyala äthi.'

The police have instructed us to let them know if any couples check in. The receptionist would have informed them already.

Dammit!

Ravi put his arm round Tanya's shoulder and walked casually past the reception counter ignoring the suspicious stare of the boy at the front desk. In the room they started packing in frantic haste, stuffing their kit bags with whatever came to hand.

Ravi checked the window.

A white car was parked across the main gate. It had a bank of blue, red and white lights fitted across the hood and the word POLICE printed on the bonnet and boot. The cops were already inside the building and might well be halfway up the stairs. Ravi knew they had, at best, a few seconds to get clear.

He felt it again, that heady mix of fear and exhilaration that seemed to envelop him in moments of extreme danger.

He grabbed Tanya by the hand, scooped up the bags in the other, and ran. He turned right, away from the main stairs and towards the rear stairs leading down to the restaurant. The corner seemed to stretch and stretch away from them, and Ravi expected to hear a challenging shout at any moment. Then they turned the corner and started down the narrow stairwell at the back of the building.

Ravi pushed the glass door and found himself in a long room with tables for dining arranged in rows. It was empty except for a uniformed waiter setting places for dinner. The man glanced at them incuriously and turned back to his task. The door at the far end of the room was open and led to a ten-foot passage between the building and the boundary wall. The wrought iron gate leading to the Marine Drive stood at the end of the passage. But to leave by that gate would bring them into full view of the police car parked across the other gate.

There was a hefty generator standing against the wall. Ravi climbed onto the casing and helped Tanya up. The boundary wall now came up to his chest and he was able to see the roof of a small shed on the other side. He dropped the bags over, then climbed up and gingerly lowered himself on the roof below. Tanya dropped down beside him and crouched immediately when they heard a commotion on the other side.

'Ung koheda giyey?'

Where did they go?

'Pārata yanawa äthi, ralahamy,' a deferential voice spoke Sinhala with difficulty.

They must have gone to the road, officer.

Ravi jumped down and caught Tanya when she followed. They picked up their bags and ran up the broad driveway between the apartment blocks. Fifty yards of hard sprinting brought them to a corner that allowed them to take cover and catch their breath. A careful peep rewarded them with a glimpse of a white car moving slowly down the Marine Drive.

'They can't turn into the flats from that side. They'll have to drive round the block and get to Galle Road.'

'We'd better be going then, hadn't we?' Tanya asked calmly.

They ran till their chests began to heave. One or two people looked at them sharply but no one interfered with them. When they passed the row of shops that fronted the main road Ravi saw people milling around with shopping bags, buying groceries. He stopped and drew Tanya into the crowd. They stood behind a pillar watching the gate that led to Galle Road. Their caution was rewarded in less than a minute when the white police car turned in at speed and disappeared into the complex behind them.

Ravi led the way across Galle Road and up a lane on the landside.

'Where are we going?' Tanya gasped for breath.

'Those cops will be back in a minute. We have to get away from the main road for a start.'

'Let's go to Aunty Nora's. It's close by.'

'Mm, I thought of that. I just wondered if they'd start checking on your relatives.'

'Oh, we've got stacks of relatives. Anyway Aunty Nora isn't related. Her daughter and mum were schoolmates.'

Ten minutes later, having climbed over the wall at the back end of the lane, they were tapping at Aunty Nora's door.

'Tani?' The old lady chirruped happily when she realized who it was. 'Darling, what are you doing here?'

'Aunty No,' Tanya folded the frail body in a fond embrace. 'I can't go home at the moment because some people are looking for me … to stop a story I've written. Can I stay with you for a day or two?'

'Of course you can, darling. Stay as long as you want,' Nora said with a pleased smile. 'Come in. Have you had dinner?'

'No aunty, but please don't worry. We'll pick up something from outside.'

'Nonsense. I'll make you omelettes and there's bread.'

The house had just two bedrooms and a tiny box room full of broken furniture and suitcases. The old lady conducted Ravi to his room, and led Tanya gently but very firmly to her own bedroom. Tanya looked at the scowling Ravi over Nora's head and pulled her tongue at him.

A shower and change helped Ravi push back the tide of exhaustion that had gradually engulfed his body. Tanya joined him in the sitting room looking, as she always did after freshening up, bright and sparkly. They could hear Aunty Nora pottering about the kitchen.

'What the hell is she protecting you so much for?' He asked grumpily. 'Does she imagine you're a kind of vestal virgin?'

'Of course she does. Anyway she doesn't approve of nice Burgher girls getting involved with Sinhala *yakkos*.'

'What?' Ravi had only been fooling around but now the outrage in his voice was genuine. 'What's she got against the Sinhalese?'

'Oh, Aunty thinks most Sinhalese are nice people in their own way,' Tanya went on unctuously. 'It's just that they are a little uncouth … there's no refinement in them. No class! Aunty thinks we Burghers can do better.'

'I like her bloody cheek. I've half a mind to go in that kitchen and …'

'Show her your couth?'

They started laughing.

Ravi thought how strange it was that his mum had always warned Tilak and him about getting entangled with Burgher girls. Sinhala mothers thought Burgher girls were flighty and frivolous, and were always trying to trap their precious sons into marriage. And now he was being told that the blasted Burghers thought they were too good for the Sinhala in the first place.

Aunty Nora might have perverse views about Sinhala boys, and Ravi meant to take up the issue sometime, but he had to admit she could make a superior omelette. They were light and fluffy and stuffed with onions and cheese. A shower, fresh clothes, a tasty meal and the prospect of a good night's sleep in a safe haven. Ravi couldn't have asked for more.

He sighed contentedly.

Aunty Nora asked with a worried frown: 'Darling, why are these men looking for you? What have you two been up to?'

'It's just some photographs …,' Tanya stopped suddenly and looked at Ravi. 'Oh dear.'

Ravi looked thunderstruck.

They'd left the cassettes taped to the fan at the Great Eastern.

Ravi stood up immediately.

'No. Not now Ravi. It's too dangerous.'

'I have to get it back.'

'If they've seen it, it'll be gone already. If not, there's no rush. Let's plan this thing.'

'What's happened?' Aunty Nora asked anxiously. 'What have you lost?'

'A roll of film,' Tanya said quietly. 'We left it in a restaurant we visited.

Don't worry, we'll collect it later.'

Aunty Nora was a TV addict. She had studied the TV guide and used a black pen to circle the programs she had selected. Quite fond she was of Sinhala teledrama, Ravi thought, even as she held Sinhala boys in low esteem.

She cleverly kept the two of them apart by motioning Tanya to sit beside her on the sofa facing the TV, leaving Ravi to languish on one of the cane chairs.

Ravi remembered something and went to his room. Tanya cocked an eyebrow at him when he returned. Waiting till Aunty was properly distracted Ravi opened his fist to show her a key in his palm.

She understood.

They'd never checked out of the Great Eastern. The key to the room had been in his pocket.

Ravi said: 'Aunty. I'm going out a little later. I'll be back in an hour or so.'

'Are you going to look for that ... film?'

'Yes.'

'I'm coming with you,' Tanya said immediately.

'No.'

'Shut up,' Tanya's voice was unexpectedly harsh, uncompromising. 'I'm coming.'

Aunty was shocked. 'Baba, girls should not be out so late in the night. It's not safe.'

'Please don't worry, aunty. I can take care of myself. Anyway Ravi's there.'

21

They had waited till midnight before leaving the house.

Ravi surveyed the main road carefully from the top of the lane. Long distance buses roared up and down the road. The pavements were deserted except for a man sleeping in a doorway. No police car.

Ravi waited in the shadows till a three-wheeler came by. He waved it down and bundled Tanya in when the man swung to the pavement. It cost them Rupees 20/- to be dropped in front of the flats. Five minutes later they were by the boundary wall of the hotel.

The flat dwellers appeared to have turned in for the night, for there was hardly a light showing through the frosted glass windows. Ravi pulled himself carefully onto the roof of the shed they had used earlier. He pulled Tanya up, and a minute later they were crouched near the door of the restaurant. It was closed for the night.

And locked.

Ravi was wondering whether he'd have to bluff his way past the receptionist when Tanya tugged at a window and it came open with a squeak.

This is going to work!

He signaled Tanya to wait and climbed in. He began to feel his way between the tables hoping fervently the waiter slept in his quarters elsewhere. He wasn't really anxious to step on some goof's face in the dark. He found the door and released the latch to allow Tanya in.

They would have found it difficult to negotiate the back stairs if not for a flashing neon light from the road providing the faintest illumination. They got to the second floor and moved cautiously along the corridor. A light hanging over the main staircase lit the far end of it.

Ravi took the round knob of the mortise lock in his hand and tried to turn it.

Locked.

Maybe housekeeping had locked it afterwards. He inserted the key, turned the lock and eased the door open. The room was in darkness but the light filtering through the blinds was enough to make Ravi realize that something was wrong.

The fan was working.

The boy who cleaned the room had left it on or…

Ravi turned off the fan, switched the lights on … and nearly died of shock. An old couple was asleep in the double bed. The light disturbed them and they opened their eyes, first the man and then the woman. Eyes that quickly widened in terror.

As if in a dream, Ravi took note of the straggly greyish-black hair of the woman spread out on the pillow. She had covered her mouth with her hand. On the bedside table stood a tumbler with a set of dentures. The man had a fine head of white hair above a seamed and wrinkled nut-brown face.

'*Vendiathi eduthu kolunga. Engalai summa vidungal,*' he quavered in Tamil.

Take what you want. Leave us alone.

The tendons in the woman's neck were taut and distended; the mouth behind the hand was half open. Ravi knew she was bracing herself to scream.

They were Tamils, probably here on a rare visit from Jaffna. They would not want to create a scene if they could possibly avoid it. But they were very frightened. He put his finger on his lips and then joined his hands together in a universal gesture of greeting.

It was a near thing but he saw the old woman's eyes flick across to Tanya. Then the tension went out of her and she drew back, slowly but surely, from the edge.

Ravi made the gesture of supplication again and then stepped on the bed. The old woman's eyes widened again and the man lifted his arms as if to ward off a blow. Their expressions changed from fear to puzzlement when he reached up to take hold of the fan. It only took a moment to yank off the little cassettes and hand them to Tanya.

They backed out of the room slowly. Ravi placed his finger on his lips once again in an unspoken warning before switching off the light. Minutes later they were climbing over the boundary wall. The roof of the much-abused shed wobbled under their combined weight but they jumped down unharmed.

Ravi was high again and reckless. He felt himself soaring in the air. He grabbed Tanya by the waist and pulled her into the shadows. He tried to hold her close and bury his face in the side of her neck.

'Stop it, you clown,' Tanya gasped in surprise. 'You'll get us arrested.'

'No one can catch us. Don't you know that?'

She took a firm grip of the hair at the back of his head and yanked him off. But she was laughing. 'Not here.'

'Back home then? If aunty is asleep?'

'We'll see.'

But when they unlatched the gate they saw that the lights were on. Ravi muttered something under his breath and Tanya squeezed his arm. When Ravi opened the door he found aunty seated in the hall with her bible open on her lap and her reading glasses balanced precariously on her nose.

'You shouldn't have stayed up, darling,' Tanya greeted her fondly. 'I told you we'd be all right.'

'I was worried about you. I couldn't have slept anyway. Let's get to bed now. You must be exhausted.'

*

They were seated at the kitchen table with the two rolls of film lying ominously between them. Aunty had made breakfast for them and then taken herself to the garden, leaving them alone.

'Do you know which is which? It'll be a disaster if we mix them up.'

'The one with the cross is Siri's,' Ravi pushed it with his finger. 'That's the one we need to develop.'

'What about the other?'

'Premasiri in bed with that woman will be much too explicit for your feature. No studio will print it anyway. They'll call the police first.'

'Even Siri's film will cause problems. The technicians will recognize the Minister.'

'Yeah. It's a problem all right. We need to find someone who works in a studio, who'll do a private job.'

'Marie.'

'Who?'

'Marie. Marie Fernando who lives down our lane,' Tanya said excitedly. 'She works at Salaka at Union Place. I'm sure she'll help.'

'Is she on the phone?'

'Her dad's name is Gamini. I think I can trace the number from a directory.'

'There's a Communication Centre at the top of the road. Let's try from there. I don't want aunty to overhear this.'

Alpha Communications offered IDD & local calls, photocopying, laminating and numerous other services. Tanya found Gamini Fernando's number and caught her friend Marie as she was leaving home.

Ravi left her to it.

Tanya came back looking pleased.

'Marie says it won't be a problem. She'll bribe one of the technicians to get the job done. We have to meet her outside the studio at about 9.30.'

'Good. We have plenty of time.'

'I want to call mum. She'll be in a state by now.'

'I have a thought …,' Ravi started.

'What?'

'I don't know how it's done but, since the cops are involved, they might have tapped your phone.'

'Can they do that?'

'Technically it's no problem. Let's not take a chance. Can you reach someone in your lane to give a message that you are all right? What about that bald coot?'

'Uncle Conrad? Yes, I suppose so,' she said grudgingly. 'And don't you call him a coot!'

They took a bus to Bambalapitiya junction, and from there another that took them to Union Place. They were early and spent ten minutes idling in the bus stand watching the crowds of working people stream off to their shops and offices. One more crowded bus pulled up and this time a plump girl in a dark blue business suit pushed her way through the throng and stepped on to the pavement.

She must have been fond of Tanya because she immediately folded her in a fond embrace.

'Where have you been? There's a rumour that the police are after you. What have you done?'

'Calm down, Marie, we haven't committed any crimes. We took some compromising photos of a Minister. He's using the police to try and steal our film.'

'Oh, is that all?' Marie was mildly disappointed. 'So you want the film developed? No problem.'

Ravi gave her the cartridge.

'Is this your fellow? He suits you, sweetie.'

'Of course not! Don't put ideas in his head.'

Marie dug her playfully in the ribs. 'Ahh, he already has ideas. I can tell.'

'Be serious, honey. How can we collect the film and prints?'

'Be at the Bambalapitiya main bus stand from 5.30. Watch for route number 155. I'll pass it to you through the window.'

'Thanks Marie. I owe you one.'

'Never mind that. Tell me all about this fellow when we meet next.'

Tanya needed to buy clothes so they went to House of Fashions on Duplication Road. The store was crowded with pre-Christmas shoppers. For some unknown reason, Tanya had been in a sour mood since the meeting with Marie. Ravi's offer to help pick her underclothing was met with an icy stare and an invitation to "bugger off".

When they finally emerged, loaded with bags, Tanya spotted a cyber café across the road. She decided to start working on her piece and left Ravi to carry her purchases back to the house.

*

Tanya had recovered her good humour when she returned for a late lunch. They chatted happily over the meal and then, when aunty complained of a slight headache, packed her off to bed and washed the dishes in companionable silence.

They were seated in the drawing room reading the newspapers. With just over a week to go, the election campaign was in full swing and the spiral of violence was almost out of control. The newspapers were filled with reports of beatings and burnings. The Government was using state agencies and security personnel to maximum effect while the opposition was retaliating with hired goons. Ravi found that their own little escapade had been relegated to page two.

SUSPECTS IN ALLEGED BOMB ATTACK STILL AT LARGE.

'This report says the police expect to arrest us at any moment.'

'Wish them the best of luck,' Tanya answered with her face buried in another page.

'Did you finish your article?'

'No. Just an outline. I'll finish it tomorrow.'

'We'll have to find a way to send it in, won't we?'

'No problem with that. I'll scan the photos and E-mail the whole thing in.'

'Clever girl.'

'Yes.' Her smile sent his heart skipping. 'I am, aren't I?'

Ravi looked at her fondly as she became engrossed in some other item in the newspaper.

He said casually, 'Marie thought we'd make a nice couple, didn't she? Maybe we should become an item.'

'What did you say?' Tanya lowered the newspaper. Her eyes had narrowed and there was a pink flush on her cheeks.

'I just said maybe we should, you know ...'

'And you thought once you've said that, I'd jump into bed with you?' Tanya's voice was arctic. 'Is that it?'

'No, that's not what I meant at all,' Ravi protested. 'You told me in Sinharaja I should decide if I wanted to be serious ...'

Ravi stopped when he saw the look in her eyes.

'Listen, you cocky bastard. If you're keen on me you'd better woo me.'

'Are you really serious?'
'You'd better believe it.'
'And how do I woo you?"
'Chocolates and flowers and on your bloody knees.'
'And after I've wooed you?'
'Ask me the question. Ask me if I wanted you.'
'What will your answer be?'
'You're not bloody getting any answer now. When you've done your wooing and you ask the question, I will decide. It'll depend on my mood at that moment.'

Tanya stood up without waiting for a response and stalked off into aunty's room. The door slammed with an impact that shook the house.

The bus stand at Bambalapitiya stood directly in front of the market. Impatient motorists were honking their horns in frustration as traffic got snarled up between the lane turning right into Station Road and the bus stand on the far side. Commuters stood on the pavement ready to rush towards each crowded bus that pulled up.

It was just past 5:30 when a route 155 bus came by. It didn't stop at the main stand but went on to another shelter some thirty yards further down the road. Marie was leaning out of the window and waving.

Ravi ran after the bus and reached it just as it was starting off again. Marie tossed him the packet and yelled: 'They're awful.'

Then she was gone.

They'd waited till they got home before opening the packet. Aunty was still pottering about in her garden, so they were able to examine the photographs at leisure. There were just four of them and, of those, two were blurred and out of focus.

The other two had hit the jackpot.

One showed the Minister emerging from the bedroom with just the head of the woman seen over his shoulder. The second showed them both, naked as Adam and Eve, stumbling into the verandah. The Minister, belly drooping obscenely like a toad's, was clearly recognizable in both photographs. Siri had done his job well.

One glance at the photographs and Tanya's mood changed in a flash.

She squeezed Ravi's arm in her excitement.

'We did it. We've got the bastard.'

Ravi looked down at her. She was grinning from ear to ear and her eyes were dancing. He realized he should have been excited too, for he finally had his enemy by the throat.

Ravi was excited all right, but not only on that account. He realized, with some surprise that he was getting really fond of this crazy, unpredictable creature. And she was sitting very close to him.

He kissed her gently on her nose and then her eyes and cheeks. When he felt her arms tighten round his shoulders he ran his tongue over her lips.

Marshmallow lips, soft and incredibly sweet!

They heard the door latch and sprang apart guiltily before aunty limped into the room, complaining bitterly about caterpillars.

22

Tanya had E-mailed the photographs and exposé to her editor the previous day. An hour later she'd had an ecstatic call from Pali Ranatunga. Yes, it was a great piece and yes, the publisher had given the green light to run the feature in the centre page on Sunday.

Tanya had walked on air for the rest of the day, humming a tune and laughing for little apparent reason.

They'd sat for a celebratory dinner at the little pantry table. Aunty Nora had not been clear as to what the party was about but, like a good Burgher, had thrown herself into the spirit of the festivity.

They'd bought balloons and streamers and decorated the house. They'd also overridden aunty's protests that it was too early and assembled her white Christmas tree in the hall, carefully hanging the ancient decorations on the branches with a dainty little figure of an angel at the summit.

Ravi had gone to Pilawoos to collect packets of chicken biriyani, and aunty had contributed a bottle of red wine she'd been saving for a special occasion.

'Let's all have a glass,' Tanya said. 'You too, aunty.'

'No, darling. It goes straight to my head.'

'We'll carry you to bed,' Tanya insisted. 'Come on. It's no fun if you don't join.'

So they'd poured aunty a glass from which she took a few cautious sips and then a few more when she found it nice. Tanya and Ravi had a couple of glasses each before they sat at the narrow pantry table with aunty at the head. Aunty insisted on reciting grace before they opened the wonderfully aromatic parcels of biriyani.

Biriyani was an ancient Mogul preparation of Basmati rice with chicken, onions, potatoes, tomatoes, curd and loads of spices mixed together and cooked in ghee. It was also the most delicious recipe for heart decease. Ravi loved it.

They set about finishing the rest of the wine. Tanya surreptitiously placed her foot on his lap. When he looked up in surprise he found her engrossed in her plate, ignoring him. Ravi found his throat so dry and constricted he couldn't swallow. The biriyani no longer tasted right either.

He'd held her foot with his left hand and continued to eat with his right. Aunty was a bit giggly afterwards and knocked over her chair when she tried to stand up. Tanya staggered a bit as well as she helped the old lady to her room. Ravi heard them laughing in the room as they prepared to go to bed.

He waited impatiently in the drawing room for Tanya to come out again after aunty fell asleep. She never came.

This woman was surely going to drive him out of his mind.

He finally took himself off to bed wondering if a cold shower would help.

*

They had slept late.

Ravi had finally dragged himself out of bed and into the shower. He went down to the road later to pick up a newspaper and fish buns from Caravan. When he got back, Aunty Nora was clipping a hedge in the garden and Tanya seated in the drawing room holding her head.

'Why did you make me to drink so much?' She asked Ravi accusingly. 'One glass is the most I've taken before.'

'How was I to know that?' Ravi was secretly pleased that she was suffering a bit. 'I thought all Burghers are great topers.'

'Shut up,' she said wearily as she stood up.

'You put your foot on my lap during dinner.'

Tanya stared at him. 'I'd never do that. You're just making it up.'

'It's true. Were you so sloshed you can't remember?'

'Rubbish. You're just imagining things.'

She was still in her nightclothes.

The edge of her silk shorts just escaped from below the oversized T-shirt and her legs stretched endlessly from there to her bare feet. Her hair was a tangled mop, her face free of artifice and she was now frowning malevolently at him.

But she took his breath away!

Ravi had never imagined that any woman could be so infuriating and unpredictable and yet, at the same time, so desirable. She reminded him of a leopard he'd once nearly stumbled on while trekking in the jungle with his father. The animal had stared at them for a long moment before turning and moving into the forest. Heart stopping beauty you wanted to reach out and touch, yet a promise of danger to keep you at a safe distance.

He had an overwhelming impulse to just fold her in his arms and carry her, scratching and spitting, into his bedroom. He couldn't summon up the nerve.

A steaming cup of coffee slowly eased the scowl off Tanya's face. She settled down to read the papers sitting cross-legged on the carpet.

Aunty came in from the garden and turned the radio on before going to the kitchen.

Tanya said, 'I see here Wendy's staging a musical show tomorrow, at the BMICH.'

'Who's Wendy?' Ravi asked.

'My friend Wendy Martin. She arranges events. You know, musical shows and such.'

'So? Are you planning to attend? Or take part?'

Tanya grinned pleasantly. Her earlier grumpiness had lifted a bit.

'No. I just thought you'd be interested.'

'Mm.'

'The National Alliance has gained ground. This paper says the election is evenly poised.' Tanya had her nose buried in the newspaper again.

'Then your scoop might be enough to swing it for them. I can just see the headline. Daring Reporter Topples Government.'

'I wish.' But she was grinning happily when she said it.

Ravi heard the music stop and the DJ announce 'News in Brief'.

' ... fire at newspaper office ... arson suspected. And in sport it's cricket.'

Ravi felt the skin on his forearms tightening into bumps. He saw the shock in Tanya's eyes.

It couldn't be. Surely it couldn't be!

They called Pali Ranatunga.

Busy signal.

Tanya tried the office numbers but there was no ringing tone, just a high-pitched whine.

They called again and finally got through to the editor.

'Ranatunga. Who is this?'

'Ravi Perera. Is it true about the press?'

'Yes, yes it's a disaster,' he answered tersely. 'Is she with you?'

'Yes.'

'Keep her there and stay out of sight. I'll call back later'

They waited.

It was mid afternoon when Ranatunga called. His voice was calmer but still raw with emotion.

'Ravi? The office and print shop are badly damaged. Some men had come in two vans, assaulted the security and tied them up. Terrible loss. Insurance will pay, but we can't recover our records.'

Ranatunga paused for a minute. Ravi stayed quiet.

'Anyway that's another matter. We are determined to get the paper out on Sunday. It's the last edition before the election. We want to tell the country about this and why it happened.'

'How will you get the paper out, without the press, I mean?'

'We can borrow the newsprint and there's a party with a web press who's agreed to do the printing.'

Tanya was leaning against him with her ear pressed against the back of the hand phone. Ravi felt the warmth spread through him.

'That's good,' Ravi murmured more to her than to Ranatunga and that earned him an impatient frown.

'It is critical that we publish Tanya's scoop. It will show the public who had the motive to attack the press. But the publisher wants the negatives in his hand before he gives the go-ahead,' Ranatunga continued. 'Seems his lawyers want to be sure there's been no doctoring of the photos.'

'We have the negatives, Mr. Ranatunga, but how do we get them to you?'

'Hmm, yes. That's a problem. I think I'm being followed. We are all under surveillance.'

'All right,' Ravi said confidently. 'We'll think of a way.'

'I have to have the copy as well. Tell Tanya it must be in my hands by Friday night - latest.'

'I'll call you.' Ravi rang off.

They spent the rest of the evening arguing about it.

Tanya preferred a simple, direct approach. Have Ranatunga assign some trusted employee meet them in a secret place and take delivery of the package.

Ravi said: 'He may be one of the guys already in the pay of the other side. We were betrayed once, remember? Or the guy might be followed. Anything can happen. If we lose the negatives then it's all over. We just can't take a chance.'

'The election's next Wednesday. If we don't make this Sunday's edition then all our effort will be wasted.'

'Yes, I know but ...'

Someone rang the bell.

Had the enemy traced them already?

Ravi felt his pulse racing as he crawled to the front window and peered cautiously over the sill. A stooped figure in a long sleeved shirt buttoned at the neck, and baggy trousers stood by the gate, looking hopefully at the front door.

Mr. Batcho from down the lane had come to borrow the newspapers.

Something clicked inside Ravi's head while he watched Tanya and aunty collecting the pages of the newspaper scattered all over the carpet.

'Hold on. Where's the notice about that show, by that Cindy Barton character?'

Tanya scowled. 'Wendy Martin.'

'Whoever. Where is it?'

They found it eventually in the very last page they examined. Ravi tore off the section he wanted, and sent old Batcho off happily clutching the rest of the newspaper to his chest.

Tanya was looking at Ravi with a frown.

'Why the sudden interest in music?'

'Cindy ... Wendy sounds a sexy sort of bimbo,' Ravi drawled lazily.

'If you like them big and chunky.'

'No. I like them slim with nice long legs.'

'Oh, get lost. What's this all about?'

'Can you find that Wendy female's number?'

'Yes. I suppose I can. Are you going to tell me what's going on or not?'

He did then and was happy to see it pleased her very much.

*

Wendy Martin was standing on the stage of the main auditorium and yelling at someone in the wings to 'Stop arsing around and get those props up on stage'.

Her angry features dissolved into a grin of genuine pleasure when she saw Tanya. She gave her a hug that made the slighter girl gasp, and then took Ravi's hand in a vice like grip.

'So this is your fellow, is he?' Wendy enquired loudly, looking Ravi up and down as if measuring a horse. 'Not bad looking for a Sinhala bugger.'

'He's not my fellow Wendy,' Tanya protested. 'We're just partners in this project.'

'Yeah right,' Wendy mocked. 'No time to go into that now, there's work to be done.'

She turned and yelled, 'Simon. Simon. Where the hell are you hiding?'

A thin fellow in jeans, an earring and long hair came ambling out of the wings. He had a T-shirt with four words printed on it. The first two were "THE MAN" and an arrow above the words pointed to his chin.

The two words in the bottom line were "THE LEGEND" and the second arrow pointed to his crotch.

Ravi took to him immediately.

'I like your T-shirt,' Ravi told him when he was introduced.

'Thanks man,' Simon smiled. 'It's only the truth. Ask Wendy.'

'Yeah, yeah! Two inches of pure steel,' Wendy sneered. 'There's no time for this shit. Simon, Ravi's here to help. Take him backstage and make use of him. Sylvie. Sylvie. Where's this girl got to now?'

The Bandaranaiake Memorial International Conference Hall, everyone called it the BMICH, had been a gift from China, way back when Sri Lanka had been in the vanguard of the Non-Aligned movement. Like an aging beauty queen, it was now well past its best but still an imposing structure, majestic in an ocean of green turf.

The crowd began to arrive by 6.00 p.m. A trickle of enthusiasts first and then a steady stream as curtain time approached. There were to be six ushers standing near the door to help ticket holders find their seats.

Tanya was smartly turned out like the others in a hastily purchased black skirt, white blouse and red sash. There were seven of them now and Tanya, with another girl called Swini, was to handle the VIP invitees.

Ravi had to use all his powers of persuasion to convince Tanya, then Wendy, and finally Pali Ranatunga to fall in with his plan. Ranatunga had been the most difficult, flatly refusing to attend the function because he was so busy, and because he thought it was too risky.

Ravi, standing in the wings by the side of the stage, laughed to himself when he remembered parts of their conversation.

'What do you mean the safest way to pass secret documents is to do it in public? You must be out of your mind.' Ranatunga sounded angry, not buying Ravi's plan. 'You'll ruin everything with these crazy schemes.'

'That's the whole point sir,' Ravi had said soothingly. 'No one will expect us to do such a crazy thing. If you go to the toilet, they'll watch like hawks but out in the open, it'll work. Trust me!'

The hall was nearly full when Tanya saw her boss walk into the vast foyer followed closely by his wife, a sweet-faced lady in a Kandyan sari. The entrance to the hall was elevated above the level of the foyer and had to be approached by a flight of steps. From her vantage at the head of the steps Tanya saw two men come into the foyer after Ranatunga.

They didn't approach the entrance to the hall but hung back in the open area, watching Ranatunga and his wife. They didn't look like music lovers.

Tanya's hand phone pinged. She reached for it but retreated into the hall before putting it to her ear.

'Ravi?'

'Don't give it to him. Give it to the wife.'

'Why on earth ...?'

'Do it!'

'Oh, all right!'

Swini had already greeted Ranatunga and guided him inside. Tanya took over and led the couple down the aisle to the front of the hall with VIP seating. No invitation had been sent to Ranatunga but two seats had been reserved for them, and Tanya knew the numbers. She got them seated and handed each of them a magazine-souvenir. She took the copy for Ranatunga from the top of her pile and the one for his wife from the bottom.

When Tanya walked up the aisle again she found the two men already inside the auditorium, standing menacingly at the back of the hall. One of the men, with a badly pitted face, looked at her sharply and looked away. They kept their eyes on Ranatunga, waiting to see who approached him.

The performance began at 6.30.

Tanya left Swini and the others to handle latecomers and went backstage to find Ravi. She found him sitting on a bench chatting with Simon the legend. They were both sucking on ice lollies.

'Hi scrumptious,' Simon greeted her breezily. 'You're far too hot for this loser. Why don't I drop by and see you sometime?'

'Are you sure? You're not just funning me?' Tanya asked innocently. 'Will you bring your legend along?'

'Course I will. You're in for a treat,' Simon grinned as he stood up. 'Gotta go see what my dummies are up to.'

He sauntered off waving his fingers jauntily over his shoulder.

Ravi suppressed a spasm of irritation. 'How did it go? Were you able to pass it?'

'Sure, that part was ok, but there were two men following them. They are standing at the back of the hall now, watching Ranatunga.'

'How did they get in?'

'They showed some security ID and scared the girl at the entrance. They saw me seat Ranatunga and give the souvenirs. I don't know if they suspected anything. I told him to stay till the end and leave with the crowd.'

It was nearly 9.30 when the curtain finally came down. The crowd began to stream out of the auditorium and down the stairs on either side. Ravi and Tanya had gone down earlier and now stood near the rest rooms with some of the other helpers. The Ranatungas' finally made their appearance at the first landing and then came slowly down the final flight.

Tanya squeezed his arm but Ravi had already spotted the pursuers, two tall men who stood out of the crowd like piranhas in a goldfish bowl. They were jostling some of the others in an effort to get close to the Ranatunga couple. The poxy fellow was immediately behind the editor when they reached the foot of the steps where a small crowd had assembled. The other man stayed several paces back.

The first man shoved Ranatunga from behind, making him stagger into the man ahead of him. In that instant, the man behind reached over his shoulder and snatched the souvenir in Ranatunga's hand. Before the editor could gather his wits and his balance the man had melted away. The second man remained where he was, watching Ranatunga and the rest of the crowd.

Mrs. Ranatunga took her shaken husband by the arm and led him towards the exit. Her copy of the souvenir, with the negatives and notes nestling safely between two gummed pages, was clutched openly in her left hand.

They took a three-wheeler to Bambalapitiya junction, got off and picked up another to drop them near Dickman's Road, well past their destination. Ravi bought *godamba roti* to take home for their dinner.

'Do you think they'll attack Mr. Ranatunga again?' Tanya asked anxiously.

'No way to be sure but I don't think they will. They wouldn't find anything in the souvenir and he didn't collect anything else.'

Tanya squeezed his arm as they turned into their lane.

'How did you guess they'd grab his souvenir? That was quite good.' Ravi felt chuffed.

He said modestly, 'Lucky shot! I just asked myself what I'd do if I was the watcher.'

'What about the other roll? What are you going to do about that?'

'I've given it some thought. Those photos have value only if we don't use them.'

'What do you mean?'

Tanya stood outside the gate, reluctant to go in.

'No newspaper will publish those photos. We can give prints to the opposition to distribute copies everywhere but that will be terrible for that poor woman, whoever she is. Anyway once we use it, its value is shot. But if we keep it with someone reliable, then it has value.'

'Tell me.'

'I thought, well ... after Sunday, we can try to get word to the Minister. If he harms either of us, copies will be released to his political enemies. If he leaves us alone, the film will never be developed.'

Tanya stood still for a moment, digesting the thought.

'I'll be able to go home,' Tanya's eyes lit up in delight.

She touched her lips with her index finger and then placed it on Ravi's cheek, but when he reached for her, she slipped away and went into the house.

23

Ravi was in the kitchen trying to make an ancient toaster work without blowing up. He heard the front door click open, and a moment later, aunty came in having been to mass at Holy Family Convent across the road.

'Isn't Tanya up yet?' She put the kettle to boil. 'Do you think she'll like some coffee?'

'Still asleep, but I'm sure she will.'

Tanya came in just then rubbing her eyes sleepily. She dropped into a chair with a groan and held her head in her hands. Her hair was an untidy mess, her baggy T-shirt was crumpled and she seemed only partially awake.

'Morning Tani girl,' Ravi said breezily. 'What a ray of sunshine you are today.'

'Oh shut up, will you. I can't stand cheerful buggers early in the morning.'

'Don't worry her, son,' Aunty Nora gave Tanya a steaming mug. 'Here you are baby. You'll feel better after this.'

Tanya sipped for a moment and seemed to wake up. She sat up suddenly, 'The papers, Ravi. Didn't you get the papers?'

'I'm going to the market now, dear. I'll get them for you.'

'How long will you be, aunty?' Tanya asked. 'Will you need any help?'

'Not at all. This is my Sunday treat. I meet lots of my friends at the market. I'll be back about noon. It's my day off so no cooking. There are lamprais in the freezer.'

'You go on then, darling' Tanya told the old lady fondly. 'Enjoy your morning. Ravi can fetch the papers.'

As Ravi walked to the newspaper kiosk at the top of Asoka Gardens he felt the tension rise in his veins.

Had they managed to get the Statesman printed and out into the stands? Did it carry Tanya's piece?

Yes, Yes, Yes!

They had managed to get the Statesman out all right, badly printed and crudely put together. But readable. And how very readable! From a glance at the front page Ravi knew they had made it. The inch high headline screamed: MINISTER CAUGHT IN LOVE NEST!

One photograph of the naked Minister with a woman standing beside him was spread across four columns.

They sat on the floor in the drawing room and read the full article on page eight again and again. Tanya had written it well, stating explicitly what she could prove and conveying by innuendo what she couldn't.

The Minister had been caught in a highly compromising situation with a young woman. It was cleverly implied that the Minister had misused his powers to coerce the woman into providing sexual services in return for political favours. And there was an additional sting at the end of the piece. The much publicized bomb attack on the Minister had been no more than a few crackers lit by some unknown prankster. It had been enough to make the Minister run naked out of the room.

Tanya was jubilant.

'They've run the whole thing,' she murmured again and again. 'I simply don't believe it. They've run the whole piece.'

'Don't they normally?'

'No. The editor cuts and chops the piece. You don't recognize it in the end.'

'Good for you, sweetheart,' Ravi patted her on the head. 'You're a star now.'

Tanya looked pleased for a moment and then asked seriously, 'Do you think this is enough to swing the election?

'It will have an effect, I'm sure. Premasiri is one of their top men and you have shown the public what these Ministers are up to. Whether it will swing the election, who can tell?'

They sat in companionable silence for a while, trying to absorb the enormity of their victory.

'I must call Pathirana. I need a line to whoever's in charge of the Minister's security.'

Ravi dialed the number Pathirana had left with him. Switched off. Ravi called back in fifteen minutes and managed to catch the man. Pathirana told Ravi a fellow called Buddadasa had replaced him in the MSD. He gave the contact number.

Tanya placed her face against his ear while he waited for someone to pick up the phone. Ravi tried to turn his face to peck her on the cheek but she caught his nose firmly between thumb and forefinger and turned his face away.

'Hullo. Sergeant Buddadasa please. Yes. My name is Ravi Perera.'

'*Vesigey putha. Umbawa kääli walata kapanawa.*'

Son of a whore. I'll cut you to pieces.

'You'd better listen,' Ravi went on calmly. 'I have an important message for the Minister.'

'Minister don't want your message,' Buddadasa yelled with fury. 'Minister want you dead.'

'I have the other film. The film from the Minister's camera. I haven't developed it yet. Do you understand what that means?'

'You want to sell it to the Minister?' The man calmed down slightly. 'How much do you want for it?'

'No sale, only insurance! I will leave the undeveloped film with a friend. If anything happens to Miss Koch or to me, my friend will give the film to Mr. Tennakoon. Explain to the Minister that his action photos will be sold at every street corner.'

'You fucking bastard!'

'Shut up and listen. If no harm comes to us, the film will never be developed. Do you understand? Explain it to the Minister. If he leaves us alone, he has nothing to fear.'

Buddadasa was silent for a long time.

'Will you pass the message?'

'Yes. Yes, I'll pass the message.'

Ravi rang off.

Tanya asked, 'Who'll hold the film for us? Or were you bluffing?'

'Bluffing's no good. Your friend Wendy, do you think she'll keep it for us?

Tanya clapped her hands. 'Sure she will. She's perfect.'

'Good. That takes care of everything.'

'Can I go home then? I miss them so much, especially mum. Do you think it is ok?'

'Yes. I'll take you home once aunty gets back.'

Something in his tone made her look at him.

'What is it, baby? You're worried about something.'

'No. Nothing important.'

'C'mon, you can tell me.'

'Since mum and dad were killed, I've felt an unbearable pain … like a … a malignant growth in my belly. I thought I had to kill someone — or kill myself to stop the agony.'

Ravi was lying on the carpet staring at the ceiling. Tanya crawled over to where he was and gently took hold of his hand.

Ravi went on, as if speaking to himself, 'But when I'm with you, I don't feel it so badly. The pain … it's bearable. When you go, I'm afraid it'll start again.'

Tanya was silent for a while, then said softly, 'That's the only nice thing you've ever said to me.'

Ravi looked at her in surprise. Her eyes, greeny black like a bottomless pool, had an expression he hadn't seen before. She drew his hand under her T-shirt and placed it on her breast, covering it with her own hand.

Size of a teacup with a marble perched on it, scalding the centre of his palm.

Tanya lay down beside him on the carpet still holding his hand in place. Her eyes were closed. Ravi held himself back with a supreme effort of will, determined to savour that one moment, not sure at all if it would last. He lay on his side, close enough to feel the sleep sodden warmth of her body, and just looked at her.

Her hair was untidy, as if she had carelessly run her fingers through it. Her skin seemed to glow in the sunlight streaming in through the window, creamy soft — like cheese. Her T-shirt was partially rucked up and he could see the flat waistline moving gently as she breathed. Skimpy silk sleeping shorts below.

He nibbled her ear and then gently bit the side of her neck. He kissed her eyes, tip of nose and finally her mouth, touching her lips with his tongue. Tanya opened her eyes and her mouth widened in a lazy grin that seemed to spread from ear to ear.

'What the hell are you doing? Do you think this is food fair?'

'I'm checking the scents and flavours of Tanya.'

'Have you found anything you like?'

'The ears taste of butterscotch, sort of crunchy sweet,' Ravi mumbled, 'but your lips are definitely honey. Coffee flavoured honey.'

'Mmm.'

'I'm just going to check on your belly button.'

Ravi rested his head on her bare midriff, feeling the firm muscle under the soft creaminess of her skin. His eyes were inches away from the waistline of her pyjama shorts, pink flowers scattered over the filmy silk material, held in place by a thin cord tied in a slipknot. And below that her bare legs seemed to stretch and stretch towards the horizon.

Those flimsy pyjamas had never left his mind, not after the titillation at Sinharaja and the fiasco at Hambantota. The promise of it made his heart stop. He leaned little further, grasped the end of the cord with his teeth and pulled the knot free.

He felt the painful grasp of her fingers in his hair.

Oh man! Here we go again.

But this time she didn't pull his head up; Tanya-like, she did exactly the opposite.

Ravi held onto her as if he were drowning. 'I wish you didn't have to go.'

'You know I have to, darling. My mum must be frantic,' she replied gently, 'but we can be together in the evenings, if you want to.'

'I want to.'

'Will it be safe for you?'

'I think so. I'll come anyway.'

*

Wendy had been intrigued by their story.

'You guys are crazy. Let's just release the photos and fix the bastard for good,' she had said. 'What good is it to keep it hidden?'

'It's a deterrent, Wendy,' Tanya had explained. 'This really is a serious matter, the only way to stop them killing us in revenge. You must keep this quiet. Just mail the package to that address if you hear we've both been attacked. Will you do this for me? Exactly as I said?'

'Oh all right!' Wendy said with a resigned sigh. 'Anything for you, love. Just don't get yourself killed.'

The Koch household had exploded with joy when Tanya walked in. Pam Koch had been leaning over the wall chatting with a woman in the next garden.

She uttered a squeak of delight, came trotting up to the gate and hugged Tanya. 'Baby, baby I was so worried about you. Are you all right?'

'Yes mummy, I'm fine. We just stayed out of sight till the paper came out. Ravi took good care of me.'

Pam looked at Ravi uncertainly, not sure if she wanted him taking "good care" of her daughter. Her innate good nature won in the end and gave him a hug of welcome before leading them into the house.

'Dick. Dick, look who's here,' she called to her husband.

Richard Koch was holding the TV remote in his upraised hand and his younger daughter Tammy was wrestling him for it. They all started talking together.

'Hullo Chubby! Saw your scoop in the paper. Great ...'

'Sis, have you run off with this fellow ...'

'Shut up, Tam.'

'Would you like some tea, Ravi?'

'Sis, have you married the bugger already?'

'Shut up Tam. Go do your homework or something.'

'Sit down, Ravi. Don't take notice of the little brat.'

Pam hurried off to put the kettle on. Tammy flung herself into her sister's arms and hugged her joyfully. She picked up Tanya's bag and followed her to her room like a puppy. Questions in a childish treble came floating back to the drawing room.

Richard Koch asked, 'I know those buggers burnt the press. Is Tanya in any danger?'

'I don't know, Mr. Koch. They wanted to stop the story. Now that it's out, there's no benefit in attacking us. But she needs to be careful. At least till the election.'

'What's all the fuss about a bomb attack? What did you all do?'

Ravi gave the man an abbreviated version of their escapade, glossing over the parts that might have alarmed him. He loved the story, slapping his thigh and laughing when he heard that the Minister had panicked at the sound of firecrackers and run naked from the room, straight into the photographer's camera.

'Serves the dirty bugger right,' he said with typical disdain that most Burghers had for authority figures. 'These bloody tree climbers think they are kings when they get into power. Good to fix them now and then.'

Pam came back pushing a rickety trolley with a pot of tea and some cups. Richard looked at the cups with disgust.

'What's this rubbish? Give this boy a proper drink.'

'It's not Ravi who wants to drink, it's you.'

'What's wrong with having a drink to celebrate?' A new thought seemed to strike him suddenly. 'Why have just a drink, let's have a party. Tammy, Tammy come here!'

Tammy came running, followed more sedately by a curious Tanya.

'What's up, poppo?'

'We're having a party. Tam, go down the lane and tell Uncle Conrad to bring a bottle this time. The fellow's always cracking my booze. Tani, go tell Marie and her parents to bring their dinner and come. Also the Edemas'! I'll tell the others.'

'But Dick, I haven't prepared anything, and tomorrow's a working day,' Pam began uncertainly.

'Ahh don't be a wet blanket Pammy. This is bring and come. Just put normal dinner on the table.'

It didn't take an hour for the neighbours to start trickling in. The Edemas, a distinguished looking elderly couple, were first.

'How, how Richard? So now our little Tanya is a star reporter. Where is the young lady?'

The Ponniahs came next, shyly placing a food carrier on the table Richard had pulled into the garden. In small family groups they came in with their offerings and greetings.

'How are you Pam? What's Dicky up to now? Where are the girls? My, how Tammy has grown! Like a coconut tree, no? Read the paper today. Can't believe our Tani has fixed a Minister. He deserves it, the shameless old bugger.'

Ravi sat in the garden watching the party slowly gather momentum and a life of its own. The women got together on one side for a good gossip, the men to the makeshift bar, and a noisy gaggle of children trooped into the hall to watch a cartoon.

Conrad the bald man came armed with an ancient piano accordion, followed by a hefty woman, much like a tug hauling the Queen Mary to a berth. When he saw Ravi he grinned widely, then turned and whispered something to his wife.

'No. Really?' The fat woman exclaimed loudly looking directly at Ravi. She then turned and said something that made another woman look in his direction.

Ravi felt his cheeks burning. He called Tanya over.

'That bald moron is spreading the word,' he complained, 'they're all laughing at me. Can't you do something.'

'If I tell them you've already seduced me, they'll break your kneecaps,' Tanya laughed callously. 'You're better off if they think you're harmless.'

'You're a big help, I must say.'

'Don't worry about them, baby. Only my opinion counts,' she went on. 'And I think you're ok. Not up to Burgher standards — but ok.'

'Oh shut up.'

It didn't take long for the men folk crowded at the bar table to get warmed up. The piano accordion was hauled out and Conrad yelled for everyone to gather round. They started soberly with Christmas carols, then to Irish ballads and finally to the inevitable Baila.

The little kids started dancing first and then the adults led by Conrad's wife, the massive Maureen, started cavorting in the verandah and in the garden. Old Mr. Edema was clearly risking a heart seizure as he pranced about with a laughing Tanya. Ravi, emboldened by a stiff arrack someone had forced on him, hauled a giggling Tammy to the floor. She was self consciously awkward for a while but gradually let herself go, dancing with the grace of a gazelle.

Ravi was surprised to find that he was enjoying himself immensely.

He looked around. Conrad, with a red-faced Richard singing in tandem, kept the raunchy verses coming in a smooth flow that must have come from long practice. Maureen with her arms like legs, and legs like logs, was a surprisingly deft dancer. She continued to dance by herself even after her exhausted partner retired to the bar. Pam was busy trying to sort the dishes the visitors had brought in, from the Ponniahs' parcel of dosai to someone else's pittu and pol kiri.

She called Tammy to help her. Ravi found a seat on the garden wall to cool down and get his breath back. Tanya joined him.

'Are you put out by all this? My dad gets carried away sometimes.'

'Surprised, not put out. They're all having such a good time. I think it's great.'

'I'm glad you like our ways,' she squeezed his arm. 'Our parties get very lively.'

'Mm.'

'Let's grab something to eat. At a "bring and come", if you wait till the end you only get parippu and rice.'

PART THREE

Strike & Counterstrike

*He knew that the essence of war is violence
and that moderation in war is imbecility.*

Thomas Macauley

24

The newspapers had reported a few early results and predicted sweeping gains for the opposition. The electronic media had trumpeted fresh results through the day, and by early evening finally confirmed that the Peoples Front government had suffered a stinging defeat in the polls. Four senior Ministers including Mudalige Premasiri had lost their seats. The National Alliance had the numbers and would form the new administration.

Ravi felt a glow spreading through his body. They had refused to be cowed by a bully with unlimited power. They'd taken the battle to him and had finally crushed the bastard. Sure, there was a swing against the government, but who was to say that theirs had not been the critical blow that tilted the balance?

And the king cobra, Mudalige Premasiri himself was out of parliament. Out of power!

Awesome!

He wanted, more than anything, to share the moment with Tanya.

When his tuc-tuc turned into Campbell Place, Ravi noticed that people had come out of their houses and were standing by their gates, talking in small groups. Some bystanders from the main road were running down the lane.

Something was dreadfully wrong.

At Tanya's house, the gate was open and the garden full of people. He saw faces he knew from the party, but their eyes were frozen in shock and looked at him without recognition. Conrad was there, his arm thrown protectively over the shoulder of a visibly distraught Maureen.

The house had been blitzed.

The glass panes of the windows facing the road were all shattered. The centre of the roof above the drawing room had collapsed, leaving a hole through which wisps of black smoke still spiraled up to the sky.

Ravi walked like a zombie up the front steps into the drawing room. The floor was slippery with soot-blackened water dribbling slowly through the hall door and into the garden.

They had thrown all the valuables in the house in the centre of the hall and set fire to the lot. The flames had reached the roof, destroying the cross members to leave a gaping hole in the centre. Some men were trying to clean up the mess. They were reaching into the pile of broken furniture, household stuff and piles and piles of books looking for anything that could be salvaged. Ravi could see they were just going through the motions. The water had finished what the fire had started. Very little would be saved.

Where was Tanya? Where was the rest of the family?

He ran to where old Conrad was standing.

'What happened? Who did this?'

'They came in a white van, six or seven thugs ... iron rods. Only Pam and Tanya were there. They smashed the house ... set fire,' the man grimaced as if in physical pain. 'Pam tried to stop them, they hit her with a club, broke her arm.'

Maureen was staring at the ruined house with glazed eyes, tears dribbling unheeded down her massive cheeks.

'Tanya,' Ravi asked hoarsely. 'Did they hurt her? Where is she?'

'They had beaten her and thrown her into the garden!' Conrad's voice was anguished. 'Tanya was unconscious when we came. Pam was screaming in pain.'

'Where are they now? Where's Tanya?'

'Dicky took them to hospital ... Ponniah's car.'

'Where? Where did he take them?'

'Accident service at General.'

'Did you see them? Did you see the men who did it?'

'Dicky was at my house. We came out when we heard a big commotion. Saw them getting into the van. Rough looking bastards. Some in shorts and caps, some in longs. One bugger was smartly dressed ... stood near the gate shouting for the men to get in the van.'

'Describe the man.'

'Uh. Long hair, like a bloody ponytail. Average height but heavily built. I noticed a thick gold bracelet on his right wrist.'

Ravi turned to leave, then stopped. 'What about the little girl? Tammy. Is she all right?'

'She's ok. Luckily she'd gone to Mrs. Edema for a music lesson. She's there now.'

'I'm going to the hospital now,' Ravi told Conrad. 'Here's my number. Will you call me if there is anything I can do?'

'Don't worry, son,' the man said kindly. 'We'll look after Tammy girl and the house. You go and see to Tani and Pam.'

As he held onto the seat of the three-wheeler, Ravi tried to calm his racing mind. In his arrogance he had thought the enemy had been crushed. He had been so confident the game was over that it came as a shock that the vanquished enemy could strike back with such ferocity. And poor Tanya and her family had taken the brunt of the attack.

As if in a dream Ravi felt his horror and outrage change into cold calculation.

And anger.

It is still early in the day of reckoning. I have time to settle accounts.

He called Pathirana.

No response.

The accident service at the National Hospital was crowded. Anxious family members milled around as the blood soaked victims of yet another motor mishap were rushed in for emergency treatment.

Richard Koch was seated on a plastic chair with his head in his hands. Ravi sat quietly beside him and touched his shoulder.

The man shuddered and turned his tear stained face towards him.

'Did you hear? Did they tell you what those bastards did to my family?'

'Yes uncle, I heard,' Ravi said helplessly. 'How are they? Have they been attended to?'

'They set the fracture in Pam's arm. She's in pain but ok, I think. Tani … Tani …,' his voice broke and he started sobbing. 'She's in intensive care. She's still unconscious. They … they hit my little girl on the head with an iron bar.'

Dear God, don't let her die. Just don't.

'Will they let me see her?'

'No. No, she's in ICU. The nurse promised to let me know if there is any change.'

'I'll stay with you.'

Richard Koch just nodded, staring at the floor. He didn't care.

Ravi rang Pathirana again.

'Sergeant? It's Ravi. Ravi Perera.'

'How are you Sir?' Pathirana greeted him effusively. 'Your photos were brilliant. They swung the election. Remember to tell Mr. Tennakoon that I helped you.'

Upali Tennakoon was the National Alliance candidate who had defeated Mudalige Premasiri. He was the individual who had benefited most from the scandal.

'Yes. I'll tell him,' Ravi lied effortlessly. 'But now we've had a problem.'

'What? What problem?'

'Miss Tanya and her mother were assaulted a couple of hours ago. Their house was wrecked.'

'Assaulted? When? Were they badly hurt?'

'Tanya is unconscious, still in Intensive Care.'

'I'm sorry.'

'I want to know who did it. Is the MSD involved?'

'Can't be. The Minister has resigned. I hear he's retired from politics as well.'

'Who's behind this then? I need to know.'

'I'll try to find out. I'll call you back in a little while.'

Post election violence was taking its toll. In ambulances, three-wheel taxis and private vehicles they were brought into the emergency service, broken gory combatants screaming their pain. Ravi tried to take his mind off Tanya, fighting for her life in the ICU, by studying the wrenching anxiety written on the faces of the family members bringing their wounded.

The phone buzzed gently in his pocket. Pathirana.

'Mr. Ravi, I made some enquiries. There's definitely no MSD involved.'

'Who did it then?'

'I hear it's a contract job. An underworld gang has taken it!'

'Who gave the contract? The Minister?'

'No. Not him. It's Shalindra. He's the one behind this.'

'What? What were they supposed to do?'

'Teach the girl a lesson she wouldn't forget. I suppose they've done that part already.'

'Is that all?'

'No. No. That's not all. I hear that he's offered half a million Rupees to have you killed.'

Ravi felt his blood curdling in his veins. He kept opening his mouth but no sound came.

Hired killers were hunting him! This couldn't be true.

'Sergeant? Are you serious?' Ravi made a valiant effort to keep the fear out of his voice. 'Do you know who's taken the contract?'

'Some gangster from Wanathamulla. I don't know his name.'

'Can you find out? Can you get a description? I need to know.'

'I'll try. I'll have to ask around.'

'Do it soon.'

'All right,' the man said slowly. 'Mr. Ravi, these men, they'll do anything for money and this is a very big reward. You have to be very careful.'

'Yes.'

How can I be careful when I don't know the assassins, and where they'll come from?

'To remain safe you have to stay hidden,' Pathirana went on, 'but that alone isn't enough. You have to think like the killers and then make sure you're one step ahead of them.'

'Mm.'

Pathirana rang off promising to make more enquiries.

Richard Koch had retreated into a dazed stupor and seemed reluctant to talk. He sat staring at the wall, his hands resting limply on his lap, and his shoulders slumped against the backrest of his seat.

The killers could be anywhere, even standing behind him right now. He cringed when a rough looking fellow pushed his way through the row of seats immediately behind him. The enemy had no face. In this country where killers were available for small sums, what wouldn't they do for half a million?

Ravi knew he first had to master the panic rising in his chest.

Think!

Think like the killers. What would they do next? They'd finished the first part of the assignment. Would they now give it a rest? Of course not! They'd want to make the big bonus. They didn't know where he lived so where would they find him?

At the bloody hospital, of course. His girlfriend was in ICU. Where else would he be but in the waiting room of the Accident Service?

The Police Post was near the entrance, and there were too many people in the waiting area, so there'd probably be no direct attack while he sat there. They'd be waiting outside among the parked vehicles and shadows of the gloomy street.

Would they have a man inside keeping watch?

Yes, they certainly would.

Ravi stood up and walked slowly towards the Nescafe vending machine, allowing his eyes to slip over the faces of the people slumped listlessly in the seats. He saw anxiety, despair and patient acceptance etched on those faces, but no obvious killers. It could be anyone.

The National Hospital was a sprawling complex, bordered by several main roads. Ravi knew if he could get past the security guards manning the entrance to the wards, he'd easily find his way to some other exit and slip away.

But there were difficulties.

The guards were there to prevent relatives and friends from getting to the wards and disturbing the patients. They seemed to be doing their job well. How was he to get past them? And how was he to do that without being noticed by the killers?

He waited.

In twos and threes, people drifted away, but their places were soon taken by others accompanying victims of fresh tragedies. Midnight brought the diversion Ravi had been waiting for.

A number of vehicles drew up at the entrance. Doors slammed, commands were yelled and a moment later a small mob crowded through the entrance ushering a fat man in national dress. Blood dripped onto his face from a long cut on his forehead and someone was trying to hold a pack of ice against the wound.

Another man shouted the magic words, *'Amathithuma.'*

Minister.

It had to be a former Minister, of course. Someone had performed a public service by cracking his head.

There was no time for goodbyes. Ravi was on his feet and moving no sooner the disturbance started. By the time the injured man had been escorted to the nurse's desk, Ravi was near the entrance to the wards. He was standing with his back to the two guards, pretending to be interested in the commotion.

He heard the security men talking behind him.

'Oi Kolitha ämathithuma neda?' One fellow asked.

Isn't that the Minister Kolitha?

'Ow. Oka hari chandiya ney? Däng kawda uta deela,' the other answered unfeelingly.

Yes. He is a real thug. Now someone has given it to him.

One of the henchmen near the Minister yelled at the nurse to fetch the House Officer immediately. The others crowded threateningly round the flustered girl. The two security men moved a few steps past Ravi to see what was going on.

Ravi stepped quickly through the gate and into the darkened corridor beyond. He stood in the shadows and looked back. The two guards were still engrossed in the drama around the nurse's table. No one in the room had seen him leave.

No one?

One man leapt over a row of empty chairs and came charging towards

Ravi. The two guards were caught by surprise but recovered quickly, holding their arms out to restrain him. He was a short but sturdily built fellow with a shaven head, three quarter length trousers and a very tight T-shirt. He wasn't ready to be stopped. He lowered his shoulder and charged straight into one of the guards sending him sprawling. But the other guard grabbed him by the waist and held on grimly, yelling at the top of his voice.

Ravi turned and ran.

He was out of breath and lost.

Ravi stopped to take stock. There was no way that thug could find him in the maze of corridors and wards in the hospital, so there was no immediate danger. But he was stunned by the accuracy of his own deductions. They had indeed kept one man on watch inside the waiting room. That meant the others had been waiting for him outside the Accident Service. If he had walked out, as he might easily have done, he'd probably be dead by now. As it happened, he had escaped only because of the courage of the second security guard.

Ravi was shaken by the ferocity of the man who'd come after him.

Ravi used the sound of traffic to guide him to the exit on Kynsey Road. The security staff at the gate looked at him curiously but didn't ask questions. He found a three-wheeler to take him to Bambalapitiya junction. He then took another to drop him near De Fonseka Road. He walked to aunty's from there.

Secure in his room at last, Ravi sat on his bed and felt his body shake.

Gay, laughing Tanya with her unfathomable green-black eyes. What kind of men would strike a girl like that on the head with an iron rod? How could they throw her unconscious body in the garden as if she was a dead cat? Who would callously break the arm of a gentle lady with another blow?

Would they stop there? Were Tanya and her family still in danger?

How could he help them when the same men were out to kill him?

25

It was nearly mid-day.

Ravi had been lying curled up in his bed, unable to find the strength to get up. Aunty Nora had tapped timidly on his door a couple of times, asking if he was all right, if he wanted anything.

He'd been up most of the night with the same jumbled thoughts spinning through his mind endlessly. It had been his fight but he had allowed Tanya to get involved and thereby expose herself, and her family, to deadly danger. He had then made a bigger blunder by assuming that all the power and the menace had originated from Mudalige Premasiri, the Minister. Neutralize him, Ravi had convinced himself, and the fight would be over.

He had forgotten about Shalindra Premasiri.

His mobile phone buzzed on the bedside table.

'Mr. Ravi? It's Pathirana.'

'Yes. Have you got anything?'

'There's a gangster called Maru Ajit from Wanathamulla. I'm told he's taken the contract.'

'Maru?'

'It may be because he's always smartly dressed, or maybe it's short for Maruwa.'

Maruwa.

Killer.

'Did you get a description of this man?'

'I've never seen the fellow. My contact only mentioned his clothes,' Pathirana told him. 'Oh, he also said the bugger had long hair.'

Conrad had seen a well-dressed man with long hair leading the thugs who'd thrashed Tanya's house!

Ravi called Reshane and caught him at home.

'Hi, it's Ravi.'

'Ravi, you bugger,' Reshane yelled. 'I've been trying to locate you for weeks. Where the hell are you?'

'I've had reason to stay out of sight.'

'When I saw the scoop and that girl's name in the paper, I guessed it was you behind it. You really fixed old Mudalige, didn't you?'

'Yes machang, but now I have a problem. Tanya's been assaulted by some thugs. She's in the ICU at General. Can you get your pal, Doctor Anula, to check on her? I need to know if she's all right.'

'Sure. I'll call her up,' Reshane said hesitantly. 'But machang, Anula thinks you know, that I'm keen on her. When I keep calling, she'll …'

'Bugger it! Just call her. This is important.'

'Oh, all right. I'll call you back.'

It was late in the evening when Reshane called.

'I just spoke to her,' he said morosely. 'She wants me to come for her birthday party next week. She'll parade me in front of her ghastly relatives.'

'I don't give a rat's arse about your love life. What about my friend?'

'Oh that? Yes. She's suffering from concussion and is under observation,' Reshane said, as if repeating a lesson. 'Anula says she's out of danger … could be sent back to the ward tomorrow.'

'Other injuries?'

'Four stitches on her head, I think, and bruises on her arms and back.'

'I want to see her tomorrow. Can Anula take me?'

'Use the bloody visiting hours, 12.00 to 1.00. Open to the public, pal.'

'There's someone there I don't want to see,' Ravi said carefully. 'It has to be at some other time.'

'Her boyfriend waiting to hammer you? Is that why?'

'Something like that. Will you speak to your friend?'

'You're putting me in the shit.'

'What shit? She has a lovely face. With a bit of dieting she'll be a stunner,' Ravi told him. 'Useful to have a doctor in the family, no?'

'Oh fuck off.'

*

Dr. Anula was all dimpled smiles when she met Ravi and Reshane near the entrance. She led the way, waving them confidently past the security guards. She spoke to the nurse at the entrance to the ward and then, telling Reshane to wait outside, led Ravi to a screened bed at the far end.

Ravi waited till Anula went back to join Reshane. He lifted the screen out of the way and moved quietly near the bed. In spite of his mental preparation he felt a wrenching pain in his chest.

She lay on her back, looking up at him dully. They had shaved the left side of her head and covered it with a dressing. Her forearms were also bandaged and there was an ugly purple bruise under her eye.

'Honey, I'm so sorry …,' Ravi choked, unable to continue.

She didn't say anything but continued to look at him. Ravi saw a tear forming at the edge of her eye, then roll down the side of her face. He had never seen her cry before and it left him feeling physically crushed.

'It's my fault baby. I thought blocking Mudalige would keep us safe. I was so wrong,' Ravi went on. 'It was Shalindra. I should have thought of him …'

Tanya continued to look at him and Ravi thought there was an expression of infinite sadness in her eyes.

'Tani, I …'

'It was awful … so awful,' Tanya's voice was a whisper; so ragged Ravi had to lean closer to her. 'My poor mum. They beat her and beat her.'

Tanya turned her face away.

'I'll fix him for this,' Ravi's voice was chilled with an implacable anger. 'I'll make his life unbearable.'

'No! You mustn't. You mustn't.'

'What?'

'Those horrible men … only mum and I were home. They held knives on us and told us to be quiet. Then that … man with long hair came in. He spoke very softly, but his eyes were strange … frightening. He said this time it was only a warning. If we caused more trouble they'd come back.'

Tanya struggled to find words. Another fat teardrop dripped down the side of her face. Ravi touched her fingers in an effort to comfort her, but she jerked her hand away.

'They said next time they'd catch Tammy and take her away … that they'd all enjoy making her a woman.' Tanya closed her eyes. 'It was horrible. Unspeakable! She's only a baby.'

'It's all right,' Ravi was stunned by the sheer obscenity of the threat. 'We'll find a way to protect her.'

'How can you protect her every minute of the day? How can anyone protect her? No, I brought this on them. Now I have to get them out of it.'

Ravi watched her anxiously, wanting to help, unsure how to set about it.

'I'm giving up my job.'

'You can't. There must be another way.'

'I've brought too much pain to my mum … to all of them.' Tanya's eyes were looking inward. She spoke in a whisper, as though to herself. 'They told me the house was burnt. All mum's things …'

'Mm.'

She looked at him and there was a look of anguish in her eyes now. 'That man … he said if I had anything to do with you again, if I even spoke to you, they'd … they'd come for Tammy.'

Bloody hell!

Ravi felt his body rock back as if under a blow. The taste of bile was strong in his throat.

'I just can't stand the thought of Tammy being in danger. You mustn't come. I'm so sorry. You mustn't ever come to see me.'

'I can't give you up.'

'You'll have to make peace with him then. You'll have to end this first.'

How can I make peace when the bastard wants me dead?

'I'll find a way out, Tani. You know that.'

'No, not this time,' she said firmly although the tears kept rolling down. 'If it was my life, I'd trust it to you, but this is my family. They can't hide forever. You must go now. Don't come again. Just don't!'

She turned her face away.

Ravi looked helplessly at her still form for a moment and then walked away. He nearly bumped into Tanya's editor, Pali Ranatunga at the entrance to the ward. The man seemed preoccupied and brushed past him without a second glance.

*

Ravi had spent most of Sunday brooding in his room.

He knew he would never get over the pain of losing Tanya. Never erase the memory of how his enemies had found just the right lever to break her spirit. How was he going to survive losing her as a friend to confide in, as a colleague to depend on, and as a lover to find comfort with?

But lost she was and there was nothing he could do about it. Any action he took to win her back would immediately put her, and her family, in the most awful danger. He was dealing with animals.

Could he make peace with Shalindra?

There was no chance of that. Pathirana had told him that Shalindra had felt deeply humiliated that his mighty father had been disgraced and toppled from power by a pair of amateurs, insects of a type he normally stepped on. He wanted to save face by showing his world that he could reach out and crush those who crossed him.

So what options, Ravi asked himself, were left to him?

He could try to leave the country, find work in the Middle East perhaps and come back when Shalindra had cooled down. He thought about it seriously for a while. But there was a core of pride in him, driven by an unquenchable rage that wouldn't let him run away.

You bastard. You will pay your debt before the final sunset. Oh how you will pay!

So what were the options? He couldn't stay hidden all the time, not with a price on his head and hired killers on his track. In the end they'd find him and earn their money, so that left him with only one option.

Fight back.

How do you fight a man like Shalindra Premasiri?

He was obviously very wealthy. Who but a wealthy man would offer half a million Rupees to have an obscure student killed? He must already have paid for having Tanya beaten up. Pathirana had told him Shalindra ran a successful used car import business called Dilini Motors. Should he go after his business? Maybe if his business was destroyed he'd not have money for hiring killers.

Then there was his "face". Shalindra had escalated the violence, even to the extent of murder, just to save face in front of his friends. What, Ravi asked himself, would be the harvest if he managed to ruin his reputation?

Could he do it? What were his strengths?

Ravi realized he had, without really meaning to, acquired one priceless strength. Ever since this stupid quarrel started the Premasiris' had lashed out at easy, helpless targets. His mum and dad, their family business and now Tanya and her family. There were no more soft targets left.

If Shalindra wanted to strike back he'd have to find him. So long as he, Ravi, stayed hidden, Shalindra had no target at which to direct his violence.

Ravi called Nonis at the Bank of Lanka.

'Ahh Mr. Perera, how have you been?' The man was surprisingly cordial, a far cry from the dismissive tone he'd used when they had last spoken. 'I've been trying to reach you. Head Office has released your account. You can utilize your funds now.'

Thanks a lot!

Ravi fought to suppress his rage. When Mudalige was all-powerful, a word from him had been enough for some high official in the bank to illegally block his account. Now that the mighty had fallen, and not knowing if Ravi had connections in the new government, the little arse licker had rushed to put matters right.

'I want to withdraw some funds. Can I do that?'

'Of course you can sir. But you really should consider putting the rest of the money in a deposit account. We offer some very attractive …'

'Yeah, I'm sure you do,' Ravi said and rang off.

Ravi sat for a while, lost in thought. He wanted to get his money out of the bank as soon as possible. He knew he could walk into the bank and collect it, but a little niggling worry at the back of his mind made him hesitate.

Ravi knew he'd have to change his life style, plan every routine move with the greatest care. He had to keep reminding himself that there were ruthless men looking for him. They needed to get it right, or get lucky, just once. He had to be a step ahead of them all the time.

How would they try to locate him? Ravi tried to put himself in Shalindra's place. He'd ask his men to watch the hospital and Tanya's house - that would be obvious. What else? Had he, Ravi, any other contact points?

Not one.

Unless it was the bank at Milagiriya where his money was. Would Shalindra think of it? Of course he would. His father had blocked the account and now it had been released. Shalindra knew that Ravi would go there sooner rather than later. It wasn't practical to watch the bank day after day, so how would Shalindra cover his bet? Simple! He'd get some bank employee, preferably Nonis himself, to notify him when Ravi came in; then delay him on some pretext till the killers got there.

Nonis had done that once already, and it had nearly worked.

Ravi called Nonis again.

'Yes Mr. Ravi?'

'What's the balance in my account?'

'Just a minute, let me check.'

All the proceeds from the sale of his house had gone into that account. The bank had deducted all their loans, with penal interest and other charges, and left the residue for him. Ravi knew the balance would be significantly less than he expected.

'Ah Mr. Ravi. Your balance is Rupees 762,504/-.'

'I want to draw some funds and need a new chequebook. I'll come at 11.30. Will that be convenient?'

'Er ... I'm a little busy,' Nonis said hesitantly. 'Can you make it 12.30?'

'Yes. Yes that's fine.' Ravi hung up.

You little shit, isn't there a limit to your treachery?

Ravi started leafing through the official section of the telephone directory. Police Department, then Colombo South District III, Bambalapitiya, and finally OIC Crimes IP Mendis. 2581352.

Busy signal. He tried again and again till he got a gravelly grunt at the other end.

'Inspector Mendis mahaththayada?'

Is that Inspector Mendis?

'Ow.'

Yes

'Mamá Pālitha Guruge, Rajagiriyen. Kāranawak kiyanna kathakeruwey. Wanathamulle Maru Ajitge kattiya Milagiriyey bänkuwata gahanna yanney.'

I'm Palitha Guruge from Rajagiriya. I want to give some information. Maru Ajit from Wanathamulla and his gang plan to hit the Bank at Milagiriya.

'Kawadada gahanney? Kohomada umba danney?'

When is the attack? How do you know this?

'Ada dawal 12.30,' Ravi ignored the second question. *'Kattiya trishaw wala bänkuwey issaraha indiwi. Äthulata yanna dunnoth minissu vedi kai.'*

Today at 12.30. They will come in trishaws. If you let them enter the bank, people will get shot.

'Umba kohomada danney?'

How do you know this?

'Sir, māwa viswasa karanne epa. Welawata giyoth penevi.'

Sir, you don't have to believe me. If you go there at the correct time, you can see for yourself.

'Hittapang ...'

Wait ...

Ravi rang off.

The Bank of Lanka at Milagirya was housed in the ground floor of a two-storey building that had been constructed in the front garden of a stately home facing Galle Road. The stately home itself was now an International School. Across the road from the bank was another school, St Paul's.

Ravi had decided that the best place to watch the bank without exposing himself was The Caravan restaurant situated some twenty-five yards further away on the other side of the road. He wondered if he was getting paranoid. Was he imagining all of this? Should he just go directly to the bank and get his money?

As he walked with a travel bag slung across his shoulders, he juggled these questions in his mind.

No. Taking extra precautions and staying one step ahead was his only hope of staying alive.

He had to pass the bank to reach the restaurant. What if Ajit and his gang were already close by waiting for him? There was a real risk of being spotted if he walked past, even on the other side of the road. He stopped a passing three-wheeler and ordered the man to circle the block going up Dickman's Road, then along Duplication and down Nandana Gardens, to bring him back to Galle Road past the bank.

He dived into The Caravan, bought himself a roll and a coke and found a seat near the plate glass window facing the main road. He checked his watch.

12.20.

Galle Road was buzzing angrily with impatient motorists, mostly buses and school vans. Pedestrians were scurrying along the sidewalks and occasionally risking their necks by dashing madly across the road. Ravi saw that some vehicles were parked in front of the bank. His pursuers could be in any one of them, if they were there at all. Why the hell had he told the cop they'd come in three-wheelers?

12.25.

Maybe they were already inside the bank, waiting for him.

This wasn't working. What was he to do next? Take a chance and walk into the bank or leave now and try another day?

Some vehicles had backed up trying to U-turn opposite Bambalapitiya Flats. Still intent on watching the bank, he glanced idly at the vehicles lined up in front of him. Several vans, a fancy red BMW and two trishaws.

Trishaws?

As he turned his attention to them, the traffic on the other side eased up and the vehicles began to swing around. Ravi couldn't see anything remarkable about the three-wheelers as they followed the other vehicles and slipped into the stream of traffic going towards Fort.

Except that they moved to the left lane and stopped, both of them, directly in front of the bank. No one got off! Ravi felt the shock as the adrenalin hit him. His limbs seemed to tingle with a mixture of exhilaration and dread. He had casually dropped some bait into a dark, forbidden body of water. Now suddenly he could see the shadowy outline of a Great White Shark coming out of the depths.

Where the hell were the cops?

Would that cop believe the tip off without confirmation? He must have his doubts, surely? But Maru Ajit was a well known underworld thug, and the OIC wouldn't want a bank robbery to take place right under his nose, especially after he'd been tipped off. He would want, at least, to check it out.

So where were they?

Some vehicles had again pulled up in front of him, waiting to U-turn. Ravi glanced at them and sat straight in his chair. The second vehicle in the line was a midnight blue Pajero with POLICE painted in white across the front door.

Was this it?

Ravi watched as the blue Pajero swung round and slotted itself in the stream of traffic going the other way. His heart sank when it seemed as if they were not stopping, but just as they passed the double-parked trishaws, the driver swung the vehicle viciously across the road. The 4 x 4 came to a screeching halt with its nose across the leading trishaw and its rear end jutting dangerously onto the road, blocking the lane of traffic. Armed policemen began scrambling out of the back of the vehicle almost before it came to a halt.

Pandemonium reigned.

Men seemed to erupt from the trishaws like wasps from a hive stirred up with a stick. Ravi saw at least four men scramble out of the vehicles and run along the sidewalk towards the flats, hotly pursued by the policemen.

The men split up.

One of them dived into Frankfurt Place and disappeared, another fellow darted into the traffic, dodging and weaving to reach the other sidewalk. The leading cop got within range of one of the remaining men, a squat fellow in a batik shirt, who had lagged behind the fourth man. Ravi saw the policeman swing his gun, catching the man with a solid blow on the head, bringing him crashing on the sidewalk. The other cops pounced on the fallen man, twisting his arms up behind him. The fourth man disappeared in the direction of the flats.

Ravi picked up the travel bag from under the table, crossed the road quickly and entered the bank. The police vehicle was still angled across the road and one policeman had the trishaw drivers squatting on the sidewalk with their hands on their heads. Customers were crowding near the door to see what was going on and the lone security guard stood near the sidewalk nervously fingering his single barreled shotgun.

Ravi walked directly into the manager's room. Nonis seemed jolted by his sudden appearance.

'I know what you did. Those men came here to kill me. Did you know that when you gave the information?'

'I don't know what you mean. What are you talking about?'

'Shut up! There's no need to play dumb buggers,' Ravi snarled roughly, leaning over the cringing man. 'I can go to the police with this. To your superiors as well, and make real trouble for you. Do you realise that?'

The man sat staring at him as though petrified. His forehead was damp despite the chill of the air-conditioning.

'I will make a bargain with you. Release my money right now, without any hassle, and I'll drop the whole thing. Do you understand?'

Nonis nodded faintly.

'One thing more,' Ravi said menacingly. 'If you touch a telephone, I'll break your arm.'

Nonis appeared anxious to give him his money and get rid of him. It didn't take long for Ravi to draw out 700,000/- in thousand Rupee notes and stuff them in his bag. Another thought had struck Ravi as he prepared to leave. The longhaired Maru Ajit hadn't been with the men who had come in the two trishaws. Had Ajit stayed away for some reason or had he hidden himself somewhere close by to watch the operation?

Ravi threw the bag over his shoulder and went to the back of the building pushing his way past a protesting security guard. The corridor led past the staff meal room and fell into a small yard common to all the business houses in the block. The yard, in turn, fell into the driveway leading to the school.

On reaching the main road, Ravi hailed a passing trishaw and asked the man to take him towards Wellawatte. Ravi tucked the sling bag firmly between his feet and held on to the sides of the speeding vehicle. He looked back cautiously but there was no way to find out if anyone was following him. He just knew he couldn't take a chance.

On a sudden impulse Ravi ordered the driver to stop in front of Wellawatte market. He thrust a fifty in the man's hand and dived into the malodorous interior lined with vegetable and fruit stalls. He ran past housewives busily haggling over prices and escaped to daylight and fresh air through the side exit falling into Manning Place. He took the first trishaw in the stand and ordered the puzzled driver to make a wide circuit and take him back to Galle Road via Hampden Lane, Canal Road and Vihara Lane. On Galle Road once again he paid the man off and took a bus to Dehiwela.

Ten minutes later Ravi was walking down Campbell Place. The Koch residence had a derelict look to it with its boarded windows and collapsed roof. Where would they be? He tried old Conrad's house, further down the street.

Conrad was lounging in the verandah reading a newspaper.

'Dick, Dick! It's that bugger who caused all the trouble.'

Ravi glowered at him but didn't say anything. Richard Koch came out frowning worriedly.

'Don't take notice of Conrad, son,' he started kindly and then went on. 'But you mustn't come. Those bastards said they'd harm my Tammy if we had anything to do with you.'

'I've got my gun ready, Dicky. I told you,' Conrad said pugnaciously.

'I'll whack one or two of them if they try their larks.'

'Don't worry, Mr. Koch. I'll not come again. How is aunty? And Tanya?'

'They're better now. Tomorrow, they'll come home.'

Ravi proffered the sling bag. 'I've brought you some money. Use it to send the two girls away for some time. The rest can go for repairs to the house.'

'What? I can't take your money,' Richard Koch recoiled in surprise. 'Pam will be furious.'

'Uncle, I'm responsible for all these problems. I should have foreseen it and taken precautions! Now I must put things right.'

Richard Koch stared at him uncertainly.

'You must get the girls away. I need a few weeks to sort this out. In the meantime I want to be sure they are safe,' Ravi dropped the sling bag on a chair. 'Use the money.'

He turned and walked away.

26

Ravi had been awake since a magpie robin stationed itself on the TV antenna on the roof and began its morning concert. His dad had loved these cheerful little black and white birds that infested the home gardens in Colombo, and filled the city mornings with their melody.

They sometimes came in small flocks and his mother would say:
"One for sorrow, two for joy.
Three for a wedding, four for a boy!"

His heart filled with unbearable melancholy when he realized he'd never hear her say those words again. He tore his mind away from his regrets to take stock of his situation.

The police swoop on Maru Ajit's gang had given him an opening to collect his money but would not deter them from their main pursuit. Even the man they'd caught would have to be released unless he had had some concealed weapon. Ajit might have guessed by now that he, Ravi, was based in Bambalapitiya. His men would be snooping around the area, and Ravi knew it wouldn't take them very long to spot him.

He would have to give up his comfortable little hideout with Aunty Nora. Where could he go next? What if he had to leave in a real hurry? How best could he prepare for that?

He took out the cash he had kept in an old envelope in the drawer of his desk and counted it. Seventy-three thousand Rupee notes, all that was left from selling the furniture and household effects his mother had left behind.

He got dressed and walked down to House of Fashions on Duplication Road. He bought a broad leather belt. He remembered seeing an old-fashioned tailor shop on Thimbirigasyaya Road and hired a trishaw to look for the place.

"Modern Tailors – Under Taking Cushions and Curtains", were housed in a roadside building, one dilapidated step up from a shanty. An old man was seated at an equally ancient pedal activated machine staring at the road and smoking a beedi. Ravi watched the puzzled but willing man, as he skillfully cut away the stitching along the lower edge of his new belt, opening the cavity between the two sections. He then hand stitched a plastic zipper along the opening, creating a wide concealed pocket along the length of the belt.

Back in his room, Ravi took out his money and started inserting notes into the belt. A thousand folded in two lengthwise fitted in neatly and he was able to pack ten green notes into his makeshift money belt. He then took a pair of pliers and snipped off the tab of the zipper. He wore the belt and looked at himself in the mirror. With the zip on the under side of the belt, no sign of the secret money compartment could be seen by anyone standing up and looking down at it.

He sat cross-legged on the bed and stared at the rest of the money on the bed. How could he keep it safe yet accessible whenever he wanted it? After some time he went to the top of the road, and from a shop there, purchased a roll of adhesive tape. Getting back to the room, he packed the notes into a tight bundle inside the envelope.

He opened the front door and sat on the doorstep to have a close look at aunty's letterbox.

She had installed a wooden contraption painted in an appropriate pillar-box red, an extravagant affair to accommodate monthly utility bills and an occasional letter from her daughter in Australia. The box was securely bolted to the gate with a narrow slot facing the road. A small, hinged door secured with a hook, was set in the rear of the box for collecting the mail.

The narrow road shimmered emptily in the blazing heat of the afternoon sun. Ravi tore off strips of adhesive tape and wrapped them across the cash filled envelope, leaving the sticky ends free on either side. He then opened the letterbox and, inserting the bundle, fixed it securely on the inner wall above the door. He closed and latched the door, glanced around casually to make sure he was not under observation, and went back to his room.

He lay down on the bed again staring sightlessly at the ceiling. He felt the misery of his situation wash over him. He had told Tanya the simple

214

truth - with her at his side it had been bearable. But now?

What the hell was he to do next?

His hand phone buzzed.

Reshane. Inviting him for a drink at the Golf Club.

Ravi, ever cautious, didn't tell him where he was staying and Reshane didn't ask. He had asked Reshane to pick him up opposite Vajira Road. Twenty minutes later they were ensconced in armchairs overlooking the 8th green. Ravi looked at the cheerful, spectacled face of his friend with fond relief. His invitation had yanked him out of the depression that had threatened to engulf him and couldn't have been better timed.

'How have you been, you bugger?' Reshane asked when the steward had taken their orders for Lion draft. 'You just dropped out of sight. I finally got your mobile number from Tilak.'

The memory of Tilak's betrayal seared Ravi's mind like the flame of a blowtorch.

'You know about the troubles I've had with the Premasiri family. I have to lie low for a while. Although the Minister is out of the way, the son has taken it up.'

'Shalindra's not such a bad fellow when you get to know him, you know,' Reshane said airily and then added, 'I hear he's even got himself nominated for the committee at the next AGM in March.'

'That arsehole? Are you buggers crazy?' Ravi's voice had risen.

'He's made himself popular with the membership ... donations and stuff. Lots of members buy their cars from him. Big business. Dilini Motors.'

'That's why he's sucking up to them, to get them to buy. He's just a common thug.'

'No machang, you may be wrong about him. He wants to settle this quarrel amicably, that's why he wanted to meet you here.'

Ravi stared at his friend in horror. 'He wanted to meet me?'

'Yes! He called and asked me to bring you,' Reshane sounded uncertain for the first time. 'I'm sure he was quite sincere.'

'You bloody idiot,' Ravi snarled. 'You've fixed me.'

'No ... surely ...'

'That bastard's put a contract on me. Half a million!' Ravi said rapidly. 'The killers didn't know how to find me. That's why he asked you to bring me here.'

'You don't mean …?' Reshane stopped with his mouth open, a picture of dismay.

'Yes, I do mean! They must be waiting for me. In the car park most likely.'

'How can you be sure?'

'I'm sure, pal. I'm sure.'

Reshane sat in stunned silence while Ravi stared sightlessly at the lush green fairways stretching into the distance.

'Do you keep your clubs here?' He asked finally.

'Yes. In the dressing room locker. Why?'

Minutes later, Ravi left a badly shaken Reshane in the clubhouse and strolled casually across the putting green towards the starters box and the first tee. He held a comforting nine iron firmly in his hand.

Where would they be waiting?

They would have come in force, determined not to miss such a good chance. There was only one exit for vehicles, Model Farm Road. An ambush on the road was the obvious choice but there were risks in trying to stop a moving vehicle.

No.

They had to be waiting in the car park.

There was a steep footpath from the starter's box leading down to the practice range that nestled between the tenth and fourteenth fairways. The rise in the ground and the clubhouse screened him from the car park. Ravi had seen a gap in the fence and a footpath near the fourteenth tee that caddies used to get to Lake Drive. If he was able to cross the 14th fairway unseen, he knew he had a good chance of getting away.

Ravi surveyed the deserted fairway as he walked down and across. He saw a course marshal on a motorbike riding slowly away towards the thirteenth. Ravi was halfway across, fighting the temptation to hurry, when a man stepped out from behind a tree directly in front of him. One glance was enough to identify him as the shaven headed thug who'd chased him in the hospital. He lunged at Ravi, slashing at his chest with a heavy knife in his right hand.

Fear must have lent Ravi the strength and the timing, for the head of the swinging nine iron caught the man on his forearm with a solid crunching sound. The knife flew from his fingers as the man clutched his damaged hand to his chest.

But he yelled loudly and wordlessly, a sound full of fury and pain. He must have been heard for there was an answering yell from the direction of the car park. Another man was running towards him from the fourteenth tee so there was no escape that way either. The only way left was the eleventh green and the boundary wall at the back of it.

Ravi ran.

He ran till he was exhausted and then ran some more, for he knew there would be no mercy if they caught him. He heard them close behind. Too close. He heard one man shouting to encourage the others.

'Bälligey putha kääli walata kapapang.'

Cut the son of a bitch to pieces.

He reached the green and the ivy-covered wall at the back of it, at least ten feet tall. But he remembered the footholds carefully chiseled out of the block work by urchins in the neighborhood. He dropped the club and flung himself at the wall, scrabbling for hand and footholds. He made it to the top and threw himself recklessly over the edge to fall, in a tangle of arms and legs, on some low shrubbery on the far side.

Ravi tried to orient himself. He was in a shantytown that had sprouted behind Castle Street Hospital, bounded by the Golf Club on one side and the railway line on the other. He knew that running in the open was futile, so he had to find refuge in the midst of the squalid plank and zinc-sheeted hovels that spread out before him.

Ravi dashed down the first alleyway ignoring the women folk who stopped their activities to stare at him in surprise. Another, meaner alley opened on his right and he dived into it.

Someone said, *'Sir, mehe enna.'*

Sir, come here.

The caddie, Eetin, gestured urgently. He reached out and pulled the exhausted Ravi into a bat cave made of block work and boxwood.

'Ohoma inna sadda nätuwa. Mama balagannang.'

Stay here quietly. I'll look after things.

When the three men came running into the alley seconds later Eetin was seated quietly on his doorstep.

One of the men yelled roughly:

'Kalisang kārayek meheng diwwaney? Koheda giyey?'

A man in trousers ran this way. Where did he go?

'Rail pāra pāththata giyā,' Eetin answered calmly and then went on. *'Mey Wapara Somegey bajarr eka. Eyāgen ahalade āvey?'*

He ran towards the rail track, but this is Wapara Somey's territory. Have you asked him if you could come here?

Ravi, cowering inside the flimsy structure, had a sudden urge to laugh. Shantytowns were ruled by gangs that protected their fiefdoms with the utmost ferocity. These men had clearly crossed a line by entering it. When they next spoke, the intruders sounded a little uncertain, *'Apeng kachal nähä. Minihek allaganna āvey.'*

We mean no harm. We just want to catch a man.

But they turned and walked back the way they came. Eetin watched them impassively till they were out of sight.

Eetin addressed Ravi in Sinhala.

'I think those men will watch the roads round our *watta*. Better for sir to wait some time.' Then he went on: 'Is it still Shalindra sir who is after you?'

'Yes.'

'Very rich. Powerful in Club also. Committee member next year, it seems. But caddies don't like.'

'Why?'

'Bad man. He kept wallet in golf bag once, then accused caddie, my sister's son, of stealing money. The boy was suspended for three months. Blames caddies when he misses shot. Always complaining and giving bad reports.'

'Mm.'

'Cheats also.'

'Really? How?'

'Puts *hora* score. If he gets seven, he say six. Like that.' Eetin added slyly, 'Can put him in big shame if you want. Cost a little money.'

'What do you mean?'

'Toyota tournament on Saturday. Shalindra sir never marks card, always tells caddie to enter score, then signs card without looking. Useless looking because he never wins, even after cheating a little.'

'So?'

'So can get caddie to put very good score for him. Enough to win tournament. But other members sure to challenge. If there is enquiry he will get caught and big shame. No committee for him then. Maybe resign from club.'

'Will the caddie agree?'

'Senior caddies maybe say no, but young fellow say yes if we pay.'

'How will we know who the caddie will be?'

'Once the draw is out, can fix.'

'How much for whole thing?'

'Two thousand Rupees?' Eetin asked hopefully.

Ravi knew if he gave all the money the old rogue would stay drunk for the whole week.

'I'll give five hundred Rupees now. Get the job done and I'll give you another two thousand,' Ravi told him and saw the old man's eyes light up.

'Don't worry sir, it will be done, you'll see. How will I find you afterwards …?'

Ravi thought for a moment. 'Call me and I'll tell you where to come for the money. Here, I'll write the number on the wall.'

*

Tita's golf column in the Daily News said it all. Ravi felt a familiar rush of exultation as he read the headline.

TOYOTA GOLF TOURNAMENT IN DISSARAY,
Prominent golfer disqualified in cheating scandal.

Got you, you son-of-a-bitch! Say goodbye to your chances of getting on the committee.

Then he felt a featherlike cloud of fear touch his mind. It always did
– afterwards. Shalindra was sure to guess who was behind the frame-up.
How would he strike back?

Ravi's hand phone rang.

Eetin.

*'Sir? Harida wädey? Eka secretary mahaththayatath gahannna giya.
Dhäng club eken aswenawalu.'*

Sir? Is the job OK? He tried to assault the club secretary. Now he is
resigning from the club.

'Bohoma hondai.'

Very good.

'Salli ganney kohomadha?'

How can I collect the money?

'Dickman pāra langa patrol shed ekata enna ada havasa pahamārata.'

Come to the petrol station near Dickmans Road at 5.30 this
evening.

'Hondai.'

Good.

Ravi stood near the little office and watched the cars and trishaws
pull in for petrol. He knew some of the attendants by sight and nodded
to them as they hurried about their thankless tasks.

Eetin came hurrying in from the road a good five minutes before then
appointed time. He looked about anxiously till he spotted Ravi standing
in the shade and came shuffling over, an expectant grin on his face.

Ravi looked over the old man's shoulder and felt a jolt in his chest. He
knew he had made the terrible mistake of underestimating his enemy. A
trishaw had turned in from the road but, instead of heading towards the
pumps, came directly at him. A man leapt out before the vehicle came
to a halt.

Shalindra had done his homework. He must have found out that
Eetin had a hand in the plot. His men had followed Eetin, knowing he
would lead them to Ravi.

Ravi thrust the two green notes into Eetin's hand and ran. He threw himself blindly across the three rows of rush hour traffic on Galle Road, forcing more than one motorist to brake and swerve to avoid hitting him. Traffic was lighter on the far side of the road and he was soon racing down Milagiriya Avenue towards the sea.

Ravi tried to force his brain to think rationally. He'd flung himself across the road knowing that the trishaw couldn't follow, but the men could and would pursue him on foot. Running alone wouldn't save him.

Where could he hide?

He was gasping by the time he reached the unfinished Marine Drive at the end of the lane. The dual tracks of the coastal railway ran between the road and the sea. An overcrowded office train had stopped for the signal near Kinross Avenue. It must have been stuck there for some time because many of the passengers had stepped down beside the track and were walking about aimlessly.

Ravi ran across the tracks to the far side of the carriages. Once out of his pursuer's direct line of sight he eased himself through the clusters of office workers standing around and climbed into a crowded carriage. The two transverse seats were all taken and other passengers stood, packed like sardines, in the space in between. Ravi turned his face to the sea, found himself a handhold and waited.

Five agonizing minutes later an almost empty train, the probable cause of the holdup, rattled past on the seaside track leading to Fort station. A whistle blew and the stationary train gave a jolt. The remaining passengers hurriedly squeezed themselves aboard as the train began to move.

Would the gang have boarded the train to follow him?

It was certainly possible but Ravi thought it unlikely. The train was absolutely packed to the roof so there was no possibility of moving from carriage to carriage looking for him. It would stop at each station and hordes of passengers would get off. An army of watchers would be needed to spot one face in that crowd.

They must have guessed by now that he was based in the Bambalapitiya area. The sure way to nab him was to post men all over the area to spot him when he returned.

There was no going back to Nora's house.

Ravi needed a place to stay, at least for a couple of days, till he worked out a plan of action. Reshane was out, for they'd definitely watch his house. Who else could he go to? Mohan had been another good friend at Warwick, Mohan Edirisinghe. Now where the hell did he stay? Moratuwa – that's it. Watson Peiris Mawatha in Moratuwa and this train, bound for Panadura, would take him there.

Wellawatte, Dehiwela and Mt. Lavinia, the train laboured to each of these stations and people disembarked wearily with their briefcases and shopping bags. A well-dressed man with an enormous behind vacated a seat in front of him and Ravi was quick to seize an opportunity to rest his feet. The man had left a newspaper on the seat and Ravi picked it up. He opened the newspaper and pretended to read, covering his face as best he could.

Another chubby fellow was asleep next to him with his arms crossed over his chest and his face resting comfortably on his multiple chins.

A commotion at the far end of the carriage made Ravi look up in alarm. The standees still jammed the centre aisle and they heaved and moved as people craned their necks to see what was going on.

'*Horek. Horek. Magey pocket ekata gähuwa,*' a man was yelling
Thief. Thief. My pocket's been picked.
'*Kauda?*' '*Däkkada?*' '*Allaganing,*' other passengers took up the cry.
Who is it? Did you see? Catch him.
'*Kauruth bässey nähä. Okkogema sarkku balamu,*' another voice added.
No one has got off. Let's search the pockets of the passengers.
The fat fellow next to him never stirred.

Losing interest, Ravi was lifting his newspaper again when he felt, rather than saw, something drop into the narrow gap in the seat between him and the next passenger. He looked down casually.

A brown wallet.

Ravi looked up in shocked surprise. Standing directly in front of him, and clinging to one of the vertical supports, was a young girl in a faded blue dress that hung loosely on her slight frame. She was looking directly at him with a half smile on her lips.

Surely she couldn't be a pickpocket? Yet she continued to look knowingly at him. He opened his mouth to call out, but for some reason he never understood, the words didn't come.

It was probably her eyes that stopped him - laughing eyes, dancing with mischief and daring him to denounce her. Ravi then did something completely out of character, something so impulsive and risky he'd look back on it with wonder.

He folded the newspaper and placed it over the wallet.

An action committee, seemingly regular commuters, had started searching the passengers amid yelps of protest and outrage. They were moving towards his end of the carriage and Ravi began to regret his hasty action, wondering what he had let himself in for.

Then somewhere deep inside he felt again that strange exhilaration, half dread and half fizziness, which danger seemed to trigger in him.

The searchers came to the girl and she lifted her arms with a saucy smile while a burly woman patted her pockets perfunctorily and passed on. Ravi realized with relief that they were only searching the standing passengers. They had reached the end of the carriage when the train pulled into Ratmalana station.

The man who'd lost his wallet got off calling loudly to the God of Kataragama to strike down the thief that very night. The girl's grin broadened when she heard the threat. The man with the extra quota of chins who'd been dozing in the seat next to Ravi collected his parcels and rose to his feet.

The train pulled out with a jerk. The girl in the blue dress casually took the vacant seat next to Ravi.

'I give half to sir.'

'What?'

'The money,' she explained as though to an idiot. 'I give you half. Truly.'

'I don't want the money.'

She gave a puzzled look but didn't say anything for a minute. Then, 'At Bambalapitiya … I saw men chasing. Sir have to give them money?'

'No,' Ravi was mildly amused that everything seemed to revolve round money for this girl. 'No. They want to kill me.'

If Ravi thought she would be shocked he was disappointed. She just nodded her head as if that kind of thing happened everyday.

'Sir go where now?'

'Moratuwa. I have a friend there.'

'Mm. My home also Moratuwa.'

She was quiet for a while as the train screeched to a halt at Lunawa station. Many of the passengers shuffled out leaving a half empty carriage. Ravi lifted the edge of the newspaper and found the wallet had disappeared.

The girl's eyes were on him as he looked up. Small face with a tip tilted nose that fell just short of prettiness but made up for that with animation. A mass of untidily cut curly hair, looking like a chimney brush, above it. She looked so unlike a thief. Ravi wondered why she insisted on conversing in her awful, broken English.

'Why do you steal? Isn't it wrong?'

She frowned in apparent puzzlement. 'Is my *rassawa,* my job no? How it can be wrong?'

'You just escaped today,' Ravi said quietly. 'One day they will catch you and send you to jail.'

'Yes. Very hard when work alone,' she admitted seriously.

'So where is your partner?'

'I belong Kadu Piyal. He is in Welikada.'

'Your husband is in jail?'

'Yes , jail,' the girl said unemotionally. 'Not husband. He own me.'

'What do you mean, own you?'

'*Booruwa gahala dinuwa. Eda indang mama eyata aithei,'* she said simply, reverting to Sinhala to express herself better.

He won me at a card game. Since that day I belong to him.

Ravi looked at her sharply. He thought for a moment she was joking but then was shocked to realize she was quite serious.

The train began to slow down.

'Moratuwa,' the girl said. 'Where your friend's house?'

'Watson Peiris Mawatha. I have to go there and ask.'

'Mm.'

The train stopped at a dingy platform. Ravi followed the girl to join a queue forming at the exit where an elderly man wearing a khaki railway uniform was collecting tickets.

'I don't have a ticket,' Ravi whispered to the girl.

'Mang ekka enna.'

Come with me.

Sure enough, when it was their turn the old man greeted her with a betel stained smile.

'Ahh Janaki. Kohomada ada?'

Ahh Janaki. How are you today?

'Marma, meya mamath ekka.'

Uncle, he is with me.

Betel mouth just grinned and waved them through the gate. Janaki stopped under the lights of the station entrance and turned to Ravi.

'Turn to *wamata* at main road,' she said solemnly waving her left arm, 'then again *wamata* ... Watson Peiris.'

Ravi realised again how young she looked and how scrawny she was under her tent like dress. He felt a tinge of unease. How could such a childlike creature survive in the shark-infested waters she swam in?

He reached out and touched her arm.

'Thank you.'

She reacted as if he had stabbed her.

'Allanna epā,' she said harshly. *'Kavadarwath allanna epā.'*

Don't touch me. Never touch me.

She turned abruptly and stalked away leaving a dumbfounded Ravi staring after her.

Ravi found Watson Peiris Mawatha without difficulty. The first man he spoke to belched and staggered away mumbling to himself, the second was a visitor himself and couldn't help. Ravi walked through the open gate of the next house and rang the bell. A middle-aged woman in a housecoat answered the door, giving him the bad news.

The Edirisinghes' had lived close by but they'd moved away. Somewhere in Dehiwela, she thought. No, she didn't have an address.

Shit.

Ravi tried to consider his options as he walked back. He could take a bus back to Bambalapitiya and try in sneak into Aunty Nora's house but he knew that was very risky. Should he try to look for a cheap hotel?

A small figure stepped out of a shadow as he turned onto the main road.

Janaki.

'Sir's friend not here?'

'No.'

'Sir help me today,' she said softly. 'No one help like that.'

'It's all right,' Ravi murmured without interest, wishing she would go away.

'Can give sir place to stay. If sir want.'

Was she setting him up to be robbed?

Ravi was tired and dispirited enough to try anything. He needed a safe place to get some rest, to plan his next move.

'I will pay …'

'No money,' she said firmly. 'Sir come.'

Janaki led the way across the main road. She disappeared into a small eatery by the roadside and came out in a couple of minutes swinging a shopping bag. She led the way down an unlit lane and then to a gravel track. Ravi noticed with some trepidation that they were in a poorer section of the town with houses gradually deteriorating into not-quite shanties.

Janaki turned into the small yard fronting a marginally better building that might have been a small shop, now shuttered for the night. She led the way through the gap between the side of the building and a barbed wire fence, stepping carefully over the roots of a large mango tree and what looked like a pile of shuttering planks and props from a building site.

Ravi realised that the back of the building faced the Bolgoda Lake and the gravel track ran parallel to it. He saw the black water glinting as ripples caught the faint moonlight. Janaki led him to the back of the building that ended in a narrow open verandah.

'Sir, wait,' she said and disappeared.

A moment later Ravi heard footsteps above his head. A narrow trap door opened in the wooden ceiling. A shaft of light streamed down, and in it he was surprised to see an improvised rope ladder made by tying knots at regular intervals on a thick coir rope.

Janaki, leaning over the trapdoor, said: 'Sir come.'

Ravi had to remove his sneakers and throw them up first because he needed his toes free to grip the rope. He was breathing deeply from the awkward climb as he surveyed his surroundings with amazement.

It wasn't really an attic, just a space between the ceiling and the asbestos roof. Space enough for one girl. A single twenty-watt bulb hung precariously from two exposed wires and dimly illuminated the strange dwelling. The ceiling planks had been nailed to the underside of the rafters and looked unreliable. The girl had used shuttering planks, placed across the rafters, as a base for her mat. The room was bare except for her mat with two pillows at one end and three cardboard cartons under the eave of the roof.

*

Ravi felt a sense of unreality as he struggled to find a comfortable position.

He lay on his back looking at the low roof above his head. He had used more shuttering planks to form a makeshift bed over the rafters and the girl had given him some boxboard to lie on. He had quietly slipped the stained, coverless pillow under the cardboard to keep it away from his head but that only added to his discomfort. Watery moonlight filtered into the room through the narrow gap between the roof and the block work wall. Ravi could see the branches of the mango tree swaying gently in the breeze and changing the sky pattern. That gap was Janaki's secret entrance.

He had to be dreaming.

Just a few hours ago he'd left his comfortable room to meet Eetin. Soon afterwards he had found himself running for his life, and then fate had thrust him into the company of a young pickpocket. He couldn't believe that he'd allowed himself to become an accomplice in her theft and was now actually taking shelter in this crazy attic.

They had sat at the edge of the rear verandah and eaten the packets of rice and curry the girl had bought with her stolen money. Ravi had washed his shirt at the shallow well in the next compound and hung it out to dry.

They had not spoken much when they settled down to sleep at either end of the small space in the ceiling. Janaki had pulled up the rope ladder and secured the trap door with a stout stick. Just before turning out the light she had pulled a long knife from under her mat and pointed it at him. The heavy knife was incongruous in her tiny fist but the face above it was serious.

'*Mang langata āvothin maranava,*' she had said quietly.

If you come near me, I'll kill you.

Ravi hadn't the slightest intension of going near her, but the seriousness of her threat made him curious. He remembered that she had reacted with uncharacteristic violence when he'd touched her arm. He wondered idly if she was nursing some trauma related to physical contact.

He didn't really care. He'd leave in the morning and never see her again.

Janaki was still awake. Ravi heard the planks creak faintly as she turned.

'Why those men are trying to kill sir?'

Ravi wondered again why the silly creature insisted in conversing in her broken English when they could so easily communicate in Sinhala.

'For money. They are paid.'

'Who is pay them?'

'My enemy.'

'Is sir going to kill this enemy?'

'No,' Ravi said more vehemently than he intended.

'Then how is sir going to stop them? For money they will look and look till they find and kill sir.'

'I don't know.'

Janaki was quiet for a while and Ravi hoped she'd gone to sleep at last.

'Then have to take away his money,' she said suddenly. 'No money, no *chandiyas.*'

Ravi didn't answer for a moment, surprised by the simple clarity of her thinking. How do you stop a man from paying a reward for your death? Take away his money. No money, no hired killers.

'What this man's business?'

'Cars. He imports cars.'

'Can burn all man's cars, then he have no money.'

'Mm,' Ravi answered casually. He felt a small sliver of an idea flitting across his mind.

'Magey haturata gahanna udaw keruwoth mama sir ta udaw karannang,' Janaki switched to Sinhala suddenly.

If you help to attack my enemy, I will help you.

'Mona hathurada?' Ravi wondered where this was going

What enemy?

'Madamey sir. U thamai apiwa suddanta deela ridduvey.'

The sir at the orphanage. He gave us to white men to be hurt.

Bloody hell!

There'd been rumours from time to time that this kind of thing happened but Ravi had never taken it seriously.

'Which *madama*?'

'Premila Home. In Lunawa.'

'What is his name, this man?'

'Wije sir, madam's husband.'

'You were in the *madama*? For how long?'

'Don't remember. From baby time.'

'Wije sir, what did he do?'

'He stay in Colombo, come there only Friday, Saturday. He take one, two girls to place near beach. White men take pictures ...,' Janaki's voice faded. 'Then do bad things ... hurting.'

'You ran away?"

'Yes.'

'And now you want to attack Mr. Wije?

'Yes,' Janaki said fiercely. 'Yes. Kill him.'

'I'm not going to kill anyone.'

'Something else then. Make him sorry.'

Ravi didn't reply.

After awhile the girl spoke. 'Will sir help me?'

'I'll think about it.'

Ravi struggled to put his whirling thoughts in order. Going back to Aunty Nora's house was a big risk, so he had to find another place to stay.

There'd be plenty of offers in the Sunday Observer classified but that was in five days.

Until then?

An aphorism he'd picked up somewhere passed through his mind.

Where do you hide a tree? In the forest, of course!

So where do you hide just one man? Where else, but in a crowd?

He felt most comfortable in his own middle class environment. Well middle class – wannabe – upper class, Ravi thought in a moment of self-mockery. But that was where they'd look for him. They'd not look for him, nor would he be easy to find, in the mass of poorer people in the city. But to be safe he'd have to literally submerge himself in that mass.

Could he stand it?

Should he stay here for a few days till he found something more suitable? How could he do that without getting involved in this creature's bizarre project to punish "Wije sir"?

PART FOUR

War

*If you're going to put a stick in someone's eye,
you have to drive it all the way in.*

US Official in Iraq

27

Sunlight was filtering into the room when Ravi woke. The trap was open and when he climbed awkwardly down the rope ladder he found Janaki seated at the edge of the verandah looking at the river. She smiled cheerfully at him, pearly teeth flashing in the sunlight.

She casually handed Ravi the pink plastic cup she'd been drinking from. Hot sugared tea probably collected from a kiosk on the road. It would have been churlish to refuse, so Ravi stifled his qualms and took the cup. He took care to take the handle in his left hand, so that he sipped from the unused side of the cup. He found the tea tasting of ginger and surprisingly good.

'Sir will stay here?'

'For a few days, maybe. I must pay something.'

'No money for stay. Can buy food if sir want.'

'All right.'

'I know sir have ten thousand in belt,' she smiled slyly, 'but Janaki won't take.'

Ravi stared at her in surprise. How had she managed to find that? She must be very good at her work, better than he had imagined.

'What is this place?' Ravi covered his annoyance, pointing at the shuttered building behind them.

'*Cementhi gabadwak. Mudalligey kadey thiyenne towmey.*'

Cement store. The mudalali's shop is in the town.

'*Loriya enava cementhi geniyanna. Wena kawruwath enney nähä,*' she continued.

The truck comes to take cement. No one else comes here.

Bolgoda Lake spread out before him, broad and still in the morning sun. To his right Ravi could see traffic on the bridge spanning a narrower section of the lake. Fishermen in small outrigger boats were casting and pulling in their hand nets. Some Bramminy Kites were circling the sky in their search for scraps on the water.

There appeared to be a small house in the next garden beyond the mango tree. Ravi could hear a woman yelling at some children. Although the rusty zinc sheets of the roof could be seen, the overgrown live fence screened off the house. The land on the other side was vacant with wild scrubs growing head high in the swampy ground.

Ravi tried to arrange his thoughts. Returning to pick up the threads of his life was not possible while Shalindra Premasiri had a contract on him. Running and hiding was fine for a few days but to carry on like that indefinitely was out of the question. So where did that leave him?

Just two options.

Shalindra had to be forced to withdraw his contract, or he, Ravi, had to leave the field; he had to go abroad and get a job of some sort. Despite his simmering anger and instinct to go after Shalindra's blood, Ravi knew in his heart that the latter was the sensible course. The job agencies demanded money and he might have enough – just. He would need the passport he'd left at Aunty Nora's.

He dialed the old lady's number, feeling guilty that he'd neglected to call her in the night. Someone picked it up on the first ring.

'Nora isn't here right now. Who is calling?' Ravi felt a cold sensation at the back of his neck when he recognized Pam Koch's gentle voice.

'Uh, it's Ravi.'

'Oh Ravi! Are you all right? Where are you?'

'I'm fine Aunty, truly, but why are you there? Where is Aunty Nora?'

'Those awful men. They came here last night looking for you. They roughed up poor Nora … broke some of her things …'

'Oh God! Is she badly hurt?' Ravi felt his stomach churning. He wanted to throw up. 'She must be devastated. It's all my fault.'

'They kept her at Durdans for observation but I think she's all right. Just bruised and shaken. It's you she's worried about, wondering if those ruffians caught you.'

'I'm ok. Please tell her I'll repair all the damage. I'm so sorry for all this.'

'I'll tell her, Ravi, but you mustn't blame yourself.'

'Tanya … is she all right?'

'The girls are in Melbourne, with my sister.'

'I see.'

'I couldn't thank you for what you did. Dicky and I were so relieved to send them away for a while. I hope this will end soon.'

'Yes.'

'Ravi, those men, they've taken all your things, clothes, papers, everything.'

'What? What about my passport? I had some important files there.'

'There's nothing left. Nothing.'

Ravi sat for a while trying to absorb it all. Without documents, he couldn't apply for a new passport. His idea of leaving the country was a non-starter. He had to stay, and that meant a fight to the end. In a secret corner of his heart, he was glad it turned out this way. He could almost taste it in anticipation, like some forbidden pleasure.

You want war, you bitch-bastard? I'll give you war – up to your throat.

Janaki was looking at him quietly.

'I need to buy some things. Will the shops be open now?'

She nodded and stood up, her oversized dress billowing around her. 'I'll come with sir.'

They traversed the gravel track and then the metalled lane that led directly to the bazaar. Janaki led Ravi to a zinc-sheeted warehouse where readymade clothing, factory rejects most likely, was laid out on long racks for customers to pick. Ravi bought himself a pair of denims and a couple of T-shirts, a sarong and a towel. He made another stop at a pharmacy for toiletries.

Janaki seemed to know everyone.

A thin man with a scraggly beard and a skullcap greeted her with a vast yellow-brown smile. He stepped carefully out of his boxwood stall, full of old keys and key cutting tools, just to speak with her.

'Ahh Salim aiya, business hondaida?'

Brother Salim. Is your business good?

'Hondai. Hondai deiyangey pihiteng,' the man answered.

Good. Good by the grace of God.

A crippled beggar leaning on his crutches called out so loudly that bystanders turned to look. *'Ahh, apey duwata ada kollek innawa wagey.'*

Ahh it looks like our daughter has got herself a boy today.

To Ravi's embarrassment, Janaki just grinned and stuck her tongue out.

She bought two neat brown paper wrapped packets of rice from a villainous looking vendor, another friend, who'd set up a table under a jam fruit tree on the pavement. If ever there was a man who needed to be screened for communicable deceases, this fellow was a prime candidate.

'Aren't you going to work today?' Ravi asked jestingly.

'No need! Have money now. Work when money gone.'

'Who taught you to speak English?'

'Madam. Good, no?'

She seemed so proud of her accomplishment that Ravi didn't have the heart to tell her what he really thought.

'Yes. Good.'

Janaki wanted to visit the owner of the cement store to pay her rent. She led the way to a surprisingly spacious structure, opening into a yard off the main road, filled with cement, lime and piles of bricks. Shuttering planks and bamboo scaffolding was piled outside. Mudalali was a dark man with thinning hair and bloodshot eyes of a boozer. A substantial belly spread around him like a lifebelt.

Ravi, standing quietly in the yard, saw him greet Janaki with a broad smile. Ravi wondered what it was about this little thief that made people take to her. He left her to her business and gazed at the lake shimmering in the background.

There had been a time when his dad had been keen on fishing.

The season for trolling off the western coast was during the northeast monsoon when the sea was reasonably calm. Sunday mornings would find them chugging out of the Kelani mouth in a hired boat, just as the sun peeped over the treetops behind them.

David would put out two rods marking one for himself while Tilak and Ravi took turns with the other, thirty minutes at a time. When it was Tilak's turn to mind the rod, Ravi would lie on the engine cover with his hands under his head and watch the birds in the sky above him. Terns and Gulls soared and wheeled in the wind. Of them all, it was the occasional Sea Eagle that captured his imagination. Gliding over them with motionless wings while it searched for an unwary fish to come to the surface, it presented a spectacle so irresistible that Ravi would forego his turn at the rod if he spotted one close by.

He had thought the world was like that.

Below the surface of the water, hidden and unseen, were the poor. To his childish mind they were a faceless multitude that was unimportant and uninteresting, of no consequence in his world. His family lived on the surface, as did all middle class people, breathing God's air and living normal lives. A little dull perhaps, but still …

The rich were different. They had privileged lives soaring in the air above, wild and free, like the Terns and the Gulls.

Hovering above even the Terns and Gulls was the majestic White-bellied Sea Eagle, remorseless and deadly. Watching and waiting! When the moment was just right the Eagle would plummet out of the sky with those awful talons stretched open to take its prey from the surface of the water — or below it.

The super rich! The super powerful!

Ravi had longed to be an Eagle, rapacious and untouchable!

Instead of being an all-powerful Eagle soaring in the air, he'd now been forced to submerge himself in the water, a fugitive instead of a predator. In the world of the poor under the surface, he had expected to see faceless robots, eking out their miserable existence like termites in a mound. Instead he was surprised to find life under the surface pulsating; full of colour and character.

He felt like a snorkeller looking at a coral reef for the first time and being startled, perhaps even charmed, by the life forms he found there.

When he turned back to the shop, he saw a handwritten sign in Sinhala — "Bajaj for hire. 200/-". It struck him that he needed a means of transport if he wanted to take the fight to Shalindra and had been wondering if he should buy a second hand motor bicycle. He'd never driven a trishaw and didn't have a license. On the other hand, it was perfect cover. Trishaws buzzed around the roads like flies making a perfect nuisance of themselves to other motorists. But no one took any real notice of an individual driver.

The trishaw was ancient, with chipped red paint and a canvas hood with patches sewn on older patches. The mudalali only glanced at his driving license before returning it to him. He was more interested in collecting Rupees 1400/- being rent for a week in advance. The trishaw started readily though and moments later he was nervously first-gearing his way along Galle Road.

Janaki was delighted. She bounced about in the rear seat, now leaning out of one side and now the other, waving her arms and yelling to shoo traffic out of his way. He was in a bath of nervous perspiration, and still in first gear, when he crossed the main road and reached the relative safety of his lane. He stopped with a jerk under the mango tree and climbed down.

Ravi sat on the step pulling the wrappings off his purchases when Janaki casually reached under her dress and pulled out a pair of black denims and then a black T-shirt. Her eyes were dancing with merriment when she offered the clothes to him.

Ravi realized she'd been shoplifting. He guessed that she had some kind of elastic strap round her waist and wide slits in her pockets to help practice her trade. His first instinct was to belt her one for the unnecessary risk she had exposed him to. He turned angrily towards her but found her looking at him anxiously, like a Spaniel he had once owned, waiting for his approval. He found his fury fading into a kind of resigned amusement.

She obviously was a reckless idiot without any conception of right and wrong, but there was something in her personality, some innocent charm, that made people like her. He felt it too and knew that it was dangerous – for him.

Ravi spent the afternoon checking the trishaw and then driving it up and down the gravel track for practice. He walked back to the bazaar to buy a length of chain and a stout padlock and secured the vehicle to a low branch of the mango tree.

Janaki had wandered down the lane to catch up with neighborhood gossip so Ravi tried to effect some improvements to his end of the attic. Nails in the rafters to hang his clothes, a line for his wet towel and a cardboard carton to store his new clothes. The sun went down in an explosion of red and orange over the bridge on his right, but Ravi saw a mass of dark clouds building up and covering the eastern sky. An evening thunderstorm, a feature of the northeast monsoon, was due at any time.

It began to rain soon afterwards and Janaki came running back giggling, soaked hair plastered to her skull. Her friends in the neighbourhood had all wanted to know about her new lover she reported, laughing.

The rain lashed the little verandah forcing them to climb into the attic for shelter.

Janaki asked, 'What about your *hathura*? His car place you know?'
Hathura. Enemy.
'Yes.'
'Rääta gihin okkoma kudu karamu.'
Let's go at night and smash all his cars.
'No.'
She was silent for a while, then, 'Piyal put sugar in car one day. No start afterwards.'
Ravi felt a shiver of excitement.

He remembered reading about it. How vehicles could be disabled by putting sugar in the petrol tank. The engine seized up very quickly. Shalindra would be badly hit if all his cars were disabled.

Shalindra had destroyed every single thing that was dear to him. But by those very actions, Shalindra had also set Ravi free. He now had no property or business to defend, no loved ones to be concerned about. He could strike at Shalindra and his interests whenever and however he chose and Shalindra couldn't strike back. He knew that the power had tilted back to his side. All he had to do was remain hidden.

He wanted to think it out carefully before he decided on his next step. He changed the subject before Janaki could continue.

'This Piyal, how long have you been with him?'
'Long time.'
'Why do you call him Kadu Piyal?'
Kadu meant sword.
'He carry big knife,' her eyes grew larger. 'Always.'
'Is that the knife you showed me yesterday?'
'No. He have big knife.'
'Why is he in jail?'

'Minihekkwa käpuwa.'
He cut a man.

*

Ravi had no difficulty in following Pathirana's instructions. Shalindra had named his business, Dilini Motors, after his daughter, the little girl he'd seen prancing about at the Golf Club. The name was proudly emblazoned on a long board that spanned the road frontage. The open yard was filled wall to wall with Japanese cars and off-roaders, with a small office building forming one lateral boundary. The road frontage had a five-foot metal fence with a small guardroom at one end.

Ravi parked the trishaw some distance away and walked in. A bored security officer in a dark brown uniform waved him inside. Ravi inspected several cars and finally seemed to settle on a white Nissan, parked in the third row from the front. The salesman, who had been hovering around hopefully, bustled up.

'Full option, sir! Three years old, but only twenty four thousand on meter.'

'What are you expecting?'

'Seventeen lakhs, but I'll speak to the manager and get a reduction of fifty.'

'Can you arrange the lease?'

'Definitely.'

Ravi pretended to think it over.

'I want to test drive this one.'

The salesman looked satisfied but just a little less obliging now that he thought the fish was firmly hooked. He looked glumly at the mass of vehicles that had to be moved in order to get that particular Nissan on the road, shrugged his shoulders and went towards the office.

Ravi followed close behind.

The manager, a short fellow with massive forearms, was leaning back in his seat and talking loudly into a mobile phone. He waved the salesman towards a metal cabinet that stood against the wall. Ravi watched the salesman as he unlocked the cabinet to reveal a wooden board with keys arranged in neat rows and columns. Ravi saw him count under his breath, selecting the fifth key in each of the first three rows.

Ravi stood near the entrance to the office. The door was fitted with a Union night latch but there was also a hasp and staple fitted, so they must padlock the door as well.

The salesman cleared a way by parking the other two cars on the pavement and took him for a quick drive round the block. Ravi promised faithfully to come back the next morning to complete the deal.

It was just after sunset when Ravi drove past the Majestic City complex to Bambalapitiya railway station. He didn't realize that there was a regular rank for three-wheelers in a shadowed area across the road, till the driver of the first vehicle came towards him truculently.

'Hire ekak nevai malli,' Ravi said quickly, 'nangi ekka yanna āwey.'

I'm not here for a hire, brother. Just to pick my sister.

The man wasn't convinced but moved away slowly. A nearly empty train going towards Fort pulled in, and minutes later, a crowded commuter train screeched to a halt at the near platform. Weary passengers began to stream through the narrow exit and squeezed between them, a small figure in a dress like a pillowcase.

Grinning broadly.

Ravi took off as soon as she climbed in, not wanting another argument with the regulars.

'Sir went to car place?'

'Yes. We'll go there again now.'

She had gone off to work that morning, but Ravi had persuaded her to get off at Bambalapitiya on the way back. She had grumbled that the journey from Fort to Bambalapitiya hardly gave her enough time to attend to business, but had finally fallen in with his plans. Ravi felt her moving about in the rear seat and guessed she was fishing out the wallet she'd lifted.

'Ū māva rävättuwa,' she complained, sounding thoroughly aggrieved.

He cheated me.

'Mokkadda prashney?'

What's the problem?

'Hondata ändagena hitiyata, sarkkuwey hulang.'

He was so well dressed but no money in the pocket.

Ravi laughed to himself as she uttered a disgusted oath and flung the wallet into a pile of garbage on the roadside.

They parked across the road next to a stall selling hoppers and *kotthu roti*. Business was good, as a constant stream of vehicles pulled in to collect their dinner. The *kotthu* man made a loud drumming noise every time he pounded the skillet with two sharp-edged metal plates.

Janaki asked for some money and bought stuffed rotis. Ravi hadn't eaten since that morning, and found the nameless filling delicious. They watched the yard across the road as they ate. A security guard stepped onto the pavement to chat with a man carrying a shopping bag, probably a servant from a neighboring house. There appeared to be only one guard on duty, a silver haired man in a brown uniform.

Janaki waited till the man with the shopping bag moved off.

'Sir can pick me up in five minutes?' She asked over her shoulder as she eased herself between the vehicles and across the road. Moments later she had struck up a conversation with the guard.

The man was obviously cautious at first, but after a few minutes Ravi could tell that he was falling under her spell. He could see the man grinning and waving his arms. Ravi eased the trishaw into the stream of traffic then made a U turn to bring the vehicle in front of the yard. Janaki waved to the guard, trotted across the pavement, and dived into the vehicle.

'His name Ratna,' she said gaily as Ravi drove off. 'On duty every night.'

'Mm.'

'He has daughter, age like me. He is very sad I am doing *vesi* work.'

Vesi. Prostitute.

'You told him you were a prostitute?'

'Hmm. *Vesi!*' She giggled. 'I told you were my *pimpiya.*'

Ravi felt outraged to be called a pimp but realized it was really a good cover. In the strata of society he was now moving in, a pimp and his prostitute would blend in very naturally.

*

Ravi found it strange that his conscience was quiet. Just months ago the thought of wreaking another man's property would have appalled him, yet here he was on his way to do just that and he had no qualms.

But he had not slept well.

His mother always wanted Christmas celebrated just right and by the whole family. That meant mass in the morning, followed by a vast and boring round of visits to sundry relatives, but the high point was the Christmas dinner just for the family. There'd been four of them when his brother was alive and after they lost him, Tilak filled the gap.

He could not bear the thought that it was all gone. Forever gone. He cried then, lying there in a wretched attic on a sheet of cardboard. Bitter tears that did little to ease his pain and loss. All his agony had been caused by one ruthless foe, a man who would go to any length to crush anyone who stood up to him.

In the grey early hours his sadness slowly turned again to anger, cold and implacable. He knew that he would not turn away till Shalindra Premasiri was crushed.

Salim, the key maker, was grumbling that there was no room for his feet. Janaki was whining that she was hungry and wanted to eat first. Ravi ignored the moaning and tried to concentrate on keeping the trishaw steady in the stream of traffic. He was getting proficient now, able to weave in and out of traffic and stay clear of the private buses. He already had painful calluses on his fingers and palms from handling the throttle and the hand clutch.

The 50 kg bag of sugar did take up all the leg space at the back. Salim and Janaki were crouched on the seat clutching a funnel and a metal scoop. Salim's bag of keys was pushed down the vacant space behind the rear seat.

Ravi allowed his plan to unravel inside his head one last time. Now that he was about to actually carry it out, he had again expected to feel some inner revulsion.

He felt nothing.

Salim started his refrain again, leaning over Ravi's shoulder. Ravi felt the man's breath in his cheek and turned his face away in disgust.

242

'Magey salli dhenawa kiiva ...,'
You promised me the money ...
Salim was Janaki's friend, the key cutter from Moratuwa town who'd promised to do the job for Rupees 2000/-. He was demanding payment in advance but Ravi didn't trust the man.

'Sir salli devi, ivasala inna, aiya,' Janaki placated the man.
Sir will give the money. Be patient.

It had been Janaki's idea to act like a tart.

It gave her an excuse to hang around near the car yard every evening. So she dressed in her best clothes, no different really to the other clothes she wore, and did her face using a pilfered stock of cosmetics. Liberal applications of rouge and lipstick in her inexpert hands did make her look older and, Ravi had to admit, whore-like.

Ravi had dropped her near the car yard every evening and it had not taken her long to charm the old guard. Twice Ravi had forced a thoroughly embarrassed Reshane to drive by, pick the girl up and drop her further off on Dickman's Road. On other days, Ravi would allow her an hour to chat up the old man and then pick her up in the trishaw. The guard believed she'd failed to make a score on those days.

From the second day, Janaki had carried a large handbag on a shoulder strap and in it, a 375 ml bottle of arrack. Janaki had shown the guard her secret weapon, saying that her clients were always more generous once they'd had a couple of tots. It wasn't long before she had offered the guard a small sample which he knocked off with relish, throwing the contents of his glass down his throat and then wiping his mouth with the back of his hand with a stifled 'Ahh!'

After that, the old man had allowed her to wait inside the guardroom.

Only today, when she planned to pour out a more liberal dose, the arrack would be doctored. Ravi had carefully crushed 20 tablets of Valium and dissolved it in the arrack. If Janaki gave the man two shots of 50 ml each, he'd have taken the best part of seven tablets. The old toper knocked the shot back with one huge swallow so he'd never notice a change in taste. How long would it take for him to pass out?

Longer than Ravi had expected.

He had parked the three-wheeler near the food stall across the road and could see the guard chatting animatedly with Janaki. The food stall put up its shutters for the night as the last car pulled away. Ravi put the trishaw on the road knowing a stationary vehicle, specially a three-wheeler, would invite police attention. He circled the block slowly, ignoring Salim's grumbling from the back.

He noticed the change during the third circuit. The guardroom light was out. Ravi drove the trishaw up to the gate and found Janaki holding it open. He drove through and Janaki closed it after him.

'Vädey hari. U hodhatama budhi. Märillada danney nä.'

The job is done. He's fast asleep. Don't know if he's dead.

Ravi rushed into the darkened guardroom and took stock. He scanned the road carefully but couldn't spot anyone taking an interest in the yard. The old guard was still seated in his chair with his upper body slumped across the table. To Ravi's relief he was breathing noisily, half snore and half gurgle. Ravi turned the old man's head to ease his breathing and then examined the panel of switches behind the desk. By trial and error he turned off the lights illuminating the center and back of the yard leaving just the ones by the road.

Salim got to work on the office door. He had been nervous and fidgety all evening, but once on the job he settled down like a professional.

The bastard had done this kind of work before.

The door was secured with a padlock in addition to the Union night latch. Salim opened his sling bag to reveal a number of wire loops, each having dozens of old keys strung together. He knelt down before the door and began trying his keys with Janaki leaning over him, holding a small flashlight. Ravi stood in the guardroom watching the road.

A Police car went by. The cop in the passenger seat glanced at the yard and said something to the driver. The car slowed nearly to a standstill as the cops stared suspiciously at the yard. Ravi held his breath as the car drifted past and then picked up speed. Would they swing round and come back? He had locked the gate so the cops would have to force it open to come in. If they did, Ravi and his friends would have to scale the high wall at the back to escape.

He glanced impatiently at his watch. Salim was taking too long. Then Janaki was at the door.

'Hari.'

Ok.

Ravi left Janaki to watch the road and went into the office. He shut the door and switched on a light. Ravi pointed to the metal cupboard. Salim started to say something but changed his mind when he caught Ravi's eye. Five nerve wracking minutes later the lock squeaked back and they had the cupboard open.

They left Salim on watch and got to work. The keys were arranged neatly on the board in rows and columns, just the way the cars were parked. Ravi unlocked them all, leaving only the front row that was well lit and visible from the road. It was tiresome work thereafter to collect a full measure of sugar into the metal scoop and, using the funnel he'd brought along, carefully pour the contents into the petrol tank of each vehicle. He continued doggedly ignoring Janaki's pleas that she was tired and hungry and Salim's near panic when the patrol car went past again.

It was close to midnight when the last vehicle was done. Ravi spent more time making sure there were no traces of sugar on the ground. He then locked all the cars and carefully replaced the keys in order.

Salim got to work again, locking the key cupboard and the office. Ravi examined the guard. He was still sprawled across the table but his breathing was quieter now. Ravi hoped he'd wake up before his relief turned up in the morning.

Time to leave.

Salim had got off at Lunawa junction, still grumbling that the agreed amount was not sufficient to cover the time and the risk.

It was well after midnight when they got back to Janaki's attic. Ravi bathed at the well in the next garden but the girl had thrown herself down on the steps and was lying there with her head cradled in her arms, refusing to move. Ravi, unable to stand the sharp stink of her sweat soaked clothes, finally chased her off to wash herself and change her clothes. She came back complaining about the cold but cheered up when Ravi took out the parcel of roti and curry they'd bought at an all-night boutique.

'I help sir today, no?'

Ravi, cautiously: 'Yes.'

'Now sir's job finish, sir will do my thing?'

'What thing? What do you want to do?'

'Premila House!. Punish Mr. Wije.'

'Ahh. What can I do? You'd better forget about that.'

'But sir promised,' Janaki wailed, sounding close to tears. 'I helped sir also.'

Ravi looked at her with resigned exasperation. He had no interest in her battles but she was an amusing little devil, and she had indeed been a great help today.

'All right. I'll think of something. Be patient.'

The promise was enough. She grinned and brightened up immediately.

28

Pathirana had helped Ravi to locate Shalindra Premasiri's home at Charles Drive, off Duplication Road. Seeing the comfortable bungalow set in a large garden made Ravi realize he'd need to do a lot more than damage a few cars to bring this man to his knees. He'd been watching the house for four days now and was beginning to pick up their routines. Shalindra in his silver Montero had passed him several times with a casual glance but no sign of recognition.

Ravi started parking his trishaw next to a tiny kiosk a crippled man had set up two doors from Premasiri's home. It wasn't a great place to pick up hires for a three-wheeler but it gave him an excuse to hang around, and he did get an occasional hire to drop someone on Galle Road.

There appeared to be two live-in women servants in the Premasiri home. An obligatory security guard sat in a little green box near the ornate metal gate. A driver came in every morning at 7:00, an egg bald man dressed in a spotless white shirt and sarong, to drive the little girl to nursery school. Maduri Premasiri seemed to be a good mother for she never failed to accompany the child in the morning and again to pick her up at 11.30.

Except on Wednesday.

On Wednesday, Maduri dropped the child at school and went for her game of Bridge. The old driver dropped her at the stadium of the old racecourse that now was home to the Bridge Federation. She would be gone all day, so the driver went by himself to pick the little girl from St. Bridget's nursery on Maitland Crescent.

Shalindra Premasiri kept irregular hours. He'd leave the house anytime between 9.00 and 11.00 for his office at Lucky Plaza. He'd be back for a late lunch after the school traffic settled down at 3.00 p.m. Later in the evening he'd dress up in a trendy tracksuit and head for the Sports Ministry grounds on some days, and on others it was the gym at The Hilton.

Lost your taste for golf, have you pal?

That Saturday morning had been a busy time for Maduri, taking the little girl for tennis lessons and then for ballet. Shalindra came bursting out of the house just after 10.30 yelling for the guard to open the gate. He backed the big vehicle recklessly on to the road and raced away. Ravi took off after him but had no chance of keeping up. He lost sight of the vehicle on Duplication Road and turned back.

Shalindra was back in about an hour still apparently in a foul mood. He nearly rammed his own gate, yelling at the guard to get off his butt. He drove out more sedately a little later and Ravi followed him to the Capri Club.

Saturday afternoon beers. Sacred.

Ravi calculated that it was safe to leave Premasiri there for a while. He had arranged to pick up Janaki outside Fort station at 12.30 and it was about time.

His phone rang.

'Kotuwata enna epā,' Janaki sounded shaken. *'Kollupitiyata enna. Ikkmanata.'*

Don't go to Fort. Come to Kollupitiya. Quick.

'Mokada wuney? Kiyanna.'

What happened? Tell me.

But she had rung off. Ravi turned towards Galle Road, through the traffic lights at Kollupitiya junction and into Station Road. The station was deserted when he got there but a down train pulled in a few minutes later. A few passengers trickled out and then Janaki came running towards him.

She dived into the back of the trishaw.

'Yanna. Yanna.'

Go. Go.

Ravi started the vehicle and pulled away from the station. He heard the girl trying to catch her breath.

'What happened? What's the problem?'

'Piyal hireng eliyey. Māva allanna hāduwa.'

Piyal is out of jail. He tried to catch me.

Ravi felt cold.

Kadu Piyal was out of jail and looking for the girl he owned. What the hell was he, Ravi, doing in this mess?

Ravi turned left at the lights and drove straight to Galle Face green. The umbrella lovers were out in force even in the blazing heat of the early afternoon. Ravi found a vacant space under a half dead Palmyra tree and parked the trishaw. He took the girl by the hand and made her sit by his side. Just one more Galle Face couple.

'Tell me what happened. Are you sure it was Piyal?'

'Yes, Piyal. Was waiting at going out place in station.' Relating the incident seemed to agitate the girl. 'He tried to catch. I ran back into station and hiding.'

'Is he your husband?'

'Husband, no, no,' she seemed appalled he'd even asked. 'Piyal like boys! He keep me to bring money.'

'Why are you frightened of him?'

'He beat me. Tie up and beat with belt when money not enough,' she turned her head and looked into Ravi's eyes, gripping his arm tightly. She seemed terrified. 'Don't let him take me. Better to die.'

'Does he know the place we stay — in Moratuwa?' Ravi asked cautiously.

'No. No. He keep me at Ragama, work on Negombo and Kandy trains. When police take Piyal, I run away. Find this place.'

'How did he find you today?'

'He know I work on train. He know I come to Fort in morning then take office train back. He wait.'

'Hmm.'

'Can't work on train now,' she was calmer now. 'Maybe I start *hora salli* business.'

Ravi looked at her sharply. *Hora salli* meant counterfeit notes.

'Where do you get *hora salli*?'

'I know the man. I give Rupees 500/- in good money, he give Rupees 1000/- note in *hora salli*.'

'Then?'

'Maybe I sell to shops for Rupees 600/-. Make Rupees 100/- every note. Good no?'

Ravi stared at the sea trying to put his thoughts in order. Janaki had helped him when he was desperate. She'd been a staunch ally during the attack on the car yard and would be helpful in the future. He owed her and wanted to help.

But not to the extent of getting chopped up by some sword wielding thug.

On the other hand Piyal didn't know where they were hiding, so they were safe for the moment. If she stayed off the train!

Ravi decided to carry on with his surveillance. He drove back to the Capri but the silver Montero was gone. He breathed a sigh of relief when he found both vehicles parked safely at the Premasiri home. Shalindra had come home for lunch and a nap.

He noticed that once she had unloaded her worries on him, Janaki lost no time in recovering her normal high spirits. She loved the big houses on either side of the road, being particularly taken with a garish monstrosity with blue glass and pink walls. She chattered on till she suddenly realized she was hungry.

She didn't waste a moment telling Ravi about it.

Ravi groaned inwardly knowing she'd keep moaning till she was fed. He thought for a moment and decided to try Perera & Sons, on Duplication Road. The place was half full but he managed to grab a table near the front window. Janaki was clearly impressed with the place and gazed around with awe, especially at the people with fat wallets crowding round the cashiers desk.

Ravi recognized that look in her eye. 'No. Not here.'

'Is easy.'

'No!'

She shrugged her shoulders in resignation and then brightened up when she saw the plate of pastries the waiter set before her. She adored *"chainis"* rolls and immediately asked for more.

As he watched her stuff herself Ravi realized he was fond of the little thief. Her mop of untidy hair above the small delicate features made her head seem too big for her body. Stick like arms emerged incongruously from the oversized dress but her hands were beautifully formed with long delicate fingers. She had grasped a *chainis* roll with both hands and was feeding herself with a small frown of concentration.

Ravi knew he couldn't possibly let her fall into the hands of some thug who'd abuse her. He wasn't equipped to fight a knife-wielding killer either. Was there some other way?

'How old are you?'

'Duh nuh,' she had her mouth full of food.

'What?'

'Don know. Before run away madam say maybe I am 15. Not sure.'

'How long is it since you ran away?'

'Two year. Maybe three.'

Janaki went off to find the washroom.

Ravi found a newspaper on the chair next to his and glanced idly at the headlines. The main story was about a massive racket in customs. Another described a robbery of a jewellery store in Sea Street. And on the side, as if of lesser importance, "AMC vows to leave coalition. Another general election likely".

An idea began to form in his head, something that would bring Shalindra to his knees. He needed to think it out.

Janaki came back looking cheerful. Too cheerful! Ravi knew immediately that she'd lifted some poor bastard's wallet and wanted to whack her on the side of her head. He paid quickly and bundled her out of there before the loss was discovered.

Charles Drive was quiet when they got back. The two vehicles were still parked in the porch and the security guard was asleep in his little green box. The French windows in the large sitting room were open and, ghost like through the lace curtains, Ravi saw someone moving about.

It was nearly 5.00 when the family came out dressed for the evening. The little girl's voice could be heard down the road as she pranced around excitedly. They climbed into the Montero and Shalindra drove off. First stop Majestic City shopping complex. Ravi parked the trishaw on Station Road and hurried into the atrium dragging the girl behind him.

'If you steal anything I will beat you,' he said severely. 'I really will.'

She just grinned showing all her teeth, then squeezed his arm. 'Have enough for today.'

Before Ravi could think of a suitably crushing response he saw the Premasiri family coming up the corridor from the underground car park. Ravi took firm hold of the girl to avoid losing her in the crowd and also to keep her out of mischief. She liked that and kept pointing out the wonders she saw in the display windows.

The Premasiris' walked slowly through the shops stopping only to buy the little girl a pair of sneakers. Then they entered the Food City supermarket for what looked like their weekly groceries. Ravi watched them patiently till they carried their heavy load of parcels down to the car park. He raced round to the exit and managed to follow the Montero to MacDonalds.

Janaki was getting bored and starting to complain she was hungry again. Ravi had just started the trishaw to head for Moratuwa when his phone rang.

Pathirana: 'Mr. Ravi, you are a hell of a fellow. You never told me you were going to hit the cars.'

'What are you talking about?'

'Engines seized in three new cars. I hear the buyers are going to courts,' Pathirana sounded jubilant. 'Shalindra is stripping the engines of all the others.'

'Good.'

'So it was you?'

'Forget about that. There's something else. If I could get Salindra to commit a crime at a shopping complex, how can I get the Police to keep watch and catch him in the act?'

'What crime?'

'I'll tell you later.'

'You'll need a plain clothes man.'

'OK. Can you arrange it?'

'No. I don't have the authority, but what about Tennakoon? He's a Deputy Minister now. If there's an election, Shalindra will be his opponent.'

*

They were standing on the exposed platform at Slave Island station. The stink of urine from the waiting room behind him was like a foul blanket someone had flung over his head. Office workers stood around him patiently clutching their lunch boxes and briefcases, waiting for the train to show up.

Getting on another train was the last thing Ravi wanted to do, but it had turned out that the only contact Janaki had with the fake currency dealer was on the 5.05 train from Fort to Panadura. They had to board that train and locate the man.

With Piyal stalking them, Ravi had decided that going to Fort was too dangerous, so he'd picked the next stop. Janaki stood tensely at his side, looking about her nervously. No chatter today.

The train was crowded already but the new passengers somehow contrived to squeeze themselves into the carriages. Janaki led the way into the first compartment. Once inside she left him and skillfully wormed her way first to the upper end and then down the compartment looking for her quarry. She was back with a disappointed shake of her head just when the train began slowing down for Kollupitiya station. They drew a blank in the second compartment as well and changed again at Bambalapitiya.

Janaki spotted the man as soon as they stepped into the third compartment and squeezed Ravi's arm excitedly. She leaned forward and spoke to a thin fellow with long oily black hair and funny eyes that never stayed still. Ravi thought he looked more like a druggie than a counterfeiter. Probably just a small-time broker.

Yes he could supply the goods, the man had said, his eyes darting all over the carriage. Bring Rupees 5000/- in cash for the Rupees 10,000/- Ravi wanted. The Buhari Hotel in Maradana, at noon the next day, was the meeting point.

The train was just picking up speed after Wellawatta station when Ravi heard Janaki scream. A short thickset man dressed in black had grasped her by the neck. As Ravi watched in horror the man, who had his back to him, almost lifted her off her feet and shook her as one would a rag doll. Janaki's eyes were terrified but she didn't utter another sound.

Piyal!

'*Vesa balli,*' he said loudly as he lifted his right hand to strike her. Prostitute bitch.

Ravi reached out and hauled on the emergency chain with all his strength. The brakes locked with a loud screech and people inside the carriage were thrown violently into each other. Luggage from the overhead rack crashed onto passengers seated below and added to the screams and confusion.

Piyal had been thrown against some passengers making him lose his balance and release the girl. Ravi braced himself behind the man and hit him just above the hipbone, where he thought the kidneys would be. He put all his strength into the blow but it was like hitting a wall. It must have hurt though, because the man arched his back and was slow to turn around. Ravi hit him again and pushed him roughly so that he lost his balance again and fell, with a roar of anger, on some other passengers trying to get off the floor. Ravi grabbed the girl by the hand, pushed his way roughly to the carriage door and jumped out of the stationary train.

And ran.

The road was badly lit so he couldn't tell if Piyal was close behind. And he was too frightened to stop. They ran till they were exhausted and finally reached the friendly lights of Galle Road, just by the Wellawatte Police Station.

The pavements were teeming with working people on their way home. Ravi crossed the road to a crowded bus stand. He stood at the back with Janaki at his side; the other passengers screened her tiny figure. Ravi felt he could safely look over their heads knowing that Piyal had never seen his face.

Ravi saw him then, frog-like in black, with long wrestler's arms. He was standing at the top of Hamer's Avenue and looking up and down the main road. A bus pulled up in front of him and Ravi used his strength ruthlessly to push his way in, dragging the girl behind him.

Through a slit in the window as the bus pulled away he saw Piyal still standing on the far side. But he was staring at the bus.

Janaki was sprawled on the rear steps pretending to be asleep. Ravi prodded her with his toe. 'Go and bathe.'

'No.'

Ravi could smell the stale sweat from her clothes and was not overjoyed by the prospect of it filling the little attic above. At the beginning Janaki had been in the habit of just sleeping in her day clothes and only washing up in the morning. She hated going down to the well in the dark and Ravi had to use all manner of threats to persuade her to bathe at night. Words had no effect on that day, so Ravi finally had to rap her on the head with a single knuckle.

She howled as if he had fractured her skull.

She jumped to her feet in a fury and stood glowering at him for a while. Seeing him unmoved, she finally turned and went off, dragging her feet and muttering to herself.

Ravi scrolled through the memory chip of his hand phone and located Sandika's number. Pathirana had told him that Sandika was an important man now, Coordinating Secretary to the Deputy Minister Tennakoon.

Sandika was pleased to hear from him and more than happy to co-operate in the scheme to fix Shalindra.

'Sure, Mr. Ravi. I can arrange for a plain-clothes cop to stand by. Give me the full details.'

Ravi described what he had in mind and they promised to stay in touch.

When Janaki came back her mood had improved. She was running her fingers through her mop of wet hair and stopped to flick some water on him.

'*Napura.*'

Wickedo.

'*Podi oora,*' Ravi replied.

Small pig.

She prodded him with her foot as she passed behind him.

'Why you beat me?' She demanded.

'Good for you to bathe,' Ravi smiled. 'You smell better.'

Strangely his reply seemed to mollify her. Ravi had a suspicion that despite her grumbling, the imposed discipline made her comfortable. More secure.

She wanted to eat then and brought out their parcel of hoppers.

Ravi enjoyed the quiet evenings in the back porch. The gentle wave motion of the lake made a rhythmic sloshing sound against the reeds and mangroves at the waterline. It was still and quiet after the children in the next compound were put to sleep. A tiny fishing boat drifted past from time to time, kerosene lamp flickering in the breeze. He was getting used to the faint odour of mud and stagnant water now.

Ravi sat with his back to the wall, staring at the water.

Block out the past – it was over and done. Focus on bringing Shalindra down. Nothing else matters.

Janaki lay sprawled on the floor near him, chattering away. She always had something to talk about. A new dress she'd seen in a shop and wanted to buy, or steal. An injury to her foot she had sustained when jumping from the train or a new pimple on her forehead.

But mostly she talked about people she knew.

A crippled lottery ticket seller who induced her to buy just one ticket each week! She didn't know how to check the result so she simply gave it back to the man the following week and he told her if she had won — or not. She hadn't yet. Lahiru aiya, the one eyed man who sold bundles of green vegetables harvested from his *kira kotuwa* by the lake. He had been bitten by a snake but saved from death by Weerawansa Vedamahaththaya, the ayurveda specialist living near the bridge. Sarpin, the carpenter from three houses down the lane, had run off with his sister-in-law, leaving his wife and two children destitute.

'What sir doing with *hora salli*?' Janaki changed tack suddenly. 'Going to put jeep man in trouble?'

'Yes.'

'Sir want my help?'

'Yes.'

'I help sir always but sir never do my job.' Janaki said it softly but there was a strange note in it, expressive of both disappointment and resignation. As though she could expect no better from anyone and that touched Ravi.

'All right then. I'll do your job.'

Janaki sat up, grasping his hand in her excitement.

"Really? Sir won't lie?' She shook his arm for reassurance. 'We go there and hammer all?'

'No. Something better than that. Where is this Premila Home?'

'Lunawa, Station Road.'

'How many children there?'

'Don't know. Many children.'

'Madam's husband, Mr. Wije, he only comes on weekends?'

'Yes.'

'And he takes children to the suddhas where?'

'Take in van. Same road have motel near sea.'

'Only girls?'

'Boys also, sometimes.'

29

Premila House was old.

It must have been an impressive building in its day with its high, tiled roof and imposing portico. Erected like many of its kind, Ravi felt, by a businessman who had struck it rich. He'd have wanted to impress his neighbours, and must have done too. But later generations had found the money all gone and the old monstrosity too costly to maintain. So now it was an orphanage where, if Janaki was to be believed, fresh horrors were inflicted on already traumatized orphan children.

Ravi parked the trishaw further down the road and strolled past the entrance. Old wrought iron gates leaned drunkenly on corroded hinges, permanently open. The white van parked under the brightly lit porch hadn't been there when Ravi surveyed the premises on the previous day.

Mr. Wije had come down for the weekend.

Ravi went on till he came to the corner of the property. The yellow boundary wall was strictly for show, just for the road frontage. A live fence, with ample cattle created gaps, ran down the side separating the orphanage from the vacant lot next to it.

Satisfied that there was no one in the garden, Ravi walked back to the trishaw. He was surprised to find the girl, who'd been keen to walk in and assault everyone, nervously biting her lower lip.

'*Māva thaniyama thiyanna epā. Ung māva allaganivi,*' Janaki said in a small voice.

Don't leave me alone. They'll catch me.

He took Reshane's Sony Camcorder she'd been holding to her chest and found it damp from her hands. He held the unfamiliar device in his hands; going through the routine he'd practiced all morning. He had already taken a copy of that morning's Daily News and scanned the front page onto the stick. That would help establish that the recording was made on, or after, today the fifth of January. He started the trishaw and drove it to the vacant lot.

He ushered the still nervous Janaki ahead of him, and using her as a screen, scanned the name board over the gate. Ravi stood for a moment at the corner of the property till the road was clear and then pushed his way through the fence and into the garden. He had noted that there were several mango trees in the garden but none of them big enough to hide behind. But there was a hedge of some thick stuff lining the driveway that would cover them, provided they sat on their haunches.

Someone opened the front door.

Janaki turned as if to run away and Ravi had to grasp her firmly by the arm. He felt her trembling. A sari-clad woman walked into the porch and collected something from the van. The front door closed behind her.

They reached the hedge safely and sat down to wait. Ravi checked the Camcorder again. Janaki was seated with her back to the hedge, looking away from the building with her hands crossed tightly across her chest.

His knees were killing him. He could feel the girl shivering as she sat close to him and knew she wouldn't be able to hold her nerve much longer. Ravi was beginning to wonder if they had drawn a blank, when the front door opened and a man came out in a cloud of cigarette smoke. A heavy man with a full head of jet-black hair. Well-pressed pants held high over his hips by a pair of old fashioned suspenders.

He walked to the edge of the porch and looked up at the sky. The end of his cigarette glowed red in the middle of his face. Ravi started his recorder praying that he'd get it right.

A moment later the woman came out again leading two girls. Ravi couldn't believe it.

These bastards were still up to the same game.

One girl said something in a tearful voice and the woman shushed her. She opened the rear door of the van and bundled them in. Janaki turned around when she heard the girl's voice. She started shaking again and clung to Ravi's arm.

The fat man threw his cigarette away and climbed into the van. The woman went inside closing the door behind her. Ravi waited for the headlights to sweep over his head, then turned and ran for the gap in the hedge.

By the time he got the trishaw on the road the taillights had disappeared. But Janaki had shown him the motel she'd been taken to years ago. Were they still using the same dump? Ravi raced the vehicle towards the rail tracks and turning on to Beach Road, saw faintly in the distance the brake lights of a white vehicle brighten for a moment before it turned off the road.

He took the trishaw past the motel, leapt off almost before it came to a standstill, grabbed the Camcorder and ran. He got a distant, and very fleeting, scan of the girls being helped down and through the open front door.

Was it enough?

He scanned the dilapidated blue and yellow building for good measure.

Ravi bought string hoppers from a kiosk in town and drove back to the attic. Janaki hadn't spoken a word and went off meekly to bathe when he told her to. Ravi replayed his recording and found the images jumping all over the screen, but the clarity was amazing. If he went to the police with this they'd have to investigate and question the girls.

Then Mr. Wije and his wretched wife would be well and truly screwed.

They had finished their meal when dark clouds built up over the lake and the wind picked up. They hurried into the attic when rain swept through the little verandah. The girl had been unusually quiet and subdued all evening. As soon as they climbed into the attic she curled herself in her corner and went to sleep.

No chats tonight.

The rain beat down with a heavy drumming noise close to his head. It kept Ravi awake for a time but he got accustomed to it and dozed off. As if in a dream he heard someone moaning and wailing. The noise went on and on, haunting through the beat of the rain.

Ravi came awake with a start. The wailing was coming from the other end of the attic. He realized that Janaki was having some kind of a nightmare. In the frequent flashes of lightning he could see her trashing about and calling out.

'Epā, epā, epā. Mata bähä.'

Don't, don't, don't. I can't.

Ravi spoke her name but she continued to moan and mumble, lashing her hands about so violently he thought she'd hurt herself. Ravi crawled over to the edge of her mat. Unable to listen to the piteous sobbing, he finally stretched himself on the rafters and, keeping his body well away from her mat, reached out and put his arm gently round her shoulders.

She continued to call out some words Ravi couldn't understand, then repeating the words, 'epā, epā.'

At a loss for words, Ravi said, 'Baya wenna epā, baba, mama innava.'

Don't be afraid, little one, I'm here.

He must have reached her at some level of consciousness because she stopped calling out after that, but continued to cry with a low keening sound, her sobs wracking the slight body from time to time. She reached for his arm then and hugged it across her chest using both her arms. After that she seemed to settle down and grew quiet.

Ravi waited patiently till her breathing became regular and slowly released his hand from her grasp. When he returned to his mat he realized that the rain had stopped.

*

Ravi had the trishaw parked under the Kottang tree near Shalindra Premasiri's gate. There was little movement in the houses down the lane except for some boys playing cricket in the next garden.

Ravi passed the bundle of fake notes to Janaki in the rear seat.

'You are sure you can do this?' Ravi wondered again if he was taking too big a risk. Premasiri was a very violent and dangerous man.

'Prassnayak nähä aiya,' she said confidently.

No problem brother.

Janaki had not spoken about the previous night at all. Perhaps it was all a forgotten dream. But from that morning, she had started calling him *aiya* – older brother. Was that a step up or a step down?

Ravi was bemused by the change he saw in himself. Just weeks ago he would have felt offended if someone of her class addressed him like that. Now he was touched, honoured even, by the assumed relationship.

He couldn't just abandon her when this was over, that was certain. She'd be forced into slavery with Piyal or end up in jail. He had to do something, get her trained for some honest job perhaps. She wasn't educated but was smart enough and had those wonderful people skills. Everyone liked her. He'd have to whack the thieving out of her, of course.

But his primary task had to be finished first.

Not being quite sure how the system worked, he had refined his plan by calling Pathirana several times. Sandika had used his clout to get a policeman from the Fraud Bureau positioned just where he wanted him. Now it all depended on Shalindra repeating last Saturday's routine.

If he didn't, the plan would fail and they'd have to try again next week.

The little girl, Dilini, came prancing out of the house at 5.00, almost exactly on schedule and Ravi found his spirits rising. Her parents came out soon afterwards. The silver Montero went towards Duplication Road but there, instead of turning left towards Majestic City as Shalindra had done last week, turned the other way.

Bugger it!

Ravi swallowed his disappointment and followed the vehicle in heavy Saturday evening traffic. Shalindra pulled into a vacant slot outside Liberty Plaza, and Ravi's heart sank. Maduri Premasiri got off alone and hurried inside, giving him a slight glimmer of hope. Ravi drove past them, parked by the side of the road and watched the vehicle in his rear view mirror.

Maduri came out carrying a small parcel. They turned left at the lights and then onto Galle Road. They stopped again at the Fairline Building and this time the whole family went inside.

Ravi felt a pulse thudding in his forehead.

Get on with it, you bastard.

They came out in the end, shopping bags in hand and calling to the little girl who was skipping excitedly ahead of them. This time they headed for Bambalapitiya, and to Ravi's infinite relief, turned into the Majestic City complex.

Ravi hurriedly parked the trishaw on Station Road and walked in through the main door. He had a mobile number for the cop and needed to make contact. Ravi stood in the center of the atrium and called the number. A phone trilled softly and a man seated on the steps by the water cascade held it to his ear. The man looked up and caught Ravi's eye.

A slim man in a white shirt and beige trousers stood up to greet him, 'Mr. Ravi?'

No handshake or smile. He looked at Janaki with cop's eyes, remote and uncaring.

'Yes.'

'I'm Tissera. Is your man here?'

'Just coming in.'

'I have briefed the manager. He will co-operate,' Tissera said unemotionally. 'Point Premasiri out to me when he comes in. Don't contact me after that.'

Moments later Ravi saw the family walking in. They had Dilini by each hand and the child was swinging off her feet with shrieks of delight. Shalindra seemed preoccupied and withdrawn while his wife spoke fondly to the little girl, trying to calm her down.

Ravi saw Tissera looking at him and held his thumb up, receiving a nod in return. Now it was up to him to spring the trap.

The family took the escalator to the first floor but Ravi stayed where he was. Janaki wanted to loaf around but Ravi, not trusting her to stay out of trouble, cowed her with a furious glare. The Premasiri family came down the main staircase in a little while and, passing the seated policeman, went directly to the supermarket.

This was the critical moment. Janaki had to carry out the task but this was not a crowded train and Shalindra was not some harried office worker. If she was caught, he might do her some serious physical damage. Ravi wanted to be close by so he could take a hand if things went wrong, yet there was the risk that Shalindra would recognize him. He had a week's growth of beard on his face and a cap pulled low on his forehead, but was that enough?

Ravi decided that he would go in, but stay well away from Shalindra.

Ravi picked up a basket and walked inside. Janaki, looking relaxed now that she was on the job, passed him without a word. Shalindra was pushing a big trolley, while Maduri inspected the shelves, picking things as they moved along slowly. The little girl skipped about picking up brightly printed packages and putting them back cheerfully when her mother shook her head.

Janaki was very good. She brushed past Shalindra just when his trolley got entangled with the trolley of a fat woman coming the other way. In that instant Ravi knew she'd lifted his wallet although the action was far too swift for his eye to follow. Janaki walked across the aisle and disappeared. Ravi knew she'd circle around and come up behind Shalindra again. She now had to pull out the Rupees 1000/- notes from the wallet and replace them with an equal number of fake notes, and do it without anyone noticing.

He kept his eye on Premasiri who was nearing the check out counter. She was taking too much time.

Where the hell was she?

Janaki walked past him but Shalindra was already at the checkout with just one customer ahead of him. Would she have time to slip the wallet back in his pocket? She was halfway there when the other customer finished up. Maduri started unloading her groceries on to the counter and Shalindra reached for his wallet. Ravi saw his mouth open in surprise as he found his pocket empty.

Janaki had seen it happen. She immediately cut across the aisle once again and vanished from view. Ravi felt bitterly disappointed. His careful plans all wasted. They had been so very close to success.

Ahead of him, Premasiri was yelling that his wallet had been stolen, the bull voice rising above the chatter. Customers and staff rushed forward and craned their necks to see what the commotion was about. Ravi saw it then; just ahead of him on the ground was the wallet where Janaki had dropped it.

Oh you wonderful, wonderful creature.

Ravi turned away, circled the shelves and eased himself out. He heard someone shout that the wallet had been found. Janaki was seated coolly on one of the benches in the atrium waiting for him.

It had been a real close call but the girl's quick thinking had saved the operation. He looked fondly at her, then on impulse reached across her shoulders and gave her a quick hug. She glowed.

Only one uncertainty remained. Would he pay by cash or would he use a credit card? If he used his card, once again all would be lost. But he was a car dealer, not the kind of businessman entirely open with the Inland Revenue. Ravi guessed that he'd deal mostly with cash. He hoped he would today.

He did.

The manager of the store was there by the checkout girl to pick up the three crisp Rupees 1000/- notes and hold them to the light. Tissera moved in then and pandemonium erupted. He heard Shalindra's voice behind him, venting his outrage with a full-blooded roar. Shoppers from other parts of the complex were hurrying over to see what was going on.

Ravi grabbed the girl by the arm and hurried on to the road. His work for the day was done.

Driving back, Janaki spotted a place called Raheemiya Hotel in Ratmalana and announced she wanted to celebrate by eating biriyani. Ravi in a mood to indulge her, stopped at once and Janaki ran inside to pick up two hefty parcels.

Back at the attic, Ravi opened one pack and was dismayed by the stale, rancid smell that rose from it. He threw the parcels into the shrub-covered wasteland and told Janaki he'd fetch more food from the town. She had thrown herself on the floor as soon as they got back and now pretended to be asleep.

Ravi prodded her with his toe.

'Go and bathe.'

'Hmm.'

'Now.'

'Passey.'

Later.

Sharper prod with the toe. 'Right now.'

'Mona karadarayakkda mey? Vadeth karala dunna.'

What a nuisance this is. After I've done the job for you also.

But she got up wearily and trudged off, still mumbling to herself. Ravi smiled as he watched her go, then drove the trishaw to town.

Just to please her, Ravi thought to try another Moslem hotel on the main road. He had parked the trishaw and was about to get off when a man walked out of the hotel tearing the cellophane off a pack of cigarettes. There was something familiar about the silhouette that made Ravi's skin prickle. The man paused to strike a match and Ravi knew his first guess was right. The man drew hard on the cigarette, mounted his motorbike and eased into the traffic going back to Colombo.

What the hell was Pathirana doing here? At this time?

It could be a weird coincidence of course. On the other hand Pathirana had known all about the operation that evening; known that Ravi would be at Majestic City. Had the man followed them afterwards? If so, what was his motive? Had he only followed them into the town or right up to the attic?

Pathirana was his ally. He had helped Ravi in his campaign against the Premasiri family. Just the same Ravi felt uneasy. Not uneasy enough to move from a very convenient hideout, but wishing he knew what the man's motives were.

*

The report in the Daily News shook him just a little. Tennakon must have had a hand in it because the report appeared at the bottom of the first page. The headline was damning.

POLITICO ACCUSED IN FAKE CURRENCY CASE

Shalindra had been charged in the Magistrates Court and released on bail. The silly bastard must have tried to punch that cop, Tissera, because he was also charged on that account. The case was coming up again in a few weeks.

The Golf Club caper was a blow to his pride. Next Ravi had dealt a serious blow to the man's business. Now Premasiri was facing a criminal charge in court and his political career might be ruined as a result. Shalindra knew he had been set up, and he knew who was behind all his current problems. A violent and ruthless man to begin with, he might now be out of control.

Ravi wondered if he had gone too far? For the first time he felt nervous about leaving his safe little burrow in Moratuwa. He had promised to return Reshane's video recorder, and anyway needed help to get his recording on videotape. He called Reshane and arranged to see him when he came home after work.

Ravi drove past Reshane's house to make sure there were no obvious watchers. He parked the trishaw on the Marine Drive and walked back. When Janaki had complained of a headache and wanted to stay back, Ravi had been secretly pleased by the prospect of a quiet chat with Reshane.

'I saw the papers today. Was that more of your doing? You're giving the fellow a real workout, aren't you?'

'I just want him to pull his thugs back, machang,' Ravi sank into a comfortable chair for the first time in many days. 'I don't know what else to do but keep hammering at him.'

'Well maybe this will show him he can't beat you. Maybe he'll give up.'

'I hope so. I'm not too sure what will happen next.'

Ravi put the Camcorder on the table. 'I have about ten minutes on stick. Can you put that on tape for me? I need two copies.'

'I'll need to buy new tapes so I'll do it tomorrow night,' Reshane agreed readily. 'That ok?'

'Sure thing. Can you put it on a CD as well?'

'Sure.'

'Thanks pal. You don't know how much you've helped me,' Ravi rose to leave. 'I'll call you in a couple of days.'

'Don't go,' Reshane said quickly. 'Stay and have a beer. I want to know the details of your scam.'

It was nearly 8.00 when Ravi dragged himself away. On a sudden impulse he decided to drive past the Premasiri house before heading back to Moratuwa. He turned up Fifth Lane, swung around and drove slowly past the house. The lights were on and there were several other cars parked on the drive and the roadside. Had a gang gathered to lend moral support to the victim or had he gone and killed himself?

A security guard was standing by the road. Ravi stopped the trishaw in his usual place next to the shuttered kiosk and walked back casually. The guard was wearing a new cream and brown uniform. Shalindra had changed his security service.

'Ayubowan. Mahaththyagey gedera pārtiyakkda?' Ravi asked
Greetings. Is the master having a party at home?
'Oyā kauda?' The man was suspicious.
Who are you?
'Mama methana purudukaraya. Sirwa anduranawa.'
I am the regular here. I know the master.
'Ahh. Pārtiyak nevei. Mahaththaya karadareka vätilaney. Yāluwo ävilla.'
No party. The master is in some trouble. His friends have come over.
'Oya aluth service ekenda?'
Are you from the new service?
'Ow. Ape sir gema service eka. Mama policien uswuna witharai, meheta bänduna.'
Yes. The security service belongs to the master. I just left the police and joined up.
'Mokada policiya atha ärala security ekakata bänduney?' Ravi asked casually as he turned to leave.
What made you leave the police to join a security service?
'Magey sergeant mahaththya bänduna, ithin mamath āwa.'
My boss the Sergeant joined, so I also came.

An alarm began to ring inside Ravi's head, like a distant fire siren. He turned back slowly and looked directly at the man.

268

'*Sergeant mahaththyagey nama mokakkda?*'
What is your Sergeant's name?
'*Pathirana mahaththaya.*'
Mr. Pathirana.
'*Eyā dhän Premasiri mahaththayage service ekeda?*'
He is now in Mr. Premasiri's service?
'*Ow. Eyā thamai manager.*'
Yes. He is the manager.

Ravi turned quickly before the man could see his reaction. He felt as if his body had been thrust in a bath of icy water. He shoved his hands in his pockets to control his shaking fingers and had to grit his teeth to stop from running to the trishaw.

The treacherous bastard had followed him all right. He must have wanted to give Premasiri a gift of information when he joined the service. What did they plan to do now? The obvious step would be to send Maru Ajit and his gang to kill him. Now that he was forewarned all Ravi had to do was to find a new hiding place.

But what if they moved tonight? Janaki was alone in her little attic.

Ravi tried to reassure himself as he raced the trishaw through the evening traffic. It would be all right. There was no special need for them to do this today. He had time to get Janaki to safety.

He had to have time.

It took him over an hour to make the journey. He parked the trishaw at the turnoff and walked carefully down the gravel lane. Thankful for once that there were no lights in the dingy footpath, Ravi kept to the shadowed edge along the live fence that bordered it. The other houses were shuttered for the night although muted sounds of teledrama dialogue filtered onto the road.

The attic was dark.

Ravi eased himself past the mango tree and the pile of shuttering timber by it. He stepped onto the little verandah. Maybe she had gone to sleep.

Why was the trapdoor open and the rope hanging down? Had she left it for him?

He had to climb that rope.

Ravi removed his shoes and gripped the rope. He listened again but couldn't hear anything other than the lapping of water in the reeds. He took a deep breath and began to climb. He pulled himself inside and breathed a sigh of relief when he made out the dim figure of the girl stretched out on her mat.

Ravi switched the light on, and choked back a scream.

No. No. No..

Her face was purple.

There was a strip of cloth protruding from under her chin. The same pink print as the nightdress she normally used. Then he saw the rest of the ripped nightdress thrown on the side of the mat. They had torn a strip to tie around her throat and strangle her.

She had been stripped naked. Her hands and feet had been stretched apart and tied to the rafters with coir rope. There were ugly black cigarette burns on the inside of her legs and breasts. Blood, still glistening moistly, dripped from her groin. On her stomach was a savage burn, still covered with ash. They had, as a final indignity, ground out a cigarette on her belly.

He felt the awful taste of bitter bile in his throat as he knelt down and touched her feet.

Cold.

He fought to keep from throwing up.

He wished fervently he could tear out his eyes to shut out the horror. He felt his chest getting tighter and tighter and knew if he didn't bellow his rage and grief, he would burst.

Something made a creaking sound behind him.

Ravi turned his head, almost resenting the intrusion at that moment. Nothing. There it was again, the faintest of creaks but this time he saw that it came as the rope tightened against the edge of the trapdoor.

Someone was climbing up.

Ravi knew he was in mortal danger. It was to kill him that the men had come. The poor girl just happened to get caught in the middle, and they had amused themselves with her while they waited for him. Now they were coming to finish the job.

Ravi grasped the single bulb that lit the room. He twisted it out of the holder plunging the room into darkness. Laying the bulb on the floor he crawled to the end of the room. He squeezed himself through the gap, grasping a branch of the tree to support his weight as he wriggled out. He panicked for a moment when his hips got wedged in the gap but then he was free and sliding down the branch.

Ravi picked up a length of wood from the pile of timber and eased himself round the edge of the building. In the faint light coming across the lake, Ravi saw the figure of a man standing under the trapdoor and looking up. He wasn't capable anymore of thinking or planning so he just took one silent step in his bare feet and swung the club at the back of the man's head. There was a dull thud and the man lurched drunkenly against the wall, then slowly slid to the ground.

The rope moved. The other man was climbing down.

Ravi just stood there.

When the man was half way down Ravi took a full swing of the club and hit him across the middle of his back. The blow swung the man against the wall, but the give of the rope also lightened the blow. The man yelled as he fell across the other body then sprang to his feet, but Ravi had his measure by then. Another swing of the club caught the man on the side of his head. Ravi saw him collapse in a dark heap.

Ravi's legs gave out under him.

The club slipped out of his fingers and he collapsed on the back steps. The bile rose in him again, unstoppable this time. He threw up again and again, leaning over and soiling his own feet.

Unable to move and not caring.

Ravi didn't know how long he'd sat there in a stupor. He realized that someone was coming only when the beam of a flashlight swung round the edge of the building. Whoever it was stood very still and moved the cone of light across him and then on to the two unconscious men. He didn't utter a word.

Ravi's eyes followed the beam. In a remote part of his mind he noted that the first man he'd hit was Pathirana. He had guessed that already. The other man's face was obscured but the long hair tied in a ponytail was distinctive. It had to be Shalindra's hired killer, Maru Ajit.

The man with the flashlight still hadn't spoken. He stepped up to the rope, inserted the flashlight in his waist and climbed up. Ravi heard him moving about in the attic.

Ravi knew he had to take his chance and run now, get to the trishaw and away. Yet he felt so immersed in his misery that, try as he might, he could not summon the energy to stand up.

Then it was too late.

The light came on in the attic, streaming down through the trapdoor.

He heard the man ease himself on to the rope and then jump down, landing like a cat. Ravi could see him clearly now. Black clothes and black face, dark and unshaven, black pits instead of eyes. Kadu Piyal had finally caught up with him.

He stared at the man, like a hare mesmerized by a snake.

Piyal walked over to Pathirana's inert body. He reached behind his own neck and, from a scabbard fitted between his shoulder-blades and under his shirt, drew out a long knife. The blade made a faint hissing noise as it slipped out and Ravi saw the light glinting off the wickedly serrated edge as it moved over the man's shoulder. Piyal then took a fistful of Pathirana's hair and lifted his head up.

What happened next was so quick and so horrifying that Ravi wondered if it was an illusion. Piyal flicked the blade across the unconscious man's neck and a thin black line seemed to run across his throat from one ear to the other. Then the line opened up as if a zipper had been pulled and gobbets of thick crimson blood erupted onto the floor.

Ravi heard Pathirana's lifeless head hit the ground with a soggy thud. The dark figure turned and stepped over the other man, lifting the head up as before.

Ravi squeezed his eyes shut but it was too late.

His stomach heaved and erupted like a fountain and vomit, steaming and acrid, filled his mouth, spewed out of his nostrils. He couldn't stop retching and the bitter taste seemed to eat into his brain. He threw up again and again till the dry retching began to knot his throat. When he was finally able to wipe his eyes weakly and look up, he found Piyal standing directly before him on the steps.

Ravi knew this was the end. In a strange, detached way he was glad. He even yearned for some external pain that would erase the agony in his mind. He just looked up at the man before him without fear or feeling, noting the long heavy arms that hung down at his side, the right hand still holding the knife that glistened wetly in the light.

Do it, you bastard. It will be over then.

Ravi couldn't tell how long the man stood silently looking down at him. It seemed a long time. Piyal stooped suddenly, picked up a yellow mango leaf from the ground and wiped the blade. He then turned and walked away round the corner of the building and out of sight.

Ravi sat in a pool of his own vomit and couldn't move.

PART FIVE

Coup de grâce

Beware the fury of a patient man.

John Drydon

*If someone puts his hand on you,
send him to the cemetery.*

Malcolm X

30

Ravi had no clear recollection of the ride from Moratuwa to Reshane's house that night. His eyes had been blurred with an endless welling of tears, his mind struck numb by too much sorrow. He had an impression of disturbances along the way, a kaleidoscope of flashing lights and blaring horns, of screeching brakes and verbal abuse, of stopping and starting off again.

No memory of how he had found Reshane's gate in the early hours of the morning.

For two days he'd been too depressed to move. He would leave his bed for meals when Rashane's mum called him, only to toy with his food, leaving most of it uneaten. Then he'd return to lie on his back and stare sightlessly at the ceiling.

The images kept coming back. A radiant face under an unruly mop of hair. She had been a truly free spirit who had learned to trust him enough to adopt him as a brother. He had been so chuffed when that happened.

Then they had abused and killed her with bestial savagery.

What extreme price must he extract for that? How much pain would even the score? It's getting towards evening on settlement day, Shalindra. You will pay before the sun goes down.

Only the prospect of massive retaliation kept Ravi from slipping into the abyss. He chose and dismissed plan after plan, till he finally made a decision. Soon after breakfast on Saturday morning Reshane found him in a better frame of mind.

'Are you feeling better?' Reshane asked and then went on worriedly. 'You have to figure out what you're going to do. The papers are full of the story. Gruesome Multiple Murders, they call it.'

'What are the police doing? Is there any report?'

'No. Just that a special team is investigating.'

'Mm.'

'Those were Shalindra's men, right? And they killed the little girl?

'Yes.'

'Did … was it you who killed them?' Reshane's voice didn't sound as if he wanted an answer.

'No. No machang, it wasn't me,' Ravi looked fondly at his friend. He was grateful that Reshane had looked after him even when he didn't know if he was harbouring a killer.

'A man called Piyal, a friend of Janaki's! He saw what they'd done to her and killed them. I thought he would kill me as well, but in the end he didn't.'

Ravi stood up and went to the window. He could see the edge of the garden and the lane going down to the sea. He felt as if his mind, like an ancient windmill, was slowly beginning to grind around again.

'Where's the trishaw?'

'I pushed it to the back of the garage. It can't be seen from the road.'

'Good,' Ravi nodded and turned back. 'I'm more grateful than I can say for what you've done but it's not fair for me to be here till this is settled. I'll move out tomorrow.'

'Where will you go?'

'I'll find a place.'

'You're sure you'll be able to manage?'

'Yes, pal. Truly.'

'You have to find a way to end this.'

'Yes. I have to end it. I know what to do.'

A fresh thought seemed to strike Reshane as he got up to leave. 'You're not going to kill him, are you?'

Ravi thought for a moment. He realized that he had, in some subtle way, changed from an easygoing student into something else. Even Reshane had sensed it and was afraid.

Ravi said quietly, 'No. I'm not going to kill the bastard.'

Killing will let him off too easy.

*

Ravi had spent Saturday afternoon altering the numbers of the trishaw. Although his deposit would carry him for a few more days, the owner might well have gone to the police when he heard that Janaki had been killed. The registration number of the old Bajaj was painted under the front windshield and again under the rear taillight. Red numbers on a white panel. Using two small tins of enamel paint and an artist's brush, he changed 201 – 1338 to 201 – 1883.

Late that evening Ravi had walked up to Elfindale Avenue. The lights in the drawing room were on and the muted sounds of the TV drifted to the road through the open window. Ravi longed to walk in and talk to Aunty Nora but knew it would only expose the old lady to more danger.

Ravi eased through gate and opened the letterbox. He was relieved to find his parcel of cash intact. He pulled it out and put it in his pocket.

Sunday morning found Ravi poring over the classified advertisements in the Observer. He had decided to find a place in Wellawatte and circled several possibilities. He left the trishaw at Reshane's and hired a three-wheeler on the road.

He liked the sparsely furnished single room annex at Frances Road because it had a separate entrance and the landlady was more interested in the advance than in his references. When he returned in his own trishaw the woman looked at him strangely but agreed to let him park the vehicle behind the house.

Ravi drove down to Premila House soon after lunch. He parked the trishaw in front of a bakery and walked the rest of the way. He was pleased to see that the white van was parked under the porch. He rang the bell and waited. A young girl with prominent teeth and a bad attack of acne opened the door and looked at him with wide-eyed interest.

'Madam innawada?'

Is the Madam in?

The child nodded, then turned and led Ravi past the main hall to a room at the end of it. A painted sign on the door announced that "The Directress" was in. Ravi walked in without knocking. A woman with heavy arms resting on the table sat working on some papers. She looked up with a slight frown, peering at Ravi through thick lenses.

'Yes?'

'You are the Directress?'

'Yes, I'm Mrs. Wijesiri,' she was watchful, clearly put out by his tone. 'Who are you? What do you want?'

'Is your husband here?' Ravi sat without being invited to. 'You'd better call him.'

'What's this about?' Ravi noticed the woman had small eyes, magnified unnaturally through her thick lenses. She was unafraid but getting annoyed. She stared at Ravi belligerently for a moment, and then finding him unmoved, hit the top of a small bell with the heel of her hand.

The pimply girl came trotting in.

'Madam?'

'Tell sir to come.'

'Sir' must have been close by because Ravi heard heavy footsteps, then a smell of stale cigarettes wafted over his head. The man addressed the woman from the door.

'What's the problem?'

'This man says that he has something important to tell us both.'

The man stood by Ravi's side looking down at him suspiciously. 'Who the hell are you? What do you want?'

A heavy, handsome face under a magnificent head of black hair. But the white roots near the skull, once seen in daylight, spoilt the effect.

Ravi ignored the question. 'Have you a video deck?'

'Yes. But ...'

'It will save a lot of explanations if you'll just watch for five minutes. It has to do with Premila House.'

The big man hesitated, then shrugged and walked out of the room. Ravi stood politely by the door till the woman stalked past him. Ravi followed them to another large room with a TV fitted at one corner and chairs arranged in neat rows before it.

Ravi took the videotape Reshane had prepared and held it out. Wijesiri hesitated, then took the tape and inserted it in the deck. They stepped back few paces, kicking some of the small chairs aside.

The Newspaper scan appeared first and Ravi heard the fat man click

278

his tongue in annoyance. Then came a sharp inhalation when the screen showed the woman ushering two girls into the van, and later, the man leading them into the blue motel.

Despite Reshane's editing, the tape was wildly amateurish with the images swinging riotously on the screen. But it was enough.

Ravi leaned forward and ejected the tape. The Wijesiri couple was staring at him wordlessly. Ravi waited.

'Who are you?' The big man asked again, his voice no longer as strong and dominant as it had been earlier. 'What do you want?

'I'm the man who has the original of this tape,' Ravi tossed the tape on a chair. 'I also have a witness. A girl called Janaki, who ran away from here some years ago.'

'We don't have money to give ...'

'I don't want your money. There's something else you can do for me.'

When Ravi explained his requirement, the couple looked surprised but also visibly relieved.

Very relieved.

*

He followed the blue Toyota down Cambridge Place and Albert Crescent, right at the traffic lights, and then left to Maitland Crescent. The little girl was dropped at the gate with kisses and waves and the driver took Maduri Premasiri straight back home.

The driver studied the overcast sky for a minute, scratching his shiny skull, then unraveled a garden hose and began washing the car. At 9.30 he took Maduri for her Wednesday game of bridge.

The Bridge Federation was housed in the grandstand of the Colombo racecourse, along with a host of other sports bodies from carom to hockey. The car turned through a gate opposite the Royal Pool on Reid Avenue, followed the road past one antiquated grandstand to stop at the second one overlooking a playground. Maduri got off and walked inside. The driver took the car home.

Ravi retraced the route the car had taken on the way to school but this time continued up to the traffic lights at the Horton Place junction. He turned there into what was earlier called Green Path and immediately left again to the now abandoned Municipal Sports Club.

The playground and clubhouse had once been a prized possession of the Colombo Municipal Council but President Premadasa, in his arbitrary way, had taken it over ostensibly to construct a cultural centre there. Many years had passed since the President had passed on but the cultural centre had still not seen the light of day. Meanwhile the clubhouse stood at the corner of Green Path, forlorn and abandoned.

Ravi parked his trishaw just inside the broken gate where it was shielded from the road. He checked his watch. The driver would be coming along Albert Crescent by 11.00. Ravi had thirty minutes to get in position. Plenty of time!

Ravi rolled down the Rexene rain covers at the back of the trishaw and, using a thin roll of wire, tied the sheets firmly to the metal upright by the driver's seat. He left a small section loose to be fastened later.

He looked thoughtfully at the knife he'd bought. It had a short, but wickedly sharp blade, and had come with a convenient little scabbard. He tucked it in his waist under his T-shirt. He then left the vehicle and strolled along the pavement in front of St. Bridget's Convent till he came to the traffic lights at the junction of Albert Crescent and Independence Avenue. Ravi checked his watch again, then crossed the road to the centre island on Albert Crescent and stood there watching the approaching traffic.

The blue car was dead on time. Although traffic was fairly heavy at that time, there weren't many vehicles turning right from Albert Crescent. The old driver was third in line when he came to a halt at the red light.

Ravi walked past the vehicle and in one quick motion opened the rear door and seated himself directly behind the driver. As the man jerked his head around in surprise, Ravi inserted his right hand between the seat and the door and jabbed the point of the little knife into the driver's ribs.

'Kägähuwoth kapanawa,' Ravi's voice was harsh with tension.

If you shout I'll cut you.

Ravi caught the driver's eyes, rheumy and terrified, in the mirror.

'Monawada oney? Mata baby ekka enna thiyanawa.'

What do you want? I have to pick the baby up.

The green light came on.

Ravi pressed the knife into the man's side, making him gasp and try to lean away.

'Härenna epā. Kelling palayang.'

Don't turn. Go straight.

The car jerked and stalled when the driver released the clutch. The driver of the vehicle behind them immediately sat on his horn and the old man began to shake.

Ravi said quietly, *'Haddissi wenna epā. Ayi start karanna.'*

Don't be in a hurry. Start the car again.

The man restarted the engine in his second attempt and took the car towards Horton Place junction. Then under Ravi's direction he turned left into Green Path and left immediately afterwards into the compound of the Municipal Club.

He was a wisp of a man, and old. He didn't resist, except to utter a low moan when Ravi caught him by a skinny shoulder and drew him out of the car. Ravi looked around carefully and, finding the place still deserted, picked up the roll of plastic tape he'd left in the trishaw and ushered the man towards the buildings.

The back of the clubhouse, all peeling green emulsion, faced the car park. An open pavilion stood to the left of it facing the playground. A corridor led into the derelict building.

He pushed the protesting man inside. Ravi had, during his inspection the previous week, found a small recess at the back of the open pavilion that might have been used for storing the groundsman's equipment. He made the driver sit on the floor and taped his feet together, and then his hands behind his back. The driver was breathing rapidly and Ravi wondered for a moment if it was safe to leave him like that.

The hell with it!

The man whimpered weakly when Ravi stuck a broad adhesive strip across his mouth.

Ravi checked his watch impatiently as traffic backed up in front of St. Bridgets'. He'd already lost too much time. Everything had to be exactly as usual.

The little Toyota handled beautifully. Ravi was tempted to keep the car a little longer but he knew that was dangerous. Just stick with the plan. He eased the car into Independence Avenue, and then left to Maitland Crescent where the Bridget's nursery was located.

A queue of vehicles had formed on the side of the road, each pulling up in turn at the little gate. A young teacher, hardly out of school herself, stood by the gate keeping the children inside and under control. The teacher would recognize a familiar vehicle and call out a name. A child would then trot outside carrying her bag and drink bottle and climb in.

A black X-Trail pulled up at the gate, a chubby brat waddled out and then he was next. Ravi looked straight ahead, avoiding the teacher's eye.

Look at the car, woman. Don't look at the driver.

She didn't. Who looks at drivers anyway? With the corner of his eye Ravi saw an arm wave. A moment later the back door opened and a school bag in the shape of a teddy bear was flung inside. The little girl followed, slamming the door shut with a bang.

Ravi released the clutch and swung the car into the stream of traffic going towards Horton Place.

Little Dilini was leaning over his shoulder, trying to study his face.

'Ko Dharmey?' She asked curiously. 'Adha udey hitiyaney.'

Where is Dharmey? He was here this morning.

'Eyata una. Thāththi māva kanthoruwen evvwa.'

He has fever. Father sent me from the office.

She was a cheerful little thing. Ravi watched in the mirror as she settled back in her seat and unscrewed the cap of her drink flask.

'Thāththi kiwwa car eka hadanna deela, trishaw ekey ekka yanna kiyala.'

Father said to give the car for repairs and bring you home in a trishaw.

The child, with her mouth circled snugly round the bottle just made a gurgling sound. What did she care? Ravi studied her for a moment in the mirror. Straight hair cut in a little bob. The centre had been gathered in and tied with a ghastly red ribbon that stood like a little crown on her head. Pretty little face underneath all that.

Ravi drove the vehicle through the traffic lights at the end of Horton Place and into Green Path. He turned the little car into the compound and ran it to the end of the car park where some GI sheets had been nailed against the boundary wall. He left the key in the ignition, took the child by the hand and led her to the trishaw.

She was skipping as she walked along, holding on to his hand. Ravi felt a sharp pang of regret, quickly suppressed. She was a trusting little thing with no exposure to the evil of the world.

Ravi lifted the edge of the rain cape and the little girl wriggled inside. He pulled it down and quickly wound a bit of wire through the eyelet securing the Rexene in place. Now the only way out was over the driver's seat.

Ravi told the child to wait a moment and ran over to the pavilion to check on the old driver. The last complication he wanted was for the idiot to suffer a heart attack or choke to death.

He need not have worried. The man must have more spunk than Ravi suspected because he had inched his way, on his bound hands and feet like a snail, halfway out of the pavilion. He looked up despairingly when Ravi walked in.

You're doing fine, pal. At this rate you'll take another hour to reach the road and find help. That suits me just fine.

He left the man where he was and turned away.

The child was delighted with the pack of Smarties. Ravi heard it rattle as she shook the sweets on to her hand.

'Ammi doctor langata gihin Dharmey ekka. Kiwwa babywa aunty kenekkge gederata geniyanna. Ammi passey äwith babywa ekka yai.'

Mum has taken Dharmey to the doctor. She wants me to take you to an aunty's house. Mum will come later to take you.

She was quiet for a while thinking about it. Ravi waited anxiously, unable to see her face.

'Ayi mata gedera yanna bäri?'

Why can't I go home?

'Dharmege una babytath hädei kiyala bayai. Doctorgeng ahala thamai ammi enney.'

Mum's afraid you will get Dharmey's fever. She wants to ask the doctor first.

She stayed without speaking for a while, thinking it over. She was clearly not happy. Then the pack of Smarties rattled again and Ravi knew he was through.

'Ikkmanata enna kiyanna,' she mumbled through a mouthful of sweets.

Tell her to come soon.

It was a long drive and the little girl was getting restless by the time he turned into Premila House. Ravi parked in the empty porch and rang the bell.

Mrs. Wije must have been expecting him because the door opened immediately and she stood across the threshold, staring impassively at him. Ravi picked the child and held her out to the woman.

The little girl took one look at the woman, howled and clung to Ravi's arm.

'Mata bähä. Mata bähä. Māva gedera geniyanna.'

I can't. I can't. Take me home.

Ravi felt his resolve crumbling and gritted his teeth. He thrust the child at the woman and stepped back. The terrified girl was struggling and crying piteously.

'Take good care of her,' he told the woman. 'If any harm comes to her, you'll be sorry.'

'I agreed to keep her for a few days,' the woman took no notice of the struggling child. 'She'll settle down in a little while.'

'No one must know about this.'

'I will see to that. Then you must take her away and give me the original tape. That is the arrangement, isn't it?'

'Yes.'

Ravi turned away without looking at the child. She wailed loudly and then he heard the door slam behind him. He found his hands shaking when he tried to steer the trishaw onto the road.

Ravi stopped at the top of Frances Road and found a call box. He dialed the Premasiri house and waited.

Maduri picked it up, tense and agitated. 'Hullo? Hullo? Who is this?'

'Mrs. Premasiri? I have her. She's safe for the moment.'

'Ohh. Please, please. She's only a little girl … please.'

'Shut up and listen very carefully,' Ravi snarled. 'Tell your husband. No police and no publicity. Do you understand? If you want your daughter back, keep the police out of it and nothing in the papers. Tell me you understand.'

'Yes. Yes. We'll do as you say. Please …'

'No. He's a fool. You convince him. I'll call again.'

'Wait, wait …'

Ravi rang off.

Ravi walked into his room and let himself collapse, face down, on his bed. The little girl's cries had shaken and depressed him but his resolve was strong. He knew he had to be utterly ruthless if he was to see this through to the end.

He turned and stared at the ceiling thinking how strange it was that he had always been one to avoid conflict and violence, the easygoing boy at school who never got into fights. Even during the riotous university years in England he had always been the peacemaker, settling disputes and bar brawls before they got out of hand. Especially Tilak's escapades.

First the memory of Tilak's betrayal helped harden his heart. Then the image of Janaki's broken body flitted across his mind, and as it did, cold, implacable rage began to fill his mind like a cancerous tumour. Shalindra Premasiri had ordered that gruesome killing and now it was his turn to feel some real pain.

It is nearly over, Shalindra. Your time has come!

31

Premasiri picked the phone on the first ring.

'Yes? Who is this?'

'Premasiri?'

'Yes. Yes. Who's speaking?'

'It's me. Have you followed my instructions?'

'You fucking bastard! I'll drink your blood,' the bull voice blasted Ravi's ear. 'If you harm my child ...'

Ravi rang off.

When he called again at noon it was Maduri who picked it up. Her voice was tearful.

'Yes?'

'Your husband's actions brought this about. Do you understand that?'

'Maybe. I don't know.'

'Believe it,' Ravi said harshly. 'If he continues to behave like a moron, you'll lose your daughter. Do you understand this?'

'What do you want us to do?' Maduri was sobbing. 'Oh. Please, please! She's only a baby. Don't punish her for someone else's mistakes.'

'Have you brought the police into this?'

'No.'

'Are you sure? If I find them involved, you will never see the child again.'

'No. No. I promise you.'

'What about the newspapers?'

'We haven't told anybody.'

'Make sure nothing comes out. Do you understand?'

'Yes. Yes. I'll do anything ...'

'Shut up and listen carefully. Tell Shalindra I want one million. Get it in thousands. Put it in a briefcase and have it ready tomorrow morning at 11.00. I will call and tell him where to go.'

'Yes. I'll make sure he does what you want,' Maduri sounded relieved by the modest demand. 'We'll be ready.'

'If I see any sign of police or any publicity, the deal is off. You won't hear from me again.'

'Yes. I understand. We'll do exactly what you want. I beg of you, please don't harm my baby.'

'What is your husband's mobile number?'

*

Ravi knew that it was at the point of collecting the ransom that the kidnapper was most exposed. That was the critical stage of the operation. He needed just the right location from where he could see Shalindra without being seen himself. He had to be able to see if Shalindra had informed the police or brought along his own goon squad.

He also needed a neat escape route in case things went wrong.

Ravi drove to Reid Avenue and parked near the entrance to the Bloomfield Sports Club. The next gate led to the abandoned grandstand of the Turf Club. His father had been an avid punter and had harsh words for the populist politician who'd abolished the thriving industry in 1956. The land of the racecourse had been distributed for various projects but the magnificent grandstand still towered over Reid Avenue.

The road turned along the front of the first gallery and then up to the entrance of the main grandstand. The area in front of it had been converted to a playground. Ravi walked past the empty buildings. There was a viewing stand with a terraced floor rising in tiers to some thirty feet at the rear edge, another floor of terraces above and a metal girders supporting a roof arching high over it. An aisle at ground level bisected the tiers and led to the back of the building. Ravi found it turned to a labyrinth of corridors leading to the bowels of the building. A variety of sports bodies seem to have been housed in those dank and musty rooms.

That included the Bridge Federation where Maduri Premasiri spent her Wednesday mornings.

A heavy metal door set in the rear wall must have opened onto the pavement on Reid Avenue but was locked tight and almost welded in place. A tunnel like corridor branched on to either side, running along the rear wall of the building. Ravi followed it, stepping carefully over empty paint tins and piles of broken furniture, till he came to another opening in the wall, a much smaller one, boarded up with planks.

He'd seen this exit from the road. Maybe it had just been an opening for dumping the garbage in the old days. Ravi didn't care. He pulled out the heavy screwdriver from under his shirt and began to loosen the planks covering the narrow aperture. Sections of the timber had already perished and came away easily; others required all his strength to shift.

He left the structure in place still covering the exit, but now loose enough to be yanked off, if he had to leave the building in a hurry. He went outside again and moved the trishaw across the road, opposite the boarded aperture.

Ravi called the house at 10.45. An apparently chastened Shalindra picked up.

'Is the money ready?'

'Yes.'

'Have you a briefcase big enough?'

'Yes. Yes, I have one. It's packed and ready.'

'Okay. Bring it in the Toyota. Come alone.'

'All right,' Premasiri went on with an undertone of anger. 'How do we exchange? I must be sure my child is safe.'

Ravi took a deep breath so it would be audible over the phone.

'You miserable piece of shit, you have no leverage in this set up. None! Do you understand that? You will do exactly as I say. Exactly! Otherwise I'll ring off and that will be the end of it.'

'Okay. Okay.'

'Shut up and listen carefully,' Ravi snarled. 'Put the briefcase on the passenger seat and drive to the racecourse. Turn the car and park in front of the grandstand. Come alone.'

'Then what?'

'Keep your mobile handy. I'll instruct you when you get there.'

'All right.'

'Get there at 11.00 sharp. Be late and I'll be gone.'

'Wait. Wait. There's no time ...'

'There's time. Move.'

The blue Toyota came round the corner with a minute to spare. It moved slowly up to the entrance, turned and parked. From his perch high in the stands and safely ensconced behind a pile of boxwood, Ravi studied the vehicle with the little binoculars Reshane had given him. Shalindra, his heavy body incongruous in the little car, seemed to be alone. Ravi studied the empty playground shimmering in the noonday heat and the buildings on the far side. Everything seemed to be in order – so far!

He called Shalindra's number and watched the man put the phone to his ear.

'Yes?'

'Put the briefcase on your lap and open it.'

'Huh?'

'Do it.'

Shalindra tucked the phone behind his ear, pushed the seat back further and did as he was told. The briefcase seemed to be packed with bundles of green notes.

Ravi was about to go on when something moved in the periphery of his vision. Two men walked onto the far end of the playground on his right. They were swinging their arms as though loosening up for exercise and walking slowly towards Shalindra's car.

Only they were not dressed for sport and they didn't look like sportsmen.

'You stupid son-of-a-bitch! You're still trying to play games with me,' Ravi shouted harshly. 'You'll never learn.'

'What? No. No wait ...'

'No.'

Ravi switched off his phone. If those two were Shalindra's goons then he'd have more men covering the area. It was time to get out. As he crawled over to the edge of the tier and dropped into the aisle below, he heard someone shout. Ravi raced down the rear corridor and began to pull the planks away from the boarded aperture. They didn't come off as easily as he had expected and he had to heave and strain, bruising his hands in the process, before he had an opening big enough to crawl through.

He heard running footsteps behind him.

Ravi fell onto the pavement, startling some women waiting for a bus. He ran across the road, and blessed himself when the trishaw started at the first yank of the handle.

*

He had played them like hooked fish all weekend.

At first he had called, listened to their pleas and rung off without speaking a word. By Sunday Maduri had been reduced to incoherence, sobbing uncontrollably every time she picked up the phone.

On Monday he calculated they would be ready.

Ravi had called again and Shalindra picked up.

'I might give you one last chance,' Ravi said quietly. 'Do you want to take it or do you want to be clever?'

'No. No. Please, it will be all right.' The voice was still gravelly but the arrogant tone was gone now. 'I'll do whatever you say. Truly.'

'I'm not promising anything. Have the money ready tomorrow morning, and we'll see.'

'No wait, is our baby all right? Please, please don't harm her.'

Ravi rang off without answering and then switched the phone off. He knew he was working on a fine line. How to inflict the maximum amount of pain and anxiety while still giving them hope? If they lost hope they'd run to the cops and he didn't want that.

Not yet.

Tuesday morning and Shalindra was still at home, standing by the phone. He picked it up on the first ring.

'Premasiri? This is your final chance. Don't screw it up.'

'No. No. Nothing will go wrong. Just tell me what to do.'

'Drive to St. Anthony's Church at Kochchikade. Park in front of the church and keep your mobile handy. Be there at 11.30 sharp.'

'All right. I'll leave now.'

'Come alone and use the Toyota.'

'Understood.'

"Premasiri?"

'Yes?'

'This is positively your last chance. Foul this up and you'll never see her again.'

'No. No. Please, she's life to us. Please …'

'Be on time,' Ravi said as he rang off.

Shalindra pulled up just a couple of minutes ahead of schedule. The church was packed with Tuesday devotees to St. Anthony. Shalindra double parked behind a row of cars and looked around. Dozens of beggars jostled each other to tap at his window till he lowered the shutter and snarled at them so furiously, they fell back as though hit by a high wind.

Ravi had seated himself in a tea kiosk across the street. He could just see the figure of Shalindra hunched over the steering wheel. He switched his phone on and called.

'Did you bring the money? The full million?'

'Yes. Yes, it's all here. Where is my girl?'

'Shut up! Just follow the instructions.'

Ravi heard the man take a deep breath.

'Yes. Tell me what to do.'

'How is the money packed?'

'Bundles of 100,000.'

'Take out one bundle and step out of the car.'

Ravi watched as the man stepped out of the car with the phone against his ear and a puzzled frown on his face.

'Now distribute it to the beggars.'

'What? Are you mad?'

'DO IT.'

The number of beggars seemed to multiply before his eyes.

They formed a seething mass around the heavy figure of Premasiri, screaming and milling about frantically for their share. They pressed him back against the car, pulling at his clothes and arms as he held the bundle of money above his head. A woman fell and was stepped on, her screech cutting through the hum of traffic. Premasiri roared with disgust and flung the notes away from him, an eruption of green confetti. The beggars went wild, leaping about frantically to snatch at the banknotes flying through the air.

Shalindra dived into the car and shut the door quickly.

Ravi called again.

'Now what?' Shalindra was clearly put out by the melee.

Ravi was silent for a minute and then asked, 'Why did you kill the girl? Why did you order her raped and tortured?'

'Oh fuck, what does it matter? Who cares?' Shalindra shouted in exasperation. 'She was a slut from the streets.'

Ravi felt the incandescence erupt inside him like molten lava. He bared his teeth but didn't say a word. As the silence stretched and stretched, Shalindra realized he had made a terrible mistake.

'I … I'm sorry. I didn't mean …,' his voice tailed off.

'You shouldn't have said that,' Ravi whispered. 'You should never have said that.'

'I'm sorry. I'm so sorry …'

'Tell your wife that you had a chance to save your little girl. Tell her you screwed it up because you're such an arsehole!'

'No. No. Please.'

'I hope you have photos of your daughter to remember her by. You'll never see her again,' Ravi said with quiet, deadly calm. 'It's over.'

'No. Wait, wait. Oh please. I beg you. I'll do anything. Anything. I'll come to you on my knees …'

Ravi switched his phone off and walked away.

32

The sky was on fire.

A mass of cloud on the horizon had engulfed the sinking sun and turned into a magical mix of colours. A riot of reds, oranges and yellows filled the western sky reminding Ravi of happier days. Warm, happy, playful days long gone. Days when those things mattered.

Now the only sensation he experienced was cold. Arctic cold in his body and in his mind.

The dilapidated boundary wall of the Kinross Club stood in tasteful forest green to his left and the Wadiya restaurant to his right. The beach, so full of life and laughter during the weekend, was deserted in the heat of the late weekday evening. Ravi eased himself on to the rude seat someone had fashioned out of a plank, balanced on two coconut stumps. The sea itself had a lazy languor, small whitecaps moved slowly up the beach and out again, as though the effort was too tiring.

Had he covered everything? He began a mental checklist.

The old woman had taken the CD without a smile, staring at him suspiciously with her little pig eyes.

'How can I be sure if this is the only copy left? You might come back with more demands.'

'What have you got that I might want?' Ravi shot back. 'I wanted the child looked after for a week. I don't need you anymore.'

'You said you had a witness, the girl who ran away. What about her?'

'She's dead. She can't harm you now.'

'Was she — was she the one killed in that massacre?' She was clearly relieved at first but then it struck her that Ravi had to be involved in the killings. Her face seemed to crumple into worry lines as she stared at him.

'Yes.'

She tapped her bell, and a minute later Dilini had come out holding the hand of an older girl.

The child had been overjoyed to see him and had flung her arms round his shoulders when he lifted her up.

'Ammi langata geniyanna dämmama.'

Take me to mama immediately.

'Ow baby, ammi balagena innawa.'

Yes baby, mama is waiting for you.

'Yamu. Yamu.'

Let's go. Let's go.

She must have hated it at Premila House, or maybe it was just the old witch, because she kept her face firmly turned away.

Ravi looked at Mrs. Wije for the last time.

I've already mailed a copy of the CD to the National Child Protection Authority. You can enjoy two, maybe three days of tranquility, then you will wish you hadn't been born. You and that pimping husband of yours!

Remember little Janaki?

This is my gift to you — from her.

Dilini had been puzzled and confused when, instead of going directly to her home, Ravi took her to the beach.

'Äyi gedera yanney nätthey?'

Why aren't we going home?

'Ammi meheta ävith ekka yanawa kiwwa.'

Mama said she'd pick you up from here.

The little girl stared at him uncertainly for a minute. But she was still a good-natured child despite all that had happened. And she really loved the beach.

She nodded wisely and sat down to pull her shoes off.

Ravi watched with remote disinterest as the child ran down to the waters edge to fetch wet sand for her castle.

He took the letter from his pocket and read it one last time:

Shalindra Premasiri,
14/1, Charles Drive,
Colombo 03.

By the time you read this letter your daughter will be gone. I want you to know, and never forget, how your own actions and crimes brought this tragedy on your head. Allow me to remind you of just some of them.

1.   You used your father's political position to destroy the small business belonging to my family.
2.   Your security personnel murdered my mother by triggering an attack of asthma and taking away her medication.
3.   Thugs hired by you assaulted and robbed my father. He suffered a heart attack and died as a result.
4.   In Moratuwa last week, your thugs tortured, raped and killed a young girl who was under my protection.

I have given much thought to punishing you adequately for the crimes you have committed, the misery you have caused and the lives you have destroyed. I could very easily have killed you and, believe me, I considered that option for a long time. In the end I decided that death would be an easy release for you – and far too kind.

Instead I want you to live, but to live with unbearable sorrow. I also want to deny you the satisfaction of having a target for any further revenge.

I will now make incisions on each of your daughter's wrists and hold her in my arms till she passes on. When she is gone, I will slash my own wrists and so achieve my own release.

I hope that my actions will always remain engraved in your thoughts.

Ravi Perera

Ravi folded the letter carefully and put it away in his shirt pocket. He reached under his T-shirt and took out the little knife he'd used to frighten Maduri's driver. He placed it on the bench.

The little girl was kneeling in the sand, scooping sand with her hand to build a tower. She giggled and uttered a loud '*aiyoo*' when one sidewall collapsed, then cheerfully started building it up again.

She looked over her shoulder when Ravi called her, shook the sand off her hands and walked obediently towards him.

The sun was now an immense orange sphere directly ahead of him on the horizon. A flight of cormorants flew across it in a loose V formation. As Ravi watched them, wondering idly where they'd go to roost for the night, something floated high above his head. He recognized the unmistakable silhouette of a Sea Eagle gliding out to sea, searching for that one last victim before darkness descended. The Eagle moved across the setting sun and, in that instant, stretched its claws and plummeted out of the sky and into the water.

That's exactly what he wanted to be, wasn't it? A pitiless raptor that could swoop out the sky and tear his enemy apart.

Ravi gritted his teeth, knowing he had to be strong now.

He picked up the knife.

Her arms were covered with sand and her face was smudged. She skipped as she walked. She came up to Ravi and stepped on his feet, one small foot on each of his and stretched out her arms for him to hold.

'*Māva paddawanna,*' she commanded.

Rock me.

As if controlled by some outside power, Ravi slipped the knife under his leg and held out his hands. He had forgotten how tiny a child's fingers could be, how soft and delicate the touch. She grasped each of his forefingers and balanced herself on his feet. Through all this Ravi had kept his eyes averted, looking at the sea, trying to pick out the Eagle again, determined not to look in her eyes. Then she began to bounce up and down impatiently, urging him to lift his feet.

He looked down.

The pretty little features looked up at him, mouth half open and eyes wide in anticipation. His vision blurred and he felt an unbearable stinging sensation in his eyes.

Dear God in heaven, how had he turned into this monster?

Ravi felt as if, by some illusionist's stratagem, his world had been flipped over. Everything was now reversed, like a mirror image. What he had accepted as unqualified and inescapable truth was ... what?

Had he, not Premasiri, been the trigger that had precipitated this endless tragedy?
Was it his doing then, that resulted in all this sorrow, all this loss?
Could he, Ravi, have averted the spiral of violence, this relentless chain of events?
He had come to innumerable forks on the road he had traveled. At every fork had he, believing there was no choice, selected the wrong turn? Had each road only led to yet more violence?
If he had only taken the other road, would his parents be still alive today? And little Janaki, would she still be grumbling about having to bathe in the dark?

And here he was, seriously contemplating the final, unspeakable obscenity.

The day of revenge and retribution was far spent.
Was it too far spent for him?

*

The security guard tried to stop him but fell back when Ravi said, 'Mama babywa hoyagaththa. Nona langata geniyanawa.'
I found the child. I'm taking her to the lady.
He walked slowly up the drive and turned into the lawn. He heard the heavy footsteps of the guard behind him.
Lacy drawing room drapes moved listlessly in the slight breeze, just

enough to reveal Shalindra Premasiri slumped at one end of a long settee. He seemed to be looking intently at his feet stretched out before him. Maduri was seated across from him, still as a statue, her eyes riveted on the telephone on the side table. Only her fingers were moving, twisting a handkerchief endlessly.

Ravi stepped in through the window and Maduri's strangled scream cut through the still evening like a knife. Ravi put down the child and she ran to her mother with a joyful cry:

'AMMEEE.'

Ravi stood near the window and looked at them.

Shalindra came halfway out of his seat with an angry grunt, hesitated and slowly sank back when he saw the child run to her mother. Ravi walked into the middle of the room and looked intently at the man.

Shalindra stared back malevolently. But in many ways, he wasn't the man he had once been.

The heavy cheeks and neck still dominated the face but did the jowls hang down just a little? Was that a touch of grey at the edge of his temple? The angry eyes held Ravi's for a long minute and then turned away. Had the old arrogance waned?

Ravi didn't care. Not anymore.

He turned to look at Maduri.

'I have given your child back. Whatever you people choose to do now, I won't retaliate,' he looked into her eyes. 'Do you understand? Whatever you do, for me, IT IS OVER.'

The woman and child had their arms wrapped round each other in a tangle, as though clinging to life itself. The child had her face buried in her mother's neck.

Ravi turned to the window.

He heard the woman's voice behind him, strong and loud.

'It is over for us too. On my daughter's head, I promise.'

Ravi stepped into the garden and walked slowly away.

He didn't look back.

When you plan revenge,
get ready to dig two graves.

Chinese Proverb

Epilogue

Ravi found he had wandered back to the beach near Kinross. He walked across the railway tracks, sat once again on the plank he had used earlier in the day, now a lifetime in his past.

The sea was dark and sluggish, like a vast basin of used engine oil. Faint moonlight glinted off the crests of the gentle swell as it gathered itself lazily to run up the beach.

It seemed to Ravi his feet had no contact with the ground.

He felt as if some crushing burden had been lifted from his shoulders that now allowed him to float at will; as if all he needed to do was to spread his arms and he would glide swiftly over the coconut palms and out to sea.

But he didn't want to fly.

No longer did he yearn to be an Eagle.

He took the letter he had prepared with so much care, holding it as he would a venomous snake. He tore it across and across and flung the scraps into the air.

All he wanted was to find Tanya.

He had not realized how desperately he wanted to find her, how incomplete he was without her. But he knew he would have to start all over again.

How had she wanted to be wooed?

With Chocolates and flowers and on his bloody knees.

Knowing her, Ravi knew he was destined to spend a lifetime doing just that. She would drive him insane with her unpredictable moods.

With her inscrutable Burgher ways.

But he didn't mind that.

He didn't mind at all.

Afterwards he'd go looking for Tilak.

They'd find a decent pub and climb on two high stools right by the bar. He would look the barman in the eye and order two ice-cold beers, making sure they were served in frosted glasses.

Ahhhhh!

They would sit together and he would tell Tilak about Tanya, tell him how incredibly lucky he was to find a girl like that.

Maybe Richard Koch would organize another "bring and come" party for them. He would take Tilak along to show him how simple, good-hearted people got together to enjoy themselves; how wonderfully well they did. He would even get the hefty Maureen to dance the wheels off Tilak.

He wanted to watch Tilak's face when he introduced Tanya to him. To compel Tilak to admit that it was he, Ravi, who had hit the jackpot.

When that was over and his triumph was clear, they would plan how to get old Reshane fixed up with the plump Anula.

That would be good for a giggle.

Of one thing Ravi was certain. If Tilak picked a fight with anyone when they were out together, he was going to sit back and watch the fellow get a well-deserved flattening. He wasn't getting involved.

But he now had a serious decision to make.

Should he thump Tilak first and then take him out for a beer, or save that little pleasure for afterwards?

He rather thought afterwards would be better.

Nihal de Silva
<wtrmrt@sltnet.lk>

Also by Nihal de Silva

THE ROAD FROM ELEPHANT PASS
Winner of Gratiaen Prize 2003

An army officer's routine assignment to pick up a woman informant near Jaffna turns into a nightmare when the Tigers launch a massive attack on the peninsula and the camp at Elephant Pass. The two adversaries are forced to escape together through the rebel held Wanni and later, cross the abandoned Wilpattu National Park on foot.

Bitter enemies at the start of their journey, Captain Wasantha and the activist Kamala face innumerable threats from wild animals and from a gang of deserters who make determined and violent efforts to capture the woman. The constant external danger, and their enforced dependence on each other, gradually erodes their enmity and distrust.

But a shocking revelation confronts Wasantha when he finally reaches Colombo. He is now compelled to choose between his friend and his country.

*

Out of the cannon mouth – death and the deathlessness of love.
- Carl Muller

A captivating mix of exciting narrative and picturesque descriptions.
- Sunday Observer

Holds the reader's interest from start to finish.
- Sunday Times

A useful contribution to the process of building bridges between communities.
- Dr. Jehan Perera

A gripping novel.
- Sunday Island

STATE LITERARY
AWARDS – 2004

We certify that the
State Literary Award
in the category of

NOVEL

relevant to the year 2003
was awarded to the book entitled

THE ROAD FROM ELEPHANT PASS

By

NIHAL DE SILVA

President
Arts Council of Sri Lanka

Chairman
Literary Panel

Director
Department of Cultural Affairs

Date: 05/10/2004

The Gratiaen Trust was set up on the initiative of Michael Ondaatje after his book, 'The English Patient' was awarded the Booker Prize. 'The English Patient' was later made into a successful film.

The Ginirälla Conspiracy

COLOMBO IS UNDER A TERRIFYING THREAT

Sujatha Mallika, a girl from a remote village in the south, has been deeply traumatised by events in her own past. When she enters Jaypura University she faces and survives a sadistic rag carried out by a student union affiliated to a radical political party.

Even as she suffers the rigours of the rag, she is deeply impressed by the rhetoric of a messianic leader of that party who promises to sweep away the corrupt establishment and find a place in the sun for the rural poor. When the rag is over she joins the party and works hard to bring them to power.

Although deeply committed to their just cause, Sujatha is repelled by the violence the party uses to suppress its opponents and punish 'traitors'. She also becomes aware of a mysterious plan called the 'Ginirälla project' aimed at seizing power in the country. Dismayed and fearful, she leaves the party when she graduates from Jaypura.

As a journalist, Sujatha battles the demons of her own past even as she works to unravel the Ginirälla Conspiracy. What she finally uncovers is a plot so terrifying that it is almost beyond belief.

But the discovery comes too late for her, and for the city Colombo ...

A Tribute to Nihal de Silva

By Professor D.C.R.A. Goonetilleke

Nihal de Silva began his career as a novelist late in life, but he rapidly established himself as a truly professional novelist. He delivered three novels in three years, a novel per year - The Road from Elephant Pass in September 2003, The Far Spent Day in September 2004 and The Giniralla Conspiracy in mid-August 2005.

He started with a splash: The Road from Elephant Pass won both the Gratiaen Prize and the State Literary Award - oddly, this concurrence between the two panels of learned judges has occurred only twice in thirteen years since the inception of the Gratiaen Prize in 1993.

Nihal de Silva is, in fact, a phenomenon, embodying the essence of the recent efflorescence of Sri Lanka's literature in English. In 1987, Dr Lakshmi de Silva commented: 'Sri Lankan novels for the most part suffer from structural weaknesses; they ramble, meander and peter out, or else jerk with spastic rigour through a clutter of uncoordinated and unconvincing climatic episodes.' The firm structures of Nihal de Silva's exciting and complicated narratives is worthy of admiration.

His skill in characterization is at its best in The Road from Elephant Pass - in its projection of Captain Wasantha Ratnayake, the Sinhalese soldier, and Kamala Velaithan, a female Tamil LTTE cadre, a seeming informer, and the interplay of their characters as they move from Jaffna, through LTTE-controlled areas, through the Wilpattu game sanctuary to Colombo. Nihal de Silva begins his career as a novelist by confronting Sri Lanka's most urgent problem at present - the terrorist problem. He handles it in the manner of a novelist by presenting opposed views through these two main characters and by depicting the ground realities of the war.

In The Far Spent Day, Nihal de Silva courageously exposes another aspect of our contemporary world – the misuse of power by politicians (the use of violence as a weapon, the amassing of wealth illegally, by the use of power to indulge in sexual harassment). He also focuses on areas of experience hardly explored by our writers in English - the urban underworld of thugs and pickpockets and the world of the destitute.

In The Giniralla Conspiracy, Nihal de Silva turns his attention to left-wing, revolutionary politics and captures its kind of thinking and the socio-economic conditions that create it. He also exposes the notorious rag at universities in Sri Lanka. The physical harassment of first-year undergraduates by the seniors and the political factor are common knowledge; though it is difficult for someone of an older, different age group to judge whether such behaviour as introducing cockroaches into a leafy vegetable and forcing the new undergraduates to eat it is possible, it looks as though nothing seems beyond the present-day senior undergraduates during the rag. Yet not all senior undergraduates are horrors during the rag. Those who perpetrate the undesirable deeds in the novel belong to a radical party and thereby their party is discredited. Nevertheless the party itself is shown as emerging from the inequities in our social system. Nihal de Silva is not in sympathy with radical politics, whether it be at university or national level, but he understands it.

At one level, Nihal de Silva's novels are effective thrillers. It is his acute awareness of our contemporary political, social and economic problems that make these more valuable than mere exciting narratives. Tragically, Nihal de Silva was a fatal victim of LTTE terrorism, caught in a landmine explosion at Wilpattu National Park on 27 May 2006. His novels indicate that Sri Lankan literature in English has undergone a great loss. Ave atque vale! (Hail and farewell!)

Professor Goonetilleke is the Professor Emeritus of English at Kelaniya University and is the author and editor of 14 books published by prestigious publishers including Penguin and Routledge. In September 2006 he was conferred the *Sahityaratna*, the most prestigious literary award of the Arts Council of Sri Lanka.